Christ House Books

2013

Publisher: James Ward Kirk Fiction/Christ House Books
Website: jwkfiction.com
Twitter: @JamesWardKirk
Facebook: James Ward Kirk Fiction

**W. Franklin Lattimore**
Twitter: @ImpactWriter
www.facebook.com/WFranklinLattimore

Cover art and design by Megan Reid.
Model: Hanna Reid
Photographer: Angela Reid

Biography Photographer: Christy Brothers
Christy Brothers Photography - Columbus, OH

**ISBN-13: 978-0615837734 (Christ House Books)**

**ISBN-10: 0615837735**



Christ House Books

To my loving "Mamaw"

Myrtle Tennessee Hamilton

(1915-2012)

I can hardly wait to see you again.

# FREEDOM FIGHT

Book One of the Otherealm Trilogy

W. Franklin Lattimore

## Prologue

It was dark.

It was black.

There was absolutely no light where he was, and yet he had no trouble seeing his hands when he lifted them before his face. Looking down, he could see his stomach, his legs, his feet.

He could see that he stood on an old railroad tie. It was mostly black due to what looked like tar or oil that had long ago become part of the wood. It lie close to another. In fact, he realized now that he was surrounded by them; an unending field of blackened lumber.

It appeared that there was no specific order or pattern to their placement, though they seemed to be mostly end to end and side by side, creating an almost flat surface. They were all close to each other, though not pressed tightly together. He could see space between most of them, but he couldn't see what lay beneath due to the lack of light.

He got the impression that the place in which he stood was massive. He thought to call out to listen for an echo, but didn't. He wasn't even sure that he could if he wanted to. Using his mouth and vocal cords seemed like a distant memory.

He felt more alert and more observant than he'd ever experienced before. There was no hint of murkiness or confusion in his mind. His mind was sharp, keenly aware.

And he was aware that he was alone.

Completely and utterly alone.

He knew that in this place no one else existed. He was fully cognizant that his was the only presence in this vast expanse of lonely pitch darkness.

He stood.

He stood longer.

He breathed, and he stood.

Never had he been so aware of absence.

*I'm alone. There is no one else. I exist completely alone.*

He bowed his head. He looked at his hands and feet. *This is all that I can see of ... me. I will never again see another person, and I cannot see, now, my own face. What do I look like?*

*I look ... sad.*

He began to weep. He wanted to call out for help, but instinctively knew that there was no ear to hear his cry.

*This is my existence. I am here. I am alone.*

*I am afraid.*

He turned, but in no way did his perspective change. It was utter blackness for as long as the place stretched. And he knew in the core of his being that it stretched forth without end.

He looked upward. Complete darkness. He'd never seen complete darkness before. Even in a dark room with one's eyes shut, a person sees imaginary pin-pricks of light. Here, though, where his eyes were perfect, there was nothing imagined.

He listened. As complete as the blackness was, the silence was equal in its power. He could hear nothing. Not the air entering or escaping his lungs; not the beating of his own heart. Again, he didn't bother opening his mouth to make a sound. He knew it would be of no use. Yet, he knew that his ears were working as perfectly as his eyes.

There would be no comfort here. No one would ever console him. No one would ever take his hand or stroke his brow. He would never feel the touch of another person again.

He stood for endless ages. Eons. Time had no meaning.

He stood looking into the eternal darkness of his futile existence. He did not matter any longer. Had he ever? He couldn't remember. He was not important. His life held absolutely no significance; no value at all. He was forgotten.

His heart broke. *I want to matter.*

Silent tears fell from his eyes. He knew there was no hope to be found, or to be given, in this place. He had never experienced a place of such profound truth.

He deserved this.

*This is where I belong.*

He stood.

# Part One

## Freedom Rings

"There is a way which seems right to a man, but the end of it is the way of death."

Proverbs 14:12

# Chapter One
## 1981

### Friday, January 9 – 10:35 p.m.

*Please, don't let them start. Don't let the voices come tonight.*

The glow of the alarm clock on his nightstand was the only illumination in the bedroom. It wasn't enough light. Any more light, though, and he'd never get to sleep, even if his nightly "visitors" remained at bay for once.

"Is it even worth trying to ask you for help?" he whispered into the darkness. "You never answer."

*They're coming, all right. It's only a matter of time.*

Brent Lawton lie in bed, staring at the dark ceiling. The darkness pressed in against him from every direction.

*How did I end up like this? This wasn't the plan. All I wanted was a little control.*

*Five bottle caps and a penny. It all seemed so ... so safe.*

He took in and released a long breath. The tension didn't dissipate even a little bit.

Brent had just turned sixteen-years old. A starter on his high school basketball team, he lacked neither athletic prowess nor intelligence. Not that either seemed to matter anymore.

*No, not anymore.*

The best jump shot on the team and the ability to ace nearly every test put in front of him wasn't—at least so far—helping him out of the trap in which he now found himself.

He felt isolated. Alone. Especially amongst his family.

Except for Lydia, of course.

His thirteen-year-old sister still looked up to him, though even her admiration was usually tainted by gray.

His thoughts drew him back in time to where and when it all started.

Three years earlier—*could it have been longer?*—the day-to-day stresses of living in the Lawton household had become nearly intolerable. Brent had come to realize that he was tensing up every time he'd head home from school, knowing that it would only be a matter of time before another 'discussion' erupted between his mom and dad. If just two days passed without heated words, yelling, and impassioned threats, it was hailed as a miracle.

Most times, just after the shouting would start, Brent would hear a light knock on his bedroom door. Lydia would wait for him to open it and then, with eyes filled with fear and cheeks dripping with tears, ask if she could "come in for a little while."

Brent always said yes.

*She's the only one in my life who makes me feel important anymore.*

Sometimes he would just hold her, rocking her gently, while assuring her that things would soon settle down. A thirteen year old consoling a ten year old. It shouldn't have been made to happen. And yet, three years later it continued.

The fights between his parents were a carousel of emotional diatribes. In fact, Brent could usually forecast with some measure of accuracy what day the next flare-up would occur, and sometimes even the subject matter.

Just two days prior, his mom demanded to know why his dad had been fifteen minutes late from work...

"Don't start with me, Sharon."

"I suppose it was traffic again? Or are you going to tell me you stopped off at the store with nothing—once again—to show for it?"

At the top of the stairs, in his bedroom, Brent heard the whole thing play out. His mom seemed to be insinuating unfaithfulness. But, it could also have been that she was a control freak, having to be so in charge of life events that Keith Lawton was allowed no freedoms of his own.

To be fair, though, the yelling didn't always start with his mom. The *need* for another altercation would sometimes begin even before his dad entered the house. Envelopes with the name Keith E. Lawton behind transparent-plastic address windows would show up in the mail box, the senders of which had all-too-familiar names: Sears. J.C. Penney. L.L. Bean; names not coincidentally tied to his wife's limitless stacks of catalogs.

Heated words, yelling, and impassioned threats.

Brent was *sick* of it!

However, about a year and a half earlier—July of 1979, to be exact, the summer prior to his first year in high school—life took what, at the time, seemed like a fortuitous turn.

While outside playing ball with some friends, Brent's attention was drawn to someone walking toward them from down the street. He recognized the individual instantly. It was Kim Cox.

*Kim*. What kind of parent names a boy *Kim*? He was the guy on the street that everyone pretty much avoided. Older by some five or six years, Kim wore black a lot, had long blonde hair, and kept company with others who looked pretty much the same. All the kids at this end of the street knew to walk on the opposite sidewalk if they ever had to pass his house.

"John. Tim. Look."

The three of them stood in the yard with muted stares as Kim continued his advance. Five houses away, then four, then three, until he got to the property line of Brent's home.

"Hey, you guys. You wanna see some magic?" he asked.

John, Tim, and Brent looked at each other momentarily; all eyes saying the same thing: *Who's going to say no?* But, out of nowhere, with a slight shrug, Brent said, "Okay."

Strained whispers gushed from his friends. "Are you crazy?"

Ultimately, they did approach Kim Cox, but John and Tim made sure that Brent had taken the lead.

Kim took something out of the right pocket of his jeans. He squatted down on the sidewalk and waved the boys closer.

"Let's see if you can outsmart me. See these?" He held out his right hand, and in it were five bottle caps from Coca-Cola bottles. "These are yours to control." He laid them on the ground before them. Now, more curious, the boys also took squatting positions on the sidewalk.

"What do you want us to do with them?" asked John.

"You are going to take this penny and cover it with one of the bottle caps. I'll turn my back while you line them up any way that you want. Let me know when you're ready, and I'll turn back and tell you which one of the caps the penny is under."

Breathing a sigh of relief, Brent asked, "That's it?"

"That's it. Pretty simple," Kim Cox replied.

The three boys looked at each other, smiled, and accepted the challenge, no longer as nervous.

Kim turned his back.

Each of the boys had done his part to make it impossible to know which cap the penny was under. Two of the caps were twisted to get the Coca-Cola name to face other directions; the placements of two others were shifted a bit, while yet another was made to remain exactly in the same spot and position that Kim laid it down. It was under this cap that they had decided to put the penny. "Okay. We're ready," said Tim.

Wanting to be skeptical, but overcome with a hopeful curiosity, the boys watched as Kim turned around, closed his eyes, and began to pass his right hand over each of the caps, palm down.

*What the heck is he doing?* Brent was transfixed as he looked up from Kim's almost ghostly-white hand to look at his closed eyes. *This guy needs some sun,* he thought to himself, both amused and struck by Kim's pale appearance.

After a couple passes with his hand, Kim opened his eyes. He simply reached down and picked up the second cap from his right, revealing the penny.

"That was pretty cool," said John. Brent and Tim agreed. "Let's see if you can do it again."

Kim smiled with confidence, with a *knowing* that caught Brent's attention. "You got it. But nothing you can do will cause me to make a mistake."

Time after time they played his game. Each time Kim's hand came down to the hidden penny. For a short while John and Tim thought it was fun, but they were getting restless to do some things that, in their minds, really took some talent; things like throwing supposed "sliders" across home plate on their makeshift front-yard ball field. Tim taking the lead, all three of the boys stood up.

Tim asked, "So, what's the trick? How'd you do it?"

After he picked up his caps and the penny, Kim Cox stood, silent. With his black clothes and additional inches of height, the guy was daunting.

He looked Brent dead in his eyes—that's how Brent remembered his eyes, too. Dead. After several painfully-long seconds, Kim said, "Powers." That's *all* he said. And with that one word, he turned around and began walking back down the street.

The boys stood there for a moment, unsure whether they should maybe try again for a real answer or just accept what they'd been given. In the end, though, John turned to Tim and said, "Your turn to catch."

That had pretty much been it. Fifteen minutes of tricks that shouldn't have affected anything in his life. Except that in that brief period of time Brent was sure that he had seen something that went much deeper than a mere trick.

‡‡‡

That evening at home, as it turned out, was one of the "miracle" nights. It was peaceful; a welcome respite from his normally tight gut and on-edge nerves.

As his mom and dad lounged in the family room watching Family Feud, Brent sat down at the dinner table nearby with a deck of playing cards.

*If it can be done with a penny and five bottle caps,* he

thought, *maybe it can be done with playing cards.* It was worth a shot.

Brent rifled through the playing cards, pulling out four red cards and the ace of spades. He lay them face down on the table, closed his eyes, and mixed them up. He then situated them into a row, confident that he had no idea which was the ace.

Looking down at his neat little row, he placed his right hand over each of the cards, wondering what that was supposed to accomplish. It was obvious to Brent that Kim's trick had something to do with having marked one of the bottle caps. But after a moment's thought, Brent realized that Kim would have had to mark the right bottle cap *before* the penny was placed under it; something else seemingly impossible.

*Okay,* Brent thought, *There has to be something to this hand-over-the-cards thing.* Was it a sense? A feeling? Brent refocused. *Okay, the ace of spades. Ace of spades. Which one are you?* He suddenly grabbed for the nearest card. He turned it over. *Two of diamonds. Well, that didn't work.* He flipped the card back over and mixed them up again.

*Kim had closed his eyes while moving his hand over the bottle caps.* Brent, too, closed his and leaned his head back as he had seen Kim Cox do. He began to move his hand over the cards again.

"What are you up to?"

Brent jerked upright. It was his mom. She sounded a bit amused and was now standing behind his chair. "Umm ... just working on a card trick I saw earlier."

"Oh yeah? Are you any good?"

"We'll see in a few minutes, I guess. Gotta figure it out first."

"Well, you've got my curiosity piqued. Let me know when you're ready to amaze me and your dad."

As his mom went to sit down near his dad, each in his and her own recliner, he returned to the task at hand. *Okay, let's try this again.* He closed his eyes, leaned back his head, and placed his hand over the cards, moving it back and forth.

Thinking it was about time to drop his hand, he did so. He opened his eyes, flipped the card, and saw the annoying red of the seven of hearts. He sighed. *What's the trick?!*

Then it hit him. Kim had never said anything about it being a trick. He had initially used the word magic, and later, when asked, he had said, "Powers."

*What did that mean? What kind of power? Power that the penny had? That* he *had?*

"Power, huh?" Brent said under his breath. "Well, then, let's get a little hocus-pocus weird with this." Once again he shuffled the cards and set them in line. He, again, closed his eyes and leaned his head back. He, again, placed his hand over the far right card and began moving it to the left. *Power. Power. What kind of power?* He began making a second pass back to the right.

Determined that something would be different this time—that something would stand out—Brent kept his hand hovering and moving over the cards. With eyes closed and his brow furrowed in concentration, a thought sparked in his mind. *Power to see!* He believed he was onto something now.

*The ace of spades. Black. Shaped like a ... spade.* The picture formed clearly in his mind. He could see the card. He also visualized the tiny words printed below the spade. *Maybe the name of the card company*, he thought.

Without warning, what felt like a blast of heat shot up into the palm of his hand!

*What the...?* He opened his eyes and jerked his hand back. He did *not* just imagine that. He examined the palm of his hand, but didn't see anything unusual. Turning his attention back to the row of cards, he lowered his hand to the one over which his hand had just been. His heart began to beat hard with anticipation. Had he done it? Had he just figured it out? He flipped the card over.

There it was in all its black beauty. The Ace!

"Yes!" he nearly shouted.

"Figure it out, Hon?" inquired his mom.

"I think I actually did!"

"Good for you."

Brent reshuffled, redistributed, and reattempted.

It happened again. Heat. The secret was heat! He saw the card in his mind, and he actually *felt* heat rise up from it. *This... this is amazing!* He took a steadying breath. *Okay... Okay... Let's see. I'll bet it doesn't have to be five.*

He reached for the deck of cards and looked for an additional two red cards. He shuffled them, placed them in a line and, once again, found his ace. *I'm three for three with this!*

Again he reached for the deck. *Let's make it thirteen.* Another attempt, and another success. *Twenty-five?* Success. *Thirty-five*? Success!

He could hardly contain his exhilaration. Even more exciting was that he was accomplishing the feat with black cards mixed into the rows.

*All fifty-two? Why not? Why shouldn't it work?*

With all fifty-two cards spread out in neat rows, taking up

most of the table, he closed his eyes and concentrated on his card. As he moved his hand over the first row of cards he felt no heat, just normal room temperature. He opened his eyes and gathered those cards to the side.

"Okay, you've got us both curious now." It was his dad. "What's the goal?"

Brent looked over his shoulder. Both were standing there. "Well, I'm looking for the ace of spades."

His dad cleared his throat, and with humor playing in his voice, asked, "Isn't part of performing an illusion the knowledge of where the card is while your *suckers* remain clueless?"

Brent found humor in that, too. "You'd think so, huh? But, this isn't an illusion. This is just as exciting for me as it is for anyone watching." He turned back to the table. "Okay, no talking. Give the Great Brent the atmosphere he needs to astound you." He heard his mom restrain a laugh.

He concentrated. He moved his hand. He felt some warmth. He pushed aside the cards that had remained cool. The card that had just generated the warmth didn't quite feel right, though. He'd leave it for the moment and continue his search. He cleared another six cards before coming upon another card that was generating some warmth. *I wonder what that means?* He continued on.

After his hand had passed over the last of the fifty-two cards, he looked at what remained. He was down to seven cards that had caught his attention because of the heat they seemed to generate. He took a deep breath and looked back at his parents who were watching intently. His dad, with arms folded and a slight smile on his face, was obviously entertained.

As Brent was about to continue, his dad said, "Sharon, hand me that pile of cards our magician just pushed to the side. Let's see how impressive he is before he makes his final pick." His mom picked up the pile and handed them to her husband. He re-formed the deck and then began to search through them. Brent held his breath.

"Well, Brent, you've got something going on here. Your ace of spades is not in this deck." He set the cards down on the table.

"Okay," said Brent, "Let's see how impressive I really am."

## Chapter Two

Brent couldn't stop thinking about his initiation into darkness back in July of 1979. The innocence of it all. The stupid card "trick" wasn't even about gaining control! It was just a stinking grab for attention! Something that was supposed to be fun! No torment! No *voices!*

As it turned out, Brent's parents had been very impressed with what he'd done with the cards that first day. In fact, his father had gone so far as to sit down at the table with him and even reshuffled the deck himself. Then he arranged the cards on the table himself. Apparently, it had been time for a reevaluation of the card trick.

Brent had passed the test again, with flying colors. Though his dad couldn't find them, he had been sure there were markings on the cards. There had to be. Right? Because, obviously, there had to be a naturalistic reason to produce such astounding results.

When pressed, a third time about how he'd done it, Brent simply said, "It's a secret." He was beginning to enjoy that he knew something that no one else could figure out.

However, as the days and weeks went on, his family and friends, who were initially very impressed with his ability, grew more and more indifferent. It was rarely brought up any more to brag about. Brent didn't like the waning of interest in his ability and began to wonder what other attention-grabbers his *giftedness* could secure.

He tried the shell game that had originally been done on the sidewalk with Kim Cox. Yes, he'd been able to duplicate it, but to everyone else it just seemed even more a parlor trick.

He was getting frustrated.

Late one night while lying in bed, a few weeks into his new *skills*, he had the spark of a new idea. It was obvious to Brent that he was able visualize what he wanted to find and then find it, but what if he could visualize what he wanted to *happen* and then cause it to take place?

But how? If it was at all possible, he was going to find out.

Brent realized that *this* was the moment... this was the decision that had set a dark and dangerous new course for his life. He wanted to ebb the flow of memories; bring them ultimately to an end. He desperately wanted to stop reliving the beginning of his life's end.

But the memories persisted...

*Okay, what do I want to happen? It would have to be something ... something so unusual that* if *it actually happened it would be obvious that I was the cause.* He pondered the idea for several minutes, and then it struck him. *Ohh... what* if!

*Michele.*

*Impossible! Now you're just being stupid.*

*But ... what if ...?*

If he were able to get Michele Atwell to go out with him, he'd know, without question, that he had a *truly* astonishing gift. Not one time had he been able to catch her eye. He didn't understand why. He wasn't exactly hideous to look at, and he was an athlete...

*Okay .... I've got my goal.* He smiled to himself. What if he were really able to make this happen? He would sure turn some heads at school with *her* on his arm!

Brent knew it was an impractical pursuit. It was ridiculously improbable. ... Which made it the perfect test. The question was: How does one go about manipulating someone else's desires? Would he have to be able to see her in order to throw a *whammy* on her? Could it happen as he lay in bed? Was there a way to study up on this?

He chuckled and shook his head. *It's a stupid idea! Idiotic!*

*Still...*

It took a full day before he got past all the moral objections he had to manipulating another person's will. First, he doubted that it could really be done. So what real harm would come as a result anyway? Second, if the impossible happened and she *did* go out with him, she'd be getting someone who wanted her for more than her body, though that body was certainly a perk! And who's to say that in some cosmic sense it wasn't supposed to happen anyway? After all, if it was a gift—a gift that had to have come from God, since he probably did exist—then wouldn't he just be accomplishing what he was gifted to do?

Moral constraints out of the way, he began to practice. *Practice* was probably the wrong word to use since he didn't have a clue what he was doing. But then, a lot of the practice he did on the basketball court to acquire his skills had been little more than trial and error; pretty much just like this.

He had one class with Michele; English Composition. He'd have to choose a seat somewhere behind hers. Then he could try to ... well, do *something*. He'd figure it out then.

Monday morning Brent walked into his first period English Comp class. He got to the classroom early so as to get the best possible seat for getting a good look at Michele. The problem was that she never showed up. She wasn't there the next day either. As it turned out, she was home, sick with the mumps of all things.

At home he resorted to Plan B. Okay, there really wasn't a plan, but he was going to at least attempt to make some sort of headway. So, locked in his room he sat at his desk with his eighth-grade year book before him; and in it, a picture of Michele. He focused on the photo and strained to make his thoughts known to her.

*You like Brent Lawton. You want him to be your boyfriend.* Conjuring those two sentences in his mind was enough to cause him to laugh out loud. "Oh, brother! Have I lost it." But Brent felt a niggling to go at it again. So he did.

The more he said it, the more he also felt like he was making some sort of mistake. It wasn't a conflict of conscience, but something else. He was doing something wrong.

He sat back with a sigh and rubbed his eyes.

"If you're not sure that anything you're doing is right to begin with, how can you be certain that anything you're doing is wrong?" he asked out loud. He leaned forward and looked at Michele's picture again. "I want this girl," Brent murmured. "I need this girl."

"I'm going to *have* this girl."

He attempted again to speak to her mind—believing it had to somehow be possible—that she wanted him. Then a thought occurred to him, almost like a whispered voice. *You're saying it wrong. She needs to believe the thoughts are her own.*

"Her own thoughts," Brent mumbled. *Yes! That's it! She needs to think that the thoughts I'm sending are her own!* Brent gave himself an I-could-have-had-a-V-8 pop to the forehead and looked again at her picture with renewed enthusiasm.

*I like Brent Lawton. I want him to be my boyfriend.*

The thought voice spoke to him again, *Out loud. Be more subtle.*

He stared into her eyes; willing himself to see their greenness; seeing more than a photograph. He was looking at the object of his desire face to face.

"Brent Lawton," he began again in a whisper. "Brent Lawton." He felt like he was drilling Michele's eyes with his own. "Brent Lawton. I wonder why I never really noticed him before. Brent Lawton. Now that I think about him, he is kind of cute. Brent Lawton. I wonder why I never really noticed him before. Brent Lawton. Now that I think about him, he is kind of cute."

The repetition of just his name and those two sentences went on for nearly an hour until Brent felt a rivulet of sweat travel down his back. The chill of it alerted him. He blinked and sat up. He blinked again and looked at his alarm clock. "What? No way." He looked at his watch. "An hour?" He rubbed his eyes and pushed back from his desk. He felt weak, as though he had been through a hard workout.

"Okay, that was a little weird." He stood up and went downstairs for a snack. "I need some protein."

‡‡‡

The following Monday, again early for school, he sat at his desk hoping. The classroom was about half full when she walked in. Michele Atwell in all her long-legged beauty, looking none the worse for the type of ailment she had suffered through. She was laughing with a girl named ... Hmm ... He couldn't remember. Michele's best friend. A mixed pair to be sure: nerd and absolutely-not-nerd.

As Michele and friend started looking for seats, Michele turned toward the back of the classroom and caught Brent's eyes. For a moment—a brief, *glorious* moment—her eyes widened in surprise. She caught her breath, smiled a quick smile, and darted her eyes toward the floor as she took a seat.

Brent's heart skipped a beat. Maybe three or four beats! She had just noticed him! She didn't just see him, as she'd done countless times, but she *noticed* him!

Brent nearly exploded in song! *Nearly* being the operative word. Good thing, too, because the only lyrics that erupted in his mind at that incredible moment were *The hills are alive with the sound of music!*

Good grief! How embarrassing would that have been?

He smiled.

No, he didn't ... he grinned.

He grinned like a Cheshire cat!

‡‡‡

Brent and Michele were now an "item." Guys and girls alike throughout the school were either high-fiving him or looking at him in utter amazement. *Good grief,* he thought while walking to class one afternoon. *Every girl in this school must have thought I was a total loser!*

After a while, though, even the wonder of bagging Michele

Atwell wore off in the minds of his classmates. And he was once again relegated to the life of the average.

Much like an adrenaline junkie, Brent needed his periodic "fix" of popular opinion. So he began making it a practice of learning more ways of exploiting his *gift* for glory.

It was becoming much easier to manipulate situations to his liking now that he was listening more attentively to his *thought voice*. It was a bit eerie at times, as he was growing to believe that it might really be a voice. And if it was a voice that was guiding him to do things he didn't know how to do himself, was it *his* voice he had been hearing?

The question both troubled and fascinated him. That is, it fascinated him until one night, about four months into his relationship with Michele.

It was that horrific night that the *thought voice* said something that gripped him with fear.

"Hello, Brent."

# Chapter Three

**Friday, January 9 – 7:07 p.m.**

In an old farmhouse hundreds of miles away in a small town in the eastern hills of Kentucky sat what appeared to be a frail, aging woman. She was certainly aging, but her appearance hid the strength that she kept in ready reserve. She was thin with a small frame, but she had been steadily working, keeping up her small farm for almost more years than she could count. A widow for the past seven years, Hannah Moore readily admitted her own amazement at being able to take on and accomplish all of the work the small farm required.

It was just after 7:00 p.m. and she was now allowing herself some down time. She sat comfortably in her favorite rocking chair in the bedroom. The old coal stove was ushering its heat, pushing back the wintry cold that invaded other parts of the house. Coal trucks constantly worked their way up and down the winding road of the hollow "dropped off" free fuel for the residents of this otherwise-forgotten back road. The warmth of the room soaked into her body allowing her to finally relax.

She was grateful for the rest. It had been a frigid day. But, still, the chores had needed to get done. She had awakened early to feed the chickens, hogs, and her two dairy cows, and after making sure that they were as warm as the weathered buildings would allow, she turned her attention to getting back inside and to domestic concerns. Though she certainly didn't like the cold spell that had hit, it did allow her to focus on things that still needed to be done around the house.

Her old mountain home was still in decent repair after nearly a hundred years. Her husband had been born in this house. *So many good memories*, she thought as she wrapped up folding her laundry. Their six children had known this side of the mountain as their home, as well. And, those six had given them fifteen grandchildren. It was a shame that John hadn't gotten to see and know all of them before he passed. A couple of those grandchildren were approaching marrying age. Would she get to be a great-grandmother? *God, You are so good!*

Leaning over to a corner table, she picked up her Bible and opened it to the Psalms. With so many friends and kin who lived nearby—resulting in somewhat frequent, somewhat unexpected visits—she didn't always have the luxury of reading the Word in the evenings. But, she never missed a morning. Her quiet time with the Lord was the elixir she needed daily for her loneliness.

Those first few weeks and months without her husband had been the most difficult in her life, having to enter into every new day alone. If the Lord had not been present with her each morning she'd have surely gone mad. The first words from her lips each new day were, and continued to be, *Good morning, Jesus.* No, it wasn't an instant fix for the pain, but she was determined to continue her conversations each morning with someone that she loved. There would be no more *Good morning, Honey.* No more *Ready for breakfast?* But she could still converse, and she could still drink in love and acceptance. She could still feel comfort.

To wake up with her Lord close by was a bona fide treatment that gave her a measure of what she needed to get through her days alone. Oh, how she still missed her husband.

She turned a few pages, settling on Psalm 100. She began to read aloud to herself. There was always something about hearing the Word of God spoken, even if it was she who was doing the speaking.

"'*Make a joyful noise unto the Lord, all ye lands. Serve the Lord with gladness; come before His presence with singing.*' You sure are good to me. Thank You for Your love and Your provision. '*Know ye that the Lord He is God: it is He that hath made us, and not we ourselves; we are His people, and the sheep of His pasture.*' Jesus, thank You that You are great enough and big enough to handle all of our challenges."

Tears came to her eyes as she surrendered her loneliness to Him for the ten-thousandth time. "'*Enter into His gates with thanksgiving, and into His courts with praise; be thankful unto Him and bless His name.*' You are worthy, Lord. Worthy even when things do not go the way I'd like. '*For the Lord is good; His mercy is everlasting; and His truth endureth to all generations.*'" She placed her finger between the pages to mark her spot, closed the book, and looked through her ceiling to Heaven. "You have shown me Your mercy, O Lord. You have not forsaken me. Never forsaken me. Now, that's not to say that I always felt that way. No, Sir. Thought You had abandoned me for a time, but I was wrong. You got me through. And, You still do."

She leaned back her head and just sat silent for a moment, enjoying His Presence. She sighed with contentment. Then it came. Disquiet rose up in her spirit. She sat up.

"What is it, Lord? I feel You quickening my spirit." She closed her eyes and waited for an answer. It wasn't what she expected. It was a Scripture reference that came to mind. It was distinct: Psalm 91:14-16. She opened her eyes immediately and flipped open her old King James Bible. The pages hardly stayed in the binding any longer after years of constant use. One of her grandchildren had given her a brand new New International Version Bible earlier in the year because of the condition of the one she held. She appreciated the gesture, but this was a gift from her husband. A gift that wouldn't be traded in.

She found the reference. And, until she began reading it, she didn't know what it was going to say. Again she began to read aloud. "'*Because he hath set his love upon Me, therefore I will deliver Him: I will set him on high, because he hath known My name. He shall call upon Me, and I will answer him: I will be with him in trouble; I will deliver him, and honour him. With long life will I satisfy him, and shew him My salvation.*'

"What, Lord? What does this mean? Are You warning me? Is this for me?" She fell into a wary silence. A word formed in her mind ... *Grandson.*

‡‡‡

**Saturday, January 10 – 1:07 a.m.**

He lie awake, exhausted. Brent's mind was moving a million miles a minute. It was all his fault. He should have known from the very beginning that he didn't have a "gift." Ha! What a joke. A dark, ugly joke. And the joke was on him.

How could his life end up in such a mess because of five stupid bottle caps, a penny, and a deck of playing cards? It was planned. It had to be. These things ... these dark *beings* that whispered to him every night had set him up. It was so clear now. It was clear ... *now*. And *now* was too late.

"Hello, Brent." [1]

*Oh God, no. Please, God. Please keep them away.*

"Brent, let us in. You wanted power. We can give it," the almost audible voice claimed.

*This is not happening. This isn't real. You're creating these voices yourself, and you've got to stop it.*

"Brent, you know us. We've been with you for a while, now. We've chosen *you* to give our power to. You can finally have control of your life."

[1] Go to Appendix A for information on Multiple Personality Disorder vs. Demonism

Panic began to rise within him. Would he give in this time? Would the arguments that these voices made be more convincing this time? He felt his protective resolve waning.

"Brent, take control. Take charge of your life. You've been trying to use your gifts to influence those around you. You've seen small results. You need us. You need us *in* you. Allow us to enter."

*No. I won't. I won't do this.* He felt a cold sweat seep to the surface of his skin. "Leave me alone," he demanded in a strained whisper. "I don't want you in my life anymore."

"It's too late for that, Brent. There's no backing out now. Let us give you what you've been seeking. Power."

"I don't want it anymore. I don't need it."

The gravely whisper continued in his mind, "Sure you do, Brent. You need what we can give. It's free. It won't cost you a thing. You will enjoy the pleasure that we can give you. You will feel the warm, physical ecstasy of letting us enjoy your body. We'll give you such intense pleasure that you'll wonder why you waited this long."

Brent knew what they were claiming. They were promising sexual gratification. He could have the power he'd been yearning for if he would allow them to defile him sexually. This was insane! There was a price. It wouldn't be free. And, Brent was too scared to allow it. "No! I won't allow it. Leave me alone!"

"Brent ..."

"I said *no!*" Brent rolled out of bed, tears trailing down his cheeks. Why wasn't God doing something? Maybe He didn't exist after all. No, that wasn't true, and he knew it. The fact that something was haunting him every night proved that there was a spirit realm.

Brent walked to his dresser and stared into the mirror set into the hutch above the dresser. He was terrified. He could see it in his own eyes. *I want out of this. I need out of this. I can't take it any longer.* Without breaking eye contact with himself, he opened a small drawer built into the right side of the hutch and found his Boy Scout knife. Unfolding it, he lowered his eyes to his left wrist. The scar was still there. How many times had he stood here with the same intention he had now? Only one time had he set aside the fear of penetrating the skin. He remembered how the blood had pooled on his wrist before spilling over and down onto his dresser. Could he actually do the deed this time?

*I hate my life. I* hate *it! God, please, help me do this. Help me succeed.* He placed the tip of the blade onto the scar. The voices returned.

"Brent, maybe you're right. Maybe this is the best solution. Your fears will be over. You will no longer cause your parents' marriage to fail. You will finally know peace."

"Shut up," Brent demanded through clinched teeth. He began to apply the needed downward pressure.

‡‡‡

**1:10 a.m.**

Hannah Moore knew that sleep was not an option. Not now. Not while she felt the Lord's continued call to prayer. Initially she didn't know which of her six grandsons she was to pray for. But it became clear as she began to intercede. It was Brent. She hadn't seen him in nearly seven months, not since the annual visit by her daughter, Sharon, and her family. The family came down from Millsville, Ohio, once a year for a two-week visit, something she always looked forward to. She loved all her children and grandchildren deeply.

Remembering their last visit, Hannah recalled the somber mood that Brent seemed to have upon arriving. He was distant and looked ... tired. She remembered thinking that he looked like many adults who had been shouldering too many worries. *He's too young to look that way*, she had thought then. But, a few days into the family's visit, Brent looked completely refreshed and happy, without a care in the world. With that her concerns had evaporated.

Now she focused her prayers on the boy. She knew that "old slew foot" was up to no good as far as her grandson was concerned. She was familiar with Satan's devices. She'd battled him off and on for years. He and his demonic horde were formidable. But, since the Lord was directing the prayer, she knew that God was going to move on Brent's behalf. All she had to do to keep God's hands—and His plan—moving forward was to remain diligent in her supplications.[2]

She had gotten out of her chair nearly an hour ago, falling to her knees beside her bed. She intuitively knew that this situation, whatever it was, was going to require more than casual prayer, and she grew up believing that intercession happened on one's knees.

The Spirit persisted in His urgings. Therefore she would also persist. Maybe it would be a night without sleep, but little did

---

[2] Go to Appendix A for information on Effective Prayer

that matter. She would keep a long-distance, prayerful vigil until the Spirit gave her release.

# Chapter Four

**Saturday, January 10 – 1:17 a.m.**

He had failed again. Brent wept on his knees where he had collapsed, the open knife held loosely in his right hand.

Again he had failed to penetrate the skin. He failed because he was scared. At the moment that he felt actual pain, induced by the point of his knife, he thought about something. Or, rather, some *place*.

It was a destination that he thought little of, if it even existed. As he had stood there watching the blade push against the taut skin of his wrist, a sudden recollection invaded his mind.

His grandmother, whom he'd always known as "Mamaw," had often talked about Heaven. And did she ever make it sound real. There never seemed to be a twinge of doubt in her mind that it existed. "It's where I will be with your Papaw again someday," she would say. "There are so many people that I long to see again, and many of them will be there on the opposite bank of the river waiting for me as I cross into glory."

*A river? In Heaven?* He remembered thinking how impossible that sounded. But, if she said it was there, who was he to say that it wasn't?

In none of his other attempts to kill himself had Heaven entered his thoughts. What had always stopped him was the remembrance of the pain that was created the first time he had succeeded in drawing blood. He couldn't fathom the pain of pushing it all the way in then drawing it back.

Then there was Lydia. What if she ended up being the one who found him? He couldn't bear the thought. Tonight, though, she slept at the home of a friend. If he was going to finally follow through, this would have been the perfect night.

He sighed. *So much for convenience.*

Now, new and troubling thoughts occupied his mind; thoughts that revolved around a place called Heaven.

It was a place where good people went. Certainly he wouldn't—*couldn't*—measure up like his Mamaw. But it sure would be good to dream about such a place; to have his inveterate nightmare replaced by a dream of Heaven...

He sighed again.

Why even bother thinking about it? That wasn't where he'd go anyway. And besides, the thought of the place was just one more thing that kept him locked in this devilish world for another day and night.

The notion of reliving all of this emotion and mental torture again in twenty-four hours caused him to take one more glance at his knife and contemplate another attempt. But, again, his thoughts drifted back to after-death destinations.

If not Heaven, where? Doesn't the existence of Heaven, if it truly does exist, presume an actual place called Hell? And, if so, wasn't it obvious that he was a ripe candidate for admittance there?

Brent got up and began to pace, open knife still in his hand.

In times past he would have laughed it up with friends who, usually after a few drinks, would boast of the parties that they'd have once they all arrived in Hell. Someone would usually start singing or shouting "Highway to Hell!" to everyone's amusement.

He wasn't laughing now, though. Something in his mind screamed that Hell was to be avoided at all cost.

So, there it lay, sprawled out in front of his mind's eye; a roadmap showing two entirely different destinations. Neither of the routes promised even the remotest hope of safety ... of peace.

He was at a fork in the road, and he'd arrived at it by a one-way street. To the left was life as usual. To the right was suicide. And there was no way to back up.

Only minutes ago the decision to travel to the right was paramount in his mind. But now he sat, stationary, knowing that, with no way to keep it from happening, life was going to drag him kicking, screaming, and clawing to the left. All because he was scared. For months he'd been too scared to live, but now ... now he was also too scared to die.

*I've just discovered the definition of misery,* he thought.

Brent folded his knife. He walked over to the hutch, put the knife in the drawer, closed it, and walked back over to his bed. He'd survived another night.

*Survived. Yeah, there's some irony.*

At least the voices were gone—for now. They wouldn't torment him again until tomorrow night. And now he'd be able to fall asleep.

Now, though, he had to face the nightmare.

‡‡‡

**1:23 a.m.**

Hannah felt a sense that the battle was ebbing. She didn't get up immediately, though. It was always safer to pray a little longer than needed than to assume the battle was over and stop, only to find out later that she could have done more.

"Lord, is that it? Is there more prayin' that needs to be done? I feel like the enemy has retreated. Is that true?" She waited. She listened.

Silence. Calm. Peace.

"So be it, Lord. But, Father, I come to You now with a pleadin' heart. You wouldn't have burdened me to fight tonight if You didn't have Brent's safety in mind. And I know that safety to You is a matter of eternity. Father, I don't know if that boy knows You or not. In my mind I have doubts about that.

"O Redeemer of the souls of Man, don't leave this boy alone. You trouble him. You get his attention. You put the right people into his path to share Your love with him. And, just to make sure you do, I'm going to trouble *You* day and night until that boy is safely in Your arms." She looked up and shook her index finger at the air, imagining that her Lord was looking down at it, and hopefully smiling. "You don't want an old, determined woman pestering You to no end, do You?" She smiled. "Actually, I don't reckon You'd mind that at all."

Hannah got up off the floor, her knees arguing with her all the way up. "Next time, Lord, would You remind me to kneel on a pillow?" She got into bed and pulled her thick comforter up to her neck. She was asleep in moments.

## Chapter Five

**Saturday, January 17 – 10:19 a.m.**

It had been a week since his last major encounter with the voices from hell, as he had come to consider them. But he was suspicious. Was it was all a ploy? For some reason or another they seemed to be less effective in getting to him. It wasn't that they had stopped their nightly visits. No, they still came. But just as quickly as he would hear one of these ... those *things*, it would shut up and go away; as if it had been muzzled.

This gave him a modicum of peace, but no true comfort. The fact that the voices still came, if only for a moment or two, was evidence enough that he was still in trouble.

Brent sighed.

He looked up into a near-cloudless sky and squinted; the intensity of the sunlight causing his hazel eyes to water. It was probably just below freezing, even in the sunshine. The warmth and moisture of his breath caused puffs of white to float away in the morning air.

Looking down, he saw his shadow stretching down the driveway, causing his five foot, eleven inches to look nearly twice that. His thick, dark hair stuck out around the stocking cap he had pulled over his head, something his Grandma Lawton had made for him. It was an item that was worn in the daylight *only* when there was no one else around. He chuckled. He had a matching scarf and mittens that remained in the closet. He *could* wear them ... one item at a time, perhaps, but after having seen what he looked like with everything on at the same time...

He laughed.

Yep, cap *or* scarf, but never both, and *certainly* never the mittens.

It felt good to smile. If nothing else, his grandmother's amusing gift had provided the small lift that he needed right now. He knew it would be short lived, though.

He desperately wanted to talk with someone. But to whom do you speak about voices that you hear in your head, voices that are from some dark, wicked being-*thing*? All he could think of was a Catholic priest. And the only image that would form in his mind about priests and demonic voices was 'The Exorcist.' And there was *no way* he was going to allow anybody to throw burning holy water on him!

Was he possessed? He didn't think so. But things were definitely serious.

He almost produced a contemptuous laugh. Of course things were serious. He'd been trying to kill himself, for Pete's sake! And that brought up another question...

Why had the compulsion to kill himself suddenly subsided over the past week? "Subsided" was probably the wrong word. Eased, maybe. He still wasn't happy. He still wanted out of this existence called his life, and rid of all the bad things were still happening.

Case and point—last night.

Brent had arrived at his school on time for warm-ups before the basketball game against rival Jackson High School. He had entered the season as a starting forward, and he thought he was doing well...at least well enough, all things considered. But as soon as he was done suiting up in the locker room, Coach Chamberlin called out to him and waved him into his office.

"What's up, Coach?" Brent had asked.

"Brent, I'm sitting you down tonight."

Stunned, Brent responded with, "What? I'm out?"

"Not 'out.' Sitting. You won't be starting. Randall will be taking your place tonight."

"Coach ... I'm ... Can I ask why?"

"Brent, have a seat."

Brent remained standing.

Coach Chamberlin looked straight into his eyes, pointed to the gray, vinyl-covered office chair and again said, "Brent, *have* a *seat.*"

Brent complied. He hadn't been trying to make a statement by his refusal; he'd just felt stuck in place.

"Brent, you know me. In the two seasons that you've played for me, have I *ever* been unfair to you, or for that matter, unfair to *any* of the members of this team?"

Brent hadn't had to think about that. Everyone knew that George Chamberlin was a player's coach. He was tough in practices, and he made sure that everyone pulled his weight, but he gave no one on the team a reason to dislike him for showing favoritism.

Brent liked this man. He had from the very start of his first practice with him. In fact, if it hadn't been for this coach he would never have found himself as a starter.

In that moment, he had remembered the day that the coach had taken him aside in the midst of one preseason practice and told him he was going to feel a little extra pain in his legs over the coming weeks. When Brent had asked why, Coach Chamberlin had responded, "Because I'm going to stretch you. I see something in you that can help this team, but it's going to take some extra effort on your part ... and mine. Are you willing?"

Brent had exuberantly said yes.

"Well?" His coach's voice brought him back to the moment.

"No, sir," said Brent. "I've never seen you be unfair to any of us."

"I hoped that was still the case. Brent, something's wrong. I can see it in your eyes. I can see it in the way that you've pulled back from what used to be strong interaction with your teammates. And, I can see it in your game.

"I don't have the luxury of waiting for you to pull yourself out of whatever's been beating you down. Randall has been working as hard as anyone on this team, and he deserves a shot. And, right now—and maybe it's *only* for right now—you are the weak link in my lineup."

Brent tensed, clenching his jaw.

"Can you talk about what's going on? Can I help you somehow?"

Brent wasn't prepared for any of the conversation at hand, let alone such a direct question. "Umm ... No, sir. I'll be fine. Just haven't been feeling well for a while, but I think I'm getting over it." He got up. "Did you already tell Randall?"

"No, not yet."

"I'll let him know." He had turned to go, and then hesitated. Turning back, he'd looked into Coach Chamberlin's eyes and said, "I'm sorry I disappointed you."

"Brent, you're not a disappointment to me. I can see that there's something internal going on that's had a negative effect on you and your game. Once it's behind you, you can earn your starting position back. But it's not a given. It *will* have to be earned again. You okay with that?"

"Yes, Coach. Thanks."

With that, Brent had walked back into the locker room and informed Randall that he was about to have his first-ever start in a basketball game; their *biggest* game.

On the way home from their biggest loss, his parents had apparently decided not to prod him with the why-didn't-you-start question. That was appreciated. In the midst of all the other stuff that happened at home, he still found evidences that his parents cared.

He had spent a restless, and somewhat silent, night in bed. He slept in until about 9:45 a.m. then got up, ate a bowl of

Frosted Mini-Wheats, and headed outside. He didn't know what he was going to do with his day, but he didn't want to stay inside to figure it out.

In the light of day, with the sun shining down on the snow-frosted lawn, he felt like he could think about his life situations without the fear he dealt with at night. He knew he didn't have any choice but to start trying to think things through.

To what end? He couldn't fathom.

He reached into his left coat pocket and pulled out the tiny book he had found in the attic Thursday after school. His mom had asked him to take the rest of the Christmas decorations up that she had just packed and to put them with the others that his dad had put away the evening before.

After the struggle of getting those awkward boxes into the attic, which really wasn't much more than a crawl space, he had noticed his dad's old military duffel bag. His dad had been in the Navy, and every once in a while, as a kid, Brent would rifle through it and try on his dad's old uniforms and medals. He'd also examined the little trinkets that had been collected during his dad's tours of duty abroad.

Brent pulled the bag over into an area where a single 60-watt bulb suspended in the rafters could shine down into its contents. It had been a few years, so he opened it and stuck his hand in, looking for evidence of happier times. He felt his way down toward the bottom, looking for what he used to call his dad's "Popeye hat."

As a little boy he couldn't believe that his dad had Popeye the Sailor's hat. He remembered the awe that he had felt. What had he been, six, maybe seven, years old?

Brent found it again and pulled it out. He knew that it used to be snow white in color, but it had yellowed a bit with the years. Staring at it, he recalled that it was because of this funny-looking hat that he had first tried spinach. Big mistake. Wrong thing to ask for. That experience had been so bad that he never wore Popeye's hat again.

The memory brought another smile to Brent's face.

Putting the hat back into the bag, his hand hit something that felt too hard to be clothing. As he turned his hand to grip it, he realized that it was a book. Pulling it out, he saw that it was a United States Department of the Navy-issued New Testament. He sat in the cold and just stared at it. It stirred something within him, and he couldn't bring himself to put it back in the bag. So, it had come down the ladder with him and into the warmth of the house.

He slept with the little book lying beside him on his night stand. There was a slight feeling of comfort knowing that it was close, and because of that, he had decided that the next morning he'd do some reading.

Walking down the length of the driveway he looked at the New Testament that he grasped in his right hand. It felt as though he held some sort of weapon. Odd. Even if it were true, he still didn't have a clue as to how it could be used.

He walked a few blocks up the street to a neighboring park where he knew there was an area of picnic tables. There wouldn't be anyone crazy enough to be sitting around in this weather, so despite the chill, there he would begin reading.

‡‡‡

**Sunday, January 18 – 12:35 a.m.**

Brent lie in bed thinking about how he'd failed again. *My lot in life*, he reflected. Early in the day, he had sat in the cold for nearly a half hour trying to figure out what to read in that New Testament. When he finally settled on starting at the beginning, he was faced with a litany of unpronounceable names. Every name "begat" another name.

Determining that there would be little help from the begating chapter, he had skipped ahead. He'd found some areas where Jesus seemed to be talking, text that was printed in red. He'd figured that maybe reading Jesus' words would bring the answers that he was seeking. After all, the founder of Christianity should know the most about spiritual things, including unseen evil beings.

He had come upon a couple passages where Jesus dealt with possessed people and cast the demons out; which strangely unnerved him. However, seeing as how Jesus didn't seem to be all that interested in showing up with him at the park, Brent couldn't see how this man would be able to tell his demons to depart.

*They* are *demons, aren't they? I've got demons in me.*

Searching further in the small black book for answers, he'd become frustrated with words that he didn't understand. And the uncommon words that he *was* able to figure out were foreign in today's world. What he would do for a little modern English.

*I'll never make sense of this*, he'd determined. When had the book been written? He looked at the copyright page of the book and saw that it was originally published in 1611. No wonder he couldn't understand half of what he read. With another sigh, he closed the book and treaded back home.

With his harassing spirits having paid their very brief and, again, restrained visit for the night, Brent waited for sleep to overtake him. He whispered a small prayer before drifting off...

"God, where are you? Do you even care? I need help."

## Chapter Six

### **Wednesday, March 25 – 12:25 p.m.**

Brent sat nervously in the high school principal's office. Mr. McClaren had gone to the assistant principal's office where Galen Todd was receiving his punishment, leaving him anxious and alone. His parents were going to let him have it. Again.

Galen was a kid he'd been having fights with for the past few years—fights that oftentimes got out of hand. For the life of him, he couldn't remember what had started their conflicts back in junior high school. Regardless, they didn't like each other, and rarely did it take more than a wrong look in one or the other's direction for words to let loose. Such was the case this day.

Brent had been in the lunchroom eating when Galen had passed by his table. This time it had come to more than words, and they'd been caught. Again.

Undoubtedly, this would result in a *minimum* of multiple detentions and a letter home. But he knew in his gut that they had both stepped over a line this time that would net them some suspension time.

Brent touched his lip for the umpteenth time, wondering if it looked as fat as it felt. *Man, am I going to get it.* He hoped against hope for detention. He could forge his dad's signature on the letter—proof that the issue had been dealt with at home. He could also develop an excuse for why he was spending non-basketball-related time at the school.

*You're not going to get that lucky this time, and you know it.*

Brent wanted to yell. Why had he let Galen goad him into another fight? *At least he won't fare any better.*

Mr. McClaren walked back into his office, pulled the door closed behind him, and sat down behind his desk.

"Brent, seriously, what is it with you? You're a bright kid; you're smarter than this."

"I don't know, Mr. McClaren. I'm kicking myself now," responded Brent, hoping that his sorrow-filled tone might somehow lessen the blow he knew was coming.

Mr. McClaren leaned back in his chair and folded his hands behind his head. He closed his eyes for a moment and made a few of his habitual, Morse-code-sounding hums. Then he sat back up and rested his folded hands on the desk.

"I'm afraid I can't be lenient this time." He looked Brent directly in the eyes. "Brent, I like you. You're a pretty good kid. And when you're not around Galen, you're a model student. But, that doesn't reduce the need for this punishment. It only makes it harder for me to exact it.

"I'm afraid that I'm going to have to suspend you. The two of you are getting five days. But, since Mr. Harris caught Galen starting the conflict, he's going to be sent home to serve his, and yours will be served here at the school."

"Sounds like he's still getting the better deal," remarked Brent.

"Only if his parents don't care. With five days out of school, they will count against his total absences. Yours won't. But your days here at the school will probably feel a lot like confinement. You'll do your homework, you'll get to eat lunch if you bring something with you, and you'll come out of it without having fallen very far behind in your studies. I doubt the same will be said of Galen."

"And my parents?"

"We've already called your mom," Mr. McClaren replied.

Brent sighed. *That figures.*

"Brent, you can make this time worthwhile, or you can rebel against it. It's all up to you." Mr. McClaren handed Brent an envelope with what was probably the terms of his suspension. It had *Mr. and Mrs. Lawton* scribbled on the front.

"You're probably already aware, but Mr. Chamberlin is in charge of in-school suspensions. You'll report to him first thing in the morning."

"Mr. Chamberlin? ... *Coach* Chamberlin?"

"That's right," confirmed the principal.

Brent dropped his head and brought his hands up to his face. *Great*, Brent inwardly moaned. *This just keeps getting better and better.*

‡‡‡

**1:15 p.m.**

"What is it with you? Another fight?"

"Mom, don't get bent out of shape. You heard Mr. McClaren say that I didn't start it. It was Galen."

They were on their way home in his mom's car, and Brent was getting an earful.

"Don't even try it, Brent! I also heard Mr. McClaren say that you willingly retaliated. You could have left well enough alone."

Brent shook his head and sighed. This was a fight he wouldn't win, and when his dad got home from work he'd hear it all again.

"Yeah, mom. Whatever you say."

His mom ignored the comment, probably thinking that it would make an even stronger point.

After a few minutes they were back at home. He had a few hours before 'final judgment' fell upon him, so he went straight up to his room, closed the door, dropped his books on his desk, and allowed himself to fall backward onto his bed.

"My life sucks! I hate this!" he exclaimed. "Everything is going *wrong!*" He slammed his arms down on the mattress.

His thoughts progressed toward a conclusion that he didn't want to consider. Maybe the voices were right. What if he did take the power offered to him? Could things—*would* things—change for the better? The thought made him uneasy. He rolled out of bed and stood up as if the mere idea might cause his 'visitors' to return.

*This is crazy. Stop being an idiot.*

Brent pulled the chair out from under his desk and sat down. He may be suspended, but that didn't diminish the amount of homework he had to get done. Pulling his American History book out of the pile that he had brought home, he began to read.

‡‡‡

**Thursday, 12:04 a.m.**

Brent lay on his back in bed. His hands were folded beneath his head as he thought about these latest events in his life.

It had been a long day. As expected, Brent's dad had come home and "heard about it" from his mom. Brent had listened through his closed door as his dad put up a weak defense on his behalf.

"He's a teenage boy, for crying out loud! Boys get into fights! Quit trying to baby him!" his father proclaimed.

His mom stood her ground, and then he heard his dad start up the stairs.

Upon reaching his door, his dad gave a couple of soft knocks, and entered his room. Then Brent received the obligatory right-versus-wrong speech, followed by what Brent thought was a bit of an over-the-top grounding. Two weeks of no T.V., no phone, and no going out.

Now he lie consumed in his customary darkness from hell, feeling angry at the world.

"That punk is going to get it," Brent voiced under his breath. He'd had it with Galen. The next opportunity he had, he'd make sure that Galen got the message: *Don't even breathe near me, or you'll suffer.*

"That's it, Brent. That'a boy."

Brent groaned. It was *them.*

"Ready now, Brent? Ready for the help we can give you?"

‡‡‡

**12:07 a.m.**

Hannah awoke and sat up in bed. She was wide awake and alert, and she knew immediately what that meant. This time she didn't waste a second with questions. She just began praying.

There wasn't a twinge of anger for the interruption of her rest. She held no resentment toward the boy whose life was causing so much loss of sleep. She loved him and she used that love to fuel what she needed to do.

How many times had she also thought about walking over to her son's home to use the phone to call her grandson? But each time that the thought entered her mind she dismissed it, feeling a check in her spirit, and knowing that her calls of concern might just add to the boy's troubles.

No, this war would be won by God, by His plan and His methods. She would not meddle beyond her simple obedience to God's calls to act.

Hannah swung her legs out of bed, dropped a pillow on the floor, and knelt down to pray.

‡‡‡

**12:08 a.m.**

Brent knew that he was getting weaker, getting closer to caving in to the promptings of the voices. Of course, now, many of the promptings were coming from memory, as the beings seemed to continue getting 'muzzled.' He could not figure out what was causing them to suddenly stop prodding him. There was neither rhyme nor reason to it.

But the voices were clever. They knew what to say before they were silenced.

Tonight was no different, especially with what had happened at the school today and with his subsequent grounding. He was torqued-off at the world, and he wanted to be able to force some sort of recompense.

He had given ground in his mind to the idea that, if he had additional powers, he could affect Galen at a distance. He could also further manipulate circumstances at home to his liking. He mused that it was about time he effected changes that *he* wanted in his life.

The rubber was now hitting the road. His anger fueled growing hostility within his soul. He was faced with another opportunity to say yes to these dark beings, and at the moment, he couldn't think of a single good reason to say no.

Not once had he ever entertained the notion of a one-on-one conversation with the voices, save for putting up a protective front. But now...

"Brent, think about it. Power, physical gratification, influence, and..." The words were choked off as if someone had pressed a mute button on a remote.

What happened? *No, not this time!* Brent felt a slight panic, believing his opportunity was about to be lost. "Hey ... Hey!" he said in a stiff whisper. "Not now! You can't leave! Not this time!" But it was too late. For the first time in this hellish relationship he felt robbed.

‡‡‡

**3:26 a.m.**

Brent looked down and saw his feet on the dark wood of the railroad tie. The darkness consumed everything, but he could still see. How was it possible?

He stood in 'his spot,' and once again began looking around at outstretched blackness.

Despair enveloped him. Meaninglessness. Utter meaninglessness.

*I deserve this place. I am nothing. My life is nothing.*

He stood.

He stood and wept.

*Did I have a chance to avoid this? How did I end up here?* He let out another always-silent sigh. *I belong here. I am here, because this is where I belong.*

How many times had he thought to call out for help? But in this place, sound did not travel, let alone exist.

It wasn't a place of evil. It wasn't a place of *anything*. It just was. It just existed. Devoid of any presence except his own, it amounted to nothing more than being able to inhale the dark, silent void of outer space.

He looked, again, down to his feet. He realized that his gaze always returned downward. It was the only way that he had any sense of depth perception.

Railroad ties. Blackened old railroad ties. The reason for their existence when nothing else did...? It didn't matter. Just like nothing else mattered. Though he couldn't reason out the why, he merely accepted that they were there.

Without warning a shaft of intense light shot down from out of nowhere, causing him to gasp! It was far off into the distance, but it was staggering.

Brent could hardly breathe. His heart began to race.

He stood there and stared at it, his soul aching for it.

Without any thought to consequences, he took a single step forward, then stopped. He had been in this place for a thousand million years, and never once had it occurred to him to take even a partial stride. But there had never been a reason to do so before, had there?

He took another step forward toward the light. He looked down. He saw that there was another railroad tie on which to step, and he did so. He looked up again at the shaft of white light.

His steps became methodic: Look down, see a tie, take a step, look at the light. Look down, see a tie, take a step, look at the light.

Over and over he repeated the actions. The stream of illumination was still far distant, and though he could not tell how far, he seemed to be making progress. One thing caught his attention now that he was a little closer to it. The light appeared to be coming down out of the blackness from a hundred, a thousand, a million miles up, and it fell straight down in a narrow beam to a single point, then stopped. It looked as though it came to an end on the same horizontal plane on which he was now walking.

He continued forward, carefully making sure that each step had a railroad tie below it. Each step was greeted with another surge of anticipation, a feeling of importance that was gathering like a storm in his mind.

*What does this mean?* His psyche screamed for an answer.

Forward he continued, each small step equally a torture and a hope.

He stopped.

What he now saw made no sense. The light was cast down and focused upon ... a flower; a single, long-stemmed flower.

It stood erect in a red clay pot as it rested on the surface of the railroad ties. It looked to be a white daisy. The bloom was maybe another thirty to forty steps away. The beam of light fell only upon that solitary point in the otherwise vast expanse of emptiness.

*It's beautiful! It's ... it's ... beautiful!*

Tears filled his eyes. An ache filled his heart. *If I can reach it ... If I can hold it, I can keep it ... take care of it.*

A sense of purpose and hope permeated every fiber of his being.

He looked down to take a step onto another railroad tie, but something was different. He stood a moment, unmoving, to look and ponder. The next tie, on which he would need to step, was not pressed up against the one on which he stood. It was a good six inches away, with blackness filling the gap between. Curiosity waning, he took a slightly broader step onto the next tie. He looked up and saw the flower.

He was on the verge of joy!

He looked down, again, to take another step and saw that the next tie was cocked at an angle away from the one on which he now stood, creating an even greater gulf to bridge. He stepped. He stood. He looked up.

His heart was hammering; his pulse was throbbing in his neck.

He looked down.

Fear stabbed at his heart and mind.

*Something's wrong. Something's going wrong!*

He watched as a tie to the right of where he stood seemed to sink into the blackness of whatever it was that the pieces of wood rested upon. Another, this one to his left, did the same.

He felt the tie below his feet begin to shift. Survival instincts kicked in, and he stepped forward onto the next available tie. It appeared, now, that *none* of the ties ahead of him touched another. It was as if each one had been scattered into its current resting place by a whirlwind.

Another tie ahead of him, and to his left, began to sink into the blackness below. And another did the same a little further ahead. And, then another. It was beginning to happen all over!

He looked forward into the distance and saw his flower, his hope, his *purpose*, still sitting securely upon its own railroad tie. He shuddered. *It* cannot *go away!*

He looked down again and realized an even greater terror.

He'd been mistaken. The ties were not sinking. They were falling!

As more ties disappeared, creating greater gaps between the remaining ones, he could see, through those breaches, blackened pieces of lumber falling, spiraling, and tumbling downward.

*The railroad ties rest on ... nothing!*

His breath caught in his chest. Time was running out. He knew—he just *knew*—that it was just a matter of time before two things happened: gaps too large to jump over would be created, and eventually—*God, no!*—the flower would tumble out of his existence forever.

There was no other option but to run, leaping over newly created fissures to gain purchase on another wooden surface. He jumped. He landed. He felt the tie falter below his feet and he jumped again.

*God, please! Don't let me lose it! It's the only thing I have left! It is my only hope!*

Again he jumped, reaching another tie. The ties around him were beginning to fall three and four at a time, tumbling out of sight. He made to jump for another, when it began to fall from view.

*Where?! Where?!* He kept the shaft of light as his directional goal as he continued to jump, waver, and pitch. The gaps were becoming too big to manage. *They're too far!* He leapt for the next closest one, barely making it, and fell to a knee to regain his balance.

He was only a couple of leaps away! He saw that the flower pot rested upon a tie pressed on either side by more of the same. It almost looked like a wood deck made up of maybe ten or twelve giant slats of the thick, dark wood. *Good, it's safe,* he thought, and leapt for another hopefully-secure surface. He'd made it again.

Brent knew that he shouldn't, but he looked behind him anyway. Black railroad ties were falling, dozens at a time, as he scanned the distance. He shifted his focus back to his goal. The tie on which he stood lay in a straight line, jutting toward the next closest tie. He took a running leap and made it safely.

He was going to make it! Just one more jump and he'd be there. He'd be able to touch and hold his precious, *precious* treasure! He took a deep breath. There would be no running leap this time, just a single, precarious bound across six feet of emptiness.

He jumped.

He was there! He'd made it!

His heart swelled with emotion and his eyes filled with tears as he took a single step toward the brightly-lighted flower. He crouched down. He willed his hand forward to caress the flower's delicate petals. Then, without warning, the tie on which it rested fell from sight. The flower tumbled downward, quickly enveloped by darkness; its beauty—and his hope—gone forever.

He screamed, with all that was in him, a completely silent *Noooooooooo!*

## Chapter Seven

### Thursday, March 26 – 8:01 a.m.

"Sorry I'm late," announced Coach Chamberlin as he walked into the small, windowless in-school suspension room. He stopped and stared at the lone occupant. "Brent?" His eyebrows pinched together in a disappointed wince. "Tell me what you did."

"I don't suppose starting with 'it wasn't totally my fault' is going to make much difference."

"I'd say that's a pretty good assumption."

As if it were a part of his story, Brent sighed for the hundredth time before speaking. He looked down at his notebook, unwilling to look into the eyes of yet another displeased person. "I punched Galen Todd."

"I see. And I'm assuming that he did or said something that made you feel like he deserved it. Am I right?"

"Yeah."

"Then why are you the only one sitting in this room with me?"

"Galen was totally suspended."

"Totally, huh?" The coach shook his head. "Okay, Brent. It looks like it will probably be just you and me for the next two days. Next week, though, I'm sure it will be a different story. You're not the only one in this school who lands in a seat before Mr. McClaren.

"Brent, just because you're one of my key players doesn't mean you're going to get any special privileges. You understand that, don't you?"

Brent gave a slow nod.

Coach Chamberlin sat down in a chair behind a small table at the head of the room that served as a workstation. "You'd better get started on any homework that you have. There's no sleeping, so fight the urge to lay your head on your arms. Believe it or not, in-school suspension is a form of punishment, and the days are going to feel long even with homework to do."

"It already feels long," replied Brent.

The coach looked at Brent, obviously searching for the right words. Finding them, he said, "I'm going to invade your personal space a little bit with a question. You've resisted telling me before, and I think that had something to do with your teammates always being in proximity. But the basketball season is over. It's just you and me, now."

Tension developed throughout Brent's neck and back, knowing where his coach's words were heading.

"Something's wrong. And, while you may think of me as just another authority figure doing his job, I want you to know that I really *do* care. If I can, I want to help." He paused to allow his last statement to have a little impact. "Can you tell me what's going on? Does it have something to do with life at home? Here at school?"

Brent looked up at his coach, a wary look touching his eyes. Would it hurt to trust this man? Could he just lay things out and expect someone like him to understand? He looked down at his notebook again. He'd risk it. His pride was pretty much demolished anyway.

"Coach, it has to do with a lot of things. Home, school, you name it. But I don't think you'll understand. *God* sure doesn't seem to." He shook his head. "I'm into something that even *I* don't understand; something that I can't get out of."

"I'm listening," said Coach Chamberlin. He stood and pulled his chair out from behind the table. Placing it a couple of feet away from Brent, he straddled it and sat down, the back of the chair providing an arm rest.

"Coach, I *really* don't want to talk about this." Brent began to choke up, tears pooling in his eyes.

"Brent, it's okay. You may not believe it, but you're with a friend."

Brent rubbed away the tears before they fell. "You're going to think I'm crazy." How he wanted to get up and run. The heel of his left foot began tapping the floor nervously.

"Try me."

"Coach, I'm lost. I'm lost, and I don't know what to do. I'm afraid ... and ..." Brent stopped. His tongue seized. He had actually believed he could follow through. He fought in his mind for clarity. *I can't*, he thought to himself. *I've still got too much to lose. This could get me cut from the team.*

Brent looked up, his red eyes showing the stress behind the tears. "I'm sorry, Coach. I thought I could, but I can't. I can't tell you." His eyes trailed downward again.

"Okay, Brent. Relax. I'm not going to force it." He began to get up to move back to his work area, but paused and sat back down.

"Brent? You said something a minute ago. I'm going to ask about it because you brought it up. You mentioned God."

"Oh ... yeah ... *Him*. What about it?"

"Do you believe in Him?"

"I'm forced to believe in Him. I don't really have the luxury of not believing."

"What do you mean? Are your parents forcing their beliefs on you?"

Brent released a cynical laugh. "My parents? Nuh-uh. They could use some religion, if you ask me. Coach, the reason that I can't explain what I'm going through is the same reason I can't tell you how I know there's a God."

"Okay," Coach Chamberlin continued, "Let me ask you this, then." Again he paused, making sure that he had Brent's full attention. Brent's eyes met his again. "If you were to die tonight, would you go to Heaven?"

Brent looked up into his coach's eyes, stunned. "What?"

"Would you?"

"I ... uhh ..." How was he supposed to respond to this? He panicked, searching within himself for some way out. This was cutting too close. "Yeah, ... I mean ... I don't..." Brent looked down again, knowing the next words out of his mouth were going to be a lie. "Yes," he said firmly. And seemingly without the ability to keep his mouth closed, he followed it up with, "I hope."

"Let me ask it another way. If you were to die tonight and found yourself standing before the throne of God ... If *He* were to look you in the eyes and ask, 'Why should I let you into My Heaven?' what would you say?"

*What the...* Brent was at a total loss. If he were standing on a log in the middle of a lake he couldn't have been more off balance than he was now. "Coach, I ..." He stopped. He took a deep breath and spoke the only truthful answer that he could manage. "I've ... I've never killed anyone. I don't mean to hurt people. I ..." He couldn't find any more words. *I what? I ... what?* He was staggered by his inability to produce another sentence. *That* was his best argument? *That* was the single statement that he could give to God as his defense against Hell?

Brent looked up again into the eyes of his coach, his own registering fear. He could see that Coach Chamberlin recognized it.

"Brent, listen to me..."

"Coach ... Coach, I..." Brent's thoughts were a torrent of emotions, of horrified realization.

"Brent. Shhh...It's okay."

Brent looked back and forth in his coach's eyes, looking for something—*anything*—that would steal his panic away. He wasn't seeing it.

"Brent," Coach Chamberlin said more insistently. "It's okay. Focus on what I'm saying."

The fog in Brent's mind seemed to clear a little bit.

"Brent, what are you doing tonight?"

"Tonight?"

"Yes, Brent. Tonight. What are you doing this evening?"

"I, uhh, I'm grounded. I'm grounded for two weeks. I'm not doing anything."

"Brent, my wife and I are going to an event called Freedom Rings. I'd like for you to come with us."

"I don't think I'll be able to. What is it?"

"It's kind of a get-together of people from all sorts of different backgrounds and life challenges. There will be music, someone will talk about the Bible..."

Brent cut him off. "Church?"

"Not exactly. It started off as something small, about a dozen guys and gals. They wanted to get together as a group, where no one would criticize them for their lack of Bible knowledge or the way they wore their hair or their clothes. They especially didn't want to be looked down upon because of the situations that most of them had in their lives.

"The man who pulled the group together wanted to let these people know that God wasn't concerned with what they looked like or where they came from, just that God cared about each of them as individuals, that He cared about them in *spite* of the messes that they'd landed themselves in.

"This little group grew. It now has more than 700 attendees."

"When did you start going?" asked Brent, obviously captured by what he'd just been told.

"Brent, I was part of that original small group." Coach Chamberlin let that register before he continued. "You're not the only one who knows what desperation is."

‡‡‡

**4:55 p.m.**

Sharon Lawton stood in her kitchen making preparations for dinner. Crisp, green vegetables, strewn about the counter space, were washed and ready to be chopped up for a salad. She was just opening a cabinet to pull out a large serving bowl when the phone rang. She grabbed the bowl, set it down in the midst of the scattered greens, then reached for the phone.

"Lawton residence."

"Hello, Mrs. Lawton. It's George Chamberlin, Brent's basketball coach."

"Oh, hi, Mr. Chamberlin. What can I do for you?" Sharon asked, already preparing herself for another dose of bad news from the school.

"Is Brent available?"

"I believe he is. Will you hold for a moment?"

"Yes, ma'am. Happy to," the coach replied.

Sharon set the phone down on a chair beside the kitchen counter and walked into the living room. As she approached the foot of the staircase leading to the second story of their large suburban home, she could hear Lydia laughing. Brent was saying something to her, but Sharon couldn't make it out. For all of the conflicts that periodically raged through the family, she was grateful that her children, at least, had a good relationship. Looking up the stairs she called out, "Brent!"

"Yeah?" Brent called out.

Miffed, Sharon put her hands on her hips. "Brenton Nathaniel, do you mind stepping out of your room when you answer me?"

Brent stepped from his bedroom and walked to the top of the stairs. His face had a look of indignation, with a trace of humor about the eyes. "*Yes*, Mom. What is it, *Mom*?"

"You're asking for it," Sharon threatened lightheartedly. "Coach Chamberlin is on the phone for you."

Brent's eyes changed; the humor fading. "What does he want?"

"I didn't ask."

She watched as Brent took a deep breath, let it out slowly, then proceed down the stairs. Turning to follow Brent as he passed, she returned to the kitchen and her food preparations.

"Hello?" Sharon heard him say after taking up the phone. "Hi, Coach."

Pause.

"Yes, I remember."

Pause.

"I don't know. Besides, like I said," Brent turned to look at his mom, "I'm grounded. I'm pretty sure I couldn't go anyway."

Pause.

"No ... I didn't ask." Brent sighed. "Okay. Hold on."

Brent covered the mouthpiece of the phone with his left hand, pursed his lips for a moment, then said, "Mom, Coach wants me to go to some church-like thing with him and his wife tonight. I told him I doubted that I could go, but he wanted me to ask you anyway."

Sharon finished cleaning the seeds out of a bell pepper and then turned to look at her son. "Brent, even if you weren't grounded I don't think I'd say yes to something like that. Your coach seems like a decent man, but I don't know him well enough to say yes to you going to some religious meeting. I don't want you to get mixed up in some sort of cult-like group."

‡‡‡

**4:57 p.m.**

The irony of his mom's statement caught Brent short. *Cult, Mom? If you only knew what I'm* already *involved in.* He could have laughed if things hadn't become so serious.

"So, I should tell him no?" Brent asked.

"I'm afraid so," she replied as she began to slice the pepper into long strips.

Brent put the phone back to his ear. "Coach, my mom says I can't go." There was a moment of silence on the other end of the line, then his coach responded.

"Okay, Brent. I'm sorry to hear that, but I will be praying for you."

Not knowing exactly how to take that, Brent replied with, "Thanks, Coach."

"Have a good evening, and I will see you..."

"Brent?" His mom interrupted.

"Coach, can you hold on a sec?"

"Sure."

Turning to look at his mom, Brent saw her wiping her hands and stepping toward him. "Can I speak with him for a moment?" she asked as she reached for the phone.

Brent didn't reply. He just relinquished control of the phone and listened.

"Coach Chamberlin? It's Mrs. Lawton again. Exactly what is it that you're wanting Brent to attend with you tonight?"

Brent cringed. He wasn't at all sure that he wanted to go to the meeting tonight, and his mother had been the perfect excuse not to. Now, completely out of character, his mom seemed to be taking away a perfectly legitimate excuse. In a million years, he couldn't have fathomed that his mom would have stepped out of her introverted nature like this, taking the initiative to talk with someone she didn't really know.

"And where is it?"

Pause.

"Mmm-hmm. Yes, I know the area," she replied. "And what time would he be back home?"

*Oh no*, Brent thought. He closed his eyes and shook his head.

"Okay," she said into the phone. "He said that your wife will be going as well, is that right?"

Pause.

"Mmm-hmm." She laughed at something that Coach Chamberlin said. "Sure, that'd be great. I'd enjoy meeting her sometime."

Pause.

Another laugh. "I'm sure we will."

Pause.

"No, no problem at all. He's free to go if he'd like. I'll give him back to you right now. Have a good night, Mr. Chamberlin." Brent's mom handed him the phone. "You're free to go if you'd like."

With utter lack of enthusiasm, Brent responded, "Great. Thanks, Mom."

Taking back the phone and putting it to his ear, Brent said, "Coach, it looks like I can go. What should I wear?"

"What are you wearing right now?"

"Umm ... a pair of jeans and a black t-shirt."

"That sounds good to me," was the response.

Confused, Brent replied, "To church?"

Coach Chamberlin chuckled. "It's not church. I already told you that. My wife and I are going to eat a quick meal, and then we'll head out to pick you up. We should be at your house a little bit after six o'clock."

Brent let him know that would be fine, then they said their goodbyes. Hanging up the phone, he walked back through the living room and went back upstairs.

What had just happened? And what had he gotten himself into?

## Chapter Eight

**Thursday, March 26 – 6:21 p.m.**

"Hi, Brent. Good to meet you," said Mrs. Chamberlin as she stepped out of the car, allowing Brent to crawl into the backseat of the two-door, olive-colored Ford LTD Brougham.

"Good to meet you, too," said Brent as he climbed in. The car was warm compared to the forty-degree temperature from which he came. "Nice car, Coach. What year is it, a '71?"

"Close," came the reply. "It's a '70. And, thanks. It's the only toy that my wife allows me to have and tinker with in my spare time. How're you doing?"

"Nervous."

Coach Chamberlin smiled. "I can understand that." He put the car in gear, pulled away from the curb, and they were on their way.

About fifteen minutes later, they entered the parking lot of a large church called Forest Acres Community Chapel. The parking lot was nearly full, and Brent could see a half-dozen people standing outside of the main entrance wearing suits. An uncomfortable feeling stirred within him.

"Umm, Coach, I thought you said we weren't going to church," he said.

"We're not. Not exactly. Like I told you earlier today, we started off small. But, since we've gotten so big we've had to find larger places to meet. This church graciously allows us to use their facility every Thursday evening. Don't worry, Brent. I'm not throwing you to the wolves," he said with a chuckle.

"Good," said Brent, not so sure he could count on that.

After the car was parked they proceeded through the dipping temperatures to the entrance. They were met at the front door by a man in a three-piece suit with short, well-groomed, blonde hair. "George! Good to see you! And Cheryl, I'm glad you could make it." After shaking their hands, the man turned to Brent and extended his hand.

Brent took it and began to shake it when the man said, "God bless you, brother! It's good to see you, too!"

Unsure how to respond, Brent said, "Uhh ... yeah. You, too." *What have I gotten myself into?*

Once inside the church they hung up their coats, crossed through the foyer, and entered the large sanctuary. Brent had never seen such a large church before. If his coach had been right, and there actually were close to seven hundred people attending this meeting, then it was obvious that this place could easily hold a thousand. *What kind of church draws a thousand people?* Brent wondered.

He was glad to see that there was a lot of available seating toward the back of the large room. He started for one of the back rows. But his coach stopped him dead in his tracks. "Brent, looks like there's some seating available up front, about the fifth row. How 'bout we sit up there?"

"Oh. Okay, that's fine." It wasn't fine. And how was it that a building could make him feel so edgy? He had a nagging feeling in the pit of his stomach and the mental image of a warning sign with flashing red lights. Part of him definitely did not want to be here. Strike that. *Most* of him did not want to be here.

They found seats in the fifth row in the right-most section of the church. As Brent looked around, he noted the breadth of the two center sections, a wide aisle that stretched the length of the sanctuary, and two equally impressive side sections, also separated by aisles.

On the stage were several people preparing instruments for play. Brent was taken aback as he saw electric guitars, an electric bass, drums, a piano, and several microphone stands. *In a church? This is weird!*

His attention was pulled away from the stage when he heard a man's husky voice to his left. "George! God bless you, man!"

Coach Chamberlin stood up, crossed in front of Brent, and stepped out into the aisle. Brent watched as his coach grabbed a burly, bearded man, also in a black t-shirt, and hugged him. There were tattoos the length of both of his arms and a long chain that extended from his wide, black leather belt to a wallet in his back pocket. This guy looked like he was part of the Hell's Angels.

"Chuck! It's good to see you, buddy! Man, it's been a couple months. Where've you been?" asked George.

In a voice that sounded like it been distorted by years of smoking, he said, "Went down to the Dominican Republic with some brothers and did some church reconstruction. Hurricane Samuel devastated that island. But, man, did I have a blast! Saw sixteen people come to Christ while I was there! It was awesome!"

Did he just hear this guy right? Brent was struck by the fact that a man, whose appearance could scare away his entire basketball squad, was all about doing church stuff. *He doesn't look the part,* Brent's mind retorted.

"That's great!" said George. "Praise God! That's what it's all about, isn't it?"

"Yep!" Chuck looked down and studied Brent for a moment. "Who's your young cohort in crime?"

George turned to look at Brent and waved for him to join them in the aisle. "Brent, I'd like you to meet another of the original twelve ... or thirteen ... I can never remember which..."

"Thirteen," said Chuck. "Remember how Tina used to say, back then, that we were like a coven for Jesus?" He laughed heartily, his thick baritone voice causing people around them to turn and look. "But, then, your mind was still a little fried from all those drugs you used to do." He laughed again.

*What? Drugs? Coach Chamberlin?* Brent could scarcely take it in.

"Oookay, Chuckie. That's a little bit too much information to be released to the general public," said George with an ever-broadening smile. "But, yes, now that you mention it, I do remember Tina saying that. Anyway, this young man is Brent Lawton, one of the star players on my basketball team this year."

A thick calloused hand extended toward Brent. Brent took it, expecting his fingers to be broken in his vice-like hands. But, instead, he was greeted with a firm, friendly handshake and a big smile. "Good to meet ya, Brent. Your coach is a good man and a good friend. Probably wouldn't be alive if it weren't for him."

"Good to meet you," responded Brent in mild bewilderment.

"You give me too much credit, Chuck. Besides..."

The conversation was cut off by a loud drum solo onstage. George and Chuck simply raised hands toward each other, smiled, and parted ways. George and Brent stepped back to their seats and sat down. George put his arm around his wife, a gesture that wasn't lost on Brent.

*That's pretty cool.*

The drum solo was loud, and Brent sat glued listening to it. Then it segued into music that could have been heard on any of the local rock stations. *What in the world?* Brent's mind kept getting blown away. *In a church?!*

Once the singing started he realized the difference. This music was rock-n-roll, but the lyrics were about Jesus. They spoke of his power, of his love, of his forgiveness.

*I've just entered the Twilight Zone.*

‡‡‡

**9:20 p.m.**

Time passed quickly. Brent was still sitting in the pew, and he couldn't believe what he was about to say. "Coach, that was incredible! I've never heard anybody talk about the Book of Revelation before."

"Trust me; I know what you're experiencing. I've been listening to Bob share messages like this for years, and I'm still captivated."

There was no opportunity to discuss things further, because soft music began to play in the background as Bob Naze began to speak again. "Friends, we've had a good time tonight. At least I have." There was a ripple of laughter in the crowd. "But, the sole purpose of these meetings is not to have fun, but rather to let you know that there is a God who loves you. Jesus Christ is real, He *is* alive, and He *really does* care.

"I'm going to ask that everyone in the sanctuary stand up."

There was a soft rumble of people standing, Bibles being placed down, people preparing themselves for what was next.

"Thank you. Now I'm going to ask that everyone hold still. It doesn't matter where any of us have to be in the next few minutes when you compare it with making sure everyone in here knows where they're going to be for eternity.

"There are a lot of Christians in here—most of you, in fact. Many of you came to know Christ by coming to these meetings over the years. It is for those who do *not* yet know our Savior that we dedicate the remainder of our time together this evening."

Brent felt queasiness return, and perspiration began to form on his brow and in his hands. *What's going on?*

Bob continued, "I'd like for everyone in this room to bow his or her head right now; eyes closed."

Brent glanced quickly to his right to see Coach Chamberlin and his wife bow their heads. He did the same. He was getting increasingly nervous. And now he understood why.

He recognized the awful presence, and he heard a confirming whisper. "Brent, don't listen to this. This is foolishness."

Brent forced his mind to focus on what Bob Naze was saying.

"Christians, I want you to begin praying for those in this room who do not know Jesus. Pray for barriers to be broken through and lying tongues to be quieted, in the name of Jesus Christ."

Suddenly the nagging voices were silenced! Brent's heart pounded. He was beginning to experience an entirely different power now. A power that could muzzle the mouths of his dark adversaries.

*Muzzle? Wait...*

His thought was cut off by the preacher's next words.

"All of you here who aren't quite sure what all of this is about, it is you that we are here for. It is you that we are praying for right now. And we pray for you because we know what Jesus Christ has done for each of us.

"Some of you here tonight are caught up in drugs and alcohol. Others of you are stuck in a rut of sexual addictions and perversions. And others of you are involved in some form of the occult—demonism, witchcraft, sorcery, divination, and the like. And there are also some of you here who have been struggling with the idea of suicide."

Brent's eyes shot open. He stared straight down at his feet, then chanced a look to see if his coach was looking at him. He wasn't. He and his wife were visibly praying, their lips moving silently. Had his coach told this preacher about what he'd been going through? No. How could he? He didn't know.

"Many of you men and women all over this church building have been going through such private hells that you're scared to reveal the darkness behind your torment. But, listen to me. Jesus knows. He *knows!*

"He knows ... *and* ... He loves you still. There is nothing that you have done, and there is nothing that has been done *to* you, that has stopped Him from loving you and wanting you to be *His* brothers and sisters, not to mention His friend.

"Jesus, Himself, said that those who ask Him to come into their lives will have a Friend that sticks closer than a brother."

Brent's mind was trying to take this all in.

*You want* me? *How could you? My life's a mess!*

"I'm going to extend to you an invitation in a moment. An invitation to ask Jesus Christ to come into your lives. But first, I want all of you to know what the Bible has to say about all of this. And to do that, we've got to start at the beginning.

"You see, the earth as we know it wasn't always broken. When God first created it, it was utterly perfect. A perfect Adam & Eve had a perfect relationship with God. They all shared a perfect love. There was also no death, no sickness, and no sin.

"God had told Adam that if he ate the fruit of a certain tree that he would die. Later, Satan tempted Eve and told her that God was holding back on them and that if they would eat that fruit they wouldn't die, but that their eyes would be opened and they would be like God. She fell for it and got her husband to fall for it, too.

"That first sin caused the whole of God's perfect creation to shift. Death was introduced, both spiritual and physical. Chaos erupted in, and through, the first family. Every succeeding generation has perpetuated the chaos. Every murder, every misuse of sex, every false religion, every war, and disease ... all of it ... is a result of that original sin.

"Remember, I said that *spiritual* death was also introduced. You see, Hell was not created for man. It was created for the devil and his angels. However, God cannot allow sin to do to Heaven what it first did to Earth, so no man or woman, boy or girl, will ever be allowed to bring it in.

"After that original sin was committed, God took the life a perfect animal, shedding its blood in order to cover the guilt of Adam and Eve. Scripture makes it clear; 'without the shedding of blood, there is no forgiveness of sin.' By doing that, God was showing Adam and Eve that He still cared about them; that they still mattered. He also showed that there was a high price to pay for sin: The blood of an innocent.

"For thousands of years God accepted the blood of animals to cover the sins of people, but the sacrifices were only good for one year. Each year the people were again reminded of the high cost that had to be paid for what they had done. God, though, had a plan that would result in one *final* sacrifice; one *last* shedding of blood. This last sacrifice wouldn't just cover sin for one year; it would wash it away forever.

"Listen to Romans, chapter three, verse twenty-three: 'All have sinned and come short of the glory of God.' Romans, chapter six, verse twenty-three says that 'the wages of sin is death, *but* the gift of God is eternal life through Jesus Christ our Lord.'

"See? All of us—every single one of us—has fallen short. There is not *one single person* in this room, or on this earth, that *deserves* anything other than eternal punishment. No amount of doing good can save you. It is *only* through Christ, and the shedding of *His* perfect blood, that *we* can have salvation—the forgiveness of our sins that will allow us into God's kingdom instead of Hell.

"Some of you have been beat over the head with religious dos and don'ts. You feel like God is up there on His throne with a big hammer just *waiting* for the next time you do something wrong so He can make an example of you. But, that's not how it is!

"Listen to what Jesus, Himself, said: "God loved the world so much, that He sent His one, and only, Son, so that whoever would believe in Him would not know eternal punishment, but, instead, would know eternal *life!'* He went on to say, 'God did not send His Son into the world to condemn it, but that the world, through Him, might be saved.' Isn't that great news?"

*God,* Brent asked, *is this true? Really?* A hope rose within him.

"Right now, those of you who want to know this God, this Jesus, I want you to raise your hands."

Before Brent could give himself time to think, his hand was in the air. He was so shocked by his response that he actually looked up at it. He closed his eyes again, returning his attention to the preacher.

"That's it. You, there, sir, God bless you. You can put your hand down."

*Did he mean me,* Brent wondered? He began to lower his hand.

"And you, young man, you can put your hand down. Yes. God bless you. Young lady in the back, God bless. You can put your hand down."

One after another after another, hands went up and were acknowledged, for what seemed like several minutes. Brent was stunned by the realization that he wasn't the only one whose life was messed up. But, then, Bob Naze had said that *everyone* needed Jesus, right?

Finally, Bob continued. "I want all of you who raised hands to make a bold statement. I want each of you to slip out of your pew and come down here to the altar. Come on now, don't be afraid. There's nothing to fear from forgiveness and peace."

And with that, the band began to softly sing.

*Just as I am, without one plea,*
*But that thy blood was shed for me,*
*And that Thou bidd'st me come to Thee*
*O Lamb of God, I come, I come*

Brent couldn't just stand there. He wanted to believe that all of this was true. But he was struck with a new fear: What if this didn't work?

*What if I go down there...* Tears developed in his eyes. *What if ... Oh God ... what if this doesn't work? There's nothing else. I've got* nothing *else! God! I'm scared! Do you hear me? I am* scared!

*Just as I am and waiting not*
*To rid my soul of one dark blot,*
*To thee, whose blood can cleanse each spot,*
*O Lamb of God, I come, I come.*

With a resolve that came from desperation, Brent slipped out of the pew and walked the fifteen miles to the altar. He saw that others were kneeling, so he did the same. He looked down and saw a box of tissues sitting right in front of him. *Good thing,* he thought. But he was going to try not to cry.

*Just as I am, though tossed about*
*With many a conflict, many a doubt,*
*Fightings and fears within, without,*
*O Lamb of God, I come, I come.*

The song—written just for Brent over a hundred years prior—came to an end. Dozens of people filled the front of the church. He could hear people, men and women alike, sobbing ... just like he wanted to do.

Bob began to speak again. "I'd like for everyone down here at the altar to look at each other for a moment. Look the full length of the altar area. I want you all to see that you are not alone when it comes to trials and complications in your lives. Now look up at me. I'm going to lead all of you in a prayer. I'd like for all of you to repeat it, out loud, as I say it. But I don't want you just *saying* it. I want you to *pray* it. Speak it to God. He's listening. I *promise* you, He's listening. You're not joining a church tonight, or some organization. Rather, you are beginning a personal relationship with the Creator of the Universe who takes a personal interest in you.

"Now, pray this after me: Father, in Heaven ... I come to you now ... broken and defeated. ... I know that I need you. ... I know that I'm completely lost without you. ... According to Your Word ... all I have to do is believe and receive. ... Right now, I confess ... that I believe that Jesus ... was conceived in, and born of, a virgin, ... that He led a sinless life, ... and because of that sinless life ... He was able to take my place in death, ... suffering and dying for my sins, ... to make me right with you, Father God. ... Jesus, right now ... I ask you to come into my heart, into my life. ... Forgive me of all of my sins ... Clean me up inside; ... inside my heart, inside my spirit, inside my mind. ... Tonight I give You my life. ... I will serve You and love You for the remainder of my days. ... In your name, the name of Jesus, I pray ... Amen.

'Amens' sounded throughout the sanctuary. Brent found out that trying to keep back the flood of tears was futile. He grabbed at the box of tissues, buried his face in a handful, and he wept.

He wept because God had accomplished in him what he had thought impossible.

He wept because the fears and pains of his life were gently being washed away.

He wept because he knew, now, that God really was good.

He wept because he knew ... he was free.

‡‡‡

**That Evening**

Hannah Moore, lying in the warmth of her bed, fell asleep, and enjoyed a full night of uninterrupted, peaceful slumber.

# Chapter Nine

**Thursday, April 22 – 8:15 p.m.**

It had been nearly a month since Hell had given way to Heaven in Brent's life, and there was no going back. Indeed, that was the farthest thing from his mind. It wouldn't be an exaggeration to suggest that the past month alone had been worth all of the torment that he had gone through in the past couple of years. He wouldn't trade in his new life for anything. That's not to say, though, that life was perfect. Far from it.

While his new-found faith was having a major influence in his own life, the same could not be said of 'others' in his home. In fact, it appeared that his "religion," as his parents began calling it, was having a negative impact, beginning with that night that he had accepted Christ.

Looking back four weeks to the beginning of his new Christian walk, Brent could now see that those *beings* that had lost their grip on his life had been given a new mission: Discourage him right out of the shoot.

After George and Cheryl—he was invited to call them by name now, as long as they were off school grounds—had dropped him off at home, Brent nearly exploded with the good news, explaining the events of the evening to his parents. That had apparently been a mistake.

"You did *what?!*" his dad exclaimed.

"I became a born-again Christian," Brent responded, the smile on his face fading.

With a curse, his father continued, "I thought we made it clear, before you left to go with that *coach* of yours, that we didn't want you joining anything! *Jesus Christ,* Brent!"

For the first time in Brent's life, he had come to understand just how blasphemous that statement truly was. "Dad, I didn't join anything."

His mom chimed in next. "Brent, how are we supposed to know *what* you've gotten involved in? Are we supposed to just be happy that you've joined some religious movement because your coach said it was okay?"

"Then why did you let me go? You talked to Coach Chamberlin, yourself."

"Your coach *assured* me that he wasn't going to allow you to get mixed up in anything that you shouldn't. That's why!" The tension in the room became palpable.

"You don't have a *clue* what I did. You don't have a clue what I *experienced* tonight!" Brent was so angry, so crushed, so hurt, that the tears virtually crawled out of his eyes. "What I experienced tonight was not some cult. I didn't join a church or some weird group of fanatics! I didn't join *anything!*"

His parents stared at him, slack jawed. In all of Brent's sixteen years, they had probably never seen him so adamant about an issue.

"You want to know what I did? I'll tell you! It might sound crazy—in fact, I *know* it sounds crazy—but I ended up getting to know God tonight. I got to know that He's *real.* I've never experienced anything in my life so good!"

He was interrupted by a timid voice from behind him, "What's wrong? What's going on?" It was Lydia.

Brent remembered how scared and big her eyes appeared when he turned around.

"Honey, you're supposed to be aslee..." The absurdity of what Brent's mom was about to say had stopped her in mid-sentence. "Everything's fine. I'm sorry that we got so loud. Go on back up to bed. I'll come up to check on you in a little bit."

With that, Lydia gave a curious glance up at Brent and headed back upstairs.

"All I'm saying...," Brent began again, without the chance to finish his thought.

"Brent, listen," his dad interjected in a slightly toned-down voice, "I may be getting upset over nothing. I don't know. You're sixteen years old, and you're capable of making some big decisions on your own. But Brent, there are a lot of crazies out there. Your mom and I don't want you getting mixed up in anything that's going to affect you in a negative way."

That last sentence shocked Brent. How well he had hid all of his dark practices over the past two years. His response was soft and contrite. "I understand. But you *will* see that this isn't some hokey religious thing. All I'm doing is believing in what the Bible says. I mean, we go to church as a family at Christmas and Easter every year, right? Why? It has something to do with the Bible. And, Mom, *your* mom reads the Bible every single day and loves God."

"Yes, but that's different."

"*How?*" Brent asked, on the verge of anger again. "Why is it okay for *her* to be a Christian, but it's not okay for *me*?"

"Brent, we're *all* Christians in this house," insisted his dad. "I was baptized as a baby. I think your mom probably was, and so was your sister. Don't you *dare* create some story in your mind—or better yet—don't try to convince *us* that *we're* not Christians and only *you* are! That will get your butt in more trouble than it can handle."

At that moment Brent felt properly slapped around, all he wanted to do was retreat. "I know that I can't say anything right now to make you understand. I just know that what I did feels right. And I hope that you won't stay angry at me."

He turned away, his head down, and walked slowly to his room.

Brent remembered clearly what happened next, and just the memory nearly broke his heart.

When Brent had rounded the corner into his room, he came face to face with Lydia. Tears were streaming down her face, and it only took a moment before she asked a desperate question.

"You're not going to be fighting with them, too, now, are you? I'll be all alone."

Brent knew all too well the anxiety that was behind that question, and upon hearing Lydia's greatest fear verbalized, tears welled up in Brent's eyes. Immediately he walked up to her, took her in his arms, and begun to cry with her. After a minute he softly whispered into her ear, "No, Lydia. I will never do that to you. I'm sorry I scared you tonight."

Several seconds passed by and she reluctantly pulled back to wipe her eyes on the sleeves of her pajamas. "Is everything okay?"

"Everything is going to be fine. Mom and Dad just don't understand that something important happened to me tonight, that's all."

Her voice became conspiratorial, and in a breathy whisper she asked, "What happened?" Her eyes became wide and curious.

Brent remembered asking himself, *How much is too much? How soon is too soon?*

"I don't know if it's a good idea if we talk about it now. You heard Mom; she's going to come up here and check on you any minute."

With a pouty look on her face, she relented. "Okay, but tell me tomorrow." She gave Brent a quick hug and walked off to her room.

That had been quite the night. He had gone to bed exhausted from all the emotions that he'd had to deal with. It was the next eight or so hours that had ultimately convinced him that God had done an incredible work.

No voices. No nightmare.

Today, weeks later, Brent had tried again to get permission to go to tonight's Freedom Rings meeting with George and Cheryl. As he'd expected, they'd said no. But it appeared that their resolve was weakening. His mom had said, "Maybe next time. We'll see." The miracle was that his dad had only given her a momentary glance without a contradictory word.

*So, maybe next Thursday, huh?* "God, *please* continue to work on this for me." Brent whispered. "I really want to hear more about You."

Pulling out his chair and sitting at his desk, Brent pulled out the New Testament that he'd been given at Freedom Rings. It looked more like a regular book than a Bible, but most importantly, it actually read like a book. He was excited about being able to read the Bible in today's language. And, not only did it make sense, it fed him. He couldn't get enough.

He opened up to where he had stopped reading earlier in the day—Acts, chapter nine. He read about a religious leader named Paul—could that be *Saint* Paul?— who had gone off to persecute the Christians in a city called Damascus. But on his way he was thrown from his horse, blinded, and told by Jesus, Himself, to go into the city and wait for a messenger to come to him. Brent was captivated by what happened next.

When a man named Ananias came to Paul, he'd laid hands on him. *Whatever that meant.* And Paul was filled with the Holy Spirit and received his sight again.

Verses nineteen through twenty-two went on to say:

> 19 Then he ate and was strengthened. He stayed with the believers in Damascus for a few days.
>
> 20 And went at once to the synagogue to tell everyone there the Good News about Jesus—that He is indeed the Son of God!
>
> 21 All who heard him were amazed. "Isn't this the same man who persecuted Jesus' followers so bitterly in Jerusalem?" they asked. "And we understand that he came here to arrest them all and take them in chains to the chief priests."
>
> 22 Paul became more and more fervent in his preaching, and the Damascus Jews couldn't withstand his proofs that Jesus was indeed the Christ.

Something sparked within Brent. And he immediately knew what it was. "God," he prayed, "Please, do in me what You did in

Paul. What You did in my life a month ago was huge, and, like Paul, I want to share Jesus with others. Teach me how to do that. Give me boldness like You gave Paul. Send me the people to talk with. I'll do my best to share what I know. I know it's not much, but I do know what You've done for me. I want others to come to know You like I have. In Jesus' name, I pray. Amen."

‡‡‡

### Friday, April 23 – 9:13 a.m.

It didn't take long before Brent's prayer of the previous night netted results, but not exactly in the way that he was prepared for.

Brent walked into his American History classroom. Inside there was already a smattering of other kids. A couple of them were sitting, but most were standing around listening to Galen Todd, resident jock and state wrestling finalist. He didn't hear what they were talking about, but that needn't have mattered, because as Brent made his way to the other side of the room to choose a seat, Galen stopped what he'd been talking about and focused his attention on Brent.

Galen pivoted his body in order to put his right foot on the seat of a chair. At just about the same instant that Brent put his books and notebook on his desk, Galen spoke. "Yo, Brent. Heard you got religion. You one of those Jesus freaks like they were in the 60s?"

His chiding question brought laughs from the rest in the room. A few more students walked in, and Brent saw in their expressions that they wanted in on the joke. But before they were given a chance to ask what was so funny, a surge of something akin to electricity rushed through his body causing a tingling in his fingertips. His heart started to beat harder, and with a boldness he didn't think he had, he put his right foot up on the seat of his own chair, mimicking Galen's stance. Looking him straight in the eyes, he answered, "Yo, Galen. No, I'm not. I'm a Jesus freak like they *are* in the 80s!"

The look on Galen's face was priceless. The other kids in the class chuckled at Brent's retort, some of them trying to hide that fact from Galen as hands were raised to cover smiles. Everyone was looking at the wrestler, but all he did was stare at Brent with a look that was a cross between bewilderment and unsurity. Then he dropped his foot and took his seat. He didn't say another word.

Now Brent was bewildered. *Wow. Where'd that come from?* He felt a wave of heat travel through his face as he realized that, now, everyone in the room was staring at him. He, again, mimicked Galen's movements and planted himself in his own chair.

*God,* that *was cool!*

After class, while Brent walked through the hallway toward his locker, Laura Tucker walked up from behind and tapped him on his shoulder. Brent stopped and turned around. "Laura. Hi. What's up?"

Laura was a bit of a gangly girl; not 'filled out' like a lot of the girls their age. She was a bit on the homely side and always lacked any semblance of confidence. Brent knew her only by association. His now ex-girlfriend, Michele, and she were close friends.

After what was obviously an awkward moment for her, Laura said, "Brent, I can't believe how you handled things with Galen back in class. That was amazing."

"No one's more amazed than I," Brent said. "I don't know where it came from." The introspection that took place at that moment was short. "Well, actually, I guess I *do* know where it came from. But, it was definitely not expected."

"I've never seen anyone stand up to Galen like that, and in a way that actually made him look ... well ... silly."

"Galen's not afraid of me, and trust me, he packs a good punch. If I had thought things through before I spoke, I'd have probably just kept my mouth shut and sat down."

Laura became quiet, but Brent could tell there was something else on her mind. He kept silent allowing her to formulate her thoughts. What she said next was pure gold.

"Brent, I don't know if you're aware of this, but I'm a..." she raised her fingers to make quote marks, "'Jesus freak', too."

"You're a Christian?" asked Brent with probably more surprise and volume than he should have released.

She looked up and down the hall to see if anyone had paid attention. "Yeah. Not a great one, by any stretch of the imagination. But, I did accept Jesus a few years ago. Anyway, that's the real reason I stopped you. I wanted to say thanks."

Brent was stuck for a response. He had no idea what she was talking about. "Say thanks for what?"

"For being willing to be open with your faith. You're getting a bit of a reputation in the school. But, then, I guess you know that already."

"Yeah, almost every day I hear or see someone who is

obviously having a good laugh at my expense," replied Brent, remembering a couple of instances.

"Well, I'm not sure I can be as bold as you. But I didn't want you to think that you're the only one in the school," Laura offered.

"To be honest, I *was* beginning to wonder. I'm the only one in the school who seems daring enough to carry a Bible through the hallways. Doesn't look like a Bible, though, does it?" asked Brent as he turned to show her the stack of books under his right arm.

"No, it looks pretty much like a novel of some sort."

"Well, as soon as I can afford it I'm getting a Bible that *looks* like a Bible. And when I do, I'll be sporting *it* through these halls."

"Wow. Don't you worry what everyone'll think?"

"You know what, Laura? I used to. But not anymore. If you knew what God saved me from..." He stopped and smiled. "Laura, I'm going to be loud with my faith, because Jesus is worth it. Let them make fun of me. They made fun of the Apostle Paul, too."

Laura was looking timid again as she half whispered, "Maybe someday I can do it too." And with that she turned and walked away, leaving Brent staring after her.

*Lord,* Brent prayed silently, *give her what I've got. Use her, too, like you used Paul. Help her to have courage.* Brent turned to walk to his locker, then finished his prayer out loud saying, "And help me to *keep* mine."

## Chapter Ten

### Tuesday, April 27 – 7:17 p.m.

The knock at the side door startled Hannah. *Who could that be?* She got up from her chair and clicked off her radio. She had been listening to some of her favorite old Gospel music. Walking to the door she flipped on a wall switch to illuminate the hallway. She pulled aside the short, flower-covered curtain that covered the door's window and looked out. It was her son, Joe.

She opened the door and saw behind him his old GMC pickup truck parked in the drive, the engine still running. "Good evenin', Joe. Didn't feel like walkin'?"

Joe looked at her with a smile. Ordinarily he would have walked the quarter mile to the house where he'd grown up. "Didn't have the time, Mother. You've got a phone call."

"Me? Who's callin'?" she asked, curious about the smile on her son's face.

"Oh, I think I'll let him tell you. C'mon, I'll drive you over."

Hannah grabbed a shawl that she kept hanging beside the door and walked out, closing the door behind her.

"Not nice keepin' secrets from your mother, Joseph," she said as her son opened the passenger door for her.

He whispered, "I think you'll get over it."

A minute later they were at Joe and Sally's home. As she and Joe walked through the door, she smelled a late dinner that was being prepared. Beef stew, she guessed.

Joe took the lead through the living room and into the kitchen where the nearest phone was. *Yep, beef stew*, she confirmed, looking at the stove.

"Hi, Mom," came a voice from the family room. Hannah looked over and saw Sally walking into the kitchen.

"Oh, hi, Honey. How're you doin'? Stew smells good."

"Thank you," said Sally as she reached for the uncradled phone on the kitchen counter. "Got someone waitin' to talk with you." She held the phone out to her mother-in-law.

Hannah reached for the phone. "So I'm told." She put the phone to her ear. "Hello?"

"Hello, Mamaw," said a cheery voice on the other end.

"Brent? Is that you?"

"Yes, Mamaw, it's me. How are you?"

Hannah paused for a moment. In a flash all of the months of

prayer for this boy came back to her. The Spirit's perpetual calls to intercession had come to an end over a month ago. She hadn't heard anything at all from the boy or his family since then. Questions flooded her mind as she refocused to answer his question.

"Oh, I'm real good, Sweetheart. Doin' real good. How are *you* doin'?" she asked, her heart beginning to beat faster in anticipation.

"Mamaw, I'm calling because I've got something to tell you. And I think it's going to make you pretty happy." Brent paused for a moment, and Hannah knew he was doing it on purpose.

"Well, come on, boy," Hannah said, knowing that he was playing with her. "Say it." She knew. She *knew!*

"Mamaw, about a month ago I became a Christian. Your type of Christian. I'm born again!" Brent sounded excited to be sharing his news.

"Oh, Brent! Oh, how I have been *praying* for you!" she said, unable to contain her joy. "I am so excited for you!" She was on the verge of tears.

Emotion began to rise up in Brent as he said, "Of all the people in my life, I knew you'd be the one who'd be the happiest for me."

"Oh, I am, dear. I am." Hannah wanted to press for details, but she knew that those would come if he should decide to release them. "I am so happy for you, Brent. So, happy!"

"God is so good, Mamaw. I can't begin to tell you the things that He has done ... *is doing*, for me," came his response.

The mother in Hannah that had lain dormant for so long spontaneously awakened. "Brent, are you readin' your Bible? Are you talkin' with God every day?"

She heard Brent chuckle. "Yes, Ma'am. I've been reading every day, and I've been praying constantly. I'd like to find a church, but since I don't drive, and since mom and dad..." He trailed off.

"I know, dear," Hannah empathized. "I know. You pray for your family. They'll come around. You stay in the Word, and you keep praying for them every day, as I have for you. Pray, pray, pray."

"I will, Mamaw." Hannah heard a voice in the background say something that she couldn't quite make out, then she heard Brent sigh. "I wish I could talk longer, but Mom also wants to talk with you."

"Okay, Brent. I want you to know that I love you so much. And I will pray for you and your new walk with the Lord. Brent, thank you so much for calling me."

"I love you, too. And thank you for your prayers. Well, have a good night. Hopefully I'll talk with you again soon," Brent replied. And with that, her daughter, Sharon, got on the phone.

She spoke with her daughter for about a half an hour. She tried to express her excitement over Brent's new-found Love, but it was short-lived as her daughter changed the subject and asked about the goings on with family and friends.

After the conversation had ended, she hung up the phone and told Joe and Sally the good news. They also received the news with gladness.

After their brief conversation, Joe asked if she was ready for him to drive her back home. She declined his offer. She explained that she wanted to walk and talk with the Lord. She was going to carry this new joy with her as she trekked down the pathway between their two properties.

She said her goodbyes and began walking. It was cool, and she pulled her shawl more tightly around her shoulders. If the warmth she felt inside could have radiated outward, she wouldn't have needed her shawl at all. "Lord, thank you! Thank You, thank You, thank You." A Scripture verse filled her heart and mind, and she nearly shouted it to the sky. "'My soul doth magnify the Lord!'"

‡‡‡

Seven days later Brent received a package in the mail from his Mamaw. It was an authentic, black leather-bound Bible.

## Chapter Eleven

### Tuesday, May 5 – 2:10 p.m.

Brent groaned with the idea of another 'lit' paper being due. A momentary flashback to the sheer monotony of the in-school suspension room, though, made him acknowledge that having the freedom to do *anything* outside of those walls was a good thing. Perspective. He was becoming a glass-half-full guy now. If he'd tried thinking that way a little over a month ago, no doubt that he would have failed. But, his relationship with the Lord and his growing knowledge of the Bible were purifying his mind and softening his attitudes.

Yesterday, Brent had heard two of his guy friends joking that he'd been "brainwashed by organized religion." Initially that had ticked him off. Later, though, with his emotions in check, he'd thought those comments through. He ended up agreeing with them. He *was* being brainwashed. *Good thing, too,* he'd thought. *After all the garbage I've put into my mind, my brain* needs *a good washing!*

He sat now, in front of a blank piece of notebook paper. For the past twenty minutes, he'd been trying to develop a good thesis statement. But, with the school's library being so warm, he felt he was more likely to develop a good nap. He needed to stand up and maybe get a drink of water. The thought became moot when the bell rang, signaling the end of the school day.

Brent stood up and gathered his papers and books. He paused for a moment, looking down at his new Bible. He picked it up. It was black leather with a zippered cover. In gilded letters of gold, it read "Holy Bible" on the front. Never mind that it was a *thees*-and-*thous* King James Version. It was the visibility factor that he wanted. He *wanted* everyone in the school to see him walking with it.

He unzipped and opened the cover and read for the hundredth time the inscription his grandmother had written within:

*My Dearest Brent,*

*Simple words aren't enough to tell you how proud I am of you and how much I love you. My greatest prayer for you right now is for you to know Jesus better and better every day. Never be embarrassed of Him, because He was never embarrassed of*

*you. He is your greatest friend and defender, so you can stand for Him, knowing He will always be there for you. The Lord gave me a message for you: Psalm 91:14-16*
*Always My Love and Prayers,*
*Mamaw*

*How often does God give someone a message like that?* he wondered. Brent felt blessed and honored every time he read the passage. He had taken a highlighter that first night that he'd received the Bible and marked the Scripture verse so that it would stand out.

Brent thought back to what his grandmother had said on the phone. She had been praying for him *every day*. Amazing. It's as if she knew the battle he was dealing with. Had she known? Was it possible that God had informed her? He knew instinctively that if it hadn't been for his grandmother's prayers, he wouldn't be alive right now experiencing the promises held in that Psalm.

*God, bless her*, he prayed silently.

Picking up his books he headed for the hallway. Before making his way to his locker, he made a left turn into the nearest restroom. Opening the door and walking in, he immediately regretted not going straight to the bus. Standing before him was Galen Todd and two others guys—Tim Alcorn and Joey Parks—that Brent didn't know well.

Galen saw him immediately. No backing out.

"Hey there, Bible Boy," mocked Galen. "It's funny you should walk in here like this. We were just talking about you."

Brent decided to play it casual. "Hey, Galen." He stepped toward the row of urinals, but Galen stepped in front of him, putting his right hand firmly on Brent's chest.

"Come on, Galen. Let's not do this. Okay?" said Brent in a measured tone.

"Lawton, that's not quite like you. What's wrong, turning into a pansy?

Brent didn't respond, he just locked eyes with Galen, his muscles tensing.

Galen continued. "It's about time you and I had a little talk. You see, I have a problem with you. Guess I always have. But do you know what the new problem is, Bible Boy?"

Brent took a step back, trying to distance Galen's hand from his body. But Galen stepped forward, too, and pushed Brent backward, pressing him up against a full-length mirror on the wall.

"Galen, don't, man. All right?" Brent's adrenaline level was beginning to spike. He knew that Galen and he were pretty evenly matched should it come to blows, but that's what Brent wanted to desperately avoid. His heart had changed, and along with it came a softening of his heart toward Galen Todd. He no longer hated him, but he struggled with the idea of looking weak by backing down. But a fight right now wasn't exactly in God's plans. He was sure of that.

"Lawton, you've become little more than a girl. At least before you were willing to show you weren't a wimp. You've given me all the advantage that I need; not that I needed any. Right now you and your wimpy religion are going to take a dive. After I'm done with you, you'll think twice about trying to make me look stupid in class again." Galen made a fist and forced it down upon the stack of books that Brent held, causing them to slap the floor.

Still playing the pacifist, Brent clenched his teeth and simply bent down to pick them up. Galen kicked a notebook across the bathroom into a stall.

*God, help me with this.*

"Come on, man." He stood back up. "Galen, I never meant..."

"Shut up!" shouted Galen with a stab into the air; his finger pointed at Brent's face.

Brent's fingers instinctively drew into fists. He watched Galen's eyes and saw his attention drawn toward a particular black book resting on the floor. Galen bent down, picked it up, and tossed it at Brent, who caught it.

"Take your little book, Bible Boy. Do you feel it *saving* you right now?" Galen laughed at his verbal jab. "The way I see it, only sissies carry Bibles." He looked back at his friends, expecting them to be enjoying the spectacle. Instead, they stood there, unsure, with muted stares.

That's when it happened.

Brent felt another surge of Holy Spirit boldness course through him. He took a step toward Galen, fire burning in his eyes.

Galen turned his attention back toward Brent and saw his advance. He stepped backward out of reflex, but just as quickly stopped and regained his stance.

Brent lifted his Bible up in full view of everyone in the bathroom. "You think this book is wimpy, Galen?"

Galen stared dead into Brent's eyes. "Yes. That's exactly what it is."

"And you think that I'm a wimp for carrying it around; that somehow this book makes me weak," Brent asserted.

"That's right. Your religion and that book are nothing but a crutch for people who can't handle life on their own terms." Galen looked back again at Tim and Joey who obviously didn't want to involve themselves. They were looking increasingly uncomfortable.

Brent brought Galen's attention back when he said, "Here, you take it," and extended the Bible out to him.

"What?" Galen's expression and another step backward let Brent know that the tide had turned. "No. I don't want your book."

"Why, because it's a book of weakness? Because you're too big and important to be seen holding it?"

"Lawton, right now I'd shut up if I were you."

"Galen, here's the deal. You call me weak. But I dare you... I *dare* you to take this book, and tomorrow, with it in full view, walk around the halls of this school all day."

Galen just glared.

"Come on, Galen. Take it." He took a step forward, but this time Galen didn't move. "If you think it's so easy to carry this book around, let me see you do it."

Galen's two friends looked at each other for a moment then turned back to watch Galen's response. Once again he was faced with having to deal with a situation that his own words had gotten him into. Once again he was looking the fool.

Time seemed to stop. Brent determined that the next person to say something was going to be Galen Todd. He was going to have to extricate himself from this situation on his own. Brent wasn't going to make it easy on him now that he had the upper hand in this confrontation.

After a good minute of silence, Galen's posture relaxed. He looked back at his friends and said, "Come on, guys. We're going to miss the bus." Breaking eye contact with Brent, Galen walked around him and headed for the door, Tim and Joey following.

Brent heard the door close behind him. His fingers tingled like they normally did when he was having an intense experience with the Holy Spirit. He took a deep breath and slowly released it with a word of thanks to God. Another confrontation had been dealt with by the Lord, and again he had come out of it untouched.

He knelt down and picked up his books, then walked over to the stall in which his notebook lay. Picking it up, he wondered how long his luck would hold out when it came to Galen.

*Luck?* Brent realized immediately that his word choice had been a discredit to the Lord. Luck didn't exist, and even if it did, luck would *never* again get the glory for the good that happened in his life. He was going to be grateful *only* to God.

He'd been called a wimp for believing in God. Let the everyone think so. Let them throw words at him. He knew better. He just loved his Savior.

*"Because he loves Me, says the Lord, therefore I will deliver him."* Those words from Psalm ninety-one—Brent's 'message from the Lord'—were certainly proving prophetic.

# Chapter Twelve
## 1982

### Thursday, September 23 – 10:17 a.m.

Amazing. Simply amazing.

Brent tried to digest what had just happened.

He stood in the hallway in front of the school's auditorium. Thirty seconds ago someone that he still did not know had walked away from him heading, presumably, to his next class.

*God, thank you for using me.*

*Truly* amazing.

Brent had been heading to history class when he'd been approached by someone he did not recognize. *Probably a freshman*, he thought.

What had the guy said as he approached? *Oh yeah...*

"You're Brent ... right?" asked the kid with a look of nerve-racked resolve.

"Yeah, that's right. What's up?"

He looked edgy, unsure of himself. "Umm ... I hear you're pretty tight with God. I ... umm..." His voice trailed off.

Brent placed his left hand on the kid's shoulder and directed him toward the doors of the auditorium where they would be out of the way of the other students walking through the halls.

"What's going on?" Brent asked. "You okay?"

The kid took a deep breath and slowly released it before continuing. "Yeah ... I, uhh ... no. No, things aren't okay. Someone told me you're a Christian. Is that right?"

*I guess my Christianity isn't a secret to anyone anymore.* The past year and a half, apparently, *had* been bearing fruit. "Yes, that's right," said Brent, acutely aware that he was about to hear a plea for some sort of help.

"I was hoping... I mean, I *am* hoping that you can say a prayer for me."

"You bet. Happy to."

"Thanks."

And that was it. Brent had thought he'd at least learn the kid's name, but that was apparently not to be. His "thanks" was all he'd said before turning and rapidly walking away.

*Uhh... yeah. Okay.*

Brent walked to his next class, whispering a prayer as he went. "Lord, I don't know who that was, or what that was about, but You do. Something's bad wrong in his life, Father, and I'm asking for Your help.

"God, I don't know if he's a believer or not. But something's got him shook up. Something's eating at him, and I remember exactly what that's like.

"Protect him, Father. If he's in some sort of danger, move in and protect him with Your angels. If he's not in danger, then please, help him to find his answer in You. Take care of this situation that is tearing at his heart and win the battle for him. Let him know how big You are and how much You love him. I pray this in the name of Jesus. Amen."

Looking back over the past year and a half since his salvation, he'd realized that life was going to be filled with unexpected happenings; blessings that came right out of left field.

At the beginning of this, his junior year, he was just as determined to let his walk with God shine. To his surprise and joy, he saw that someone else had also become just as determined.

Laura Tucker, that gangly friend of his ex-girlfriend, Michele—Strike that. *Formerly* gangly friend—was apparently just as determined as he to construct a new reputation in the school. When he'd seen her for the first time this new school year walking through the halls, he was immediately struck by her appearance.

She was walking between two of her friends with a bright smile on her face. Instead of looking like the timid girl he'd known the previous couple of years, she now exuded a never-before-seen confidence. Her shoulders were squared, her head was up, and she didn't avoid looking into people's faces.

Laura hadn't seen Brent as she approached, not until he said, "Laura?"

All three of the girls turned to look at him. Laura stopped, raised her eyebrows, smiled her metallic smile, and said, "Yes?" She apparently knew that Brent was sizing her up, and he could see the twinkle in her eyes.

"Wait, who are you, and what did you do with Laura Tucker?" teased Brent.

She didn't miss a beat. "Oh, I'm sorry. You must be referring to that unsure, shy little girl that you knew last year."

"That'd be the one."

"Well, I'm sorry, Brent, but you'll just have to deal with the new version."

"Happy to," he had said through a laugh. "Umm... Wow.

Okay, so what caused…"

"Jesus."

"Now you've really got my attention."

Laura stepped from between her friends and walked up to Brent. Before he could brace himself, she wrapped her arms around him, hugged him, and kissed him on the cheek. Then she whispered into his ear, "Thank you, Brent. Thank you for being an example of Christ to me."

Brent returned the hug and said, "I'm glad you saw that in me."

The embrace ended and she'd stepped back.

"So," Brent continued, "this new you is all about your relationship with God?"

"Yes," she began. "It was the relationship part that had been missing all the years that I've been a believer.

"Watching you in class and in the hallways made me realize that I was more ashamed of my faith than happy about it. And when I got honest about that, I had to admit to God that I had really been ashamed of Him.

"I asked Him to forgive me and to put in me the same resolve that I saw in you. I told the Lord that it was now going to be all or nothing and that I'd really like to do the 'all' option."

"Wow," Brent said again.

"Yeah, wow. From the day that I made that decision this summer, I started carrying my Bible everywhere that I went. When people asked if I was "religious" or a Christian, I didn't flinch. I proudly told them that I was."

"That's amazing." Brent was realizing that *amazing* was becoming a common exclamation in his life. *Who'da thought it?*

"Better than that," she had continued. "God gave me the boldness to share Christ with my two friends." She'd stopped suddenly, realizing that Brent probably didn't know them. "Oh! Brent, this is Denise, and this is Dori, two of my closest friends."

"Hi. I've seen you two around. Good to meet…" Brent began, but was cut off by the *amazing* words that followed.

"… My *Christian* friends," Laura concluded.

"What?" replied Brent, stunned. "The two of you are Christians?"

"Yes!" came an emphatic, shared response.

"That's amaz…" Brent caught himself. "That's awesome! Welcome to the family!"

The girls' smiles were as full of life as Laura's.

Denise said, "We've known Laura for years. We've hung out together, slept over at each other's houses, but we didn't know anything about her faith."

Laura produced a look that bordered on embarrassment and shrugged.

Dori then spoke up. "Well, we didn't know anything about her faith until this summer. One day she's just another nerd like the two of us..." All three of the girls laughed. "...the next she's Bible Girl!"

That last statement wasn't lost on Brent. But unlike him, Laura wore the euphemism like a badge of honor.

"Laura, I'm proud of you. I'm proud of *all* of you!"

"Thank you, Brent. The three of us have begun praying for Michele. We're hoping she'll be the next one to join this party."

Michele Atwell and he had not parted on the best of terms, unfortunately. He was glad that she wasn't present at the moment. Awkward would have been too weak a term for how the encounter would have felt. It was difficult enough having to pass her periodically in the school's hallways.

"That'd be great," responded Brent. "I hope she will be."

The bell sounded the beginning of the next class period. All three girls let out a surprised little yelp.

"We're late!" exclaimed Dori. The three began to move quickly down the hallway.

Just after the girls turned the corner into an adjoining hall, Laura called back to him, "I'll talk with you later!"

*Beyond* amazing.

‡‡‡

That evening, ten miles away, hidden on the outskirts of the Village of Pittston, a young couple began setting up their new home. To any that might have known about them, they would appear to be just another pair of giddy newlyweds. That was the illusion they hoped to convey and maintain.

But they weren't newlyweds. Their union went far beyond the "natural" order of things, and they had a plan; a plan that would envelope their lives for many years to come. With steady patience they would bide their time and do what was required of them.

It was now their turn in the succession of generations past; their turn to accomplish what had failed each time it was attempted over the past eleven-hundred-and-thirty-nine years...

The reestablishment of a dark and powerful ancient religion.

Would they be the chosen ones? Until they knew for sure, they would simply blend in. Blend in and search.

# Part Two

# Freedom Fight

"...Remain in God's love ... Show mercy to those who have doubts. Save others by snatching them from the fire of hell...."

Jude 1:21a, 22-23a, God's Word

# Chapter Thirteen
## 1987

**Thursday, May 14 – 12:17 p.m.**

Brent circled the parking lot a third time. He was going to be late now, but there was nothing that he could do about it. He refused to get another ticket.

*Parking Nazis*. That's what everybody on campus called those who funded the university's coffers by way of little yellow pieces of paper slipped under windshield wipers. Faced with being late yet again, he was beginning to agree. Why couldn't he have gotten a pass for a lot that was closer to his classes? The question often asked and never answered.

He peered down each row of cars praying for someone to leave. Wait, was that movement? He backed his car up just a few feet to see better down the parking aisle. Yes!

Giving the steering wheel a hard turn to the left, he pulled down the narrow lane. Backing lights lit up as a car began pulling out of its spot.

Brent parked his car, a blue 1985 Pontiac Grand Am, and upon exiting his car, threw his black book bag over his shoulder and ran toward the campus quad area to get to Hallis Hall.

It was a warm day. He'd misjudged the temperature again, and the sweatshirt he was wearing was starting to live up to its name. Sweat began to trail down his back, causing the t-shirt underneath to stick to his skin. He ignored it.

Summit State College was a small liberal arts school located about an hour away from Millsville. Brent had battled back and forth in his mind about staying on campus for the semester. He'd opted for the long commute rather than missing out on his mom's home cooking. Besides, it also got him out of the party-oriented dorms. He'd been required to spend his freshman year in the dormitories, but despite the benefit of not having to drive to class he couldn't handle the din that was so pervasive in dorm life.

Now approaching the end of his junior year, he was beginning to see the light at the end of the tunnel. *One more year. Only one more year*, Brent consoled himself.

He reached Hallis Hall and approached the closed door of his classroom in the hallway of the second floor. Brent paused before pulling the door open. He knew what was coming and gave a slight shake of his head.

Opening the door, he was greeted with the friendly, albeit sarcastic, voice of his professor.

"Good afternoon, Mr. Lawton! Nice of you to join us," voiced Professor Bauer.

Brent took his embarrassment in stride. It wasn't the first time, and probably wouldn't be the last.

"Sorry, Professor."

"Have a seat, Mr. Lawton. You're still first on the agenda. Get prepared. You had better *dazzle* me."

A chorus of chuckles rolled through the class of thirty-plus students. Brent took a seat near the back of the classroom, put his bag on the floor, opened it, and grabbed his outline. He was to present his argument today that the U.S. Constitution was not a living, breathing document, but rather one that said what it meant and meant what it said.

With the maturing of his Christian walk, he'd come to the conclusion that he was conservative in his ideology. How could he not be? He believed the Bible to be true.

That belief had been ridiculed by many people, from his classmates in high school to his dad, who still refused to take his faith seriously. He'd been faced many times with the argument that the Bible was out of date and that God wouldn't confine people living today with such archaic rules as no sex outside of marriage. The liberal mindset had tried to take the truth out of the Bible and replace it with pure grace—no consequences for one's actions.

He had found that the same thing happened all the time in politics.

Brent's fascination with political debate was tied to his love for God's Word. If the U.S. started as a God-fearing nation founded by godly men—men who wanted the nation to *remain* that way—then what had happened to allow such *un*godly laws to reshape the country?

To figure out the answer—or maybe to inject one—he had decided to take on a double major in college. Initially it had been just one: English. But in his freshman year he had taken an American Government class that made him both angry and determined to speak openly to a classroom full of listening ears. He was rewarded by his instructor with the opportunity to speak his opinions freely. Very unexpected.

He found that he enjoyed debate and that he could do it passionately and with well-put-together, cogent arguments. He didn't always win—in some people's opinions—but he had a voice that was getting heard.

Now he would present an argument showing that the same watering down that was happening to the teachings of the Bible was happening to the Constitution of the United States.

"Mr. Lawton."

"Yes, sir."

"Dazzle."

‡‡‡

**1:25 p.m.**

Tara Baker left her dorm room, walked down the hallway, and entered the elevator that would carry her down five stories to the lobby below. She pressed "L" and watched the door close before her. She stared passively as the numbers changed, indicating each floor. With a soft 'ding' the doors opened and she walked out.

She paid no attention to the people mingling in the lobby as she proceeded to the glass doors to exit the dormitory. Pushing the doors open, she felt the heat of the unusually warm day envelop her. Confronted by the daylight, she pulled down the brim of her hat to block out as much of the sunlight as possible.

She hated the day.

Once upon a time, though, she would have jumped at the chance to be outside amongst the blue sky, the flowers, the trees. It seemed a lifetime ago. Now she enjoyed the darkness. Thinking about it now, she corrected herself. She didn't really *enjoy* the darkness. The darkness was more ... comfortable. More *known*. It was where she belonged, where she could concentrate, where she could cultivate her powers.

Walking briskly, her long, strawberry-blonde hair trailing in the breeze, she entered the quad area. She needed food. Not having enough time before her next class to find a healthy alternative meant that she had to ingest more greasy fast food. She hated that, too.

She walked up the steps to the student union and plowed through a crowd of people with barely a notice. She even took a little pleasure in throwing a slight elbow into the ribs of an obvious goodie-two-shoes academic. The looks of surprise on his face, and that of his prissy-looking friend, were sure to be priceless. She opened the door and exited the sunlight.

‡‡‡

**1:31 p.m.**

"Ouch!" Brent kept his voice down, but conveyed his annoyance toward the girl in black who rushed past him and into the student union. "Did you see that?"

Marta Rosales, a friend and classmate of Brent, dropped her mouth open as she, too, viewed the audacity of the girl. "Not even a word of apology! You all right?"

"Yeah," he chuckled, "I'm okay. Trust me; I'm no stranger to being elbowed."

"Oh, that's right. Basketball."

"Yep. No biggie." He turned back to fully face Marta, her olive skin and long, thick, almost-black hair dropping below her shoulders. The two of them had met freshman year at an off-campus Christian event and quickly became friends, though periodically he had wondered if more than a friendship could evolve. Lately, though, the idea faded from his thoughts, regardless of how attractive she was. "You were saying?"

"I was saying," she began again, her faint Guatemalan accent paving the way, "that I wouldn't have thought to draw a parallel between how the Bible is being 'modernized' and taken out of context by atheists and anti-Christian religious sects and how the same thing is happening to the U.S. Constitution."

"It's a beautiful world, isn't it?" joked Brent, shaking his head. "Christians, and conservatives in general, are losing strategic ground to the demonic realm —the Enemy—in the name of tolerance. We're supposed to 'tolerate' shacking up, same-sex lifestyles, and abortion. We're supposed to tolerate atheistic attacks on our beliefs." Brent motioned for Marta to follow him down the steps. "Well, I, for one, am sick of it, and I fully intend to let people know, especially other Christians, that we've *got* to stand our ground. There is nothing wrong with intolerance. We've been lied to! Intolerance is *not* anti-American. Intolerance is *not* anti-biblical, and intolerance is *not* mean..." He stopped and turned again to look Marta in the eyes. "...as long as there is either a constitutional or biblical mandate for the stand one takes and it's done without hate."

"I think that you gave a convincing argument in class today, Brent. I fully expected a revolt by half the class, but only that one guy ... What's his name?"

"Jim."

"Yeah, Jim. He was the only one with the guts to go up against you. Though, I'm not sure I'd call it guts. Stupid, maybe."

Brent laughed. "Well, at least he's not wishy-washy in what he believes. He may not have been able to form a very good argument against mine, but he's firm. Half the class believes, or believed, what he argued. It's just that they were either scared or found that they—and their ideologies—don't have very solid foundations.

"Marta, a Christian who knows the *why* behind what he or she believes is a dangerous human being, not to mention a danger, to the Enemy. A studied-up Christian can topple any argument mounted against him. It's just a matter of choosing to *know* what the Word of God says and to *learn* the supporting evidence."

Marta looked down. "You shame me."

Brent paused, not knowing what to say. "I'm sorry, I didn't mean..."

"No. Don't you dare apologize. God chastises those He loves, right? I've just been chastised." She looked back up into Brent's eyes. "I'm learning that I need to change the way I handle things. I need to start turning back the darkness, too."

Brent crossed his arms and stared into Marta's eyes. "There'll be forces that'll come against you if you do."

"Bring 'em on!" she exclaimed with a wink and a smirk.

‡‡‡

**9:37 p.m.**

Tara sat in her dorm room and brooded, one question perpetually playing on her mind. *Why in hell am I here?* She was nineteen years old, and had asked herself the same question every day for what seemed like years. Sometimes it was directed toward her involvement at this college. At other times it was directed at life in general; at life on this speck of cosmic dust hurtling through what seemed a cold, uninviting, and indifferent universe.

The low light and incense burning in the room—against dorm regulations—played on her emotions. The darkness may have been more comfortable for her, but it also had a tendency to usher in mild depression. Tonight was no exception, except that it was a bit more than mild this time.

She walked to the mirror above the sink in her room and stared. Eyeliner was starting to smudge around her right eye. She stared hard and long at the way she looked. Where had she gone? Tara Darlene Baker, the naïve, strawberry-blonde girl from

Branson, Missouri, was nowhere to be found in the reflection.

*Why in hell am I here? Where am I?* Who *am I?*

She turned away from the mirror and walked to her window. Looking down at the courtyard, she could see that the lamps along the sidewalks had come on. The students below her were casually passing the evening by. Two guys laughed and pushed each other as they strode; a threesome of girls walked arm-in-arm. A guy sat with his arm around a girl on a bench underneath the huge oak tree in the center of the courtyard.

Without time to ward it off, a twinge of longing sprang up in her soul. What would it be like to be normal again? The question hung in her mind for a moment.

*What?!*

She pushed back from the window, hardly able to contain the rage that surged from her core. *Like them?! I'll die first!* She paced back and forth in her small room. Irritation fueled her. Through clinched teeth she forced out, "To hell with them. To hell with all of them."

Approaching the mirror again she stared into her own eyes and seethed. "You are *not* one of *them!* You never will be. They are weak. You have power. *Real* power." After a long moment she decided on a course of action. "I think it's time to tap into that power once again."

She felt a tingle creep up her spine. The hairs on the back of her neck prickled. She hadn't even summoned one of the dark ones yet, but she could already feel her spirit guide's presence. She walked back to the window and picked out her target. It would be that pathetic lovey-dovey couple on the bench.

She knelt down before the small table in front of her window; opening a drawer, she pulled out a rolled-up piece of black felt and spread it across the table to display her pentagram casting cloth. Two freshly-painted, concentric red circles looked like rings of blood at the center of the fabric. The center of the two circles contained a star—a pentagram—that touched the inner ring with all five points. Between the two circles and within the five points of the upside down star were symbols that very few people would recognize and, of which, even fewer could know the relevance. Next she pulled out four small black candles, set them outside the circles, creating a square, and lit them.

She was already beginning to feel the darkness swirl around her. *This* is what she knew. This is what she understood. This was her environment, and this is where she thrived.

She reached again into the drawer and pulled out a hag stone—her amulet. It was a stone that she found that had a naturally-made hole through it. Many people searched for decades for a hag stone, never to find one. The day she found hers, she knew it was a sign that she had received the blessings of the gods and goddesses. She also withdrew a chromed pentagram necklace and clasped the chain around her neck. It rested midway down her chest and reflected candlelight onto the walls. Lastly she pulled out her personal grimoire[3], her personal 'book of shadows.'

She fingered through the book, looking for a nefarious spell to cast upon the young lovers, knowing that a dark one would enter into the room with her to take on the assignment and carry it out ... if she could just find the right incantation.

A chill of fear coursed through her as she realized how close she came to a mortal mistake. She ran to her closet and pulled out another piece of black fabric and unrolled it on the floor in front of her small altar. On it were two more concentric circles of red, big enough to allow her to sit fully within their confines. Between the crimson rings were more magick symbols and the names of the spirits and gods she most often conjured.

How could she have forgotten her own protection? Several years ago she had remembered too late, and she had paid a price for it. A brutal price.

Before sitting, Tara looked at every inch of the circle to make sure that there were no breaks in it, breaks that, if penetrated all the way through, would create a hairline entryway from the outside into the protecting area. She centered herself in the blood-red circle, making sure that not a single part of her body or clothing lay outside its boundary. Grabbing her grimoire she turned a couple more pages before landing on the invocation she found suitable.

She laughed as she pictured the end result. *Oh*, she thought, *this ought to be good. Real good.*

Before beginning her spirit summons, she first spoke the spell of protection that was needed to create a barrier between her and whatever being came forth to answer the call.

"By the dragon's light
On this May night
I call to thee
To give me your might.

---

[3] Go to Appendix B for a description of Tara's items for ritual spellcasting.

By the power of three
I conjure thee
To protect all
That surrounds me.
So mote it be
So mote it be!"

Comfortable with her environment, she looked down at the handwritten words in her book of shadows and spoke forth the words that would throw a fear-filled disruption into the lives the young lovebirds sitting, oblivious, five stories below.

## Chapter Fourteen

**Saturday, May 16 – 10:21 p.m.**

"Okay, who threw that?" asked Terry. He looked up from his seat on the other side of the large round table. The group of five sat at the windowed edge of the heavily-populated student union building.

Brent looked up from his textbook to see Diane Hamilton burying a grin. Terry Carpenter hadn't seen her yet. Diane realized that Brent was looking at her and put her left elbow up on the round table and hid a quivering smile with her hand.

*Uh-oh*, thought Brent with an emerging grin of his own. *Here comes the end of serious study. So be it!* Knowing Diane was near the breaking point of laughter, Brent pretended to start sticking a finger up his nose.

Marta glanced at him, and not knowing Brent's true aim, produced a look of utter distaste as his finger got closer.

Terry, now looking at Marta, and seeing her twisted facial expression, directed his eyes over to Brent as well.

Karen McGlaughlin—the A-type personality of the group—startled everyone by loudly shouting, "Don't do it, Brent! Don't do it!"

That was all it took. An hour of concerted study erupted into uncontrollable laughter. Brent thought he would never catch his breath, especially after Diane, the initial culprit, fell off her chair and lay on the floor in hysterics.

At that point everyone knew that further study was hopeless. Terry suggested that they just close the books and order a couple of large pizzas. Everyone voiced agreement. Karen had an idea, too, and ran to her dormitory to get everyone's favorite games, Outburst and Taboo.

After tackling the layers of pepperoni, banana peppers, and extra cheese, they began a game of Outburst. Their laughter escalated, soon drawing attention from other students around them. The next thing the group of five knew, a couple onlookers from another table asked if they could join in on the fun.

It was a great evening.

By the time the "party" drew to a close and everyone had dispersed, the five friends had gained a couple of new companions.

"I needed that. Thank You," whispered Brent into the night

air. He walked alone toward the stupidly-distant parking lot.

Approaching "The Great Oak," which stood in the middle of the wide, grassy courtyard between the rows of campus dormitories, Brent listened as a strong breeze ruffled the new-born leaves of the huge tree. A sudden cold chill washed over his body. There was something very wrong about it; no way should he feel cold. It was a warm night, in the mid-seventies, at the very least.

He felt something else; something he recognized—a manifestation of evil that he hadn't felt in years.

He stopped. His heart rate spiked. Taking stock of his surroundings, he found that he was the only one in the courtyard.

"What's going on?" he asked under his breath. "God? What's ...?"

‡‡‡

**10:23 p.m.**

Tara, in the faint glow of candlelight, stood within her protective rings and stared downward into the courtyard, observing the effects of her latest harassment. A male student stopped just before passing under the massive branches of The Great Oak. He turned to look around, and she grinned.

*I know who that is. It's Goodie-Two-Shoes from the student union.*

"He's about to feel more than simply my elbow." Any moment, now, she would see the beautiful end result of her spellcast.

But Goodie just stood in place, quickly looking around. It was obvious that he was alert to the attack, however too much time was passing without the expected end result.

"What the hell is going on?"

‡‡‡

**10:25 p.m.**

Brent found his 'spiritual legs' and stood his ground. "Father, protect me," he whispered. Again he looked around, still seeing no one. Something was there, though, and very close. "In the name of Jesus, whom I serve, I rebuke you, spirit!" The command was spoken aloud, and the result was immediate.

A calm washed over him. Whatever it was that had harassed him was now gone.

His senses remained on high alert. He knew in the core of his being that whatever had just happened had been deliberate.

"Lord," he began, a hint of worry in his voice, "This isn't ... I'm not being revisited, right? I mean, that's all over. *Long* over. Right?"

The Holy Spirit's presence rose up within him. It wasn't the direct answer to his question that he hoped for, at least not one that he could recognize, but the Spirit's presence was reassuring him that he wasn't alone in this.

Unwilling to wait around for another fear-enmeshed visit, Brent started walking again, faster this time. *Just another few minutes to my car, and I'm outta here.*

Sometimes wisdom dictated a quick getaway.

‡‡‡

**10:27 p.m.**

Tara's eyes widened in astonishment and dismay. "What?! What the hell just happened?!" She stepped off her mat in order to round her altar and get a better look out the window.

She recoiled in intense pain as she felt the full force of an angry spirit lash out at her. She fell to her knees, doubling over in agony. Her intestines felt as though they were being mutilated and ripped out of her belly. She instantly knew what was happening. The spirit she'd sent out to do her bidding had been repelled! Having stepped out of her rings of protection, its wrath was now returning and with a vengeance.

She tried to utter an incantation for protection, but she couldn't focus for all the pain. "No!" she cried. "Don't!"

She rolled onto the floor into a fetal position. Her bowels squeezed, and unable to make it to the bathroom, she soiled herself.

"No, no, no," she whimpered as tears of anger, fear, and pain streamed into her hair. "No. Please, no."

# Chapter Fifteen

**Monday, May 18 – 4:57 p.m.**

Brent and Marta walked through the commons area near the student union building. Marta saw that Brent was already focused on the task ahead.

“You ready to head to the courtyard?” she asked, already knowing the answer.

“Yep.”

“At least it’s daylight. Not much going to happen under such a brilliant, blue sky.”

“I wish I could believe that,” said Brent. “But the fact of the matter is that, while people who perform witchcraft do enjoy the night to keep their practices private, demons are not opposed to working in the sunlight.”

“You sound so sure that it was witchcraft.” She paused thoughtfully before continuing. “I mean, it was night, you were alone; perfect time for a person’s imagination to get the best of him.”

Grim in his response, Brent said, “I know what I felt. A presence I haven’t felt since ...” Brent got quiet.

“Okay, Darth,” quipped Marta with a smile on her face.

“Huh?” Brent looked at her curiously for a moment, then realized he had just precisely quoted Darth Vader from Star Wars. In spite of himself he chuckled. “Oh yeah.”

They took a few more paces and Brent said, “I appreciate you, Marta. Thanks for walking through this with me. Hopefully we’ll find some answers.”

“Like you said, we Christians are only as successful as our relationships with the Lord and each other.”

“I said that?”

“Yes, you did.”

He thought about it for a moment, then said, “You know what? I’m pretty smart.”

Marta deliberately moved closer and nudged him off the sidewalk. “Uh-huh. Not to bust your bubble, but it could have been the Holy Spirit.”

“I concede.”

They entered the courtyard area and immediately Brent became wary. Marta was right about one thing: the sunlight *did* help.

"You were under the oak?" asked Marta.

"Approaching it."

"Do you think it has something to *do* with the oak?"

"No, I don't think so. But I've got to admit that I don't really know much about this stuff."

"What? You told me that you were once a practicing witch. I thought that would kind of make you, if not an expert, certainly knowledgeable."

"It wasn't until after I left the occult that I found out that I had actually been involved in witchcraft. Even then I had a tough time admitting it to myself."

They came to a stop under the shade of The Great Oak. Brent looked around, scoping out the landscape and the buildings.

"Brent, I know you wanted to come back out here. But, why exactly?"

He thought a moment then said, "Just getting back on the horse." The comment seemed to satisfy her.

Marta took a seat and leaned back against the tree's massive, gnarled trunk. "Weird place to have a nightmarish encounter. It's so beautiful and peaceful."

Brent sat down next to her. "It was beautiful and peaceful last night, too. Until the attack happened."

"That's another thing that's got me curious. How do you know it was an attack?"

"Good question. I don't know how I know. Like I said, I'm new to all of this. I guess it's the way the Holy Spirit brought up the right thing to say when I needed it. That, and the fact that it just came from out of nowhere. I mean, one minute I'm smiling, thinking back to the lunacy at the student union, and the next thing I know my skin is crawling. It *seemed* like an attack."

"What I thought you meant was that someone might have actually *sent* the demon to attack you."

"I've been thinking about that. If someone sent it, that means someone had a reason. It's not like I've got any enemies."

"You *did* ruffle some feathers in some of our classes."

"Yeah, but I never directed any of my comments at anyone in particular."

"Brent, you represent Christianity. Sometimes it takes no more than that to get someone to hate you."

"Yeah, you're right. So, now we're assuming that whoever launched this against me is someone in one of my classes."

"And lives on campus," added Marta.

"What?"

She pointed straight ahead to the six-story-high dormitory in front of them.

‡‡‡

**5:15 p.m.**

Loathing sought to reestablish itself within Tara as she peered into the courtyard. But she wasn't certain of what she saw until she was able to clearly see to the other side of the girl. Ah-ha! She hadn't been mistaken. There, sitting next to the girl against the oak was Goodie-Two Shoes himself. She could just walk right by them and go into the dorm without either of them being the wiser, but that held little interest.

Goodie was obviously one of two things: either a male witch who was able to take her spell and bend it back toward her or, more likely, a devotee of Christ. She'd had run-ins with them before. For whatever reason, her attempts to affect Christ-followers most often met with failure. *Most* often.

Back when she'd had the added fortune of being part of a coven—before deciding to further her education—her high priestess, Stephanie, had warned her about these Jesus-followers. "They must be handled with caution," she had said. "Most who have *become* Christians only *call* themselves Christians after their conversions. They are happy with being 'saved' but don't let their religion get in the way of their preferred lifestyles. With these you have little to worry about. They are not your enemies." Stephanie had then looked dead into her eyes and continued, "However, be warned. Those who *follow* The Way are not the same. It is not that they are stronger, but more difficult. Our masters are constantly warring against their 'God,' and, as in any war, there are victories and there are defeats. We win some against them, and we lose some. If you choose to battle, pick your fight carefully. In the same way that they seek to disarm those of the Dark Way, we must disarm *them* before launching an attack. Otherwise *we* can be on the receiving end of the pain. Get them to drop their guard. Then go for the jugular. To trip up or bring down a Christian is challenging, but always rewarding. The gods will sometimes reward those who engage and win against Christlings."

Tara decided as she drew closer to the oak that she was going to throw caution to the wind. *Let's see how fast I can get to the jugular.*

‡‡‡

**5:16 p.m.**

Brent stared a moment longer at the dormitory and got a chill. "You think that if someone actually did send something my way, that he or she lives in that building?"

"Not necessarily that one, but maybe one of them surrounding the courtyard. I mean, it probably didn't take much more than looking down here to find a target."

Brent thought a moment, and then said, "So, I could have just been a random mark."

Marta was about to say something when someone rounded the tree and stood in front of them. She looked strangely familiar to Marta, but she couldn't immediately place her.

The girl, wearing a black T-shirt, black jeans ... black *everything,* seemed to be composing herself to say something.

Brent broke the awkward moment of silence. "Hi. What's up?"

Again the girl fidgeted. "Uhh. I need to say something." Her right hand went up to her hair and began to tangle it between her fingers.

Brent stood up. "Are you okay?"

Tears began to fill her eyes. "I just wanted to say that I'm sorry for what I did."

Brent, now confused, asked, "For what? I don't think we've ever met before. Have we?"

That's when it hit Marta. She stood up and said, "Oh, now I remember who you are. You're the girl who directed an elbow to his rib cage a few days ago."

The girl looked down at the ground. "Yes. That's right."

Marta retorted with, "That was pretty mean."

Brent touched Marta's shoulder. "Marta, it's okay." Then, waiting for the girl to look up again, he said, "It's okay. Thank you for apologizing."

The girl just stood there, continuing to look at her feet. Her shoulders began to quake.

"Hey, now. Are you okay?" asked Marta.

The girl fell to her knees, sorrow heavy in her eyes, and shook her head. "No. No ... I'm not all right. Nothing's all right." She was on the verge of breaking down.

Brent and Marta both crouched down beside her. Marta began trying to comfort her. "Whatever it is ... It will be all right. It will."

Brent asked her for her name.

"Tara. Tara Baker," she replied, composing herself. She started to stand up and mumbled, "I'm sorry. I ... I've got to go."

"No, it's okay. You don't have to go. Would you like to sit and talk?"

Tara sniffled and said, "Really? You don't want me to go?"

"No, of course not," said Brent.

Marta took Tara's left hand in her right and reassuringly eased her down to have a seat with them on the grass. "I'm Marta."

"I'm Brent."

"I'm emotional," said Tara, bringing out the laughter in all three of them.

*This couldn't be going any better*, thought Tara. *Playing them like a ... what's the name of that violin?* She gave up on the name. *Like a Stratocaster.*

Violins were no match for a well-played, heavy-metal guitar.

# Chapter Sixteen

**Monday, May 18 – 7:07 p.m.**

She had succeeded.

Tara walked into the lobby of her dormitory, victorious. She had won them over and was now their new best friend. She giggled. How dismal she must have sounded to them. And in return, she received an abundance of their pity. *Poor, poor Tara,* they must be thinking. *She has so many problems, and we're going to help her fix them.* Rarely had Tara put on such a performance; the tears, the appearance of utter hopelessness.

"Academy, where is my Oscar?!" she nearly shouted as she entered the elevator. Pressing "6", the doors closed. She reflected on the story that she'd given Goodie and Girly-Girl. It was a story that she was going to have to keep straight in order to play her part successfully.

She had "explained" that her anguish had resulted from her boyfriend having just broken up with her, throwing her into a major depression. She had lashed out at Brent because he was a guy—a guy that happened to be in target range.

Then she told them that the reason, she thought, that her boyfriend had broken up with her was her constant alcohol binging. She told them that she hated both her ex-boyfriend and herself for creating such a mess. And finally, she said that she couldn't get her head back into her studies and that she was afraid she was going to fail the semester if things didn't change soon.

It was all lies, of course. Not a word of it was true. In fact, right now she was too busy for a boyfriend *because* she was concentrating so much on her sophomore-year studies. She was actually carrying a 3.7 GPA this year.

But they bought it all, hook, line, and sinker ... and bobber. She giggled again.

Of course, Goodie had started in with the whole "God" thing. She'd expected it once she realized that he wasn't a witch. The guy probably hadn't so much as told a white lie since he was five years old. Goodie Two-Shoes to the core.

Now, Miss Girly-Girl was a different story. She could tell that Marta had probably come from the other side of the tracks. And Tara knew she would have to watch out for her. She didn't seem as trusting as Brent. Even so, she seemed to have bought the story as readily as he.

Keeping the deception going was the key. They had offered to pray for her needs. And as long as they were praying for needs she didn't have, Tara suspected that Goodie and Girly wouldn't create too many problems when it came to using their Christianity.

Both her mentor in the craft, Stephanie O'Leary, and her spirit guide, Shalinar, had warned her against being the focus of targeted prayers. It was to be avoided at all costs. Better to have *Christlings* praying for non-existent challenges than real ones. Tara didn't understand why the warnings were given, especially if Christlings were actually misled weaklings, but caution would be maintained anyway.

The diversion would also keep them from suspecting her when it came to the torments that Goodie, and now Miss Girly, would experience. She'd have to be careful, though, and bide her time. She mustn't have any more attacks seeming to coincide with the "chance" meeting today. Yes, wisdom was called for.

Devious wisdom.

‡‡‡

**7:07 p.m.**

Brent and Marta walked away from The Great Oak feeling better than they had when approaching it a couple of hours earlier.

"Maybe God used what the enemy meant for evil last night to bring us back here to do some good today," Marta offered.

"Wow. Good thought. All's well that ends well, right? If some good comes out of my weird experience, then I'm satisfied," said Brent.

They walked a few more paces, heading toward the off-campus apartment that Marta shared with two other roommates. Brent reflected out loud. "Interesting girl."

"Yeah. Interesting," said Marta. "Pretty screwed up. But it sounds like she really wants some help. She didn't really seem interested in hearing about God, though."

"No. At least not yet. She basically gave us a list of things that we can pray for, though. When God starts answering our prayers for her, I'm sure she'll become more receptive."

"I hope you're right."

"I always am." Brent looked over and presented a big, toothy grin.

"Want another elbow?"

# Chapter Seventeen

**Thursday, May 21 – 7:45 a.m.**

Marta woke up after a restless night of sleep. Two nights in a row. She couldn't understand what the problem was. She hadn't had any bad dreams ... that she could remember.

Wiping sleep from her eyes, she walked blearily into the kitchen for her first cup of coffee. As she stepped toward the counter, she slipped on a notebook that lay inconspicuously on the floor. She caught herself from falling with a quick grab at the counter. Her heart raced and her face flushed with anger.

She bent down, picked up the spiral-bound book with the name Catlynn Jacobson on it. "Cat!" she called out. "You nearly killed me!"

Catlynn came around the corner into the kitchen with a puzzled look on her face. "Huh?"

"Your notebook was lying in the middle of the kitchen floor. I slipped on it."

"Marta, I'm sorry." She thought for a moment and said, "Lisa must have knocked it off the counter this morning."

"Lisa's still in bed. Friday—no early classes."

"Then I'm stumped. I know I stacked them with the other books right there." She pointed to her other books on the counter next to the refrigerator.

"It's no big deal, Catlynn. I'm okay. Forget it."

Catlynn went back to getting ready while Marta reached up to get a coffee cup out of the cabinet. *Maybe I shouldn't have any coffee. I'm already feeling a bit jittery.* She reconsidered. Jittery though she may be, the last thing she wanted to do was add a lack-of-caffeine headache into the mix.

"Lord," she whispered, "please, be with me today."

‡‡‡

**12:13 p.m.**

Marta walked into her U.S. Constitution class and found an empty seat. Brent wasn't there yet. She sighed. If he was late again, she'd have to wait until after class to express her emotions about the awful day she was having. The day was dragging, and it was all she could do to stay awake. Her second cup of coffee from

Mocha Manz didn't seem to be helping.

She yawned.

Professor Bauer walked in, took off his rain coat, and hung it up on a hook behind the door. He sat down behind his desk and opened his old brown leather briefcase. Taking out some papers, he set them on the desk beside him, closed the briefcase, and set it on the floor.

"Good afternoon, Professor Bauer."

Marta turned her eyes to the door. Brent was all smiles as he walked in.

"Good afternoon, Mr. Lawton." The professor made an exaggerated effort to look at his watch. "It's only 12:15. Starting a new lease on life?"

Brent chuckled. Finding Marta, he started down the row leading to the seat next to hers. "Hey, you," he said. "How're you doing?"

Marta began to say her typical "I'm good," but opted for a touch of honesty instead. "I'm having a bad hair day."

Brent smiled. "Doesn't look like it."

"It's my light way of saying it's been a bad day." She conceded a slight smile. Just being able to say it allowed a slight bit of relief.

"Sorry to hear that. Anything in particular going on?"

"No," she said. "Just a bunch of little things. It's just my day for the universe to turn its attention to me. Can't wait for the day to end, though."

She turned her attention to Brent. "You seem to be in a good mood."

"Well, actually, I am. I woke up this morning and just felt like everything was..." He thoughtfully chose his next word. "... honky-dory."

Marta laughed in spite of herself. "Nice description, Grandpa."

"So, you're not exactly feeling the same, huh?" asked Brent.

"Oh, I'll be all right. Just glad you're here to complain to."

Brent grinned and looked at his watch. "Umm, I think I've got to be someplace." Marta hit him in the arm.

Professor Bauer stood up and said, "Well, looks like everyone's here a couple minutes early today, so why don't we get started?"

Brent turned his focus to the front of the class.

Marta nervously began biting her fingernails. Again.

‡‡‡

**6:15 p.m.**

Brent finished his meal. His parents were nearly finished with theirs as well. He got up from the table and, picking up his plate and glass, walked into the kitchen. The plate was nearly in the sink when his father called in. "Rinse it, and put it in the dishwasher, Brent. Don't leave it for your mom to do."

"Okay," he mumbled under his breath, lifting the plate back up. He turned on the water, rinsed the remaining mashed potatoes into the garbage disposal, and put it into the dishwasher. He walked out of the kitchen not at all liking how he felt. A funny thing, conviction. It was certainly designed to keep people from making mistakes, but so often Brent found that it was loudest only after he'd been caught trying to get away with something. Still, it was a start.

To have moved from open rebellion against what his parents had required of him six years ago to where he actually felt conviction about such small things as a dirty plate was amazing, albeit perturbing at times. But Brent was growing. And in the midst of it, he had found that the more he was willing to give way to the Holy Spirit's leading—His conviction—the more often and loudly the Spirit could be heard. Brent was amazed that the Third Person of the Trinity was not just willing to be heard, He actually wanted to converse! Sometimes it was almost too much to fathom.

He walked back into the family room and picked up his Bible from the coffee table. Tonight was Freedom Rings night, and he was looking forward to meeting up with George Chamberlin.

As he turned around to head back through the house and out to his car, his mom called, "We received another letter from Lydia today."

"That's great! Where is it?" Brent asked.

"It's on the dining room table," his dad replied. "Part of the letter was written to you."

"Cool."

He stepped into the dining room and found the envelope that was addressed to The Lawton Family from AB Lydia Lawton at Lackland Air Force Base in San Antonio, Texas. He smiled. He still couldn't get out of his head that his little sister had joined the military. The *military!*

A year out of high school, Lydia couldn't decide where she wanted to go with her education. A friend of hers had said that she was going into the military to help pay for college. As for

Lydia, she knew she didn't need help, because their mom and dad had already set aside money for her education. But she was directionless and didn't want to go to college just to flounder. Her friend, Jessica, had asked her to go to the local recruiting station to provide a little moral support. The next thing they knew, they'd both committed their lives to four full years of active duty service in the United States Air Force. That did *not* go down well with their mom and dad. He'd seen that first hand.

Lydia had walked confidently into the house and called out, "Mom! Dad! Can you come into the living room?" When they both walked in, she announced, "I know what I'm going to do with the next four years of my life."

His dad crossed his arms and displayed a mirthful smile. "Oh really, now. And what would that be?"

Brent remembered that his mom's face showed no discernible emotion; not until she'd heard Lydia's next words: "The military."

"The *what*?" she croaked out. "Ho oohh no you're not." Her look became stern.

"The military?" asked his dad with a raised brow.

"Yep."

Brent stood there wondering if this was another of Lydia's little pranks. Sometimes she'd tease Dad just to get a reaction.

"You can't," his mom had continued.

"Well ... I..." began Lydia.

His dad narrowed his eyes slightly and asked, "What did you do, Little Girl?" The mirthful look had left, though he hadn't registered anything beyond a focused curiosity.

Lydia took a deep breath and slowly exhaled. Then she came right out with it. "I already signed up."

"Nooo!" his mom cried, immediately devastated.

It appeared that his dad took the announcement in stride. "Okay. Well, that's done. No going back now."

"What do you mean, 'No going back'?" his mom responded with a look of desperation.

"Well, if she's signed up, she's signed up. Neither you nor I can go and erase that signature. She belongs to the government now."

In that moment, his mom began to cry. "What's the phone number? I'm calling them right now. Lydia, give me the phone number."

Lydia obviously hadn't expected this sort of reaction. But, then, no one could have expected this sort of action from Lydia. She stood there, unable to respond.

"Sharon," his man said, turning to face his wife. "Sharon, if she signed, she's obligated."

It was then that Brent and Lydia had seen something take place that they hadn't seen in years. Their mom walked into their dad's arms. There she tried to take solace in the crook of his neck.

Brent and Lydia looked at each other wide-eyed. Brent walked over to her and said, "Didn't see that coming."

"Didn't see what? What I said or what they're doing?"

"Both."

After a moment, their dad looked over to Lydia and asked, "So, did you follow in your old man's footsteps?"

Lydia smirked and gave a little shake of her head. "Air Force."

"Cool," said Brent. "Are they going to let you fly?"

"*Air* Force?" Brent and Lydia both looked at their dad. "Trying to break my heart now?" But they both could see the tease in his eyes.

Brent's mom released her grip on her husband and pulled back, eyes wet, just listening.

"Yes, the Air Force," she said, a smile breaking across her face. Then turning to Brent she said, "And no, they won't let me fly. Have to have a four-year degree to do that."

"Yes! College!" blurted out his mom. "Go to college first!"

"Mom..."

"Sharon..."

The woman held up her hands. "Sorry! I know. I know. She's not mine anymore." She appeared on the verge of tears again, but fought them back. Then she put her hands on her hips and, after a deep sigh, asked, "Okay, Lydia Anne, when is all of this going to happen?"

"In seven weeks. Jessica and I..."

"Jessica?"

"Oh, yeah ... Jessica and I signed up at the same time. We'll go through basic training together and even go through avionics school together. We're going to Lackland Air Force Base in San Antonio, Texas, for six weeks first. Then we'll be going to some other base afterward for a few months of technical school. Then we'll go somewhere else for ... well ... I don't know how long."

Brent came back to the moment, holding a letter from his sister in her fourth week of basic training. He pulled the letter out of the envelope, walked over to the light switch, and turned on the dining room chandelier. Unfolding the letter, he read that she was doing well, that she was finally no longer scared of her training instructor, and that she was finally getting the feeling she was actually going to graduate. Brent smiled. *Atta girl*, he thought. Then he reached the part his dad had indicated:

*Brent, you should have joined with me. You should see all the single gals here!* Brent rolled his eye with a grin. *Just kidding. I just wanted to tell you that if I didn't have my faith in the Lord, I might not have gotten through the first half of basic training. Thank you for being a good example to me. In fact, being a good example must have rubbed off on me. Two days ago Jessica asked me to talk with her about my faith. Maybe because I keep bringing it up, or maybe she's seeing something in me that's working, I'm not sure. Anyway, we talked for a while, then I asked if she wanted to accept Jesus. She said yes! Now Jessica isn't just my best friend ... she's my sister! Thought you would like to know. Love ya!*

"Wow!" Brent whispered to himself. "Praise God!" He read through the letter a second time, folded it, and returned it to the envelope. Setting it on the table, he called out to the family room, "Sounds like things are going well for her."

His father called back, "When are you joining up?"

Brent grinned, "Signed up yesterday!"

His mom all but screamed. "What!?"

"I'm kidding! Relax."

He and his dad laughed out loud.

"Very funny," his mom retorted. "Just you wait."

‡‡‡

**8:45 p.m.**

Brent sat in the pew with rapt attention as Bob Naze preached. The topic had him scribbling notes furiously. The subject was "Infiltration of the Enemy." He still periodically attended Freedom Rings when his schedule allowed, even though he was now firmly ensconced in a church that he loved in Millsville.

Bob was drawing from all over the New Testament as he relayed the End-Times state of the world. He said that Jesus warned in Matthew 7:15 that we are to "Watch out for false prophets and teachers who dress up like sheep, but are really wolves in disguise." He went on to quote Paul, who warned that the "very elect could be deceived" by those with agendas that contradict the teachings of Christ. Jesus said that on the day of final judgment, there will be those who cry out after their sentencing, "Lord, Lord! Listen to us. You're wrong. We *did* preach and teach in your name." But Jesus will say in response, "Depart from me, you workers of sin, I never knew you!"

Brent's mind stretched to think of times when he may have been a bit naïve at the sincerity of some people who claimed to be Christians. *How many times have I been duped by people who pretended to know Christ?*

Bob wrapped up the evening with the altar call. As usual, there were several who responded and came forward for salvation. Brent loved this part of the service most. Over the past several years, his self-education in concepts called *spiritual warfare* taught him to fight in prayer for the lost when Bob was giving the invitation to accept Christ. Bob had said that the Enemy may have been specifically assigned to an individual to make sure that he or she didn't accept Christ. These demonic spirits would endure the tortures of praise and worship just to keep the altar call from being effective in these individuals' lives. Well, Brent was going to make sure that the Enemy had as little influence over a person's decision for Jesus as possible.

On his way home he thought about Bob Naze's message. He prayed, "Lord, show me. Keep me sensitive to Your Spirit. I want to know when truth is represented and when deception is at work."

# Chapter Eighteen

**Saturday, May 23 – 12:03 a.m.**

The Village of Pittston, Ohio was quiet beneath an overcast sky. The moon's luminescence pushed through the cloud cover, creating an otherworldly scene around the old farmhouse. White curtains, undulating with the soft orange glow of candles in an upstairs bedroom, suggested a warmth stereotypical of traditional country life.

Hidden behind that facade of comfort and normalcy, three young adults were cloaked in a deep unnatural power as they called on unseen forces to exact their evil intentions. The unsuspecting innocents of the local community would one day wish they had foreknowledge of this night's conjurings, for a powerful, ancient evil was now biding its time, watching attentively, at the doorstep of their picturesque village.

‡‡‡

**Friday, May 29 – 1:43 p.m.**

Marta saw Brent sitting with Tara in the Student Union eating lunch. She hesitated before continuing to the table. Why? Was she becoming jealous of Tara's encroachment into her friendship with Brent? She couldn't say, yet. She just knew she didn't much care for Tara. A twinge of guilt stabbed at her.

"God," she whispered, "please help me to have a better attitude toward her. She only wants help." Marta took a deep breath, quickly exhaled, put on a smile, and walked quickly to the table.

"Hey, you two!" she said with as much buoyancy as she could exude.

Tara and Brent looked up. Brent's already-present smile lit up.

"Hey, Marta!" he said.

Did she just see a glint of irritation in Tara's eyes? Whatever she thought she might have seen was gone as quickly as it had appeared.

"Marta, it's good to see you," said Tara, a big smile spreading across her face.

*What is it about her that's got me thinking so negatively?*

"Hi, Tara. Good to see you, too." She sat down.

Brent asked, "Well? How'd it go? Last exam of the last day!"

Marta smiled. "Hopefully it's not the first bad grade of the last day."

"I'm sure you did fine. Tara and I were talking about how to stay in touch over the summer."

"Yeah, stay in touch," Marta said, forcing her smile to remain in place. "Good idea."

"Turns out that Tara is an outdoorsy type. Hiking, backpacking, and camping and the like. Maybe we could get a couple of other people together and spend a few days in the hills in Southern Ohio this Summer. What do you two think?"

"Well, you know me," she responded, "anything to break a nail."

Marta was slightly taken aback as Tara began to laugh with an easiness that hadn't been apparent since they'd met.

"Sounds like it's time to clip mine then," Tara said with a smile. "Better I do it now, than sound like the typical girl from movies." She put the back of her right hand up to her forehead. "Oh, woe is me! I've broken a nail."

Marta sat down at the table with a smile coming to her lips. *Am I actually going to start liking this girl? Hmm... Don't know. The jury is still deliberating.*

"So," interjected Brent, "what do you think? Sound like a good idea?"

"I have to admit," responded Marta, "I'd like to have a group outing like that. It's been quite a while since I've been camping, though, and I don't have much to contribute when it comes to gear."

"Most of what we'll need I'm sure I can get," said Brent. "My family has been camping for years. We've got a new tent and a couple of older ones. Camping stove, backpacks, first-aid kits, sleeping bags, you name it. There will be some things that'll have to be bought, of course, but the cost should be pretty low."

Tara chimed in. "I've got some gear, too." Turning to face Marta, she said, "One of the most important things to get, if you don't already have them, would be a good pair of hiking boots and pairs of both nylon and wool socks."

"Nylon?" asked Marta.

"Yeah," Tara began to explain, "the two types work well together to prevent chafing and to allow your feet to breathe better. They'll help prevent moisture building up. Trust me, you don't want the alternative."

"I'm starting to get stoked by the whole idea," said Brent.

"Let's limit the number to another three to five people, though. Tara, do you know anyone who'd like to go with us?"

"I'll think about it, but most of my camping friends live out of state. So it'll probably be just me."

"No matter," said Brent. "I'm sure you'll enjoy being around some of our other friends. In fact, it'll be pretty cool taking a trip where we'll all be Christians."

Marta thought she saw a twinge of fear flash in Tara's eyes, but Tara responded with, "Sounds like a great time! I'm looking forward to it!"

Marta looked to Brent. He turned from Tara with a cheesy grin on his face and said, "Great! I'm loving this idea! I'll start researching some dates and a location."

It was then that Marta saw it in Brent's eyes—puppy-dog eyes. *Uh-oh,* Marta thought, *Brent's starting to fall for this girl.* It had been less than two weeks since they'd initially met her. She could certainly understand Brent's attraction, at least physically; Tara was runway-model gorgeous with her long strawberry-blonde hair, large green eyes, and cute figure. But behind the skin lurked something he wasn't seeing ... something that even she couldn't see clearly, yet. *God, protect this puppy dog with his tongue hanging out and his tail wagging excitedly.*

Brent looked back at Tara and grinned.

‡‡‡

**Friday, May 29 – 3:03 p.m.**

Tara said goodbye to Brent and Marta and began walking back to her dormitory. She had a lot of things to do: pack up her dorm room and get it loaded into her car and contact her spiritual mentor, Stephanie O'Leary, to let her know that she would, in fact, take her up on the offer to stay with her for the two and a half months between semesters. After all, an hour and a half away was a whole lot better than driving all the way back to Branson, Missouri; not that she had a good reason for going back there, anyway.

Also on her mental to-do list was to seek wisdom and guidance from her spirit guide. He would inform her how to disarm Brent. She would soon discover his weaknesses and use them to her advantage.

She already knew one of his weaknesses, of course: *strawberry-blonde hair and green eyes*. She grinned to herself. *Sex*. "Testosterone poisoning," she said out loud with a giggle.

Testosterone was, of itself, a powerful potion. She had what Brent wanted, and she would probably give it to him. After all, she had a body for a reason ... to be used in service.

She was no slut, to be sure. And she didn't give herself away in the hope of finding love. Access to her body was very restrictive. Private, in fact. While some in the craft were very liberal in the giving of their bodies, she kept this area of her life more off limits. She would always control the how and when. She had never been easily led to a bed and never would be. But she did make exceptions, and right now it looked like Brent Lawton would be one of them. Who knows? She might even allow herself to enjoy it.

As she walked into her dorm room, she stopped and sighed. A quick scan of the room reminded her that she was a pack rat. She had a lot of packing to do before her drive up to Pittston.

## Chapter Nineteen

**Saturday, June 13 – 12:27 p.m.**

"Sure, I can make it. Those dates don't conflict with anything," Marta said into the phone. "Let me know what I should bring. I'll head out to a store today to see if I can find some good hiking boots." She paused, then chuckled at Brent's next comment. "Yes, and *nylon* and *wool* socks! Good grief! So, who else is going?" Pause. "That's great! I haven't seen him since he transferred to Cedarville. Brent, I'm getting excited about this trip!" Pause. "So the group is going to be, you, me, Tara, Eric, Karen, and Terry. Is that right?" Pause. "Sounds great! I can't wait!" Pause. "Okay, let me know about what I can bring. You have a good remainder of your day, Brent." Pause. "Thank you. Bye!"

Now she had to go shopping in order to find what apparently were the most important articles of clothing in the whole wide world ... nylon and wool socks.

‡‡‡

**Thursday, June 18 – 2:13 p.m.**

Thursday afternoons during the summer months allowed Brent and his former high school basketball coach, George Chamberlin, to get together to talk over lunch and sometimes to go out to do some manly things: shooting at the range, a few holes of golf (a sport at which Brent knew he was rather bad), play a game of pick-up basketball at one of a few outdoor courts in the area, and sometimes, like today, go biking.

They opted for a ride along the Ohio-Erie canal; at least that's what it had been at one time. Now it was a series of broken trails, the longest of which was about 30 miles in length between Akron and Cleveland. They had never cycled the full course, but they kept talking about getting it done. 60 to 70 miles round trip would be quite the trek.

It was a beautiful day with the sun shining down through a near-full canopy of trees. Brent loved Summer. It didn't get much better than this. They were now enjoying a water break after about fifteen miles of riding, both drawing the cool liquid out of his own respective stash of sports bottles.

Another thing Brent loved was the man with whom he was hanging out.

George Chamberlin had approached Brent after graduation in May of 1983 to ask if he'd be up for a little mentoring in his Christian walk. Brent jumped at the chance. Where Brent was now in his walk with the Lord was attributable, in great part, to this man. He also believed that his dad's salvation was just around the corner. George and his dad shared several common interests, not the least of which was U.S. history—the subject that George still taught at the high school.

George and Brent sat on the dark gray wall of one of the abandoned canal locks that lined the trail. Sweat that soaked their hair also ran down their faces and necks into their T-shirts.

"So, tell me about this camping trip you're going on," inquired George, wiping sweat from his eyes with one of his shirt sleeves. "Sounds like you're pretty excited about it."

"Yeah, I am. It started out with us just looking for ways to stay connected over the summer. That is, Marta, Tara, and me. Then it got bigger out of necessity when we decided that going backpacking with some other friends would be a cool thing to do."

"Okay, I know Marta, but who is this Tara?"

"Well, she's someone that Marta and I met at the college. When we crossed paths with her she was pretty distraught." Brent went on to describe their initial encounter and budding friendships with the girl.

"Anything there on a more personal level for you, Brent?"

Brent was glad his face was already hot from the exertion of the bike ride, which probably saved him from some visible signs of having been caught off guard with the question. "Umm ... Well, she's not a Christian yet."

"Not exactly what I asked," said George with a smirk.

Brent sighed, looked at the ground for a moment, then looked over to George and met his gaze. He already knew where this was going to go.

George was a good mentor, helping Brent to steer clear of some decisions that would have compromised his walk with Christ. After avoiding some of those bad choices Brent had been glad of the man's guidance and his persistent questions about the struggles he'd been having. Most of the time, though, the questions were less than appreciated, at least initially. This held the prospect of being one of those times.

Brent couldn't help but grin as he answered. "Well, she *is* hot."

George couldn't help but laugh. "Wow. You sure know how to dodge giving a direct answer to a direct question."

"Okay, okay ... Yes ... maybe." Brent broke eye contact and looked straight ahead. "I mean, there is definitely something about her that is intriguing. She's outgoing and lives a little on the edge. She likes a lot of the same activities that I do, and ... she seems to be interested in me." Brent paused. "There, is that a little closer to the answer you were looking for?" asked Brent.

"Nailed it," George responded. "So, she's hot, has an apparent interest in you, and you two share some similar interests. So far, so good. But..."

"But..." Brent interrupted, "she doesn't know Christ."

"Pretty big element, don't you think?" asked George with a look that changed from humored to more matter-of-fact.

"Yes, it is. Very big. And it's not lost on me. In fact, Marta and I have both been praying for her and talking with her about Christ. Well, talking as much as she'll allow, anyway. It seems pretty awkward for her to talk about."

"I remember a young man of about sixteen having that same initial reaction," said George as he quickly lurched sideways to bump shoulders with Brent.

Brent smiled. "Yeah, I remember too. Don't know where I'd be if it hadn't been for you taking a chance to express your faith in Jesus that day."

"Okay," said George, once again serious, "what are your intentions with Tara on this camping trip?"

Brent blanched. "Well, nothing really ... outside of just being friends."

George shifted to turn more toward Brent. "This is where the rubber meets the road, Brent. There may or may not be opportunities for getting into trouble during your camping trip..."

"George, there's not..."

George raised a hand. "Let me finish. Brent, you're 21 years old; a full-fledged godly man. But you're a man with weaknesses. All of us have those areas in our lives where compromise is just one overwhelming temptation away. Your past with your ex-girlfriend, Michele, opened a big bad door in your life.

"The first year that you and I started getting together after your graduation you admitted to me that you and Michele had been sexually involved. With that type of experience, especially one that lasted well over a year, comes more struggle than if it hadn't happened at all. It's not easy to put the genie back in the lamp, if you'll excuse the non-Christian euphemism. And trust me, there *will* be opportunities on this trip for you to compromise, especially if you're right about this girl having eyes for you, too."

"I know you're right," Brent admitted. "Trust me, though ... more than anything I want to see her saved."

"That's great, Brent. I know that about you. You've got an evangelist's heart. But having the right heart is only part of the solution that you need to keep yourself from falling. Do you want to know what the other part is?"

Brent smiled and nodded, knowing that he'd just gotten cornered.

"The other part is a good decision, backed up by commitment. If you go into this trip wondering how far things might go with her, you're going to be looking for and *hoping* for opportunities. Opportunities to start holding hands... Opportunities to steal a kiss out on the trail when no one else is looking... Opportunities to take things—or allow for things to go—further. My guess is that you've already imagined some of those things."

Brent cringed within himself. This man knew him. Supposedly that was a good thing, but right now Brent didn't like getting caught with his hand in the cookie jar. Brent hadn't imagined that Tara and he would be 'sleeping' together, but he had fantasized about his hand running through her hair and drawing her into a tight embrace; then that lingering kiss. Brent sighed, and George must have seen it.

"Brent, I'm not trying to rain on your parade, but I am trying to keep you from doing damage from two standpoints: 1) you feeling guilty for compromising on your commitment to only date a Christian, and 2) not being different from any other guy that Tara might have had. You want this girl to come to Christ, but the biggest thing that you can do to hinder that is to compromise for the sake of a good time. Make sense?"

Brent looked at his tennis shoes and nodded. He heard George take a deep breath then stand up.

"I think I could make it a few more miles before heading back the opposite direction," said George with renewed vigor. "That is, if those formerly athletic legs of yours can handle the burn."

Brent stood up, too, and looked at his mentor and friend. "Bring it on, old man."

George laughed as he grabbed his bike.

Brent smiled, but his mind was not going to let loose of this conversation for a while. It was time to make a decision. He hoped he'd make a good one, and just as importantly, back it up with a true commitment. He knew he would, but he wasn't sure he liked ditching his mental fantasy.

*I wonder how much commitment twenty miles of praying will get me?* Brent asked himself.

## Chapter Twenty

### Thursday, June 18 – 3:19 p.m.

Tara stood on the lawn outside Stephanie O'Leary's house seething. The woman she considered her mentor and friend—her former priestess—had just called her incompetent.

*Incompetent?! Because I'm taking some bold risks, I'm incompetent?* It was all she could do not to turn around and scream at the house.

She had laid out her plan to Stephanie, describing how Brent was playing into her hands, and how the boldest accomplishment of her life was just about to take place. She had come to Pittston filled with the giddy anticipation of hearing her mentor praise her audacity.

*So much for that idea.*

Tara stood staring at her car on the street, thinking about driving off, wheels squealing, like any number of male jerks that she knew would have done. But what would that prove, that she was jerk in a woman's body? No. After being able to remain composed inside the house during her beat down, she wasn't going to lose it now; now that she could breathe again.

As she continued to stand implanted in the grass like a lawn gnome, she tried to think of where she could go to vent. Well, she could just drive around the corner and have a good rant inside the relative privacy her car.

*Not* one *word of credit for what I'm going to accomplish. Just derisive commentary on how I am putting myself at risk, and exposing* her *to risk by staying in her house while attempting it. I'm not a freaking amateur! I've been practicing my craft for eight-and-a-half years!*

The rage wasn't letting go and she still wasn't moving. She just stood there, chin nearly at her chest, eyes peering upward toward her car, arms straight down at her sides, hands balled into fists. If looks could evaporate a car...

*Get control. Let it go.* She knew the 'letting go' part probably wouldn't happen any time soon. She could, however, create the illusion of control for as long as it took to get out of visual range of the house.

Gradually she started unclenching her jaw and she began to let the blood flow to her finger tips again. She drew in a deep breath and slowly let it out. She blinked. She raised her head. She blinked again.

*Okay, steady, girl. You've proven yourself time and again. You'll prove yourself this time, too.* She unlocked her knees and began to walk to her car. A thought crossed her mind: *Maybe Marta could use a shopping partner before the trip. For right now I'd prefer her company over that of the* witch *behind me.* She smirked at her usage of the double entendre.

Tara got into her car, started it, and pulled away from the curb. After driving a couple of miles she found a pay phone in the parking lot of a 7-Eleven. Grabbing a quarter from her ash tray and her little address book from her purse, she got out of her car to make the call.

‡‡‡

**3:31 p.m.**

With a quizzical look, and no small amount of curiosity, Marta answered the phone on the third ring after seeing the caller ID: *Pay Phone*

"Hello?"

"Hi, Marta. Busy?"

*Tara. What does she want?* "Oh, hi, Tara. Well ..."

"`Cause I could use a friend right about now."

Marta breathed a quiet sigh and said, "What's wrong, Tara? Are you okay?"

"I'm just frustrated and feeling kind of alone right now. Would you like to go out and do something?"

Against Marta's better judgment she acquiesced. "Sure. Have something in mind?"

"Did you finish putting together all your camping gear?"

Marta laughed, "Gear? I own a sleeping bag, a pair of boots that *might* pass for doing some hiking and some wool and nylon socks."

This time Tara laughed. "Sounds like you got the important stuff. How about we go out and buy a few things that will make it feel like we haven't left all of civilization behind?"

"Okay, you've grabbed my attention," she said with a genuine grin. "Where are you?"

"Oh, I'm just out and about. I could be at your place in a half hour if that's not too soon."

"Nope. Come on over. Ready to take down the directions to get here?"

‡‡‡

**4:07 p.m.**

The knock on the front door of her parents' home brought Marta down the stairs from her bedroom. *This ought to be interesting,* she thought. Reaching the door, she swung it open, and there stood Tara, purse in hand and beautiful smile on her face. *She's definitely beautiful. I can see why Brent is taken by her.*

"Hi, Marta!" came an enthusiastic greeting.

"Hi, Tara. Good to see you. Ready for a romp at the mall?"

"Mall?" she chuckled. "You and I aren't going to the mall. We're going to the Army / Navy Store and to Burke's Sporting Goods."

"So, you're saying I shouldn't wear my pink pumps," said Marta with a smirk.

Tara giggled. "That's exactly what I'm saying."

"Well, okay, let's get going. I've never been shopping for Armies and Navies before."

‡‡‡

**5:15 p.m.**

Brent stood at the entrance to his family's garage and waved as George drove away. It had been a great ride; a combination of mental, spiritual, and physical workouts. *Thank You, Lord. Thank You for my mentor.*

He walked inside where he encountered his mom preparing dinner.

"Brent, you're a sweaty mess," she said with a shake of her head. "That coach of yours has been wearing you out for what..." She did a quick mental calculation in her head. "... six years, now?"

Brent laughed, "Yeah, but today I think I wore *him* out. What's for dinner?"

"Lasagna. Now go take a shower. You stink," she chortled.

With a roll of his eyes and a shake of his head, Brent went upstairs to his room to grab a fresh set of clothes.

Walking to the bathroom he called downstairs, "Any reason why I should be home this evening?"

"To spend time with your mom," came the reply. "Why? What is it you want to do?"

"Thinking about doing something with Marta."

"You two are destined for marriage. I don't care what you say."

Brent sighed. *Wish she'd drop that idea already.* He walked into the bathroom and ran the water. Luke warm. He still needed to cool down. As he stripped off his sweat-soaked clothes he thought about his mom's words. It wouldn't be a stretch for people who knew them to think that Marta and he would be boyfriend and girlfriend, but life had put them on different paths ... at least emotionally.

When they had met it wasn't love at first sight. In fact, though he found Marta to be attractive, with her long, dark hair, Latin complexion, and ever-so-slight Guatemalan accent, there was just no draw toward her. He couldn't explain it. In spite of that, though, the subject had come up about three years ago.

"Have you ever thought about me asking you out on a date?" he'd asked her one evening while studying at her home.

The question caught her off guard. "A *date* date?"

"Yes, Marta Liliana Rosales Rivas, a *date* date."

"*Enough* with my name already!" she said in mock annoyance. "I must admit, though, you are getting good at rolling those R's."

"Sorry," he said with a chuckle. "It's just too much fun to say. So?"

"Yes."

"Yes?"

"*Yes*, Brent! Goodness! I have thought about you asking me out."

Now Brent was caught off guard. "Uhh ... I didn't know that."

She laughed. "That's because I never mentioned it and you never asked. And why, after more than a year of knowing me, are you only asking now? That is, if you don't mind *me* asking."

Brent put a perplexed look on his face and looked up at her from his book at the opposite side of the kitchen table. "I don't know." He squinted in concentration before continuing. "You're a pretty girl. You're intelligent. You're fun to hang with. It just seems weird that I've never asked you out or put one of my irresistible moves on you," he said with a sly grin.

She laughed again. "Irresistible, huh?"

"Oh yeah, if I had wanted to, I could have made you putty in my hands."

At this, Marta sat up straight in her chair, crossed her arms, raised her eyebrows and said, "So ... you *didn't* want to. Is that what you're saying?"

In an instant Brent felt a chill travel down his spine and

knew that he'd totally lost control of the conversation. He wasted no time in trying to toss aside his hole-digging shovel and start trying to climb out of a crater that had only taken him six seconds to dig. "That's *not* what I meant! I just meant that if I..." *Good grief, yeah ... go ahead, stupid, and finish that sentence, too!* "I mean ... Listen, I." He gave up. "I don't know what I meant."

Marta attempted to maintain an I-dare-you-to-keep-going-down-that-path look, but once the smile began to crack across her lips she could no longer hold it. "Brent, I'm teasing."

"Thank God," he said as he drew his hand dramatically across is brow to feign the removal of sweat.

"And getting back to the subject at hand, I *have* wondered why you never asked me out. In fact, I had just assumed that you didn't think me attractive."

"Oh yeah, I'm the lone blind guy on campus."

"Well, it does make a girl wonder."

"Okay ... this isn't exactly the first time that I've wondered about this. I've just never known how to approach it. Part of me wonders why I don't get all hormonal around you like most guys. You're definitely great to look at." Brent paused to watch her reaction. She had kept eye contact, but he was sure he'd seen a little color rise through her dark complexion.

"Thank you," she'd said with a quick blink of her eyes.

"Trust me, my pleasure," he said with a big grin. "I've even wondered what it would feel like to steal a kiss from you."

"It would feel like a right hook to the jaw!" she retorted.

They both laughed.

Brent stood up from his chair and walked around to Marta's side of the table, extending his hand to her. She took it, and he guided her up and away from her seat. Brent remembered his heart beating hard at that moment. He figured that it was a moment of great curiosity for both of them, so he boldly moved forward.

He had maneuvered her directly in front of him, pulled her close, put his left hand on her waist and his right hand up into her thick hair behind her head and drew her face toward his. She didn't resist.

He kissed her.

He intended it to be a drawn-out encounter that they would both enjoy, but as if on cue, both of them suddenly burst out into laughter.

Yep, that had answered it. Friends forever.

‡‡‡

**5:21 p.m.**

“Olive green. You know, they’re saying it’s the new pink,” kidded Tara as she pulled two different types of boots off of the shelves. She handed one pair to Marta who sat on a bench in the footwear area of the Army / Navy store. Sitting down next to her, Tara took off her tennis shoes and began trying on the pair she selected for herself.

“Oh yeah. Quite the fashion statement. And they’re called ‘jump boots’ why?”

“Well, according to my father, they were designed for paratroopers in the military to give better support in the ankle area.”

“Gotcha.” Marta slipped off her shoes and put a foot into one of the boots. “They aren’t as uncomfortable as I thought combat boots would be.”

“Yeah, good thing for the military, huh? Imagine having to wear them days at a time.”

“So, things aren’t too good with you and your father, huh?” asked Marta with some measure of hesitation. Then, “Never mind. None of my business.”

“Don’t worry about it. I don’t have a father anymore.” Tara paused, as if considering the next thing to reveal. “He, uhh ... dumped my mom and me when I was fourteen. Found a bimbo, got her pregnant, and left us hanging with no income. Somewhere out there I’ve got a half-brother or half-sister.”

“You’re kidding me. You don’t know?”

“Nope. Don’t care to, either.”

“Do you know where he is? Your father, I mean,” asked Marta.

“Marta, I don’t want to talk about it,” Tara said abruptly. Silence permeated the air for a few uncomfortable moments. “Let’s get these damn boots and get out of here.” She quickly took the boot off her foot and grabbed her other shoe. Standing up, she suddenly walked away.

*Ouch. Didn’t see that coming.*

Marta stood up with one foot still in a boot, judged that it fit pretty well, replaced her shoe and followed Tara to the checkout counter.

Tara was standing behind two teenage boys who were buying pocket knives when Marta approached.

“Tara, I apologize.”

Tara turned around, anger in her eyes. "Some topics *are* off limits. Okay?" Then she turned away from Marta.

"I'm sorry," she whispered. *Something else to pray about. No wonder she secretes venom periodically. If I'd gone through that...* Her thought trailed off. She didn't want to think about it. Absentmindedly, Marta raised a finger to her mouth and she began biting a nail.

‡‡‡

**8:10 p.m.**

Tara was furious! Again she'd let her defenses down and again she'd gotten hurt. Not by a spirit this time, but by someone *she* was supposed to be putting the hurt on. She paced the guest room in which she was staying. How could she have exposed herself like that? She tried to steady herself.

Of course, the story that she had told Marta about her dad wasn't true. But the discussion about her no longer having a father had touched way too close. She had been raised in a single-parent home after her mom had died when she was a baby.

*Dad had done his best...*

Had he?

Tara broke free from the path her mind had begun to descend. She needed to deal with Marta.

*Okay ... maybe somehow I can turn this into an advantage. Maybe play on her emotions some more.* She started pacing, anger surfacing again. Regardless of the truth about her dad, she had given her—given *them*—real ammunition; an area of her life to target with prayer! *Damn you, old man!*

Tara's emotions began to flair. She walked over to the lone closet in the room and pulled out a small duffel. From it she withdrew her felt pentagram, an amulet, her pentagram necklace and her floor mat. She wouldn't need her grimoire this time. She had this spell memorized. Time to exact some more discomfort on dear, precious Marta.

*I don't think those fingernails of hers are quite short enough yet.*

## Chapter Twenty One

### Friday, June 19 – 3:37 p.m.

"Sorry about last night," said Marta. "I just didn't feel like going back out after my afternoon with Tara."

"Don't worry about it. It's okay," said Brent. "Do you think I should call her?"

"I don't know how to answer that. Part of me says yes, that she probably needs to talk to someone, but another part of me says that I saw something about her—or in her—that needs to be prayed about."

Brent and Marta sat at a table outside of Mocha Manz on the Millsville Square. It was a warm day, one that would ordinarily beckon them out to do something more eventful than just sit at a café sipping coffee. But the mood was hushed, and neither felt like doing anything but talking. So, for now, they would enjoy the soft breeze and people-watch while conversing.

"Well, couldn't I do both? I could pray on my way out to Pittston," Brent said.

"Brent, I don't think you're listening to me."

"Why do you say that? I've heard everything you've said. Tara's upset about her father; either that or she's upset about the conversation the two of you had. Maybe both."

"No, Brent. It's more than that somehow. There's more to it."

"Then, what? Help me figure this out."

"Figure it out? I *can't* figure it out! That's why I called you, remember?" Marta's voice was starting to rise. She was starting to feel her own temper begin to flair.

"Good grief, Marta! Don't you think you're blowing this thing a little out of proportion? She's hurting. She probably needs someone to lean on, that's all."

"And *you're* that someone; Brent Lawton, all-around good guy? The one who's willing to jump into whatever the problem is to save a strawberry blonde?!"

Brent's jaw dropped and his lips parted slightly. He sat there staring at Marta apparently not knowing how to respond.

Marta cringed and closed her eyes. *Oh no. What have I just done?*

She opened her eyes as Brent pressed his lips together. "Brent, I'm sorry. I don't know where that came from..."

"You're jealous?" said Brent, half asking, half accusing, in what he believed to be a moment of clarity.

"I am *not* jealous!" she said with another increase in volume.

"Then what would you call that statement? That sure sounded like jealousy. I think it was jealousy. It was jealousy, wasn't it?"

Marta stood up from her chair, but immediately had to grip the table as a wave of dizziness hit her. She closed her eyes and wavered.

Brent stood up and quickly walked around the table. "Marta, you all right?"

Marta lowered herself back down into her chair and put both hands flat on the table. "Whew. That was a big one."

"A big...what? I've never seen this before."

"Oh, it's just a dizzy spell. I probably just stood up too fast." Changing the subject, Marta said, "Brent, I'm not jealous. We're friends. Neither of us has any illusion about anything more than that. But I do love you, and I do care about you."

"Well, I love you, too."

"Good. Then listen to me." She paused for effect. "Just listen." Marta opened her eyes and looked straight into Brent's. "I haven't said anything before, but I think I need to."

Brent looked hard into her eyes and furrowed his brow in concentration. She knew he was listening now. "There's something wrong with Tara. I'm not talking about her broken relationship with her father or her lack of relationship with *the* Father. There's something else. It's been playing on my spirit from almost the moment we met her. There's something dark going on in her."

Brent interrupted, "Marta, come on..."

Marta cut him off. "Brent, don't!" She made a slight turn of her head in warning, her eyes narrowing, never leaving Brent's. "There's something that she's hiding. You don't have to believe me, but I hope you will. I believe the Holy Spirit has been keeping me alert to her."

Brent's patience was coming to an end. "Alert about *what?*"

"At first I thought it was just me, not giving her a fair chance. I felt like I was just being an unaccepting little girl who didn't want you to have another playmate. But it's been over a month, now, and every single time that I'm around her, I get this ... I don't know..."

"Say it. You're getting a check, aren't you? A check in your spirit."

"Yes. A check in my spirit."

"And why has it taken you over a month to say something?"

"Would you have believed me, Brent? I mean, you've been ga-ga over this girl since day one."

"I have not." Brent closed his eyes and hung his head, immediately remembering his conversation with George yesterday. "Yes...I have." He sighed. "You're right."

Brent looked up at Marta again and asked, "But do you really think that I've been blinded by her?"

"First, Brent, answer something for me. How many times can you remember in the four years we've been friends that I've said something to either deliberately hurt you or keep you from being blessed?"

"You've never done either," he said. It apparently gave him pause. He looked to be choosing his next words very deliberately. "Marta, I trust you. You've never given me any reason not to." He paused for a moment, then continued. "If you say there's something wrong that I haven't been able—or willing—to see, then I will take it seriously."

Marta took a deep breath and let it out in relief. "Thank you for trusting me, Brent. I just believe that whatever is going on with Tara is going to take more than just a casual prayer as you drive over to see her."

"Okay. Fair enough. Then we'd better get to it." Brent looked to reflect for a second then said, "How about we go to Belle Meadow Park, find a nice grassy area and do some praying there?"

"That sounds like a wonderful idea. It'll be the best thing we've done all day."

‡‡‡

**4:10 p.m.**

Sitting on a throw that Marta kept in her car, Brent and she stretched out on their sides facing one another, propped up on their elbows. There were only a few other people in the park, probably because for most it was a work day.

The park was surrounded on three sides by woods, sort of like being in a huge horse shoe with the parking area at the open end. The field was well-manicured and several pavilions dotted the edge of the woods where, tomorrow, people would be having family gatherings and cookouts. Marta and Brent elected for an area near the center of the horse shoe where they could enjoy the greatest amount of space available to them as they prayed.

Brent opened them up. He knew that once he began to pray

that all of the pettiness of previous arguments would fall dead to the side. When he prayed he wanted it to matter. He wanted it to be effective. He wasn't going to allow mental garbage to keep his prayers from being just so much chatter. Truth be told, he was happy to have a prayer partner regarding Tara. While he had most definitely been praying for her, he'd also been tripped up in the midst of his prayers with fantasies that he had to force out of his mind. Marta's presence offered reinforcement to his prayers; that whole "where two or more are gathered" thing that had previously been missing.

Come to think of it, Marta and he had prayed very little together regarding Tara. They had mostly just agreed to pray about her salvation whenever they thought about it. Scripture, though, had a couple of other things to say about the issue of effective prayer: If two or more come together, the Lord will be in their presence. And if any two people will focus on one thing in prayer, it will be accomplished by God. There is obviously something about agreement that the Lord really wants His people to grasp. Now, at last, in addition to these two nearly-overlooked aspects, they would add some fervency into the mix. The three—unity in cause, agreement on the target, and inexorable resolve—would come together to create a powerful weapon in a battle that they still did not see coming.

‡‡‡

**4:42 p.m.**

Tara wasn't feeling well all of a sudden. It wasn't a physical thing. It was more a feeling of loss; something that she couldn't quite put her finger on. She felt isolated. Melancholy set in as she was struck with the realization of overwhelming loneliness.

Stephanie was at work, so she didn't have anyone to talk with—not that she really wanted the woman's company. They had had another "discussion" that turned out to be another ultimatum: "Drop your plans for the Christians." Of course, she wasn't about to do that.

Having nowhere to go, Tara had spent the past hour sitting in a comfortably-padded rattan rocking chair on the front porch. As she sat watching the occasional car pass by, an uninvited memory from her past enveloped her thoughts.

She was twelve again. It was one of her favorite memories…

"Daddy?"

"Yes, sweetheart?"

"When I get married, will you give me away?"

Her dad smiled. "Absolutely, but very reluctantly. I'm in no hurry to lose my little girl to another man. He'd better be a real good guy."

"Yeah. I think he's going to be like Richard Collier."

"Who?"

"Oh, Daddy," she said shaking her head. "Richard Collier. The man in 'Somewhere in Time.'"

"Oohh… of course. How silly of me. So he's the man for you, huh?"

"If a man was willing to travel through time to find *me* I'd marry him."

Her dad laughed. "Yeah, I'd have to say that I'd be pretty impressed with him, too."

"But you'll be there?"

"Be where, sweetheart?"

"At the church, Daddy!" she said in mock annoyance.

He laughed again and drew her into a tight hug. "I wouldn't be anywhere else."

Tara snapped out of her flashback and felt tears running down her face. Her body convulsed with an involuntary sob. Then the floodgates opened and she wept; her soul pouring out in irrepressible torrents. "Oh, Daddy… Daddy… Why?"

‡‡‡

**Saturday, June 20 – 1:31 p.m.**

"I think I found the perfect place," said Brent into the phone with no small amount of enthusiasm.

"Okay, well, don't keep me in suspense," responded Tara. "Where will we be spending four or five days of our lives?"

"Shawnee State Forest. Ever heard of the place?"

"Yes! It's supposed to be beautiful! It's right on the Ohio River, right?"

"Yep, that's the place. There's a state park there with a couple of lakes where we can park our vehicles for a small fee. And, get this; there are 60 miles of backpacking trails in the forest. Not that we're going to hike all 60."

"Sounds to me like you found a great area. Have you told anyone else yet?"

"No, not yet. I'll give Marta a call when we hang up."

There was a long pause, then, "Brent, can I tell you something? Something that needs to stay between us?"

"Yeah, I guess so. What is it?"

Brent heard Tara sigh. "I'm not sure I should even say anything, and you probably won't think it's a big deal, but since we're about to spend so much time together..."

Brent swallowed hard. *Here it comes,* he thought. *This is where my test begins. God, give me strength.* Tara's pause was pregnant with revelation. Brent wondered how he was going to be able to keep this girl at arm's length, especially if she was about to admit feelings for him. Brent cleared his throat. "Yeah?"

"Well, it's about Marta," she said quietly.

"Marta?" Brent didn't see that coming. "What about her?"

"She doesn't like me."

Brent laughed with relief. "Oh, Tara."

"Please, don't laugh at me," said Tara with a tone that caused Brent to stow his grin.

Brent immediately went into damage-control mode. "Okay, Tara. I'm sorry. Tell me what's going on. Or, at least, what you think is going on."

"It's not what I think, Brent. It's what I know. And what I know is that Marta has it in for me. She is all smiles and sunshine when the three of us are together, but when it's just the two of us... Thursday she took some pretty vicious stabs at me when we went out shopping."

"You mean when she brought up your relationship with your dad?"

"Huh? What are you talking about?"

"Marta told me that she might have stepped across an emotional line with you when it came to a conversation about your dad. I'm sure it wasn't anything intentional."

"I have no idea what you're talking about. My dad? Brent, we never talked about my dad."

Brent stood in his bedroom looking out his window unable to process the sentence he'd just heard. "Wait a minute. Thursday. As in two days ago. You and Marta went shopping for camping stuff, right?"

"Uhh ... Yeah."

"Marta told me that you got upset with her because she asked about the loss of your relationship with your dad. Are you telling me that never happened?"

"Yes, that's exactly what I'm telling you."

"Okay, I'm stuck. What's going on?" Brent began to tense up.

"The only thing that you just said that actually took place was that I got upset with Marta. But it had nothing at all to do with my dad. What did she say about my relationship with my dad?"

"Umm ... Tara, maybe you, Marta, and I ought to get together to talk."

"No, Brent!" exclaimed Tara. "You promised!"

"That was before I knew that..."

"... that she was lying?"

"Marta has never lied to me, Tara. Now something's going on, and I just want to find out what it is."

"Now, I'd like to find out what's going on, too. The conversation that took place on Thursday was about *you*, not my dad."

"Me?"

"Yes. She didn't exactly come out and say it, but I know a strongly annunciated hint when I hear one."

Brent's heart sank. What was going on and how did he end up being in the middle of it? "Okay, tell me. What did Marta say that's got you so up in arms?"

"Marta warned me that since I'm not a Christian that...in a roundabout way...she has more right to you than I do."

Brent was dumbfounded. "What?"

Tara presented another sigh. "Brent, the girl has pretty deep emotions for you, and I was basically told that I'm to keep my distance."

Brent squeezed the phone's receiver in his right hand and brought his left hand up to his face, spanning his forehead between his thumb and middle finger. Now it was Brent's time to sigh. "Okay ... Tara? First, I know for a fact that Marta doesn't have a single romantic notion toward me."

"Are you sure?" Tara asked before he could get to a second assumption. "You mean to tell me that in all the time that you two have known each other she's never indicated that she wanted to be with you?"

Impulsively, Brent responded. "We've only kissed one time, and that was three years ago. And that was something that got us both laughing with the absurdity of the idea."

"Who initiated the kiss?"

"I did," said Brent, reliving the moment in his mind.

"And she was hesitant and tried to push away?"

Brent matched Tara with another sigh. "No. That's not exactly what happened."

"So, she *accepted* your approach and your kiss?"

Brent's heart was beginning to beat harder. "Yes."

"You men can be so thick-headed sometimes!"

"No, you see," he said weakly in defense of his argument, "we both burst out laughing—*at the same time*—because it was, you know, absurd." Was he defending his memory? Did his memory *need* defending? He was remembering things the right way, wasn't he? They *both* started laughing at exactly the same time, right? Or had she started laughing only because she sensed him starting?

"Brent! Oh, my god! You can't be that stupid." She paused. "I'm sorry. I didn't mean that you're stupid. Blind? Maybe. Stupid? No. But, come on; a girl accepts your lead into a romantic kiss and you think it just gets pushed out of her heart because *you* thought it was a mistake?"

Brent was speechless. He stood staring at the screen in his window. There was a green fly inside crawling on it. He stared at it as it began cleaning its legs.

"Brent, her story about my dad had to have been some sort of cover, just in case I brought anything up. She ends up being Miss Goodie Two-Shoes while I get taken down a notch and pitied. Please, Brent, don't say anything. I can handle the challenge that she laid down in front of me to stay away from you, but the last thing I want to do is come between the two of you as friends. I'm the outsider here. I hold the sacrificial position in your lives. If it needs to happen, I can be set aside in favor of you keeping your long-term friendship with Marta. I don't *want* that to happen, but I can handle it if that's what's *got* to happen. The only reason I brought any of this stuff up was to make you aware, so that you can watch out for it, not to cause a rift between any of the three of us.

"Brent, I like Marta. I'm sure that I will win her friendship if she knows that I'm not a threat. I mean, after all, you and I are only friends, right?"

"I...umm," began Brent, peering at the buzzing insect that suddenly began banging against the screen in a vain attempt to get out. *I'm beginning to feel the same way.* "I...uhh... I won't say anything to Marta. But we need to get this sorted out somehow. I don't want to lose either one of you."

"Don't worry, I'm not going anywhere if you don't want me to. I just needed to hear it. Brent, I'm sure everything is going to work out just fine."

Unfortunately for Brent, he couldn't see the smirk playing on the face of the woman on the other end of the phone.

## Chapter Twenty Two

**Sunday, June 21 – 9:35 a.m.**

The drive to church was quiet, and Brent was full of anticipation. It should have been a feeling of excitement. After all, his parents were following behind him in their car, attending church with him for the second straight week.

Instead, all he was feeling was dread. Marta was probably even now waiting for him in the church's foyer, and he wasn't sure how to act. Was he really meeting up with a girl that was in love with him? Could he have been so blind?

He knew that the ten-minute drive to the church was the perfect opportunity to do some praying for his parents' salvations, but his apprehension only allowed him to toss up a bare-minimum prayer asking that God would move in their lives somehow. He couldn't focus on anything but Marta.

It was a beautiful start to the first full day of Summer, but he barely noticed. As he and his parents pulled into the parking lot of Restoration Community Church, he saw people streaming from the parking lot toward the main entrance. They were about fifteen minutes early, but the parking lot was already three-quarters full. Finding two side-by-side spaces, they parked and exited their cars.

"Brent, it appears that last week wasn't a fluke," said his dad. "Is this place always this well attended?"

"Usually. Now that Summer's here, though, I'm guessing that we'll begin to see more empty seats. Some of it due to vacations, but I'm guessing mostly because people find a day like today to be an excuse to do something else."

"As long as I'm home for this afternoon's kickoff, we're good," his dad said with a grin.

"Keith, don't even start," his mom admonished. "We're here for Brent whether it matches up with your game time or not."

"Good grief, Sharon. Couldn't you see that I was joking?"

Brent could see that the grin was gone from his dad's face, replaced with a look of irritation. These two were masters of getting on each other's nerves.

Brent sighed. He seemed to be doing a lot of that lately.

‡‡‡

## 9:46 a.m.

Marta stood in the church's foyer waiting for Brent. She caught sight of him pulling into the parking lot, then watched as he got out of his car. *Hey! His parents are with him! That's great!* She was excited that her prayers for Brent's family were apparently paying off. "Lord, reach them this morning," she whispered in prayer. "Direct the Pastor's message to speak to their hearts and minds."

Brent and his parents reached the doors and walked in. Marta smiled and walked toward them. *Wow, Brent looks tense.*

"Good morning, Mr. & Mrs. Lawton! It's great to see you!" she said walking up to Brent's mom and giving her a hug.

"Good morning, sweetheart," said Sharon.

"Hello, Marta. It's good to see you, too," said Keith, with what appeared to be a forced smile.

*Hmm... Doesn't look like they've had a good start to their day.*

Marta walked up to Brent and gave him a quick hug and noticed that it was a little less comfortable than usual.

"I had saved a couple of seats for Brent and me," Marta began as they started walking toward the sanctuary, "but I think there are still a couple seats in the row I chose. Hopefully."

Sharon responded. "That's okay, dear. We don't all have to be in the same row."

"So, Brent, how's it going?" asked Marta.

"Oh, I'm okay," he said not looking at her. "Just looking forward to the start of the service."

"Me too. It should be interesting. It's not going to be Pastor Chuck preaching today. It's going to be his son, Jonathan."

This caught Brent's attention. "He's here? That's cool. I really like hearing him."

Pastor Chuck Sagan had been the senior pastor of Restoration Community Church for going on ten years. His son, who was in his late twenties, was an associate pastor of another similar-size church somewhere in the eastern part of Indiana. It was rumored that he wanted to earn his pastoral accreditation apart from his dad's influences. Pastor Jonathan Sagan was greatly respected by his dad, and they had what appeared to be a great relationship. The younger pastor just didn't want any favoritism for being the son of one of the area's most well-known leaders, so he decided to move out of state with his wife, Jenni.

As they cleared the doors into the sanctuary, they were met

by a man with a true look of surprise on his face. George Chamberlin stopped and put a big and genuine smile on his face. Extending his hand toward Brent's father, he said, "Keith and Sharon! It's great to see the two of you."

Marta watched as Keith lit up, as well, and took George's hand. It was obvious that, regardless of their initial disdain for the man who had "made Brent one of those born-againers," his parents had grown to really like their son's former coach. "George, fancy meeting you here," he said with a laugh. "I wondered if I'd see you today. We missed you last week."

George looked at Brent with a look bordering on amazement, then looked back at Keith and Sharon. "The two of you were here last week, too?"

This time Sharon responded. "Yes. And where were you? Playing hooky?"

George laughed as he moved to the side of the aisle so as to open it up to foot traffic again. The others followed suit. "Yeah, kind of. Last week was the graduation party for one of my nieces. Cheryl and I drove out to Fort Wayne for a few days with my sister's family."

"Is Cheryl here?" asked Sharon.

George turned around and pointed to the center section. "Yes, she's down there toward the front. There are a couple of extra seats if you'd like to join us. Not enough for all four of you though, I'm afraid." George looked at Brent and Marta. "Good morning, Marta. I must say, you look lovely in that dress."

Marta momentarily looked down at the floor. It felt good to have a man compliment her. "Thank you, Mr. Chamberlin."

"Marta, I've told you...you can call me George."

"Sorry. It's a cultural thing, I guess. Thank you, George." She smiled. "Still feels strange saying it."

George smiled and turned to Brent. "How are you feeling? Recovered from the ride yet?"

Brent laughed. "Me? I was expecting to see you using a cane this morning."

George looked at Keith and said, "Your son thinks he's better than us."

Keith looked at Brent, "He is. That is, unless you taking him golfing again."

All five of them laughed.

George told them that he'd return after going out to his car for a moment. Brent suggested that his mom and dad find seats next to Cheryl Chamberlin since Marta wasn't sure of available seating near them.

In their own seats now, seated about two thirds of the way back and to the left of the center section, Marta tried to engage Brent in conversation.

"It's great seeing your parents here. Did you have to drag them?"

Brent didn't turn to face her with his answer. "Nahh. Just asked them if they would like to come. I think they came because they knew that I knew they didn't have any other plans."

"Well, it's good they came, regardless."

Silence again.

She tried again. "George seems to really like your dad."

"Yeah."

Silence.

"Brent, look at me."

Brent appeared to still himself before turning to look her in the eyes.

"What's going on?" she asked.

"Nothing's going on."

"Then why won't you look at me?"

"I am looking at you."

"Brent," she said more firmly, "you are avoiding my question and you are avoiding looking at me. There *is* something going on."

"Marta, I..."

Brent was cut off by the rapping of a snare drum and the start of the first praise song. He stood up with the rest of the congregation.

Marta stood up as well and leaned into Brent with her shoulder. "This conversation isn't over, bud."

With that she turned her attention, as best she could, to worship. She wasn't going to let Brent's weird attitude this morning interrupt her celebration of the King of kings.

‡‡‡

**10:41 a.m.**

Pastor Chuck introduced his son to the congregation following the giving of tithes and offerings. There was no doubt of the pride he had for the younger pastor. Taking the podium, Pastor Jonathan looked into the congregation of nearly fifteen-hundred people and cleared his throat.

"Good morning," he started off, and the congregation gave him a hearty "Good morning" in response.

"I'm always a little nervous coming to this church. Most preachers who go into another church to speak don't really care how many people they blow out of the congregation with a word from God." He looked back at his dad who was seated with his mom and the other associate pastors and their wives. The congregation laughed and his father smiled and shook his head, enjoying the levity. "It'd be a real shame if I never got invited back." Another laugh.

"This morning, I hope to challenge everyone in this building. No, that's not quite true. Let me try that again. This morning, I am *going* to challenge everyone in this building. If any of you have it in your minds that my Christianity isn't as genuine as my dad's... If any of you think that I'm a preacher because it's the family thing to do... I'm about to lay that dead horse to rest.

"I love Jesus Christ. I don't, and never will, apologize for that."

A host of "Amens!" went up from the congregation.

"Today I intend to slap the sickness called *excusitus* out of hopefully everyone in here." He stopped and looked across the crowd with an intense look. He held it for a few seconds to apparently stress the point. Then he put on a big, cheesy grin. "Father, forgive me for what I'm about to do." He paused for a moment. "I'll leave it up to all of you fine people to determine which father I just said that to." Again, the place erupted in laughter.

"As I just said, I love Jesus. But I also love the Church. I'm not talking about this building or the building in which I pastor back in Indiana; I'm talking about the Body of Christ. I love being a part of the Bride of Christ. Scripture tells us that Jesus Christ is coming back for His bride; a bride without spot or wrinkle.

"Scripture tells us, also, that as Christians we are the 'righteousness of God in Christ.' That's a very important statement, and the most important word in that phrase is the word 'in'. It literally means 'a part of.' If you are a 'born-again' believer you are 'in'. By being 'in' you are righteous. Are you grasping this so far?"

Pastor Jonathan paused for affect. "Hello?"

"Yes!" came a loud response from the congregation.

"Remember, preachers, especially visiting ones, appreciate the feedback," he said with a chuckle.

"Knowing what 'in Christ' means is very important to this message. It's important to know how God sees you because of your position in Him. Folks, do you understand that you are new creations? New creatures? Now, stay with me here.

"It doesn't matter how old you are in the Lord. If you've been walking with Christ for 50+ years—and there are some of you out there who have—you are *still* a *new* creature. Your newness has not worn off. It makes no difference how many sins you've collected in your walk; you are still a *new* creation because of your station *in Christ*.

"How are we doing? You're still not talking to me." He smiled.

Several yeses and amens came as a result of the prompting.

"Now, here's the point I'm trying to make. You are—each and every believer in this room is—part of the Bride of Christ. And if Christ is coming back for a bride without spot or wrinkle, then *not one* of you is going to make it."

The congregation sat in silence while Pastor Jonathan just stood in the pulpit and looked into the crowd. As he just stood there without another word, more than a few in the congregation began to look to one another for some clue as to the meaning of what he had just said. Then the murmuring began. No one could see the smirk playing at the corners of Pastor Jonathan's lips as he waited a few moments longer.

The pastor walked to the edge of the platform and took a couple steps down toward the front row of seats. He nodded a signal to the sound booth at the back of the sanctuary and suddenly a loud crack of thunder played through the speakers.

Several gasps could be heard throughout the sanctuary as everybody's focus suddenly returned to the young pastor. Using his hands to signal a hush over the crowd, he began to speak again.

"That scared you, didn't it? And I'm not talking about that theatrical thunder clap, which I just *had* to add to dramatize the situation. I'm a little weird like that."

Nervous chuckles could be heard throughout the room.

"I wanted you to be scared for a moment. I wanted you to feel uncertainty for just a split second. In that small period of time—and please don't raise your hands—how many of you had your Christian walks flash before your eyes? How many of you were looking back on sinful actions in your life to see which ones might have kept you from making it to Heaven when the Rapture takes place?

"Fear not, beloved of God, you *are* without spot or wrinkle. Despite our fallen natures, those of us with a relationship with Christ *are* spotless in the sight of God. I just wanted to make a point; that everyone in here has sins that *should* keep him out of

Heaven. Now, to my message on the Ten Virgins, the Rapture of the church, and the Wedding Feast of the Lamb.

"Though you may be sure that you are going to make it to Heaven because you've made Jesus your Savior, can the same be said about you being one of those taken up in the Rapture of the Church for the Wedding Feast of the Lamb which is talked about in Revelation, chapter nineteen? The answer may surprise you." [4]

‡‡‡

**10:59 a.m.**

Brent was transfixed by what Pastor Jonathan was saying. He had never thought of the parable of the ten virgins quite this way before. He knew, now, that he needed to conduct his own "check up from the neck up" and evaluate his intimacy with the Lord. He'd just learned—or, at least had reinforced— that good things, without the right intentions, were pretty much worthless in God's eyes. He also knew that he still had struggles; things that he found difficult to lay at the feet of Christ; one of those things being how easily he let his eyes linger on the bodies of attractive women. *I definitely need Your help here, Lord.* He sighed, and, out of the corner of his eye, saw Marta glance his way for a moment.

Following his sermon, Pastor Jonathan transitioned into an altar call. Brent had sat through what must have been hundreds of them in the past. For as far back as he could remember he had always taken them very seriously. Scripture said that those who were forgiven much were grateful much, and the incredible grace that had been shown to him translated into an intensity for the salvation of others. At times he'd found himself with tears streaming down his face as he petitioned God for someone—anyone—in the church to make the most important decision that he or she could make on this earth.

"I'd like to ask everyone in the sanctuary to stand" the pastor said. With the rustle of movement, he continued. "Folks, you may have been in and out of churches your whole life. Doesn't matter. You may have always believed that since you were raised in a non-Jewish home or a non-Muslim home or a non-Buddhist home, that you are a Christian. But that's not how it works.

"Let's take a look at how bizarre that kind of logic is: Would

[4] Go to Appendix B to read Pastor Jonathan's message on "The Ten Virgins & The Wedding Feast of the Lamb."

going to a McDonald's every day to try to turn yourself into a hamburger? Of course not. You'd have to go through an awfully big meat grinder first ... and I'm pretty sure that you've all got limits as to what you'll do for a good burger." The crowd let out a roll of laughter, and Pastor Jonathan laughed as well, and then muttered, "I have no idea where that came from. That thought has never occurred to me before." He took a quick glimpse back at his parents and said, "My dad is never going to let me preach here again."

Following another howl of laughter from the crowd he continued, "Okay, my sick sense of humor aside, you do get the point, I'm sure. Association does not get you into Heaven. In the same vein, *not* driving a Yugo does not mean that your Chevette is really a Corvette. Not being one thing does not make you another. You may not be an atheist, but believing in God does not necessarily make you a believer. You may not be a Muslim, but that does not translate into being a Christian.

"*Being* a Christian comes only one way; through blood, sweat, and tears. Self-sacrifice, giving up your life for the sake of others, and leaving all of your wealth behind to become humble. It also takes carrying a heavy burden and one *very* brutal commitment. Now, how many of you are up for that?" A lone hand went up in the auditorium. "Sir, you are both a braver and stronger man than I. There is no way that I could live up to that.

"Let's say for just a moment that you *were* willing to do all of that, which is the equivalent to keeping the Mosaic Law. There's still one thing that you would have had to do your *entire life* before dying–live a life in which you had never done one thing wrong; never having committed a single sin. I don't think it's a stretch to say that that would eliminate most of us," he said with smile.

"One Man took care of that whole list of prerequisites for us, and He did it for each of you. He gave His all so that *you* could have His all. This Man is Jesus Christ. He lived a sinless life for thirty-plus years so that He could, one day, purposely die a horrific death on our behalves."

Brent began to pray. He hardly heard another word that Pastor Jonathan spoke, but that did not matter. He began to engage in warfare against the enemy of the men, women, boys, and girls throughout the sanctuary. "In the name of Jesus Christ," he began under his breath, "I bind every spirit that is attempting to deceive the lost in this room."

Brent could hear Marta whispering her agreement in prayer. She, too, understood her authority and wasn't hesitant to use it.

"Every lying and hindering spirit I command you to be still and shut up, in the name of Jesus Christ. Father, I ask that You would send Your angels to enter this place and engage the Enemy in warfare for the protection of those who need to hear and understand your message right now. I speak and plead the name and blood of Jesus over the people in this room. Release them, Father, to be able to make a decision for you."

"...take the next step," Brent heard Pastor Jonathan continuing. "Jesus did His part for you. Now you must do your part for Him. Jesus said that if you are embarrassed of Him on Earth, that He will be embarrassed of you before the Father in Heaven. My friends, you do not want that. There is quite literally hell to pay."

Brent thought about his parents just then. *I wonder what they're thinking?* The last time they were here, the message seemed to go over their heads and roll off of their backs. Then after service he heard the obligatory-sounding, "It was a good service. It was an interesting message." *God, I know that something has to be happening in them. You said Your Word does not return without effect. I'm just wanting this so bad.*

"There are many of you in this sanctuary who do not have a genuine relationship with Christ, and you need to know this: Every time that you think that you're not making a decision against Him, that is precisely what you're doing. A *yes* to Jesus is a *yes*. A *no*, a *not right now*, an *I'll get around to it* all equate to *no*. Listen, folks, you *are* making a decision this morning, one way or another. If you die having made a decision that is anything but a *yes*, you will not make it to Heaven. I can't be any more blunt than that. That's just the way it is."

Pastor Jonathan again walked to the very edge of the platform directly in front of the lectern. "Those of you who know Jesus as your Savior and Lord; who have absolutely no doubt in your minds about your standing with God, I want you, and only you, to please take your seats."

Brent had never seen this before, and apparently neither had Marta, as she responded with, "Wow, this is different." Brent nodded as he watched the overwhelming majority in attendance sit down.

"Brent!" said Marta in an excited whisper. "Your parents!"

Brent was looking right at them as his mom started to take a seat. But his dad leaned down and apparently said something to her. She took his outstretched hand and she stood back up. Brent's heart started beating hard with excitement. *God! Really? Really?!*

It appeared that along with his parents around forty to fifty others continued to stand. He couldn't remember the last time he'd seen so many respond to an altar call. But his focus returned immediately to his family and to Pastor Jonathan standing almost directly in front of them.

"God bless all of you who remained standing. It took some guts to remain standing, and for a few of you, even more guts to stand back up. Let me ask all of you a question. Do you want to accept Jesus Christ as your Savior and Lord this morning?"

There were a few vocal affirmations, but most just stood nodding.

"Here's the deal. You're not making a commitment to this church. You're not making a commitment to a denomination. You are making a decision for God the Father, God the Son, and God the Holy Spirit. And you will not regret it, so long as you develop a relationship with them after you've made this commitment. Now, I'm going to lead all of you in a prayer..."

Marta leaned into Brent and squeezed his arm. He turned to her to see tears forming in her eyes. She whispered, "They're doing it, Brent! They're doing it!"

Brent hadn't felt anything but astonished up to that point, but upon hearing Marta's words and seeing her tears, the floodgates opened, he leaned forward, placed his face in his hands, and he began to weep with deep gratitude to his God.

‡‡‡

**11:32 a.m.**

Brent and Marta stood in the foyer of the church as they waited for all of the new believers to come out of a conference room just off of the sanctuary. The regular counseling room at the front of the sanctuary was too small to accommodate all who had made decisions for Christ. *Praise God!* Brent reveled.

"Brent I'm so excited," said Marta almost jumping up and down.

Brent was both excited and apprehensive. He wanted to believe that his mom's and dad's commitments were real. He didn't have any reason to believe that they weren't, but he'd lived with the disappointments of this family his whole life.

He didn't have long to dwell on the thought, as the door to the conference room swung open and people began to stream out. There was a spontaneous outbreak of applause, along with a few shouts, from the people lingering in the foyer. Brent and

Marta joined in enthusiastically.

After some twenty to thirty people had exited the room, his parents came into view; both of them carrying new Bibles. Brent could see that his mom had been crying; the giveaway being her smeared mascara. He started walking toward them when something unexpected dawned on him. His mother was holding onto his dad's arm, her head on his shoulder.

Brent caught his breath and halted; stopped by the wonder of it. His parents found him in the crowd and his mom lifted her head. Grins lit up both of their faces as they started walking toward him and Marta.

George and Cheryl appeared out of the periphery of his vision and joined Brent and Marta as his parents approached.

His dad was the first to speak. "We get it. We finally get it."

Brent's heart leapt! It was real! It was *real!*

## Chapter Twenty Three

**Wednesday, June 24– 1:21 p.m.**

"So, I'll see you 7:00 p.m., then," said Brent.

"Yes. See you then," said Tara. "Oh, and Stephanie is out with some friends for the week—*thank God*—so just come on in when you get here. The doorbell is broken and if I'm in my room I might not hear you knock."

"Sounds good. See you in a little while."

Tara hung up the phone. It was getting to be crunch time. She had to make one more interesting preparation in order to make the camping trip everything she was hoping it could be.

Brent was coming over to pick her up, along with all of her camping and hiking equipment, so that they could get a head start in identifying the necessary equipment before they all left for Southern Ohio on Saturday morning. She planned a little surprise for him this evening, though; one that he was certain to enjoy; one that she was certain to enjoy showing off.

‡‡‡

**6:57 p.m.**

Tara sat before her window watching through the sheer curtains for Brent to arrive. Her hair was freshly washed and dripping wet. At the moment, she wore only a robe. Never had she done anything this brash before. She felt a twinge of nervous excitement. *This is going to be simply delicious.*

After a couple of minutes she saw Brent's Grand Am turn the corner onto her street. She got up and walked straight to her Walkman cassette player and put the headphones over her ears. Her robe dropped to the floor and she walked into the bathroom to wait.

‡‡‡

**7:03 p.m.**

Brent pulled his Grand Am to the curb in front of the house in which Tara was staying for the summer. He got out of the car and walked across the lawn to the front door. He knew that Tara had said to just walk on in, but he just didn't feel comfortable doing that unannounced. He knocked on the door and waited. He knocked a second time without a response.

Turning the handle to the door he pushed the door open and stuck his head into the house. "Tara! It's Brent. You here?" He didn't hear anything so he walked in.

Knowing that this wasn't Tara's home, he felt awkward entering as he did. However, having been in the house one time before, Brent did know where Tara's room was.

He walked into the hallway and called out her name once again. A door to his right opened and Tara walked into the hallway wearing only a set of headphones attached to a Walkman in her left hand. Brent stopped, stunned.

Tara was bobbing her head to music and looking at the player. She lifted her head and looked down the hallway toward Brent. She screamed and dropped the Walkman on the floor bringing her hands up to her chest and crossing her legs, attempting to hide that which Brent had already gotten an eyeful.

"Brent! What are you doing?! What are you doing here?!"

Brent was completely flustered and didn't know what to do. His initial instinct was to turn away, but he couldn't make himself do it. Adrenaline and testosterone surged into his bloodstream. He was unaware it was happening, but endorphins had been released that immediately led to an imprint of this moment having been seared into his memory. "Uhh ... You said seven," he said quickly in his defense.

"What? It's *not* seven!"

Brent tried to keep his eyes zeroed in on hers. He realized that she had just said it wasn't seven o'clock. "Umm ... yes. It's seven." *Why isn't she going into her room?*

Tara seemed to relax. "It is? I'm sorry. I thought I had plenty of time still." She dropped her hands and stood straight before him. "I suppose hiding myself now is ridiculous since you already got a good look." With what appeared to be an embarrassed smile, she said, finally, "But I should probably go put some clothes on."

"Yeah, okay. I'll just ... umm ... wait in the living room."

"Okay," Tara said with a smile, then she turned and walked away from Brent into her bedroom. Brent didn't turn away until she had disappeared. What he didn't see after she rounded the corner was the smirk that played across her lips.

‡‡‡

**7:28 p.m.**

Brent didn't know what to say about the incident. Tara was sitting to his right as they drove to his house. Packing the car had created a bit of nervous tension, but nothing like having her sitting right next to him.

While driving out to pick up her camping equipment he had wanted to relate to her what had happened with his parents the previous Sunday, but now he wasn't so sure that he wanted to talk about anything spiritual. He knew he was losing a small battle by not saying anything, because his real hope was that conversation would turn back to what he had seen just under a half an hour ago. He didn't have to wait long.

Without any small talk, Tara just asked him, point blank. "Did it bother you to see me naked?"

"Depends on what you mean by bother." Brent cringed the moment his little joke escaped his lips.

Tara giggled. "Well, I'm all dressed now. Don't stress yourself about it. Besides, truth be told, it's not like you wouldn't have eventually seen me naked sometime soon anyway."

Brent's testosterone levels were beyond tolerable now. He wanted to give in and just go with the flow. He wanted to reach over and take her hand and lift it to his mouth and kiss it. He wanted her to respond to his touch...

"Brent?"

Brent cleared his throat. "Yes?"

"You just missed your turn," she said with another one of her tantalizing giggles.

‡‡‡

**Thursday, June 25 – 1:15 p.m.**

It was another boring afternoon. Though the sun shined outside, Tara sat in Stephanie's living room and sulked.

She had come to the conclusion that her life was only interesting in spurts. And those spurts seemed to be short-lived. *Well, Saturday's just two days away. That will be the start of several days of interesting.* There was an anxiousness building inside of her to get close to Brent, and even Marta. Of course, she refused to allow mental or emotional connections of friendship to take place. They weren't going to reach that status in her life. The two of them were simply playthings; entertainment for the

Summer.

Be that as it may, being around either of them at least passed the time. The monotony of the afternoon was getting to her, so she decided to take a walk. Getting up off the couch, she went to her room to get her sandals.

Stephanie's phone rang. As it wasn't her phone to answer, she allowed the call to be answered by the machine. After the fourth ring she heard Stephanie's outgoing message, annoyingly cheerful: *"You've reached Stephanie. It's not that I don't want to talk with you—possibly; It's more likely that I'm just not here—possibly. Leave your message at the beep!"*

As Tara worked the buckle on her sandal Stephanie's voice came through. "Tara, if you're there, please pick up."

With a slight grimace, she walked back into the living room and picked up the phone. "Hello, Stephanie."

"Tara, there's no reason for this to be long and drawn out, so I'll get to the point. We have come to the conclusion that you are a liability to our cause. I want you to pack up your stuff and be gone from my house by the time I get back on Sunday."

"What?!" Tara could hardly restrain herself. "What do you mean? Who's 'we'?"

"The answer to that is not your concern. Suffice it to say that those that I associate with do not want you bringing undo attention to us. What you were being groomed for will not happen now."

"Groomed? You mean I was being *fashioned* for something?" asked Tara with both frustration and a sense of impending loss.

"Everything is a test, Tara. And you failed yours."

Tara went from hate and anger to repentance in the blink of an eye. "Stephanie. I'm *sorry!* I'll back out of my plans right now. If I had known..."

"... If you had known, Tara, it would not have been a test. I will expect you to be gone by Sunday."

"Wait!" said Tara in desperation. "Please wait. I can do it. I can do whatever it is you and the others want!" She began to grasp for straws. "I was the most advanced and well-practiced in my coven..."

"Coven?" questioned Stephanie, with obvious disdain. "That wasn't a coven, little girl. That, too, was a test. A qualifier. Trust me, you have no idea what a true coven is. Anything and everything you've ever done has been little more than child's play."

Stephanie continued in measured tone, "You are a danger to everything that I—that we—are working to accomplish. I want you out of my house and out of my life."

Tara heard the phone connection click dead. She lowered the phone slowly to the cradle and stared at it in disbelief. Tears welled up in her eyes as she dropped to her knees next to the small table that held the phone.

"No, no, no, no, no. This can't be happening. This can't be happening."

She was overwhelmed with emotion. The initial shock of disappointment and regret would eventually transition into anger and hatred, along with no small amount of self-loathing.

After several minutes she got up off the floor and walked back into her bedroom and began pacing and began biting the nail of her right ring finger.

*What now? What the hell am I supposed to do now?* With those questions, she heard in her mind the unmistakable voice of her spirit guide.

*Tara, you are at the end. You've missed your chance to be useful.*

"That's not true. You could be wrong."

*We are never wrong, Tara, my love. You know that. Now, do what many others have done before you. Reach for the final fulfillment. Be free. Just step across the threshold into the Otherealm. I will be here to meet you.*

"Shalinar, you're wrong. I know it. I can still be useful. I can still be used."

*Come to us, Tara, my dear one. Join us and we'll give you a purpose here, with us. There is power to be had here in the Otherealm. Leave your old broken life and let me introduce you to your true calling. Let me make you happy.*

Broken in spirit, with all pride now gone, she thought about what was being offered. She was tempted. Oh, was she ever tempted. But she still thought she could prove herself somehow. She couldn't just give up yet. Not yet.

"You have been my spirit guide for many years, Shalinar. I've done what you've asked. I've trusted you with my development. Now I'm asking for your help. Help me get back into Stephanie's favor."

*Come to me, my lovely. Come to me.*

But Tara knew that she couldn't leave this earth yet. She knew that she could still prove herself worthy. She *would* prove herself worthy.

## Chapter Twenty Four

### Saturday, June 27 – 6:20 a.m.

Saturday morning was a flurry of activity, as all of the would-be campers converged on Brent's lawn. Camping equipment by the carload was sorted out to determine what was needed, what was too much, and what was *what were you thinking?*

Tara, Marta, Eric, Karen, and Terry all showed up on time. Brent's dad had risen to the task, as well. Keith Lawton had done his share of backpacking as a young man and passed on that love to both Brent and Lydia, though Sharon had never been a big fan herself.

Sharon Lawton was also up and lending her expertise to the mix. She brought out a tray of muffins, granola bars, and fruit to give the campers a good boost into the day. Coffee was also served, much to the joy of a few who were dragging in the pre-dawn hours.

It was proving to be a beautiful day. The hikers would be cooped up in Brent's father's Chevy Suburban and Eric's Jeep Cherokee for close to four hours before getting to Shawnee State Forest in the southernmost part of the state. But it would be a fun drive, Brent was sure of it. Well, he was almost sure of it.

Last Wednesday's *situation* wouldn't leave Brent's mind. He couldn't get the mental pictures to leave. He'd tried, in a last-ditch effort, to erase his brain's video tape. But it seemed that the more he focused on ridding himself of the images the more he enjoyed recounting them. *I'm in big trouble, I think.* Brent sighed as he bent down to grab a bag of different trail foods. Seeing Tara in her tight jean shorts first thing in the morning hadn't made things any the easier.

Marta sidled up to Brent and gave him a nudge. "Ready to finish our conversation?"

"Huh? What conversation?" asked Brent with a quizzical look.

"The why-are-you-avoiding-eye-contact-and-conversation-with-me conversation."

Brent tried one last time to fend this topic off. "Seriously, Marta. You're making a lot out of nothing. Everything's fine."

Marta gave him a dissatisfied look and shook her head as she started to walk away. "Guess we'll find out this weekend."

Brent didn't like himself that much at the moment. Between

the heavy doses of lust during the past couple of days and his keeping Marta at arm's length, he found himself living in a pit of guilt.

Eric Hampton walked up to Brent as he approached the Suburban. "Hey, Brent. Do you want to take the lead on the drive down there?"

"Yeah, I think so. I've studied the map pretty well. It's not a tough drive, but I think I'll be less likely to miss a turn based on having hand-written all of the directions." *As long as Tara's not in my truck*, he thought.

"Sounds good. So, Tara. What's up with her?"

Brent turned to face Eric. "What do you mean?"

"Well, we don't really know her outside of a few comments from you and Marta."

"Oh. Well, she's a good gal. She's got a good personality..."

Eric laughed.

Brent caught the meaning behind the laugh. "Yes, she's hot. But she's got a good personality to go with it," he said with a chuckle. "Most important, though, is that she's not a Christian. We really want to show her God's love over the next several days. Marta and I have been praying for her salvation for weeks."

"So, she's heard the Gospel; right?"

"Yeah, and for the life of me I don't understand why she's still being so resistant. I can't think of why she's still holding out."

"I have a friend named Lee," said Eric in a moment of reflection. "I've had the same frustration with him. He actually told me that he knows that he's going to make the decision to accept Christ, but that something's holding him back at the moment."

"Yeah, the Enemy."

"Exactly. But he doesn't see it that way. He apparently thinks he's just some sort of an epiphany away from saying yes to Jesus."

"Well, if you'd pray for Tara during the course of these next four days, I'd be really appreciative."

Eric slapped Brent on the shoulder. "You got it. Well, guess we'd better get the rest of the lawn sorted."

Brent laughed. "Yeah. Who'da thunk we'd attempt to bring so much stuff on a hiking trip?"

Brent's dad overheard his last comment. "Now you understand why we don't go hiking every weekend," he said with a grin. "It's a lot of work just getting ready to get to the trailheads to get ready."

"I thought I had a clue," said Brent. "Thanks for your help this morning."

"You're welcome," said his dad. "I think I've had an opportunity to meet everybody in this group already. You've got some good friends."

"Don't I know it."

"Okay, how about we get everybody together and I'll teach everyone how to properly pack a backpack."

"You're a lifesaver. Thanks, Dad."

‡‡‡

**7:30 a.m.**

Brent looked around. The backpacks were packed, the vehicles were nearly loaded, and everyone seemed genuinely excited. Even Tara was apparently enjoying the company of his friends. Karen McGlaughlin had immediately taken the opportunity, upon seeing Tara for the first time, to approach and introduce herself. She and Tara had pretty much been inseparable for the past two hours. *That's awesome*, thought Brent.

It was later in the morning than he had anticipated. He had wanted to be on the road by 7 a.m., but such was life. Brent walked into the center of his yard and called out to the group.

"Hey, we're about to hit the road, so I thought it would be a good idea if we prayed first. Everyone grab a hand."

The other five gathered near Brent and formed a circle, each taking the hands of the person to each side. Each, that is, except Tara. It was obvious that she was out of her element and didn't want to join in the circle. Karen coaxed her to join the ring between her and Terry Carpenter. She looked to Brent for a moment, looking very unsure.

Brent said, "Anyone want to lead?"

There was a clearing of a throat, and Eric began to pray. "Father, we come to you with thanksgiving. First, thank you that we were all able to make it. That's a miracle in itself. Thank you for giving Karen and me the time off from our jobs that we requested. Thank you for Tara having the guts to join a bunch of strange people that she doesn't know very well. Thank you for Mr. and Mrs. Lawton who showed such kindness through food and packing expertise. Bless them, Lord. God, I pray for each one of us today, Eric, Marta, Terry, Tara, Brent, and me; that You will go before us and keep us safe on the roads we have to travel today. I come against any enemy that would try to do us any harm over the next several days, in the name of Jesus Christ."

At that very moment, Tara went into what sounded like a coughing fit. Everyone looked up to see Tara drop Karen's and Terry's hands and raise her right hand up to her mouth. She turned around, gagging, but put her left hand up in the air behind her with her index finger up, signaling that she would be all right in a minute.

Karen approached and said, "Tara. You all right?"

It was all Tara could do to nod her head. She crouched down and the coughing subsided. After a moment she got up and turned back to the group and said, "Sorry, everyone. I think I just choked on my own saliva." A few in the group chuckled. "You'd think after nineteen years I'd have the swallowing thing down." She brought her hands up and rubbed her eyes. "Sorry I messed up your praying."

"That's okay," said Eric. "I only had one more thing to say. Amen."

"Amen," came four other echoed replies.

Brent noticed that the amen never made it to Tara's lips. *God*, he prayed silently, *show her who You are during this trip.*

## Chapter Twenty Five

**Saturday, June 27 – 10:10 a.m.**

So far, so good.

They had been on the road for two and a half hours and everyone seemed to be having a good time. Even Tara. Maybe *especially* Tara. Brent didn't initially like the way things began to look at the outset of the trip, because he could see in her eyes the disappointment upon learning that she and he would not be traveling in the same vehicle.

He thought it might be a good idea for her to get to know some of the others without him being around. He had intended to suggest to Karen that she ask Tara to come with her in Eric's Jeep, but she had already beaten him to the punch. When Tara began to explain her intention to go with Brent, she turned and looked at him for confirmation.

He had raised his hand and waved her explanation off. "It's okay, Tara," he'd said, as if she were asking permission. "You can go with Karen. Maybe we'll do a Chinese fire drill and mix things up again when we stop for the inevitable bathroom break." The guys chuckled.

Well, about twenty minutes ago, that bathroom break had taken place, and he didn't end up seeing what he had expected, a forlorn Tara exiting Eric's vehicle. Instead he saw Karen and Tara get out of the back of the Jeep almost doubled over in laughter. When they had assembled back at the vehicles, Tara had approached him and asked, "You won't be too troubled if I finish the trip up with Karen, will you?" He could see it in her eyes; she really wanted him to say it was okay. After a slight twinge of jealousy, he did, and they were off again.

Terry and Marta were with him in the Suburban, and Brent overheard Terry make a remark to Marta in the back seat.

"Tara and Karen seem to be hitting it off."

"Yeah," said Marta. "Go figure. I half expected her to just cling to our illustrious leader, here."

Brent rolled his eyes and shook his head, but didn't say anything. He decided that he was happy that there weren't any additional "distractions" in the truck to deal with. Well, happy might be too strong a word.

"She nearly scared me to death when she started that coughing fit." Terry laughed. "The timing, right when Eric rebuked the enemy... a little freaky."[5]

"Yeah, that was a little weird," said Marta. "I had the same thought."

Brent retorted, "Come on, now. Let's not go overboard. There will be a lot of rocks where we're going, but we're not going to have time to look for demons under every one of them."

As Brent made the statement and looked back at Marta through the rearview mirror, he could see her lift her eyebrows and purse her lips.

*I wonder what she's thinking.*

‡‡‡

**11:43 a.m.**

They were at the southern edge of the forest, traveling west along US Route 52. Considering the need for another "pit stop," they had still made pretty good time.

"There it is!" said Marta, pointing to the road sign. "State Route 125!"

Brent made the right turn that started their drive into the heart of Shawnee State Forrest. In just under fifteen minutes they would be at the state park. Brent was also getting excited. He could feel a slight rush of adrenaline.

Terry said, "Based on what you've written down, the park entrance is 6.7 miles ahead and on the left."

Marta was feeling it, too. "You know, when all the planning was going on, I had reservations about this whole idea, but now that we're almost there, I'm really getting excited!"

Brent looked into his side-view mirror to see that Eric's Jeep had followed them onto the road. "Eric's right behind us," he said to no one in particular.

They made the left turn into the state park grounds and a little further down the road on the left they saw the park office. "We're here!"

Both vehicles were parked and the six hikers got out and stretched. They gathered near the back of the Suburban. "What's first," asked Karen?

"First we've got to go in to the office and let them know our schedule. Then those of us who don't already have fishing licenses, who are intending to do some fishing, can buy them

---

[5] Go to Appendix B for information on the authority of the name of Jesus Christ.

here."

"What do you mean about a schedule?" asked Marta.

Brent smiled. "I asked the same question when I called down here. They have hiking camp sites set up about every five miles along the trail, and with over 60 miles of hiking trails they want to know the general intentions of all of the hikers here. That way if the hikers don't eventually show up they can go out and search for them."

"Umm ..." Marta began, "This is just something you forgot to mention?"

Brent laughed. "It's just a precaution. Don't worry. This place is well hiked. We're not going to be anywhere that all of the other hikers won't also be." He was satisfied with his assurance and said, "Okay, let's make ourselves known and get to the trailhead. We've got some hiking to do!"

‡‡‡

**12:21 p.m.**

Having made it to the trailhead parking lot, they began unloading their gear. About the only things not contained in their backpacks were the two three-man tents and bedrolls that would have to be tethered to the packs. The guys had agreed that they would carry the extra weight burden of the tents, for which, the girls all called them heroes.

A can of *Off!* was presented to the hikers by Tara. "Trust me, you'll be glad of this smelly stuff by the time we head back home." She took time to spray the fronts, backs, arms, and legs of each of the hikers.

Next they put on their hiking boots, but not before the now-famous nylon and wool socks were pulled on to all of their twelve feet. And, finally, each of the men and women hefted the backpacks onto one another's shoulders.

"I expected these to feel heavier," said Marta.

Tara responded. "It's the way that Mr. Lawton packed them. You try to keep the things you'll need first at the top of the pack, and the things you'll need last at the bottom. But he also knew to shift some of the weight so that most of it was low and closer to our backs." Turning to Brent she said, "Smart man, your dad."

Brent grinned.

"Are we ready?" asked Marta. "If it's this beautiful here in the parking lot, I can't wait to see what it looks like on the trails!"

"Almost," said Brent. "First thing's first. And that is

hydration. The guy in the office said that there are water stations near every camp site, except for camp six, but there are some streams that cross through there, so we can treat some water there if we need to. Every water station that we come to, drink your fill, especially if you don't feel like it. And remember to fill your bota bags with water, too."

Tara chimed in with an over-emphasized southern drawl. "Trust him! He's prayching the *truth!*" Everyone laughed. "And besides the nylon and wool socks," she looked at Marta with a smirk, "this is the most important thing we have on the trail. Don't make someone else sacrifice his or her water for you because you've gotten lazy about keeping yours filled up."

After the trip to the water station at the trailhead, they headed off into their adventure.

# Chapter Twenty Six

**Saturday, June 27 – 12:30 p.m.**

Stephanie O'Leary took another bite of her apple. She sat outside on the porch of an old farmhouse at the outskirts of Pittston. She was barely five miles from her own home, but you'd never know it by how far civilization seemed from this piece of property. This would be the perfect place for the future coven to meet.

In fact, the group that would eventually grow into a formal coven had been meeting here for going on five years. Brendan Cadeyrn, the group's leader—known by his birth name, Brian Baird, in the Pittston community—had made sure that the property didn't lend itself to visits. The grass was kept short and the trees along either side of the long drive were well-groomed. By all accounts the grounds resembled someplace that was lived in; definitely not a place where adventurers should feel the freedom to hike into. One could never be too careful, though, so the place always had an occupant within its walls at night.

The quiet moment that she was enjoying was interrupted by Brendan walking out onto the porch. "Ah, Aileen. This is where you'd gone to," he said; his faint Scottish accent still noticeable.

Aileen Lóegaire was the name that Stephanie had adopted as a result of her research into her Scottish lineage. In fact, all six of the current members had taken names from their historical pasts. Membership in this assemblage was exclusive to a certain bloodline; a bloodline of much consequence, that would, with a common focus, bring about a highly-anticipated end.

Stephanie had been found by Brendan. At the time, she was living in Boston and had been the product of an Irish father of some repute and a brash Scottish lass who had made sure to catch his eye. Neither of her now-divorced parents had understood why she was taking off with a man that she barely knew in order to gallivant from state to state doing research on the Scots of old. If her mom knew about the bloodline from which they came, she never made any mention of it. But the records that Brendan produced were conclusive. She was Picti[6], through and through. And not just Picti, but of a royal descendancy that had been betrayed and tricked out of its rule and, more importantly, its powers, over a millennia ago.

Vengeance had a way of staying alive from generation to

---

[6] Go to Appendix B to read a brief history of the Picti people.

generation in this "family," as did the passing on of a particular legend and prophecy. In fact, if not for the prophecy, their vengeance would have been a long-forgotten enterprise.

For many generations the bloodline passed down with it a tale of treachery that had bitten deep into the followers of the *Olde Faithe*, and for many hundreds of years the bloodline had been attempting to right a wrong; a wrong that had stolen from them their generational birthright as a people.

They would have it back.

Brendan took a seat opposite her and leaned forward. "She matched the bloodline."

Stephanie frowned. "I know that. The investment of time, of belief in her, that's what's most frustrating."

"That doesn't seem to really matter to you now, does it, Aileen? You've lost her."

"Of course it matters! I know it matters!" She closed her eyes and took a deep breath and let it out. "Brendan, we've been looking for almost ten years. She had so much potential. But she would *not* listen!"

Brendan sat silent for a moment. He looked out over the field to the left of the porch. "We've got six confirmed within the Picti bloodline. Six who have made our vision theirs. It's not happening as quickly as I want, obviously." He sighed and got up from his wood-frame kitchen chair, eyes peering into the distance.

"Aileen, we'll not let this setback rattle us. It doesn't matter how long it takes as long as we are the generation to make it happen. Do you know that there are, right now, computers out there that are beginning to store up all kinds of data on people's lives? I've got to believe that one day we will have access to some of that information. The greatest challenge of former generations of the *Olde Faithe* was their lack of ability to gather information quickly. This has to be the *Redeeming Age*; I can feel it! It may take another couple of years—it may take 20 years. Regardless, we will be the generation."

Stephanie stood up and walked to Brendan and slipped her right arm around his waist, resting her head on his shoulder. In turn, Brendan put his arm around her. "Forgive me, Brendan, I know our people will rise again. Who would have thought it would happen in America, eh?"

Brendan chuckled. "Damned potato famine. Sometimes I think more Irish and Scots left the British Isles than stayed. One day, my dear priestess... One day we'll return home, but with our birthrights and faith secure."

## Chapter Twenty Seven

**Saturday, June 27 – 1:32 p.m.**

"No toilets?!" Marta was aghast. "Seriously?! No toilets *anywhere?!*"

They had been hiking for around 45 minutes following the orange blazes—orange paint used to define the trail for hikers—when Terry mentioned that nature was calling. Marta had unassumingly asked how long it would be before they got to the first campsite so she could use the bathroom. Brent saw Tara whisper into her ear, and that's when the eruption took place.

The guys chuckled and shook their heads while Tara and Karen tried to reassure her that life would be okay without "facilities."

"I had asked about the bathroom situation during the drive down here," said Karen. "I didn't know what to say when I found out." She laughed.

"It will be okay, Marta. I promise," said Tara with a chuckle. "In fact, by the time these next few days are over, going to the bathroom in the great outdoors will be old hat."

Marta did not look convinced. Not in the least. She looked at Brent and gave what could have been interpreted as a hate-filled glance, shook her head, and took the lead trudging up the trail.

Brent heard her mumbling, but couldn't make out what she was saying. He raised his eyebrows and grimaced as Eric drew an imaginary knife across his throat to let Brent know that his neck was on the line.

Brent briefly hung his head and shook it. He looked up at everyone and said, "I just assumed she knew."

Terry slapped Brent on the shoulder and headed off after Marta. Brent, Tara, and Karen set off as well.

The hike was proving to be a bit more rigorous than they had expected. If not for the hiking sticks that they brought, the pace would have even been slower. The temperature wasn't helping, either. It was easily 85 degrees, and the humidity in the air due to their proximity to the Ohio River was making things a bit harder.

Brent was beginning to think that he may have made a bad decision about coming down here with inexperienced backpackers; that is until he saw that Marta had doubled back and began walking straight toward him. He stopped and braced himself. The other hikers stopped to see what the outcome of the encounter would amount to.

Upon reaching him, Marta looked him dead in the eyes, and with a voice that only he could hear, she said, “Jerk,” and punched him in the arm.

“Ouch!” he said, not having to fake his wince.

She gave him a forced smile and said, “There. I feel a little better.” With that she turned around and joined Tara and Karen.

Terry shouted back toward Brent. “That could have been worse!”

Brent and the others laughed. Brent saw that even Marta had laughed. She then turned and gave him a quick wink. Apparently all was forgiven.

‡‡‡

In spite herself, Tara found herself laughing at the comedy routine of Rosales and Lawton. Having been so focused on how she was going to orchestrate ‘the fall of man,’ she really hadn’t considered that she might have fun with this troupe of Christian misfits. The thing that tripped her mind up the most about this trip—about these people—was Karen.

If this girl hadn’t been a religious nut job, Tara might have thought her a kindred spirit. They seemed to really connect during the drive down. No matter. In a couple of days it would all be moot. Karen wouldn’t want anything to do with her after she’d accomplished what she’d come here for.

The day was hot. Her shirt was sticking to her back and she imagined that she could literally squeeze its contents into her bota bag and not go for a fill up at the next water station.

The group had finally gotten into a steady pace. They had been walking for a little over an hour and a half. Aside from the occasional stop to acknowledge the obvious beauty of the place, they persisted so that they could make it to Camp 3, the first of the two camp sites that they would hike into today.

They came upon a sign that directed them to the Camp. It would still be a bit of a climb to make it to the site as the trail map indicated that it was about 200 feet above Turkey Creek.

After several minutes of trudging a call went up from the front of their troop. “Hey!”

It was Marta.

“Look!” She was obviously excited about something. Everyone picked up the pace and reached her in a matter of seconds. With a look of glee on her face she pointed at a fabricated latrine; the first of what turned out to be several that they would encounter on during their four-day trek on South loop of the backpacking trails.

Brent stood there looking as if he couldn't comprehend it, while Marta nearly knocked Karen over with a backpack-restricted hug.

Tara laughed. What could she say? It *was* funny!

Marta, in the midst of her jubilation, walked up to Brent and summarily punched him in the arm a second time. Same arm. Same spot.

"Oouch! Good grief, woman!" he all but screamed. "What was *that* one for?"

"Allowing me to suffer."

Terry walked up to Brent with a huge grin on his face. "My man, you just can't win."

Brent rubbed his arm. "Tell me something I don't know."

Marta retorted, "Big baby. You'll be all right. That should be the last punch of the trip."

Tara hoped not. This was getting to be a lot of fun.

‡‡‡

**8:18 p.m.**

It was still light out. Marta reflected on the day that they had spent. It had taken them the better part of three hours to get from Camp 3 to Camp 4. It had been an intensely beautiful trek. There had been a small pond with a rock cliff that rose above it with a stand of hemlock trees that towered high above. Later the trail ran along an amazing sight: Buck Lick Gorge with a quiet little stream running below. The trail had them hiking along the stream until they arrived in an area thick with large, majestic oak trees.

But with all of the beauty came work. According to their pocket guide, the trail would reach an elevation of 1160 feet before dropping 400 feet within just a half mile as they came upon Camp 4 where they would be spending the night.

Marta loved Summer evenings; they were warm and they were long. Though she'd been in the United States for nearly ten years, she had not yet fully adjusted to Ohio Winters. But the Summers... Sigh. Better than Guatemala. She sat back against one of the logs around the fire pit.

It wasn't a cool evening, but somehow the fire that Eric started was still appealing. The scent of the wood smoke, the crackling and popping of the knots in the wood, combined with the sound of rippling water from the nearby creek were intoxicating. Just what she needed to help relax after such a long day.

She looked around. Their make-shift camp site was set up; tents ready to be slept in and food stored high above the ground by nylon ropes suspended from tree branches. Apparently, while there hadn't been any black bears spotted, yet, this season, one could never be too careful.

Karen and Tara were sitting on a log on the opposite side of the fire. They were hitting it off and Marta was feeling left out. Eric and Terry had gone to fill up collapsible water containers for tomorrow morning's coffee and tonight's and tomorrow's teeth brushing.

She heard leaves crunch behind her. As she leaned her head back she saw Brent come into view from the woods. He stepped over the log and sat down next to her.

"You look relaxed," he said. "How are you doing?"

"I'm good, now that I'm able to relax. How's the arm?"

"Healing."

She chuckled. "So, what's on the agenda for tonight? Ghost stories?"

Brent laughed. "Been reading up on American camping traditions, have you?"

"Don't be such a snob, Captain America. Guatemalans also have very similar traditions when out in the jungles hiding from guerrillas."

"You have gorillas in Guatemala?"

"Oh come on, you're playing with me now," she retorted.

"No. I'm not. The only gorilla attacks that I've ever heard of were always in Africa."

"You can't be serious. You haven't been watching your national news very often. Guerrillas have been a huge problem in my country for years."

"Seriously, I honestly thought that gorillas only lived in the jungles of Africa. I had no idea that they existed in Central America."

On hearing this Marta doubled over in laughter.

"What?" Brent looked confused.

"You..." she said, trying to stifle her laughter. "You have *got* to be kidding me!" Another fit of laughter.

At the sound of Marta's laughter, Tara and Karen turned their attention across the fire. "What's going on?" asked Karen.

Still trying to contain herself, Marta responded. "Brent

thinks there are gorillas in Guatemala!" Marta wasn't sure that she was ever going to catch her breath.

"There are," said Tara. "I saw a report on them on NBC News the other night.

That was it. Marta couldn't take it anymore. She rolled over on her side and into a fetal position, laughing so hard it hurt.

Karen caught on and started to laugh, too. "Oh, Brent... You just keep stepping in it, don't you."

Brent's mouth was open, an expression of pure ignorance playing over his features. "What is it? Someone tell me!"

Tara obviously caught on, too, and fought to stifle a laugh of her own.

Karen broke the code for Brent: "Gerrrr-illas, not gorrrr-illas."

It took a second for it to register, but the realization hit home. "I'm an idiot."

At this, all three girls laughed in agreement.

Marta sat up and finally found her composure. She was able to finally talk again. "So, this is American camping! I like it!"

"You are such a brat."

Yes, she was. And tonight she loved it.

‡‡‡

**Sunday, June 28 – 6:32 a.m.**

The next morning everyone was awake at the crack of dawn. Eric started another fire for the coffee drinkers in the group. Tara, Karen, and Marta headed for the "powder rooms" together. Brent broke out a couple of bags of beef jerky and some rice cakes to pass around when everyone was back together. He joined Eric and Terry at the fire pit.

"How're you feeling this morning?" asked Eric as Brent sat down.

"Like I've been beat up by a bunch of girls," said Brent with a grin.

"You've definitely been the abuse magnet so far," said Terry.

"Yeah, well... It's not all that bad. I'd rather have all the laughter than a bunch of people grumbling about why we decided to do this backpacking thing."

"Looks like it's going to be a beautiful day again," said Eric. "Hope it's going to be a little bit cooler than it was yesterday."

Terry looked at Brent and said, "Brent, while it's just the three of us, I need to bring something up."

"Okay. Shoot."

"Last night, when we did that short devotion, did you see Tara?"

Brent looked from Terry to Eric, who shrugged, obviously unaware of where this was going. "Nuh-uh. Why? What did she do?"

"She stared."

Again Brent looked at Eric who only shook his head.

"Okay. She stared. Stared at what?"

"Into the fire. But it was weird. It wasn't like she was preoccupied. It was more like she was in some sort of trance. I don't know. It seemed like she was focusing on something." Terry sighed. "I'm not explaining this very well. I don't know what she was doing, but it was strange. At first I thought she might be having another reaction to us talking about God, but it was something more. At least I think so."

"Eric, did you notice?"

"No. But, then, I was sitting across the fire from her. The flames were too high for me to see her clearly."

"Well, then, I guess that we need to just be aware that something's troubling her." Brent thought for a moment, then, "I was going to kick off our day with prayer. Do the two of you think that we should skip it?"

"No way," responded Eric. "We're not going to compromise just because someone's not comfortable with our faith."

Terry nodded.

So did Brent.

*Okay, then*, thought Brent. *Either Marta's paranoia about Tara is contagious or there really is something strange going on with her.*

The girls marched back to the camp site wearing shorts, T-shirts—Tara in a tank top—and flip flops. It was hard for Brent not to smile. *So, that's what early morning looks like in their lives.* The mussed hair, the lack of makeup, tired eyes. *Still, all three of them are easy on the eyes.*

Karen announced, "Girls get to clean up first."

Terry had tacked up a tarp around three trees a little way into the woods that would provide some isolation from potential wandering eyes. Apparently he had also brought a shower bag that was hanging off of a limb above the enclosure.

"Pour yourself some hot water for coffee, boys," said Tara. "We're going to be warming up our showers with that pot next."

Brent had experienced camping with girls before and knew that he needed to set some ground rules. "Okay. Five minutes.

We each get five minutes." He knew what to expect with that announcement.

Marta countered. "That's not long enough. Ten minutes."

Tara came to his defense. "It's okay. We can do it in five."

Marta looked to Karen for help but got a shrug and a smile instead. Marta walked to their tent in a huff.

The guys grinned and shook their heads.

‡‡‡

Marta would be the first to shower. And as Tara and Karen waited, Karen caught Tara off guard.

"Interesting tattoo."

Tara knew exactly what Karen was referring to, as she only had the one. "Uh, yeah. Pretty cool design, don't you think?"

The tattoo was located on Tara's right shoulder blade and was almost always covered up. It was as exact a copy as she could accomplish of the one she saw on Stephanie's shoulder blade. The one time she had seen it, she did her best to burn it into her memory. She then sketched it and took it to a tattoo artist to who made it a permanent piece of artwork on her skin. At that time Tara wanted to be just like Stephanie, so if that design was significant to Stephanie, it would be to her, as well. There were some designs in the three open spaces in Stephanie's design, but as Tara couldn't remember them well enough to make them a part of her sketch, she allowed for her tattoo to be a bit more basic.

The artist recognized the base symbol and told her it was called a Triskele. He explained what little he knew about its history, but the only thing that Tara really remembered was the pain of having it applied and that it had some sort of Celtic lore behind it.

She had never shown it to Stephanie. She thought better of it. Because Stephanie always seemed to deliberately keep hers covered up, to Tara, taking the design as her own, kind of made it feel as though she had stolen it.

"Does it have any special significance?" Karen asked.

"I don't really know. A friend of mine has one just like it. I liked it, so I had one put on me as well."

Karen recognized the symbol. *Still,* she thought, giving Tara the benefit of the doubt, *it could just be innocent artwork.*

Tara's Tattoo

‡‡‡

Eric came up out of the woods with the kettle and the collapsible water container and walked up to Brent. "It's all yours." He handed Brent the containers.

Brent put the container's remaining water into the kettle and set it next to the fire. As he began to head down to the water supply to retrieve some cold water to take to the shower area, he said, "The girls are down the path a little ways with Terry. Apparently there are some baby birds that they're looking at."

"Yeah, yeah. I think I'll stick around and start packing my gear."

Brent smiled. "Okay, I'll be quick with my shower and we'll get the rest of camp broken down."

"Sounds good."

‡‡‡

Tara knew that it was shower time for Brent. She broke away from the bird watching under the guise of using the bathroom and finishing with her backpack, though, truth be told, it was the first pack completed of the group.

She stood in the woods and watched as Brent approached the shower area.

*No better time than the present,* she thought. She hoped she would have the help of Shalinar, her still-silent spirit guide. Last night she had silently made her way out of the tent, leaving Karen and Marta, to call on him and request his help. But he wouldn't speak. She had thought that he was at her beck and call, but apparently her rebellion against Stephanie's "grooming" combined with Shalinar's call to kill herself had cut off their "relationship." She would earn back Shalinar's presence in her life tonight. He wouldn't remain silent for long.

Now, though, it was time to break down the remaining

barrier between Brent and herself. They may not exactly have a chance for a warm body-next-to-body experience in the next few minutes, but she'd be able to make it evident that that's what she was looking for. She'd disarm him here, then during the course of the hike, they'd plan an after-dark rendezvous for one of the nights.

*It will be such a shame to wipe out his "Christian witness" afterward.* She laughed silently to herself. *The look on Marta's face will be priceless! I'm sure there will be some disappointed looks from the remainder of the group as well. But, Marta... It's time to rearrange your view of Mr. Goodie-Two-Shoes.*

‡‡‡

Brent had just lathered up when he heard approaching footsteps. With the soap on his face he couldn't open his eyes. He didn't need to.

"Bet you'd look good without that tarp surrounding you."

It was Tara.

Bent's heart skipped a beat, then threw itself into overdrive. "Umm... Tara..."

"Oh, don't worry, Brent. I'm not looking. Though maybe I'd like the chance to."

Different trains of thought immediately beckoned for his attention. How he'd love to say something inviting and flirtations at this moment. Thoughts of Coach Chamberlin also came to mind. Now God came to mind.

But this was his chance! Maybe. It was amazing to Brent just how fast testosterone could inject into his bloodstream.

"Cat got your tongue?"

He could hear her step closer. He pulled the cord to release water from the shower bag onto his face. He quickly rinsed the soap from his face then looked at her as she took another step closer.

"Tara. Uhh ... you've got to stop."

"Stop? Stop what?" she said with a teasing lilt in her voice.

"You know what. Trust me; part of me wants what you're offering."

Tara feigned shock. "Offering? Why Brent!" She covered her mouth with her right hand. She came closer.

"Tara, someone's going to come out here looking for one of us."

"Not likely. Everyone's either looking at silly birds or packing up, and I just happened to pack up my gear first thing this morning. I'm efficient like that. They think I've gone to use the bathroom."

"But, Tara..."

"But, nothing, Brent," she said in a serious tone. "I need you to know something, and I needed a private moment with you to express it."

Brent was curious to know what she wanted to express, but he knew that her use of the word *express* didn't necessarily mean she wanted to talk. *This is torture!*

He thought about calling out to God for help, but part of him didn't want help.

A memory sparked:

*"The other part is a good decision, backed up by commitment,"* George had said. *"If you go into this trip wondering how far things might go with her, you're going to be looking for and* hoping *for opportunities.... Opportunities to take things—or allow for things to go—farther. My guess is that you've already imagined some of those things. ... You want this girl to come to Christ, but the biggest thing that you can do to hinder that is to compromise for the sake of a good time. Make sense?"*

It had made sense. *God, I need help here. Help me!* he begged God silently.

"Can you *express* from right there?"

"I could, but it would be much more pleasant to express myself closer."

Brent's heart was pounding like crazy. His pulse was loud in his ears, but not so loud as to not hear that *still small voice.* [7]

"No, Tara. No. I can't."

Tara pursed her lips in mock disappointment. "You don't like me."

Brent knew he was being played. But he also knew that he would have enjoyed it if he hadn't given George Chamberlin his word... if he didn't have a relationship with Christ. But he *did* have a relationship regardless of what the testosterone, now coursing through his body, was screaming for him to do.

"Tara, it's not that. I do like you, and I think you know that. But I've got another relationship that I've got to honor."

A true perturbed look came across Tara's face and anger flitted across her eyes. "You've got a what?" She blinked.

"Hold on a sec. Okay? Just ... just ... hold on a sec." Brent reached up and pulled the cord again and allowed the water to

---

[7] Go to Appendix B to read about the "still small voice".

course down over him to quickly rid himself of the soap that was beginning to dry on his skin. He grabbed his towel and quickly dried off. He grabbed his clothes that he had draped over one wall of the tarp and put them on. Stepping out, he towel dried his hair while approaching Tara.

Tara was now brooding; arms crossed, head tilted down, and with a chilling look in her eyes.

Brent stopped a yard away from her. “Tara, yes, I’ve got another relationship. And it’s a relationship that you already know about. It’s with Jesus Christ.”

She stared at him for what seemed like minutes, then said, “You’re kidding me, right? You’d prefer a relationship with an invisible God to a flesh and blood woman?”

“Tara, there is room for two relationships, but one has got to take precedence. And that relationship, in my life, is always going to be the one with my God. The very same God that loves *you*, Tara.”

He took a step toward her.

She took a step back.

“Whatever you say,” Tara said with a flat voice. She turned around and began walking back toward camp.

Brent stood and watched her walk away. The taste of victory, apparently, wasn’t always sweet.

## Chapter Twenty Eight

### Sunday, June 28– 7:48 a.m.

When Brent got back to the campsite he saw Tara, backpack already on, helping Karen adjust her pack's straps. She looked up at him and her face went cold.

*What? She hates me now?*

Brent took the shower tarp, shower bag, and water containers over to where Eric and Terry were finishing with their packs.

Terry looked up at Brent and said, "Good. That's the last of the gear. You sure you only took a five-minute shower?"

Brent knew he said it with a smile, but he couldn't help getting defensive. "It was less than five minutes."

Eric heard the uneasiness in Brent's voice. "You okay?"

"Yes," he said, looking over to Tara.

"Something going on between the two of you?" asked Eric, also looking over at Tara.

"No."

"Brent," responded Terry, "you're using one-word answers."

"What?"

Eric looked at Terry with a knowing smile. "When you clam up and don't form actual sentences there's something wrong."

Brent sighed. *I can't just tell them what Tara did.*

"Tara came back to the campsite," said Terry, "...from *your* neck of the woods... looking a little peeved. Something's definitely up."

Brent looked over to see Tara, Marta, and Karen walking over to them. "Not now."

Eric took the hint and diverted conversation. Panning around the group he asked, "Everyone ready?"

Four of the six nodded yes. Eric noticed that Tara and Brent just looked at each other—Brent, with a question in his eyes and Tara, with daggers in hers.

"Great! Terry, check one last time to make sure that the fire pit is cool, will ya?"

Terry did and then they were off.

It was already in the mid-to-upper 70s as they started along the path. Brent suspected that both temperatures and tempers could prove to be high today.

‡‡‡

They had been hiking for about an hour and a quarter. Eric and Terry were in the lead; Tara, Karen, and Marta followed, and Brent took up the rear. It was mostly a quiet walk; just snippets of chatter among them. They had been advancing upward along the path when Marta saw movement below the ridge to their left.

She gasped and froze.

What Marta saw made no sense. Her brain tried to steer to a rational conclusion, but instead took an off ramp to panic.

‡‡‡

Brent watched Marta tense up and stop. He looked down to where she was staring and his eyes went wide. How had none of the others noticed it? He called out a hushed "Hey!" to the rest of the group. Everyone stopped and turned to look at him. He pointed downward off the ridge.

About 30 feet from their location stood the most massive pig any of them had ever seen. It must have just wandered out into the open, as it appeared that it had not, as of yet, seen them.

Tara got excited. "A wild boar!" she exclaimed a little too loudly.

The boar startled and looked up at them. It was a male; it's tusks way too apparent. Terry and Eric immediately drew machetes from their packs.

*What I would give for a hunting rifle just about now*, thought Brent.

The ridge wasn't steep enough to keep it at bay. The animal certainly had free passage up the slope.

The boar's stiff, black hair pointed upward from its back. The thing had to be at least 300 pounds. The slight rise to the ridge and its own massive weight would be the thing's only resistance should it decide to charge.

"Marta," Brent began to whisper, "I want you to slowly, carefully ease your way toward Terry and Eric."

Marta gave a nervous nod that Brent didn't see and started stepping toward the other guys. The boar grunted as it perceived the movement and directed its attention toward her. After a moment, though, the beast redirected its attention to Brent, who was apparently the larger threat.

Male versus male.

Brent reached back to feel for his machete.

Terry quietly told the girls to slowly—*very slowly*—move

past Eric and him. As they began to do so, the boar again glanced their way, but only for a moment. It re-fixed its eyes on Brent.

*God, I could really use your help here,* Brent prayed. His right hand finally found the grip of his machete and he began to draw it out.

The girls were now past Terry and Eric. Eric told them to keep moving along the path. With the girls safely away, Terry and Eric slowly released the buckles on their packs and lowered them to the ground. Eyes were now fastened on the dangerous scene ahead of them, they didn't see the move Tara was beginning to make.

Tara slowly reached into the right thigh pocket of her cargo pants and took out a camera. She lifted it to her eye and snapped a picture of the massive swine, the flash of which caught the animal's attention and agitated it even further.

Eric turned around immediately and glared at her. A hiss in his voice told her to *move!*

The boar appeared to shiver and tense, looking back and forth between the two men and the one. Its eyes settled again on Brent and the beast began to paw the ground with its right hoof.

*Oh God! This thing's going to charge!*

The boar grunted loudly. Then, letting out a horrendous squeal, it charged.

Brent whipped the machete in front of him. As he did, another startling sound pushed through the air.

Terry let out a terrible scream and started charging down the pathway toward Brent, angling toward the ridge and the beast. Eric followed suit with his own yell, both of them with their machetes bared for an encounter.

The boar stiffened and dug its front hooves into the dark, damp peat, skidding to a halt. It appeared unsure what to do with the new threat. It stood and grunted and squealed loudly again as Terry and Eric made it to Brent's side.

Eric whispered, "We should get out of here."

All three of them began a backward march up the path. The boar's irritation was growing again and they could tell that it meant to make another run at them. Every step backward seemed to take forever. Brent's pulse was throbbing in his neck and fingers. Adrenaline coursed through his system. He breathed hard.

Slowly they continued backward toward the three women. Terry and Eric reached their packs and the three of them paused just long enough to grab the packs and sling them up to one shoulder. Continuing their backward trek, they finally made it to a curve in the path where the trees formed a precarious natural barrier between them and the boar. There was an arising sense that they were now safe, but none of the three wanted to turn around quite yet.

Marta was beside herself with fear. She half screamed, “Come on! Come on!”

The guys backed another dozen steps and finally began to relax. With a quick look at one another they took off running toward the girls. Running was probably not the best way to express what they were capable of doing with the weight of the packs on their backs, but it was getting them where they wanted to be; as far away from that animal as fast as possible.

The girls didn’t wait for the guys to reach them before they, too, turned tail and ran.

‡‡‡

“What were you thinking?” yelled Karen. “Really? You had to take a picture?!”

Tara stared at Karen, unable to reply.

Marta’s turn. “That was stupid. You nearly got them killed!”

Tara turned wide-eyed toward the guys. “I... I didn’t know the flash was on.”

The men, one by one, dropped their packs to the ground.

“Okay, stop,” said Eric. “Relax. Let’s all just relax.”

“But,...” Marta began.

Brent cut her off. “Eric’s right. Let’s just stop. Ladies, drop your packs.”

They did so.

“Everybody gather ‘round,” said Brent. And as they did he spread his arms wide and said, “Group hug.”

Terry chuckled, as did Eric, more probably from a need to release tension than from the humor of the suggestion. The girls approached and they all put their arms around each other’s shoulders and waists. Terry bowed his head and the girls responded in kind. Brent and Eric did the same. With their heads touching they just held each other for a long minute.

When they finally looked up and released each other, Brent could see tears in the eyes of all three of the women.

Eric sat on the ground and leaned back on his hands, extending his feet outward. Everyone else followed his lead and planted themselves as well.

“Well, now,” Brent ventured, “That’s something you don’t experience every day!”

The comment produced a much-needed laugh. The tension began to leak out of them.

Eric turned to Tara. “Did you get a good shot?”

At first Tara didn’t know if she should really answer the question.

“Well?” Terry prompted.

“I uhh… I think I did, actually,” she said.

“Good,” said Brent. “Cause *no one’s* going to believe this story without it.”

They all laughed again.

“You guys were great back there!” said Karen.

Tara agreed. “You know that the three of you are heroes now, don’t you?”

Brent looked to Tara who, in turn, looked him straight in the eyes. There was a look of wonder and appreciation where earlier there had only been contempt.

Terry rolled his eyes. “We were terrified, not courageous.”

Marta retorted, “What do you think courage is? Absence of fear? Nuh-uh. It’s doing the right thing in spite of fear.” She looked to Tara and smiled. “Tara’s right. You three qualify as heroes.”

After a silent moment Eric deflected the praise by asking, “Did anyone else back there pray?”

Four other hands went up, Tara abstaining.

“You *really* think *God* had something to do with us getting away?” inquired Tara sarcastically.

“Why not?” asked Karen.

“Well, it seems obvious to me that it was three men with machetes facing a single animal, albeit a big one. That animal recognized the odds.”

Brent responded, “All the more reason to believe that God intervened.”

Tara produced a questioning look, not believing that there could be any logic in his statement.

“This isn’t the first time I’ve seen a wild boar. Now, just to make it clear, my family was in Florida in a nature preserve at the time, but those boars were still free-range animals. They could have been a cause for alarm if they hadn’t been on the other side of a small marsh area. That’s where we learned from a ranger about how unpredictable these animals are. The bigger the threat that they perceive, the more dangerous they tend to become. They aren’t your everyday turn-their-tails-and-run types. By all accounts…” Brent thumbed backward toward the path behind him. “… that animal shouldn’t have stopped its charge. It should have come at us with reckless abandon. But it didn't."

The group chewed on his words for a moment.

"God, we thank You," started Eric. "Thank You for saving us, for protecting us. You are a good God, and we take this time to let You know that we acknowledge that. Amen."

"Amen," came the group reply ... save one.

After a moment, Terry asked, "Is this the end of our backpacking adventure?"

"What?"

"Why?"

"Shouldn't we report this to the rangers? We can't let others stumble upon that thing," continued Terry.

Brent's head dropped. He sighed. "He's right. We've got to tell someone."

Eric said, "If we do, it's going to take a quite a while to get back to the trailhead to report this, and before we can even start heading back we've got to find the next forest road that intersects this trail. I'm guessing it would have to lead back to the park office. That is, of course, unless everyone wants to go back the way we came."

Karen interjected with a sigh, "And I doubt that after hiking all the way back to the office we'll want to come all the way back out here to resume where we left off."

Brent could see that everyone seemed dejected. It appeared that their four-day trip was coming to a sudden day-and-a-half end.

‡‡‡

**9:45 a.m.**

It didn't take too long to come across Forest Road 2. They made a right turn off the backpacking trail onto the dirt and gravel road. It might have been able to accommodate two passing vehicles, but it would be a tight fit. It was full of ruts and not exactly conducive to a leisurely walk.

After a half hour on the road they agreed that much of the backpacking trail they had hiked was much easier to trek than this stretch of cumbersome road. They still had quite a way to go to get back to the office—if, indeed, the road was taking them there—and the heat of the day was making it nearly unbearable. There wasn't anywhere near the amount of shade that they had enjoyed on the trail. The bota bags were being tipped back and drained into mouths more frequently.

Ahead of them the sound of a vehicle coming up the road caused everyone to stop and watch as it approached. It turned out to be a ranger vehicle, a Jeep Cherokee with a light bar on top. The group moved to the right of the approaching ranger and flagged him down to a stop.

The ranger, a man, probably in his mid-forties held his radio's mic to his mouth as he looked out the window at the group. "Dispatch show me 85 on Forest Road 2, approximately one mile West of McBride and Forest Road 13 ."

"10-4. Showing you 85."

"10-12."

The ranger stepped out of the Jeep, his badge and leather utility belt shining in the sunlight. He looked impressive in his starched beige shirt and sharply-creased green pants. His dark-complected face displayed a look of professionalism and confidence as he placed his forest-green 'Smokey the Bear' hat on his head. He was a tall man with an impressive build.

He spoke. "I'm Ranger Nathan Swope. Is everything okay here?"

"Yes, sir," Eric replied. "Well, at least it is now."

"What can I help you with?"

"We had an encounter with a wild boar several miles back. You found us making our way back to the park office to report it."

"Everyone's okay?" The ranger scanned the faces of everyone in the group.

"Yes, sir," said Brent. "It's not something we want to do again, but we came out of it all right."

Ranger Swope opened one of his shirt pockets and pulled out a small note pad and pen. "Tell me about the boar."

"It was massive," responded Marta. Tara and Karen nodded in agreement.

Brent nodded his affirmation. "It was probably about five-feet long, and, I don't know ... over three-hundred pounds?"

"That's a pretty remarkable description. You sure it was *that* big?"

This time the men of the group all nodded.

"I'm pretty sure it was a male. The tusks had to be around five-inches long."

"Where did the encounter take place? What were the circumstances?"

Brent pointed back to where they had entered Forest Road 2. "If you turn left off the road onto the trail there's a ridge that slopes down to the..." He thought for a moment. "... down to the right if you're headed away from here."

"I know the place."

Brent continued. "It was apparently rooting when we came across it. We startled it. While it focused on me we got the girls out of harm's way, then it charged me. My two *best* friends..." Brent smiled at Terry and Eric. "... had pulled their machetes and started running down the path toward me, yelling at the thing. I pulled my machete out, as well. The boar came to a stop and stared at us as we backed our way out of its territory. That's when we realized that our backpacking trip had just come to an end."

"Okay. Well, I don't doubt your story. It's rare, though, to have a wild boar sighting here. It's size though, ..."

"I got a picture," Tara said abruptly.

Ranger Swope looked at her. "Pardon me?"

"I took a picture of it."

"Miss, if you've got a picture, then we need to see what we're dealing with."

Tara drew the camera out of her thigh pocket. Walking over to the ranger she extended her arm to hand it to him. "Here you go."

Ranger Swope accepted the camera and then said to the group, "Bear with me for a moment." He stepped back to the cab of his Jeep, opened the door and sat inside. Taking the radio he said, "Base, we have a 10-11 about one mile North of NF-2 on the South loop. The report is a wild boar. Male. Five feet long. 300 pounds. Five-inch tusks. The animal has shown aggressive behavior. No injuries reported. 10-78 to incident area."

"10-4, Unit Three. 10-11 One mile North of NF-2. Wild boar sighting. 10-78."

Ranger Swope exited the vehicle once again and stepped up to Tara. "Ma'am, if I have your permission to develop the photograph on this camera I will provide you with a claim receipt for the developed film. If you have any other photographs on the film you'll need to let me know now as to whether you want them developed as well. Otherwise we'll only develop the last image on the film. However, that would ruin the other shots."

"If you'd develop all of the pictures, I'd appreciate it. There's nothing on the film that can't be viewed by everybody."

After writing Tara a claim receipt he rewound the film and removed it. After handing her the camera he said, "You can pick the pictures up at the park office when you get back there with the receipt. Thank you for the picture. It'll help us with our search."

Tara smiled at the officer as she took her camera back.

"As for this being the end of your backpacking trip… Folks, the chances of you having a second encounter with another boar is so slim as to be considered nearly impossible. Have a good remainder of your trip out here. Just head back down the road and hang a right back onto the trail. Oh, and by the way, you would have had a heck of a time finding the office using this road. I'm glad I happened across you when I did."

The group voiced their appreciation and said goodbye as the ranger reentered his vehicle. After starting the engine he looked at them one last time and said, "Men, good job protecting the ladies and each other. Well done."

With those affirming words, Brent felt like he could take on the world. Looking at Terry and Eric he could tell they felt the same way.

Brent looked at his fellow trailblazers and asked, "Do we go on?"

Marta looked at Brent for a moment then to everyone else and said, "Let's do it."

That was apparently all that was needed to get the lot of them to back in gear. They still had nearly three days of adventure ahead of them.

‡‡‡

**3:36 p.m.**

The ring of the phone startled Stephanie as she sat reading the latest in her string of Stephen King novels. Setting the book aside she got up from her couch and walked to the living-room telephone.

"Hello?"

"Aileen, it's Brendan. I've just received a call from Cowan."

"From Scotland?"

"Yes. He and his sister are still there."

David McNeill—aka Cowan Cormack—and his twin sister, Donna, were on a trip to explore and sightsee throughout the British Isles. David was using this trip to test the waters with his sister to find out if she could be lured into their numbers through the subtle means of "discovering" their family lineage.

Three months ago David had called Brendan to announce that his sister was overjoyed at the suggestion of taking the trip and fingering through historical records to discover their family roots. Of course, David already knew where to look and he knew what they would find.

The question was whether she would be properly romanticized by family legends and historical proofs that they came from royal Picti blood. Would she, like her brother, have the courage to venture beyond the facts of who the family once was to pursue who the family could be *again*? Stephanie figured she was about to find out the answer.

"And...?"

"I'm told that it doesn't look good. As much as she's loving the history and how 'tickled' she was at discovering her Picti past, she's not showing the least bit of interest in being a part of something greater than her current, rather pathetic, station in life."

Stephanie was perturbed by the news. "And that's it? She knows who she really is, a Picti princess, and wants nothing more. *That* is pathetic."

"Indeed. However, there is some potential good news on that front. In the midst of the search, Cowan discovered in the same town in which they skimmed through their family records, another family who is also linked to us through blood. If this is true, and if he can make headway with one or more of them, then we may have another long-desired link to the old country. It's too early to tell, obviously, but to have someone who can do further research for us in our native land..."

"Priceless," intoned Stephanie.

"Priceless. Cowan and his sister will be in the town for another couple of days to 'take in the sights, sounds, and the people.' He believes that the interaction that he will have with this family will appear pretty natural."

"With a true link back to the old country, will that mean a move for us?"

"Let's not get ahead of ourselves, my dear Aileen. Even if we have a couple—or a few—added to our numbers from the areas around Pictland, we've got several more here in the States. The wealth and support that we need is here, as well. Remember, it's not all about our little coven here in Pittston, Ohio. It's about the bigger picture. We'll just have to see how things play out."

There was silence on the phone for the space of about ten seconds and Stephanie was about to ask if Brendan was still there when he inquired, "Are you not going to ask of me another question, Aileen?"

Stephanie thought for a moment, coming up blank. Then it hit her. "The stone!" she exclaimed. "What of the stone? Is it the one at Tarbat?" Her heart began to beat rapidly.

Silence.

"Say it, Brendan! Out with it!"

Brendan laughed and obliged her. "Yes, my dear Aileen! The Key Stone is found! At least parts of it."

Stephanie's excitement began to wane as quickly as it had spiked. "*Parts* of it?"

"One piece was exactly where we were told, in the old Pictish village of Portmahomack on the Tarbat Peninsula. It is in the Tarbat Old Parish Church, set in a wall of the crypt, carelessly used as a piece of masonry. But it is there. Cowan asked of the rest of the stone, and the caretaker of the church took him to go look at another, similar stone, also used in a wall that circles a garden at the church *manse*—house. Cowan says it looks to be of the same piece of stone as the one at the crypt."

"But the markings, they are supposed to be on both sides of the stone."

"That, my dear, is the problem. Getting those stones pulled from those walls will be next to impossible."

"How many other pieces?"

"Cowan said he didn't know. He asked of the villagers the whereabouts of other pieces and no one knows a thing. But Cowan said that that the piece in the crypt is obviously a top section, while the one in the garden wall is from the bottom. But, there are probably five or six more pieces to be found. Unfortunately, Cowan doesn't have time to return to Tarbat to do more searching. He's got to bring his sister back to the States."

Stephanie sighed, maybe a bit too loudly.

"Dear Aileen, fear not. We know where the whole stone was, we know where two pieces are, and most importantly, we already know the location of the Key of Bridei that fits into the Key Stone. Once the remaining pieces of the stone are found—and they *will* be found—we will have our path of discovery before us. Be excited, my lovely priestess. The *Redeeming Age* is nearer than we thought only yesterday."

Stephanie's mood lightened. "You're right, Brendan. Thank you for the call. Things seem to be progressing just as you had said."

"Never doubt me, Aileen."

"Never."

"Come to the farmhouse tonight. I'm calling upon the others, as well. We will ask the spirits to advance the work that Cowan has started."

"I will be there, my priest."

# Chapter Twenty Nine

**Monday, June 29 – 8:17 p.m.**

Brent mused.

The previous day and a half on the trail went off without a hitch. No other boars, no seductive moves by Tara, and no high tension. Last night had turned into an enjoyable evening around the fire at campsite five, basking in friendship and laughter. Today's hike had started off a little later in the morning than expected, but it was nice to not feel rushed. Besides, they needed all the energy they could gather for the day's trek.

The decision to bypass campsite six had been an easy one, as there were no "facilities" and no place to get water. They did their best to make the water that they carried last. Fortunately, the day was a few degrees cooler than the previous days had been.

It was dusk, and when Brent and the others reached the camping area, they were exhausted. The additional miles of hiking had taken a higher toll than they'd experienced to this point. But they were all in good spirits as they raised camp.

As Eric and Terry set up one of the tents, Brent and Marta set up the other. Karen and Tara had gone to set up their make-shift shower and fill up the water containers.

"I'm so glad that today is drawing to a close," offered Marta, tapping in one of the tent spikes. "It'll be good to just sit around the fire tonight and relax."

Brent grunted in agreement. But he was only half listening as he pondered about Tara. She may not have made a move the previous evening or this morning, but that didn't mean she wouldn't try again.

*What is she up to? Does she really care for me or am I some sort of game for her? And why does she have to be so alluring? I can hardly take my eyes off of her.* He tapped in the last of his spikes and stood up, stretching his back.

"... who is distracted."

Brent caught the tail end of something Marta was saying.

"I'm sorry. What were you saying?"

"Brent, is everything okay?" She eyed him for a moment. "I said that you have the appearance of someone who is distracted. What's up?"

Brent made a show of rubbing his eyes and stretched again, adding a nice big yawn to the mix. "I'm sorry, Marta. Just tired and a bit sore." He looked over at her as she crossed her arms and raised her eyebrows. *Hmm... She didn't buy that.*

"Okay, yes... I've got some things on my mind."

"Tara?"

"Yes. Tara."

"Okay, talk to me."

Brent wasn't going to get into the details of the shower incident, but he did appreciate the opportunity to at least talk about some of his concerns. "She's just..." He sighed. "Do you get the impression at all that she's deliberately trying to make this a difficult experience?"

"As in this trip?" she asked.

Brent nodded. *Sure, why not?*

"I don't know about that. But she is still being very stubborn about the idea of God."

"Do you think it's that she doesn't believe? Or do you think she's putting up some sort of front because she doesn't *want* to believe?"

"Maybe she believes, but doesn't want to know *Him*," Marta remarked.

That caught Brent. "You think that?"

Marta thought about it for a moment. "I'm beginning to think so. We've known her now for, what, almost a month and a half?"

Brent nodded.

"You'd think that if she was even slightly caving to the idea of getting to know God, we'd have seen some hint of that."

Brent was forced to concede. "She doesn't want to talk about Him. She doesn't want to participate in anything remotely Christian that we do." Brent looked off into the distance where Tara had gone for the water. "What gives?"

Marta shook her head. "Why would she want to be here with us for four straight days? I mean, other than the obvious."

Brent cringed. "Which is?"

"Someone here has got her attention."

"Who?" asked Brent, hoping that the obvious wasn't really *that* obvious.

"Terry."

A look of disbelief punctuated his eyes and mouth. "What?"

She smirked. "Brent, really... you can't *possibly* think I'm serious." There was a twinkle in her eye. "She likes *you!*"

Brent didn't know how to mentally regain purchase on this shifting ground. So he blurted out the first response he could muster. "She said that?"

Marta momentarily closed her eyes and shook her head in exasperation. "Sometimes, Brent, you men can be so thick. *No*, she didn't *say* that! I said that. And I said it because it's so obvious. The woman stares at you continually. There is something about you that she's intrigued with. Maybe she's just drawn to those ruggedly strong arms of yours or your handsome scruffy face." She smiled and batted her eyes.

Brent was dumbfounded. He had no idea how to respond. He just stood there blinking his eyes with a bewildered look on his face. He didn't know if he was more surprised about Marta's revelation about Tara or her remarks about *him*.

*Rugged? Handsome?*

He finally offered, "Am I really *that* out of touch?" He hoped that she thought he was remarking about Tara.

Marta smiled. "The clueless look on your face is priceless."

"I uhh…" Brent closed his mouth, sighed, and walked over to the other guys. He could hear Marta's lilting laughter as he walked away. "Women," he said under his breath.

‡‡‡

**9:12 p.m.**

"Will you hand me the twine?"

Tara picked it up out of the small duffel that they used to carry the components of the shower and walked it over to Karen.

"Thank you."

While Karen returned to hanging the shower curtains, Tara contemplated how to broach a subject that she knew would ultimately end in her being proselytized again. She had to admit, though, that this bunch hadn't been nearly as preachy as she had expected. Not everything was *God* all the time. In fact, not once had anyone asked her about her obvious *lack* of a "relationship" with their God. For the most part she was allowed to simply be who she was. Be that as it may, she was curious about *this* Christian's religious experiences.

"So, why did you become one?" asked Tara. She knew she should have prefaced the question, making her allusion clear.

Karen didn't even look back to Tara. It was as if she had known the question was coming. "For the same reason that you're avoiding becoming one."

Suspicious and a little alarmed at the reply, Tara responded, "And that is?"

"Control."

Karen didn't say anything beyond that, and Tara knew that she was intentionally letting the word lay there, out in the open. She finished with the second of the three curtains and walked over to a sapling to begin putting up the last.

Without comment, Tara walked over and picked up the opposite end of the third curtain and began to overlap it with the first curtain, where the "door" to the shower would be. She waited patiently for the elaboration she knew would come.

Irrespective of the subject matter, though, she liked the connection that she had with Karen. They had similarities that made relating with each other somewhat comfortable. The stopping point of total relatability, though, was this whole Christ thing.

"You and I aren't very different, Tara," Karen began again. "Seems like we're cut from the same piece of cloth. We'll have to share our backgrounds with each other sometime. But to finish answering your question, I had been living my life to seize control wherever I could. In fact, I was the poster child for control freaks." Finished with the last corner of the final tarp, Karen walked over to face Tara. "And that, my dear friend, is why *you* don't really want to be a Christian, isn't it?"

Tara was taken aback. "I never said I didn't want to become a Christian. I'm just..."

"... just checking it out. I know," interrupted Karen with a smile.

*Okay*, Tara thought, *there* are *times that I'd like to smack her*. "That's right. I'm still checking it out."

Karen gazed at her for a long moment then continued. "Tara, there is something going on in you that goes beyond the typical internal struggle—or disbelief—that most skeptics have. Frankly, I think you've already dismissed the idea of ever becoming a Christian."

Tara's mouth opened slightly, more out of shock than to let something escape her lips. "I..." and that's as far as any sentence got.

Karen paused for a moment, obviously giving her a chance to continue. Tara couldn't form a sentence, so Karen went on. "And you know what? It's okay. You've made a decision that's yours to make."

Tara collected her thoughts. She had to know. "And if I *do* choose to go a different path from the rest of you?"

"Like I said, it's your decision."

"So, you're telling me that you don't *care* if I remain a..." Tara caught herself almost saying *pagan,* but finished with,

"...heathen?"

Karen smiled. "Is *heathen* the term you identify with?"

Tara couldn't believe the corner she was painting herself into. "Isn't that what *you* would call me?" She raised her eyebrows.

Karen chuckled. "Anyway... yes. I do care. But I also care about your free will. No one can make you love Jesus. Even He, Himself, won't force you. And in the time that you've been around Brent and Marta, I'm sure you've already gotten all the information that you need to make a solid decision one way or another."

Karen walked over to the duffel bag and took something out. Turning, she said, "All that aside, I want you to know something." Karen paused as she walked right up to Tara and with a genuine smile said, "Tara, you're growing on me, and I'm glad you're with us on this trip. While I sincerely love those other four camping mates of ours, I'm glad I get to hang out with *you*. And even though you don't believe what I believe, I think I've found in you a kindred spirit." With that, Karen opened her arms and violated Tara's personal space with a tight hug; a hug that was barely reciprocated, because *nothing* like this was supposed to happen.

Pulling back, Karen unceremoniously held out to Tara the object in her right hand. "Your turn to hang the water bag."

Tara couldn't help but release a short giggle.

## Chapter Thirty

**Monday, June 29 – 9:45 p.m.**

Brent walked over to the girls' tent where Marta was crouched, putting on her tennis shoes. "I wish I'd thought to bring mine," he said.

"You wish you had brought something with a little bit of pink?"

Brent grinned. "You're pretty quick-witted. Have I ever told you that?"

"That I'm pretty or that I'm quick-witted?" she asked with a slight laugh, looking up at him.

"That you're a brat," countered Brent, not missing a beat.

Finished tying her shoes, Marta stood up.

"As a matter of fact, you have told me that."

"Good. I'm glad that's settled. Ready?"

"You bet! It's going to be nice to have some alone time with you. Let me just grab my sweater."

Marta ducked into her tent and grabbed her pink sweater, which caused Brent to playfully roll his eyes at her.

"What?" she said with a mock huff. "Pink makes the world feel better."

Brent laughed out loud. The others around the fire looked back at them. Tara turned and gave them a quizzical stare. Brent felt compelled to give a quick explanation.

"We'll be back soon. Just going for a little walk."

As he began to walk away Marta took his arm. What the two of them didn't see—nor did the others—was the fire that ignited in Tara's eyes.

Brent and Marta walked along the gravel road that had led them down to the campsite off of the main trail. The backpackers would spend the night in what the trail map said was Massey Hollow. The combination of cricket song and lightning bugs made it amazing to behold. It was a beautiful, starlit night. The temperature had to be in the upper 60s; just cool enough for Marta's sweater to be a smart choice for the walk.

Though it was unlike Marta to take Brent's arm like she had, it felt comfortable, even reassuring, to him. His confidence had been waning as of late, and the fact that Marta would draw close to him, helped him realize that he was still viewed highly by her. And that, for some reason, was important to him.

The pace had been leisurely. They were near the main trail, about a quarter-mile from the camp, and still not a word had been spoken. They were so comfortable together. Why had they never been more than friends? It was a thought that played on Brent's mind, once more. Maybe it was time to change that.

Brent's mind flitted back to Tara, though. There was something about her that he desperately wanted. He was duly seduced, he recognized that. But it wasn't something that he was unable to escape. Besides, there was something in him growing toward—maybe even drawing him to—Marta, as well.

As they reached the top of the road they turned around at the intersection and looked back down into the hollow. They could see the glow of the fire pit at the camp below.

"It's almost magical," whispered Marta.

"It is," Brent replied.

Marta still had his right arm and he felt her shiver. He pulled his arm from hers and put it around her drawing her to his side. She didn't refuse his lead. He rubbed her back, hoping that the friction would generate some additional warmth. She leaned her head against his shoulder. In response, he laid his head against hers.

It just felt so right, and she didn't seem to be doing anything but drawing closer to him. His heart rate picked up. He tried to keep his breathing steady so as to not hint at how nervous he was getting during this should-I-do-it? moment.

Brent decided to throw caution to the wind. He opened his mouth to speak.

"Brent?" Marta's voice, soft and inviting, interrupted his own.

"Yes?" he said, echoing her softness.

"Will you tell me now?"

"Tell you ...?" Then it struck Brent. He'd all but forgotten what Tara had told him about Marta's desire for him, and how she was trying to make Tara out to be the bad girl.

"Tell me why you weren't comfortable speaking to me or being around me this past week." She lifted her head off his shoulder and looked up into his eyes.

The magic of the moment was over. He sighed.

Brent asked a question of his own first. "Is this why you were willing to forsake resting around the campfire to take a 'lovely stroll in the cool of the evening?'... to ask me that question?"

She smiled. "Maybe. Partly."

Brent withdrew his arm from around Marta, paused for a moment, then took a couple steps forward, sticking his hands into his jean pockets. He wondered if Marta would step up to regain her place by his side, but she didn't. She just waited for him to speak.

"Marta," he began, "I didn't mean to become so distant."

She didn't respond. He could visualize her standing behind him, eyes trained on the back of his head.

"It was something I learned. Or maybe I should say that it was something I was told."

Marta broke her silence. "About?" There was a pause, then, "About me?"

"Yeah."

Brent heard the sound of gravel as Marta took a step forward.

"Brent, turn around." It wasn't a request, but it also wasn't harsh.

He turned to face her. A look of introspection and hurt filled her eyes. "What is it? What was said?"

Brent wouldn't hold back what she so desperately wanted to know, but he didn't want to cause undue embarrassment at what he was about to reveal. "Remember when you told me about the incident at the Army / Navy store with Tara?"

"Yes."

"She confided in me her side of the story that took place that day."

At that, Marta's eyes went from hurt to curious. "She did? She told you ... what? About her dad?"

"No, not about her dad. She told me about you." Brent looked into her eyes, trying to gauge her response. Marta looked genuinely confused.

"Me? I don't get it. What about me?"

"She said that the two of you..." Brent stopped, then took a different tack. "Don't get angry."

Marta's eyes grew wider, expecting words that were, in fact, *going* to make her angry. She crossed her arms and pressed her lips together. She waited for a moment for him to continue then raised her eyebrows, as if to say, 'Yes?'

"She said that the two of you didn't talk about her dad. She said..."

"What?" Her arms shot down to her sides. "We most certainly *did!*"

Brent continued. "She said that you had basically warned her to stay away from me." He blanched at the words and looked down at her feet for a moment before looking back up to her face. He saw a change in her countenance. Her eyes grew dark and she pursed her lips for a couple of seconds before speaking.

"What *else* did she say?"

"Marta, come on, I'm sure..."

"Brent! Tell me *now!*"

Brent knew there was no reasoning with her at this point. He'd seen her angry a few times in the years that he'd known her and in those times she became unbending in her demand for answers.

"She told me that you had told her that because she's not a Christian that she can't have me. That because ..." He sighed.

"Finish."

"That because you *are* a Christian that you had more right to me, and that you made a veiled threat that she needs to back off of any romantic ideas that she might have toward me."

"¡No puedo *creer* esto! ¡Esa *perra!*" she exclaimed, barely below a scream.

Brent didn't know what the majority of that meant, but he recognized *perra. Oh boy,* he thought. *This is going to get bad.*

Marta was livid, but she hadn't heard enough. "And the rest?"

Brent spilled the rest. "She said that the two of you never talked about her dad. She said that you probably told me that story so that I'd be less likely to raise the issue with her and get the truth. Or something close to that."

Marta stared into Brent's eyes for a few seconds, looking from one to the other, contemplating something behind her own. Then, without warning she walked by him and started back down the gravel road toward the campsite at a fast clip.

Brent scrambled to get beside her. "Marta. Come on! Stop! We're not done."

"Oh, yes, we are."

"Stop!"

She didn't.

Brent raised his voice and grabbed her left arm. "Marta! Stop!"

Marta spun to face him. "What!"

"Is any of it true?" Brent searched her eyes again.

"Not ... a ... *word* of it!" She turned, shrugged off his hand and resumed her decent.

Brent jogged up beside her, and, again, went to grab her arm. Whether she sensed it, or saw it from her peripheral vision, she moved her left arm across her body, and said, "*Don't.*"

"What are you going to do when you get down there?"

"I'm going to rip the strawberry-blonde hair out of her two-faced little head!"

‡‡‡

**10:26 p.m.**

"Will you just wait?!"

The question was loud and caught the other four campers by surprise.

Karen's first thought was that Brent had done something to make Marta mad again. But when Marta rounded the stand of trees and made a bee-line for the fire pit where they were all still sitting, she knew it wasn't Brent that was on her mind.

Hatred played on Marta's face, and Karen could tell that she was aiming straight for Tara.

Tara noticed, too, and began to stand up.

Marta attempted to forcefully exert control. "*Stay down*, Tara!"

But Tara didn't, and instead assumed a defensive posture, obviously expecting physical contact of some sort.

Now the others were standing up.

Brent darted into Marta's path and grabbed both of her shoulders. He effectively stopped her approach, but not her tongue.

Marta looked around Brent to look straight into Tara's eyes. "What's wrong with you?! What is *wrong* with you?!" she screamed, tears of anger dropping from her eyelids.

To Karen, it appeared that Tara didn't know what was going on, but that didn't mean she didn't do something to instigate this confrontation.

"Marta?" began Karen, as she rounded the campfire. "What's going on?" She briefly looked back at Tara to make sure that she was keeping her distance. As she reached Brent she stood between Marta and Tara, causing Marta to look into her eyes. "Marta. Honey, what's going on?" She tried to use words and a voice that would calm the situation.

Marta wriggled her right arm free from Brent and extended it past Karen, obviously pointing at Tara. "That wench!... That *witch!...*" She had trouble formulating a sentence that would explain. "She ... she... You're a *liar*, Tara! You are a filthy liar! I knew it! I knew it!" She looked back at Brent. "I told you! I told you there was something wrong with her!"

Karen tried, again, to settle things down. "Marta, tell me. Calm down and tell me." It seemed to work as Marta's eyes focused on her own.

At the same time, Terry and Eric also circled the pit to stand a little off from Brent, Karen, and Marta. It also worked to put another layer of protection between Marta and Tara, who, though still tense, was relaxing her posture a little bit. In fact, she crossed her arms to watch what was taking place before her.

"Come on, Marta. Talk to me," prompted Karen again.

Marta seemed to find some small amount of concentration to formulate controlled sentences again. "She said that I was trying to keep Brent for myself. She said that I was trying to keep them apart."

Karen processed that for a moment. "She told you that?"

"No!" snapped Marta. "Brent did!"

Then it clicked. Tara told Brent those things. She turned to face Tara.

They all turned to face Tara.

‡‡‡

Tara tensed up again. She stood and watched the group turn to face her. She glanced at Marta for a hard second, then averted her eyes. Her brain engaged and began weighing options. The cat was out of the bag, and she wasn't going to be able to simply bat her eyes and make it all go away this time. Denying it would be fruitless; Marta's emotional state saw to that. Her only alternative was to confess to the group that she had tried to manipulate Brent.

Well, *sort of* confess.

Time to take her acting skills up to the next level.

Karen spoke up. "Tara, is that true?"

*Here goes nothing*, thought Tara. "Yes." She thought about continuing, but recognized that letting Marta have her moment of vindication was the best way to play the situation.

Brent was next. "You played me?"

Tara dropped her head and gazed downward. "Yes," she admitted just above a whisper. She heard some footsteps moving her way, figuring them to be Brent's. She looked back up. It was Terry.

He came within ten feet of her and just stood looking at her. His gaze was penetrating, but without any sign of anger. His eyes were asking *Why?*

The direction she would take was only just coming to her mind when Terry prompted, "Tara, how about something more than one-word answers?"

Tara, again, looked toward Marta. She now stood with her arms crossed, eyebrows up, waiting for a reply. She thought she heard her whisper to Karen, "Told you."

"It's true," Tara allowed. "I did say that to Brent."

Brent again. "Okay. But why?"

Tara looked into Brent's eyes. He was dumbfounded. *What a simpleton. The lights are on, but no one's home.* It was time to dive in. She took a deep breath and held it for a moment, then quickly exhaled. She let her shoulders droop a little for effect. "Really, Brent? You don't know?" She shook her head slightly. "I thought it was obvious."

Brent tilted his head slightly, his expression saying he was getting tired of her games.

"I like you, Brent."

From beyond Brent Tara heard, "Oh, here we go." It was Marta.

Tara turned her attention toward her and took a step forward, raising an accusing finger. She raised her voice as well. "That's right, Marta. Here we go!" She took another step. "I like Brent. Every bit as much as you do!" She turned her attention back to Brent. "I knew I was competing against Marta. I also knew I had little chance to..."

"What?" Brent asked in disbelief.

"...*very* little chance to measure up against her. She's got everything that I don't."

Tara caught movement beyond Brent. Marta's arms dropped to her side. She had a stunned look on her face, her mouth agape. She caught herself being stared at, then lent her own "What?" to the conversation.

"That's right," Tara continued. "You've got a family that loves you, you've got the same religion and lifestyle as Brent. You're beautiful and have that accent..." *Accent? Good grief, that may have been a bit much.* She pressed on.

Tara turned back to look into Brent's eyes. "I see how she looks at you. How you look at her." She stopped. That's all she would say until someone else spoke.

Brent broke eye contact and looked back at Marta. Both looked a little uncomfortable and neither denied a word of what Tara said.

Unexpectedly, it was Karen who spoke next. She stepped away from Marta and began to walk toward Tara. "Okay, let me get this straight. You had a conversation with Brent and told him that Marta basically told you to back off because she wants him. Is that right?"

Tara dropped her eyes and nodded.

"But there had to be more in order to keep Brent from bringing it up to Marta."

Again, Tara nodded.

Tara could see Karen walk up to Brent's left side and stop.

"Then, how did the secret get revealed?"

Tara looked up to see Karen looking at Brent, but it was Marta who answered. The anger in her voice softened a little bit, though there was still a tone of accusation. "Because he was acting weird all last week. Every time we were together he wouldn't look me in the eyes or talk with me for any length of time. He wouldn't tell me what was going on. So I finally dropped it... until tonight."

*That figures*, thought Tara.

Karen turned back to Tara. "So it was all just a bunch of manipulation to try to get the upper hand with Brent?"

Tara could see Brent squirm. She wanted to smile, but diverted her look to see the seriousness in Karen's eyes and answer her inquiry. She sighed. "Yes."

"And you really thought it would work?"

"I thought it was the only chance I had against her."

Marta walked up to Karen's left side. Terry and Eric drew up behind them. Tara saw Eric put a hand on Brent's shoulder as if to say, *I'm impressed* or maybe *It's going to be okay.* It didn't really matter to her. Despite the unexpected revealing of her ploy, this whole thing was taking a good direction. She wasn't out of the dog house, but at least she was able to keep her cover.

Marta took another step forward. "You are an inconsiderate, lying, bitch." It was stated matter-of-factly, without the volume and ranker of a few minutes ago.

Tara thought for a moment on how to handle this. She wanted to extend claws and go at it with this female, but choked it down and nodded. "You're right," she said in a whisper. Turning away, she nodded again, and then turned on the tears. "You're right," she agreed again, then convulsed into sobs.

She stood there gasping for air as pain wracked her chest. It actually scared her for a moment. It nearly felt like true sorrow. But what did she have to feel sorry about? Sorry about hurting Marta? *Whatever*. Brent? *Lame*. Karen? She fell to her knees.

Sorrow pierced her soul.

*No, damn it! Stop!*

## Chapter Thirty One

### Tuesday, June 30 – 12:18 a.m.

Something wasn't right.

Brent sat up in the tent. He looked to his left and right to see both Terry and Eric sleeping. He quietly unzipped his sleeping bag and removed the warm covering, instantly feeling the chill of the air's dampness as it made contact with perspiration in his pant legs. He unzipped the netting, grabbed his hiking boots, and silently exited the tent.

Standing fully erect, he stretched his back, then ducked back into the tent to grab the sweatshirt he'd worn earlier that evening. He pulled it on over the long-sleeved T-shirt he wore to sleep.

Embers still glowed in the fire pit. He wondered if he could stoke a fire back to life. There was still a small pile of twigs and dry leaves that they had used to initially start their fire. They would also be used in the morning to create a cooking fire. Grabbing a handful, he placed them into the pit and softly blew on the embers below. The leaves caught, followed quickly by the twigs. Within a couple of minutes Brent had another small fire burning that worked to push back the chill.

Sitting on one of the logs surrounding the pit, he crossed his arms and looked up into the starlit night. It was beautiful and peaceful. But peace could not be found in his mind or spirit at the moment.

Something wasn't right.

A realization struck Brent: While he had done his share of praying during this trip, he hadn't done much seeking. Upon accepting his failed responsibility, he felt the prompting of the Holy Spirit to do just that.

He started to pray silently, but quickly noticed that his thoughts kept wandering. Getting off of the log, he took to his knees. He remembered his Mamaw saying that "Sometimes it's the only way that prayin' can get done right." He smiled.

Since silent prayer wasn't allowing him to focus, he took to praying out loud, in a soft enough voice as to not disturb the others.

He looked over at the girls' tent. They were all in there, but they didn't all like it, to be sure. Karen was sleeping between two porcupines.

"Father, I love You." It sounded so contrived in Brent's ears. "I do, God. I really do love You. I wish there was some way to verbalize how true that is." Then it dawned on him to begin praying and worshiping in the Spirit;[8] worshiping in both spirit and in truth.

After several minutes of pressing deep into the presence of the Lord, he felt like he had reached a place of being able to interact with, rather than praying *at*, God. Now he would reach out for help.

"Lord, I feel like a fool. As I look back over the past several weeks, I realize that I've been living a life full of reaction instead of being prepared to respond. I've been more than willing to pray to You, but I haven't been willing to enter into Your throne room where You tell us to come with boldness. I've been too content to just stand outside and shout into where You are. Where's the intimacy in that? Father, thank You for Your constant grace. I'm amazed at Your continued willingness to put up with me."

Brent smiled. He knew that God's grace existed because of His perfect love. Grace wouldn't be hard to understand at all if we could first grasp the full height, depth, and breadth of His love. But that was just it... no one would *ever* completely grasp that.

He continued. "Father, tonight I felt like an idiot, because I hadn't seen how I'd been manipulated by Tara. But the truth is that I feel like a little boy around her. I never feel stable or feel like I'm strong when she's near. I feel like a hormonal dork."

Brent had a flashback to high school and Galen Todd. He then had another flashback to the spiritual incident at the Great Oak on campus.

"Yes, Lord. I get it. I was spiritually prepared for both encounters. I had been spending time in Your Presence so much that I didn't react, I responded." Brent paused, then continued, "Father, get me back to that place. I need to have stable ground to walk on again. I don't want to look like a moron anymore. I want to walk in confidence again, because of how close You and I are together."

Brent thought about how things would be in the morning when everyone woke up. He was going to need to take on the role of a man again, particularly when it came to Tara. He'd have to talk with Marta, as well.

"Father, you said in the Book of James to ask for wisdom and You'd give a bountiful supply. Well, I'm asking. Help me know

---

8 Go to Appendix B to read more about praying "in the Spirit."

how to deal with this situation correctly.

"Another thing, Lord, is Tara's salvation. I think that if she had a relationship with You she wouldn't have done what she did." Brent felt a pang of conviction from the Spirit. "Sorry. It's not about her and me. It's about her and You."

Brent thought back to how many opportunities he and Marta, and others, had had to speak the truth to her about Jesus, but she just wouldn't commit.

"God, she's fighting Your Spirit. She's fighting to keep her independence. But, God, she doesn't understand that she's being used. That *she's* the one being manipulated. Father, I know You love her. Help her to see her need. Release her from the Enemy's snare. In Jesus' name I pray!

"I don't know why she's holding back. I don't know what the Enemy is offering, but You do! Bring the Enemy's plans to nothing! In the name of Jesus I pray!"

Brent thought things through one more time, listening in his spirit for further prompting to pray, but all he felt was peace.

"Amen, Lord. So be it."

And with that Brent stood back up, took another look up at the blanket of stars above him, and went back to the tent for some needed sleep.

‡‡‡

While she couldn't make out his words, Tara could hear Brent outside by the fire pit. She knew he was praying to his God. But soon he would go back to his tent, then it would be her turn to "pray."

Several minutes went by and she finally heard him quietly unzipping and re-zipping the screened tent flap. She'd wait several more minutes before making her own exodus. She also needed to make sure that neither Marta nor Karen would stir.

After 20 minutes, by her watch, had gone by she quietly exited the tent. Her special satchel in hand, she made her way out of the camp site and up the hill to where the gravel road intersected with the main trail.

No one would be roaming the trails this late, she suspected. They had shared campsite three, and last night, campsite five, with a few other campers. Tonight, though, campsite eight was theirs alone. Add to that the late hour and she should have the freedom to do what she willed.

Kneeling on the ground she opened the satchel. She pulled from it her pentagram casting cloth, the hag-stone amulet, her pentagram necklace, and her ritual circle mat. After spreading the mat—her rings of protection—she settled within the concentric circles. She spoke an incantation for protection and then unrolled her ritual pentagram. The night was a bit too breezy for candles, so she had not withdrawn them from the bag. *Not ideal*, she thought, *but it's not the first time I've cast spells without them.*

She kissed the pentagram and decided to hold it rather than wear it this time. She would use it to concentrate with rather than the candles. Placing her amulet in the center of the pentagram, she reached into her satchel one last time and withdrew her grimoire. Tonight she would make all of the campers feel her power.

She searched the pages of her spell book for perfect retribution.

She smiled.

‡‡‡

Karen shivered. Following Tara out of the tent meant not waking Marta. And that meant not being able to grab the sweater in the corner near Marta's head. She hardly noticed the cold at this point anyway, because of what she saw before her in the moonlight. It caused her blood to boil.

Getting close to Tara had put all of her stealthiness to the test. She was close enough to see most of what Tara had pulled out of her bag. She couldn't tell what her amulet was, but saw her place it in the middle of the pentagram that would be used for spellcasting.

She was also close enough to hear.

"By the powers of the blackest night, I speak that which is vile and spite.

Merge with me my spirit guide, and let no power in you hide.

Shalinar. Shalinar. Shalinar.

I call thee forth, my medium to come, as I spellcast tonight bring me power, Otherealm from."

Karen watched as Tara extended her arms heavenward, eyes closed, bathed in moonlight. She knew that she couldn't just be a spectator during this evil moment of beckoning. She, too, had to act. But how? Confront her?

No. She instantly knew this wasn't the time or the place. Instead she would do warfare. She would make sure that whatever Tara meant for evil would not be allowed to flourish.

"Father," Karen whispered, "I ask for your protection. Put a hedge around me that the Enemy may not penetrate. Cover me with the blood of the Lamb.

"I come against the evil spirits being conjured now, in the name of Jesus. I bind them by the power and authority of the name and blood of Christ Jesus! You will not speak, for I muzzle you in the name of Jesus Christ.

Karen transitioned from warfare to prayer so that she would have wisdom in dealing with the situation unfolding before her. "Father, I want to lash out at Tara. She is attempting to come against all of us with satanic power. There is hate in her. It makes me want to lash out against her, but I know that You love her in the same way that You loved me in my pre-Christ days, and I know that You've got a plan. Help me to walk in it. Your will be done. In the name of Jesus I pray. Amen."

Knowing that she had utilized the authority that God gives all believers, she decided that there was no good reason to watch Tara's perversion of prayer. Ever so slowly and quietly Karen backed away from the site of Tara's rituals even as she continued calling on spirits to come and recognize and obey her summons. Karen, too, kept praying. Her prayers became all the more intense the further away from Tara she got.

Arriving at the camp site, she stood near the fire pit and called on God to fight on their behalves. Facing the two tents she raised her hands; left toward the men's tent and right toward Marta's and her own.

"Father, I speak a hedge of protection around these tents. I plead the blood of Jesus over Terry, Eric, Brent, Marta, and myself. Protect us, Lord, under Your sheltering wings. I pray that You, O God, would dispatch angels to protect us from the hands of the Enemy as we sleep tonight. In Jesus' holy, powerful, precious name I pray. Amen."

Knowing that Tara could come back at any moment, she thanked the Lord for His love and acknowledged His sovereignty over the situation, then she crawled back into the tent.

As she began to settle into her sleeping bag, Marta murmured, "Everything okay?"

"We're under God's sheltering wing, Marta. Everything's fine."

Karen did not know if Marta heard her or not. Marta's deep breathing indicated that she'd already fallen back to sleep.

Ten minutes later Tara quietly snuck back into the tent.

"Everything okay?" Karen whispered. She heard a slight startled gasp.

"Uh, yeah," came the response. "Just needed some fresh air

and the bathroom."

"Goodnight, Tara."

"Goodnight, Karen."

‡‡‡

Tara lay awake. This trip hadn't gone as she had planned. She had yet to trip up Brent, at least not to the degree to where his "little light" didn't still shine. It appeared that he and Marta were drawing close. And Shalinar hadn't made his presence known to her the entire trip. She could only hope that her spellcasting would produce results throughout the course of the night.

On top of everything else, she was exhausted, just like the rest of them. Mingle that with her frustration and she didn't know if she had it in her for another flirtatious presentation to Brent. Besides, yesterday morning he had made sure that Eric, Terry, and he had all gone to the shower area together to "allow the girls to have some of their own morning time."

Then there was Karen. The girl she wanted to hate, but couldn't. Karen had taken a genuine interest in her. Why? It's not like they knew each other. It's not like they had really gotten into deep conversation about anything. Well, nothing lengthy, anyway.

Even this evening's confrontation by Karen was handled with respect. Respect. She had been accorded respect when she deserved none.

Tara sighed softly. In her innermost being she knew what it was... Karen just liked her. No pretense. No expectations. No demands.

*It's like she really* wants *to be my friend.*

How long had it been since she'd had a real friend; a girlfriend to just be a girl with?

*Not since daddy...*

Tears welled up; one spilled from her right eye, traveled over the crest of her nose, and down her left cheekbone to soak into her small camping pillow. She sniffled.

She heard Karen rustle behind her. It sounded as though she may just have lifted her head to listen. Becoming as motionless and quiet as possible, brought the desired result. She heard Karen adjust her pillow and lay her head back down.

Another undesired moment of introspection flooded her mind and heart.

*Daddy...* Another sniffle, this time followed by a hard breath. *I love you and hate you at the same time. Why did you have to leave me?*

*Why wasn't I worth staying alive for?*

Tara felt a warm hand touch her right shoulder. Karen gave a slight squeeze.

Tara quietly wept.

# Chapter Thirty Two

**Tuesday, June 30 – 8:11 a.m.**

The sun was already warming the campsite when the campers became active. Marta was glad that they would be on the road home this afternoon. She was extremely glad that she and Tara wouldn't be in the same vehicle.

Twice this morning Marta had the opportunity to glare at Tara. But it seemed like any fight that Tara might have had in her the night before had gone out of her. She just looked ... tired.

*All the better*, she thought.

She ducked back into the tent and grabbed some clean—well, clean*er*—clothes and headed to the shower. Her impatience for this trip to end drove her to be the first ready to depart the campsite.

She started to walk to the shower when she heard someone jog up behind her.

"Wait up!"

It was Karen. Marta stopped and turned. As Karen approached, she could see Tara give a quick glance over to them as she ducked inside the tent.

"How about some company?" asked Karen.

"I don't think I'd *be* good company."

"None the less, let me grab a change of clothes, too. I'll be right back."

Marta stood and waited. She watched the guys as they sat near the opening of their tent, putting on their boots. She imagined that they would start breaking down camp while she and Karen took their showers. Eric looked up and saw her. He smiled and gave a slight wave.

Marta gave as pleasant a smile as she could muster and turned her eyes toward her tent. Moments later Karen emerged with a wad of clothing in one hand and shampoo, soap, and a towel in the other.

"Okay, let's get clean," she said with a smile as she approached.

As they walked Karen acted as if nothing had happened the night before.

"Looks like it's going to be yet another beautiful day. That's good, huh?"

"Yeah."

A moment of silence, then Karen said, "How are you?"

Not missing a beat, Marta replied, "Oh, I'm just peachy. How are you?" Her comment dripped with sarcasm.

"Well, mostly confused, I guess. Tara has been a hard girl to read."

"I read her just fine."

"Hate doesn't become you, Marta."

Marta stopped and turned to face Karen. "The word is *loathe*. Hate is too mild a word."

Marta watched as Karen pursed her lips for a moment, briefly look down at their feet, then brought her eyes back up to meet her own.

"You know, there is more going on in Tara than you realize. There is a lot of *loathing* going on in her, too."

"No kidding? Wow. I'm sorry. I guess I hadn't noticed that." She clenched her jaw.

Karen continued. "Okay, I know you're really not wanting to talk about this. We need to, though. And here's why... For the past month you've been telling me to pray for Tara. You said that she had some difficulties in her past that she was dealing with and that you felt that if she'd allow God into her life things would start working out for her."

Marta raised her eyebrows with an implied "And...?"

"Now you're not allowing a sinner to be a sinner."

"What's that supposed to mean?"

"It means that the job of sinners is to sin. Their job is to make life difficult for themselves and for us. They don't understand what we have. It makes absolutely no sense to them. It sure didn't make sense to me before I became a Christian. Did it to you?"

Marta relaxed her jaw and shifted it to the left before responding. "No. Not really." She thought a moment, then said, "But I didn't do to others what she's doing to us."

"Fair enough. But then, the two of you come from different backgrounds."

"What background?! I doubt that she's told the truth about anything regarding her background! She's weaving a web of lies!"

"Yes! She is! I agree with you, Marta. She's full of spite and malice. She has it in for all of us."

"All of us?" Marta frowned. "All of us? Really now. Seems to me that she's just been targeting Brent and me."

"Appearances can be deceiving. The point is that we've got to be better than that. We've got Jesus in us. We've got His love in us. That's what we've got to show to Tara."

"Ha! That's rich! What I want to do..."

"It doesn't matter what you *want* to do! Don't you understand? It's *not* about *us!* It's about Jesus' love for Tara! Marta, snap out of it! We've got an enemy who hates us. That enemy is not Tara. She is just the manifestation *of* that enemy. She is being used to hurt your relationship with God."

Marta wasn't convinced.

"Marta, how much praying have you done last night or this morning?"

Marta pursed her lips again, not answering.

"Can you find it in your heart to pray that the love of God makes itself known to Tara? Or has your heart already started to get hard against her?"

Karen sighed. "The week leading up to this trip you and I prayed twice over the phone and once face to face for her. Your heart was to see her saved."

Marta's eyes began to slowly lower. She couldn't look into Karen's eyes anymore. She saw her neck, then her stomach, her legs, then gravel. She couldn't fight Karen's words.

For a moment she tried to regain her anger, but the resolve was no longer there. Karen was right. Tara was worth something to God. *Okay, she's worth a* lot *to God*, she relented.

Marta closed her eyes and lifted her head back up. She opened her eyes to see a soft smile on Karen's face.

"Let's *choose* to love her. Okay? Let's *choose* to have the heart of Jesus toward her."

Marta's eyes misted over. She took a deep breath and slowly let it out. "You're right, Karen." She was quiet for a moment, then, "And right now I choose to forgive her."

"Ata girl. Now let's get our showers so that we can start lovin'."

Marta chuckled at a new thought.

"What?" Karen asked.

"I almost said, let's love her to death."

"Marrtaa..."

"It was just a passing thought! Okay ... I'll love her. No death involved."

They laughed as they headed to the shower.

‡‡‡

The mood among the backpackers was noticeably different from the night before. Where there had been so much anger and mistrust, there was now an air of companionship and cooperation. The three men, who had already finished breaking down and packing their part of the site, stood and watched in awe as all three of the women worked together. No words of anger. No claws bared.

"Okay, something weird is going on," said Eric.

"Uhh, yeah," agreed Terry.

Brent took it all in with befuddlement. "Obviously, Tara isn't happy. Karen, well ... she could just be displaying her negotiator side. But Marta..."

The three of them watched in anticipation for several minutes as if at any moment fireworks would launch. When they didn't, Eric said, "God got her."

In unison Brent and Terry looked at him and said, "Huh?"

"God got her. Marta, I mean. It's the only explanation. God's at work."

They turned back.

*God got her.* All three watched ... nodding.

‡‡‡

Having left the campsite and standing now on the trail, Brent asked for everyone's attention. He was about to reestablish himself as a man and hopefully leave the naïveté and goof status behind.

"Everyone take a hand and form a circle."

Five of their six did just that. Karen held out her hand to Tara, who gave a slight shake of her head and took a step backward out of their circle, arms folded tight around her. Brent watched as she turned and walked several feet away. She stopped and continued looking up the trail that they would soon be taking.

Brent continued. "This has been quite the adventure, hasn't it?"

Nods and smiles of agreement.

"We've probably learned quite a bit about ourselves during this trip. Some of it good. Some of it ... not so much."

Brent saw Marta look up into the sky.

"I know that I've seen more wrong with me than I wanted to. It's been a wakeup call. Please, forgive me for any shortfalls that leapt off page. I resolve to be better today than I was yesterday and the day before that."

"Same here," vowed Marta.

"Ditto that," said Karen.

Eric and Terry both lent their agreement, as well.

"Let's start today off right," proposed Brent.

Still holding Terry's and Eric's hands, Brent dropped to his knees. After a quick look around the others did the same.

"Father, thank You for this incredible adventure that You've given us. While we've still got today, we ask that You take the lead. You are the Good Shepherd and we are Your ... umm ... periodically dumb sheep." The group chuckled. "Help us to be strong today as we make our final push to back to the trailhead. Our aching bodies could use it. Help us to see who You are in our lives today and help us to love one another as You first loved us. God, You chose to love us before we even wanted to know who You were. Help us, on this final day ... and every day after ... to realize that You are a good God. Your heart toward us is good. Help us to radiate that goodness—that love—outward to a lost world. Help us to grow together as brothers and sisters in Christ. We love You! Bless our fellowship, we ask, in Jesus' name. Amen."

"Amen!" came the resounding chorus.

Tara walked back over, obviously uncomfortable and agitated. "Can we go now?"

‡‡‡

Tara's mindset was soured, to say the least. They were two-and-a-half hours into the hike, about an hour from the trailhead office, and Brent was steadfastly steering clear of her. The untamed shrew, however, was not. Tara shook her head. Marta was untamed early this morning, anyway. Now she was turning into Miss Goodie-Two-Shoes again.

When she had returned from the shower with Karen, Marta actually walked up and asked if there was anything she could do to help with the packing of the tent. Several times during the course of this last leg of backpacking Marta actually tried to engage her in conversation.

*Really? What the hell is going on?*

Tara just wanted to walk alone and in silence, and she made that very clear. To *all* of them.

Oh! And what about last night's spellcasting?!

What was up with that? Nothing! No affect whatsoever on this group!

Then there was Brent. How had she failed with him? Just a few days ago he had been putty in her hands. Today...

Today she wanted to scream! This trip was supposed to be her redemption! This was supposed to fix things; get her back on track, maybe even—somehow—restore her into Stephanie's good graces.

She watched Brent and Marta as they trekked ahead of her. Their periodic laughter was really getting on her nerves.

*There's got to be a way to get things back on course,* she thought. *How? Maybe Brent was closer to giving in than he was letting on. Maybe...*

"You okay?"

Tara startled and turned to see that Karen had come up beside her.

"Oh. Umm... yeah. Just thinking."

"I could tell. You look frustrated."

Tara tried to play it off. "Oh, it's nothing big."

"Oh, it's big all right," Karen said with a slight giggle, trying to lift the mood.

"What is?" Tara kicked into suspicion mode.

"How about we drift back from the group a little bit? There's something I'd like to talk with you about."

*A lecture? Really?* She felt heat rise up into her neck and face.

"We should really try to keep pace," countered Tara. "We don't want to delay getting to the trailhead office."

"Tara, we'll keep pace after we drop back. I just want to have a conversation with you."

Tara sighed in defeat. "Okay."

They slowed down and Terry and Eric passed them.

"You two okay?" asked Eric.

"Yeah," said Karen. "We're fine. Just gonna indulge in some girl talk. We don't need you guys sneaking up on us and listening in."

"Oh, yeah... exactly how we wanted to spend the remainder of the hike, listening to two girls ramble about... What *exactly* do girls ramble about during hikes?"

Karen waved at the guys. "Bye bye, boys."

With a snicker Eric and Terry moved on. Karen slowed up until they were a good thirty feet behind them then rejoined the pace.

Karen turned her attention to Tara. "It looks like you're having a tough day. What's on your mind?"

"Karen, listen, really, nothing's..."

"How long have you been a witch?"

Tara stopped. Her mind began to whirl. Her heart kicked it up a notch, and she started to feel tingling in her fingertips. She kept her focus forward, eyes darting left and right, as if searching for a quick escape route.

"What?"

"A witch, Tara. You heard me."

Tara tried to compose herself. She put a fake smile on her face and turned to face Karen. "A witch?" She faked a laugh. "You cannot be serious."

Karen faced her and looked her straight in the eyes. "You know the saying, 'You can't con a con?' Well, you can't con a former witch either."

Tara's fake smile died. She stood shocked, staring at Karen's face, unable to completely look her in the eyes. Then she knew she needed to. She adjusted her eyes to look straight into Karen's and asked, "What do you mean by witch? Are you saying that you used to practice witchcraft?"

"That's exactly what I'm saying. Now, how long have you been practicing the craft?"

"Karen, I'm not..."

"Tara, stop it. I know that you are. You're not going to succeed in convincing me otherwise."

Tara felt trapped. She had to evade this. She looked down the road to see the distance that was growing between them and the other four. She forced another laugh. "This is crazy. Look, we're falling behind. We need..."

"We need to discuss this. Tara, listen, I'm not condemning you. I'm just letting you know that I know. You and I hit it off on the trip down here from Millsville. I knew that there was some common ground between us; I just couldn't put my finger on it right away. We have similar personalities, but I knew there was more. I prayed about it our first..."

"Oh brother."

"...our first day on the trail. Yes, Tara, I prayed. I felt the Lord speak to my spirit that you and I had witchcraft in common. Then you confirmed it."

"I confirmed it. Really. And *God* talked to you." It wasn't a question as much as a statement backed with derision.

"Yes, He talked to me."

"Come on, Karen. Give me a break. All you Jesus freaks talk a good..."

"Do you have a spirit guide?"

Tara stopped mid-sentence. She was being kept completely off balance. "I'm not admitting to anything. But if I did?"

"Then I would ask why you think it's absurd for a Christian to hear from the Holy Spirit when you are able to hear from a spirit that isn't from God."

"How do you know that my spirit guide isn't..." She stopped.
Caught.
Silence.
Karen placed her right hand on Tara's left shoulder.
Tara shrugged it off.
Movement caught Karen's eye. She turned to see that Marta was coming back down the trail toward them. Tara turned, too.
"Great," said Tara under her breath.
Karen held up her hand to halt Marta's advance. Marta came to a stop.
"Marta," shouted Karen, "Can you give us a few minutes? Let the guys know that we'll be lagging behind, but we'll catch up."
"Sure. Okay." With that Marta took a last concerned look and turned away. Karen waited until Marta disappeared around a slight bend in the trail ahead.
Karen looked back at Tara. "Tara..."
"Are you going to tell them?"
"Tell who what?"
"Tell the others. Tell them that I'm a witch."
"Yes."
"Just like that, huh?" said Tara shaking her head, eyes narrowing in anger.
"They deserve to know, Tara. You've been living a lie in our midst."
"I am not! I'm just not..." Tara searched for the right word to use. "... ready to become a Christian yet."
"Are you *really* still trying to con me?"
"I'm not conning you!"
"I saw you last night."
"What?"
"When you left the tent. When you got up you woke me. I lay there for a minute, but then I felt that should follow you. You said you went to the latrines. But that's not where you went, is it?"
Tara clenched her jaw; her anger growing more apparent.
"You spied on me?"
"You're going to try to say that me spying on you as you preformed a spellcast is *worse* than what you were trying to accomplish *with* the spellcast? Tara, if anyone needs to be called out onto the carpet, it's you. And you know that. Why do you hate us so much? Why, especially, Brent and Marta?"
"Karen, you don't know what you're talking about." Tara began turning away.
Karen grabbed her arm.

"Let me go, Karen, or so help me..."

"You'll what, attempt to cast a spell on me, too? Let me ask you something, Tara. Have you ever experienced what I call a *cast back?*"

"A what?" Tara asked with contempt.

"I really don't know if there is an *official* name for it, but an instance where a demon that you cast..."

"I don't cast demons!"

"I'm sorry. Let me rephrase. Have you ever sent forth a spirit to do your bidding, only to have it come back and attack you?"

Fear threaded its way through Tara as she relived the dorm-room experience in her mind.

"And if I have?"

"Then you found that these spirits are not friendly. They are not on your side. They'd just as soon attack you as anyone else."

Tara just stared, dumbfounded.

"Do you know why?"

"I know you're going to tell me anyway, so why?"

"Because they hate you, Tara. Because there is no real love in that area of the realm that you're involved in."

"What do you mean by 'that area'?"

Karen smiled. "I wondered if you'd catch that. You're smarter than I was when that statement was spoken to me. The realm is the spirit realm, obviously. There are two areas of that realm: God's and that of God's Enemy."

"Enemy... You mean Satan, don't you?"

"Yes."

"I don't practice black..."

"Careful, Tara. Reevaluate what you're about to say. If only God is light or white, then everything else can only be, at best, shades of gray. But if you know who the Enemy is, and how this Enemy is determined to deceive us, then you'll ultimately concede that all forms of the craft are black magic."

"I don't believe in your God."

"Okay, let me ask you something? Have you ever tried to directly put a curse on a practicing Christian?"

Now Karen was wanting her to admit to actual attacks. Should she? She sighed. She'd already been called out, and if Karen really had been involved in the craft in the same way that she was currently, then lying was pointless.

"If you're asking the question, you already know the answer. Yes. I have."

"Well, I didn't know for sure. But, anyway, what was the result?"

"First, we consider Christians..."
"We?"
*Crap.* She stepped in it again. She glared at Karen again without saying a word.
"Okay," said Karen, "just finish your thought."
"Christians are the enemy. One of the enemies, anyway. It's obvious that they have power from somewhere. If the Christian is, what you people would say, 'on fire for God,' then *we* are going to have little success against him."
"Why is that, do you think?"
Tara considered that for a moment. She had pondered this question over and over and always came up with the same answer: "Because they have a defense against the spirits sent to assail them."
"And that defense is...?"
Tara's jaw clenched again. She was starting to feel jittery and weak. She was being backed into a corner and she wanted to lash out. At least something *in* her wanted to lash out. She could feel something stirring. *Shalinar?*

‡‡‡

Karen noticed something going on in her, too. She backed up a step. "Tara?"
"Shut the hell up!" She spat out the words then let out a scream at the top of her lungs! "I hate you! I hate you! Go to hell!" She screamed again, another violent scream that tore at her throat. Her body was racked with a combination of pain and pure, unadulterated loathing.
Karen took another step back. She momentarily felt shaken to her core. She should have expected something like this. "Tara!" she yelled. "Tara, look at me!"
And Tara did. And for a split second Karen felt an ice-cold fear rise up inside of her while looking into Tara's eyes.
She prayed a silent emergency prayer. *Father, help me!*
Karen stilled herself. She took a deep breath and spoke assertively at Tara. "Peace! Be still, in the name of Jesus Christ! Spirit, be bound and muted in Jesus' name!"
Tara's body relaxed and the internal strife seemed to disappear. But Karen knew better than to let down her defenses. This calm could be a deception.
"Tara... Okay. We're going to just put an end to the conversation. Okay? It's all right. We don't have to talk about this right now. Okay?"

‡‡‡

Tara was scared. What had just happened? She had just lost control. Or ... had something *taken* control? She felt unsure and totally off balance. She looked up at Karen.

Dread permeated Tara's as she looked into Karen's eyes for some measure of comfort. This time the fear she experienced was different; different from that of being alone ... different, even, than being attacked by the dark spirits. This was a fear—a foreboding—born of realization.

"Tara..."

"Karen, what's happening? What just happened? What's happening to me?" Tara looked around, unsure of everything, including her surroundings.

Karen approached her. "Shh... Tara, it's going to be okay."

Tara began to shake. Her eyes darted back and forth. "Karen, what's happening?" Tears began to flow.

Karen walked up to Tara and as best she could with the weight of the packs on their backs, she embraced her. "Shh... Sweetie, it's going to be okay."

Tara trembled.

The two of them heard the sound of multiple sets of feet rushing toward them from up the trail. They both turned to see all four of the others running. They had obviously discarded their packs to get here as quickly as they did.

"What's going on? What happened?" came the out-of-breath inquiry from Brent as they approached.

The three men had their machetes in hand, eying the area around Karen and Tara. Thoughts of the wild boar were obviously at the forefront of their minds.

Tara was now realizing that Karen wasn't preventing the group from drawing near as had been the case with Marta. Instead she waved them over in a way that allowed them to know that there was no threat; her facial expression also letting them know that they needed to be sensitive to what was going on just now. Tara choked out a whispered, "Please, don't tell them."

"It's going to be all right," Karen whispered with a comforting stroke to her hair. "I promise."

Brent, Eric, Marta, and Terry quietly approached.

Marta, apparently sensing she needed to speak in hushed tones, asked, "What is it? Are you okay?"

Karen put on a empathy-laden smile. "There's something that needs to be shared."

"No, Karen. Please, don't," begged Tara in a forced whisper.

Tara knew that she was far—*very* far—from her element. There was nowhere to run; nowhere to hide. She was in *their* environment. Whatever was going to happen after Karen shared the news was completely out of her control.

Why was she feeling shame? Why did she not want to look any of them in the eyes? Up until two minutes ago she would have lifted her chin, and with a look that spoke a challenge, announced what she was. But… But now she knew. They weren't greatly intimidated by her power.

"Tara has a confession that she needs to make to all of us," said Karen. Then, whispering into Tara's ear, she asked, "Can you tell them?"

Tara gave a slight shake of her head.

"It's got to either be you or me, Tara. Do you want me to tell them?"

A hesitation, then Tara relented, providing and ever-so-slight nod.

"Okay, gang. I want all of you to say a quick silent prayer, asking God to shower down His love and let it flow through you. Okay?"

Karen obviously didn't see what she'd hoped.

"This is a serious situation, and we're going to need some Jesus on tap. Each of you, please … pray."

They all nodded. Eric, Marta, and Terry closed their eyes and began to silently pray. Brent stood with a questioning glance, but Karen shot him a look that said, *You too*. He closed his eyes.

Tara could see him mouthing a silent prayer. She started trembling again.

Again, Karen whispered into her ear. "Peace, be still, in Jesus' name."

And again, Tara relaxed, letting out a heavy sigh.

When it became evident that they had finished praying, Karen asked, "Eric, Terry, will you help us with our packs?"

The two men came over and helped them to ease the packs off their shoulders and set them on the ground.

Karen approached Tara again and pulled her close with her right arm. She eased her head over to touch Tara's; a sign of solidarity. Tara closed her eyes, receiving what Karen had to offer.

Karen didn't mince words or make any preparatory remarks; she just laid it out before them, without a twinge of accusation in her voice.

"Tara is a witch."

## Chapter Thirty Three

**Tuesday, June 30 – 11:53 a.m.**

All four sets of eyes widened in disbelief.

Brent's eyebrows pinched together creating a stern countenance that communicated a single realization; he'd been played. "You're a *what?*" he said with a bit too much hostility.

Karen spoke up. "Brent, don't." To all four of them she said, "I, too, have a confession to make. Do you know that when you look at me, you see a *former* witch? You might say that, in a way, Tara and I are kindred spirits."

Tara received, she was sure, what was meant to be reassuring a smile as Karen looked back at her, and she felt a gentle squeeze on her shoulder.

*Why is she being kind to me? She should be as ticked off as everybody else.* Tara also knew that if the tables had been turned and she'd been the one conned, she'd have been much more aggressive than Brent had just been.

Marta spoke up next. "So, like by witch, you mean like a Wiccan or something, right?"

Karen spoke for Tara. "Not exactly. We've both got backgrounds in stuff a bit more hard core."

With her next question it was obvious that Marta was searching for a viable answer to the major question plaguing her mind. "Then you've been hanging with us these past couple of months because you've been wanting help to get out of it?

Karen brought her mouth close to Tara's left ear. "Do you want to answer this your own way?"

Again, Tara shook her head.

"Actually," Karen began, "Tara has been infiltrating our little group. She's had an agenda that, well, only she can explain."

Tara looked at Brent. He still had a look of anger and betrayal on his face.

"But it's obvious to me," Karen continued, "that she's been orchestrating a plan to cause some sort of downfall in your life, Brent."

Brent's jaw thrust forward, lips pressed together. He folded his arms, waiting for the rest.

Karen continued. "Apparently she's had it in for Marta, as well."

Tara stole a quick glance at Marta.

Marta stared back. She raised her eyebrows in a way that said, *Anything you'd like to say for yourself?*

Tara remained quiet.

Eric walked up to Brent and whispered something into his ear that Tara couldn't make out. Brent turned to look at Eric with eyes that said, *You can't be serious.* Eric nodded.

Brent looked back at Tara. She couldn't look away from his gaze.

"In case you're wondering," said Brent, "Eric just told me that I need to immediately forgive you. As a follower of Christ that's what I'm supposed to do. But I've got to tell you, Tara. I'm ticked. I don't want to forgive you." He paused, apparently considering his next words carefully. "Do you even *want* to be forgiven by me?"

Eric said, "That doesn't matter, Brent."

Brent raised his right hand indicating that he didn't want Eric's input at that moment. "It matters to *me*."

Karen turned to Tara and looked at her, as if to say, *It's your platform now* and stepped away from Tara's side.

Tara looked down at the dirt path. "I don't know what I want," she said in a half whisper.

"Well, I know what I want," said Brent, "and that's an explanation."

Karen spoke up. "Brent, before you start assuming things and making judgments, I'll remind you of your own testimony."

Brent looked at her, perplexed. "What?"

"Shortly after you and I met, you shared with me your testimony on how you came to know Christ. I seem to recall that you had used the witchcraft that you were involved in to manipulate some of the people you were around. Isn't that right?"

It was Tara's turn to go wide-eyed. "What?" she asked in a soft voice. "You?"

Brent was caught off guard, but wasn't yet ready to concede his right to be angry. "That was different. *This* is different!" he stated incredulously.

"Maybe," said Karen. "Maybe slightly."

Tara couldn't let go of the realization. "You were a witch?"

Brent obviously didn't know how to respond to that. The others in the group were now looking at him to hear more of this improbable revelation. Marta probably knew, but it appeared that Eric and Terry knew scant details of his story.

Brent apparently felt compelled to answer Tara's question. "I guess I was. But I never considered myself a witch."

As it appeared that Brent wasn't going to expound further, Karen continued. "Brent wasn't exactly a witch as Tara and I would describe one." She paused for a moment, as if considering what to say. Then she said, "I remember most of your testimony. Your involvement wasn't a practiced form of witchcraft as much as it was a belief that you had a gift; special abilities that were yours alone. That is until the demons made themselves known to you."

Everyone's attention shifted from Karen and Tara to Brent, and Tara found herself in shock at the revelation.

‡‡‡

It felt like the collar of Brent's T-shirt was constricting around his neck. What was it the Bible said about situations like this? *Don't concern yourself with the splinter in someone else's eye, when you've got a plank in your own.* Brent's plank was feeling pretty uncomfortable at the moment.

Brent knew he had to man up. "Karen's right." He looked directly at her and with true humility he said, "Thank you for helping me remember."

Taking a deep breath, he walked toward Tara. Though he could see that she grew more tense with each step, he didn't stop until he was within arm's reach.

"Tara," he beckoned.

She wouldn't look him in the eyes. His chest was as high as they were willing to travel.

"Tara, look at me."

She shook her head slowly in silence.

"Tara, it's okay. Look at my eyes."

She forced her eyes upward to meet his.

"Tara, based on my own past, I have no right to be angry with you."

"But you want to be," she said just above a whisper.

Brent had to release a small laugh. "I *so did* ... two minutes ago. But, Karen is right about me. My past is filled with trying to bend people to my will. Now that the table has been turned, do I *really* have a right to be angry with you for doing the same thing I did?"

Rage erupted in Tara. "Stop it! STOP IT!" She stepped back from Brent. Karen began to approach her, but Tara wouldn't have it. "Stay away from me, Karen!"

Karen tried to reason with her. "Tara, it's..."

"Shut UP!" Her eyes panned the group. "What is wrong with

you people? You're not *normal!*" Her hands flew up to her hair and began pulling at the sides. She screamed!

Marta took two steps backward on the brink of panic. Eric and Terry just stood their ground. Karen, because she was told to do so, didn't come close.

But Brent ...

Brent felt the peace of the Holy Spirit take control of him. This was God's moment, and Brent knew he was now in God's hands as an instrument of that peace.

He walked right up to Tara. Tara screamed again, released her hair, and brought two fists down like hammers onto Brent's chest.

Brent barely cringed. He took another half step forward and put his arms around her. Her arms were locked in his embrace. He moved his head and brought it to the left of Tara's. Whispering into her ear he said, "Tara, I forgive you."

"No!" she said with a snarl on her face.

"Yes," he softly responded. "We all do. We love you."

"Noooo! Stop it! Shut up! It's a lie!"

Brent whispered into her ear again. "I speak peace over you in the name of Jesus. You lying spirits who are controlling her mind and her body, be still, in the name of Jesus." He could feel Tara's body relax.

"Tara, God loves you. Jesus Christ is not your enemy. He is passionately in love with you."

Tara's body quaked. She sobbed. "It can't be true. It can't be true." She kept repeating the sentence over and over as Brent continued to affirm God's love. Within a few minutes of taking Tara into his embrace she seemed to lose all strength and collapsed to her knees.

She wept. "It can't be true."

## Chapter Thirty Four

### Tuesday, June 30 – 3:07 p.m.

They were all tired and hungry.

After Tara had regained her composure, she quietly resumed the rest of the hike back to the trailhead office, though she would only walk with Karen.

The subject of her witchcraft and her attempts to disrupt the lives of the five Christians had been shelved for now. Tara wasn't in a place mentally or emotionally to give or take anymore. She was exhausted and the remaining couple of miles to the vehicles taxed her even further.

Now that they were off the trail and on the road home, the group decided that gnawing on beef jerky and trail mix held little appeal for the multi-hour trip North. They decided, instead, to stop off somewhere near Portsmouth, not far from the state forest, for something to eat. Long John Silver's ended up being the restaurant of choice for the women, so the men acquiesced.

Loaded up on batter-dipped, deep-fried seafood and hush puppies, they got back on the road for the drive back to Millsville. To Brent's chagrin, the driving arrangements remained the same as they had been on the way down. He really wanted to hear more of what was going on with Tara. But that conversation was reserved for Eric's and Karen's ears, at least for a couple more hours.

Within his own vehicle, Marta hadn't said, "I told you so" yet, but Brent knew she had to be thinking it. He now admitted to himself that testosterone had kept him blind to what was going on spiritually around him, both prior to, and during, the trip. Marta had been right concerning the checks she'd had in her spirit, and he needed to humble himself and acknowledge that.

"Marta?" he said softly, looking to the front passenger seat. To Brent she had seemed deep in thought during the first fifteen minutes of the drive.

"Hmm?" she responded, gazing out her window.

"You were right."

"About?"

"I doubted your misgivings about Tara. You kept making it clear that something was going on, and I just wouldn't allow myself to believe you."

"Oh. Yeah, well... Thanks for admitting that to me."

"Forgive me?"
"Forgiven."
Terry couldn't resist. "Aww... Love birds."
Brent worked to hold back a smile and just shook his head.
Marta let out a small giggle, never breaking her gaze with the countryside.

‡‡‡

Unlike in Brent's Suburban, Eric didn't have anyone riding shotgun. Both Karen and Tara took up residence in the back seats.

The conversation that Eric wanted to hear wasn't taking place. Tara leaned over onto Karen's shoulder, as a daughter might do with her mother. The silence that permeated the cab of the Jeep was needed for the time being.

Eric looked back periodically, using the rear-view mirror, and would see Karen smoothing Tara's hair. At one point he saw her kiss the crown of Tara's head and whisper something to her that he would never be privy to.

Eric prayed.

‡‡‡

Another several minutes of silent driving was getting on Brent's nerves. "So..." he said, "Interesting trip."
Terry chuckled.
Marta was still looking out her passenger window, but nodded in agreement.
"Yeah," she said almost as a sigh. "I was just thinking about what Karen told us to do before she broke the news."
"The prayer?" asked Terry.
"Yeah," she said again. "What if she hadn't required that of us?"
A moment of quiet reflection, then Brent answered, "I'd have blown my top."
"Don't feel bad," Marta responded. "I'd have done the same thing if Karen hadn't challenged me about my attitude and my heart this morning before we broke camp."
Terry just listened.
"Really?"
"Yeah. Really."
"Hmm," said Brent in acknowledgment.
"Did either of you know about Karen's past?" asked Terry.

"Nope. Didn't see that one coming," said Brent.

"Me either," said Marta.

"One thing's for sure," said Terry. "I want to hang out with you people more often."

Brent and Marta both laughed.

*Never a dull moment*, thought Brent and Marta at the same time.

‡‡‡

They had been on the road for about an hour when Tara sat up and began watching the traffic past Eric's shoulder.

She sighed.

"Are you okay?" asked Karen quietly.

Tara shrugged. She didn't think so, but she wasn't sure she wanted to talk about anything yet.

"We love you, Tara," Karen whispered in response.

*That's the seventh time she's said that to me. That's crazy.* She wanted to call Karen out as a liar. But of all the things that Karen and the rest could say, "We love you" didn't sound like something that would escape their lips as a lie; not when they had every right to say "We hate you" instead.

Love.

What did she know about love anyway? Not much. A life built on hatred and retribution left little room for love. In the past ten years, the closest thing she felt to any kind of love was the tie she had with Stephanie. And now she knew that even that had all been just an act.

*How am I expected to believe these people? The last group of people I connected with faked it for the sake of an agenda. What's the agenda of this group of Christlings?*

*Funny ... 'Christlings' doesn't sound as cute as it did just a few hours ago.*

She sighed again. *Christians ... Brent.* She thought about him. He withstood. No other man that she had ever met would have ... or ever did.

Who was she? What in hel... Another sigh. What in the *world* was she supposed to do now?

*In another hour or so I'll be leaving this bunch to... to what? What do I have? Who do I know?*

Suddenly she remembered Shalinar's promise that he'd take care of her in the Otherealm. Was he what Karen claimed? A demon? *Is there anything about my life that isn't blanketed in lies? Is there not* one *person that I can trust?*

A voice whispered into her soul. The words, and the power surrounding them, caused her to catch her breath. She dare not breathe. *"You can trust Me, Tara."*

She was suddenly overwhelmed. Tears rose up in her eyes. Her vision seemed to cloud over as euphoric detachment began to occur. She could hear Karen asking her something, but it was muffled. Muffled in this ... place; this place that she had just entered.

She didn't feel lost. She knew she was still in Eric's car; that Karen was sitting beside her. But it felt as though she was experiencing the intersection of two realities; two existences that converged in this one small space.

She was startled. Her heart began to race. There was another presence here.

Her first mental response was, *Shalinar?*

*"No, child. Shalinar cannot inhabit My presence."*

She felt a tear travel down her right cheek. *Who? Who, then?* Her heart was beating even harder. Her soul latched onto a hope that she'd heard the right words. The words she needed.

"Please," she whispered. "Who are you?"

*"I Am."*

‡‡‡

Karen stared at Tara. She wanted to nudge her. She looked like she was in a...

No... not like a trance.

Something was happening.

Something was happening, and it was ... *holy.*

With that realization she felt the Holy Spirit rise up in her with such fullness that it startled her. Her hands went into the air as she folded herself into the presence of God.

‡‡‡

Eric looked into the rear-view mirror and did a double take. *Huh?* He started to turn around to look, but unexpectedly he felt the Spirit of God come upon him. A feeling of awe overtook him. It jarred him to his core and he couldn't help but begin to worship in the Spirit. Something powerful—something amazing—was beginning to happen.

He had to pull over. He couldn't keep driving. *There ... that closed-down convenience store.*

Eric pulled off the road and parked the Jeep. He rested his

head on the steering wheel for a moment, then he began to weep in this Presence that was just too overwhelming to handle.

‡‡‡

Brent pulled into the convenience-store parking lot behind Eric and pulled to the driver's side of Eric's Jeep. He put the Suburban in park.

To Terry and Marta he said, "I'll see what's going on."

He got out of the vehicle and walked around the front. There was a gap of maybe ten feet between the vehicles as he approached Eric's door.

Eric's door opened and he stepped out, quietly closing the door behind him.

Brent looked at his face. Tears were streaming down. Terry and Marta must have seen, too, because Brent heard both passenger-side windows roll down.

"Eric?"

"Brent..." He could barely speak. "God's doing something." He motioned back to the cab of the Jeep.

Brent looked into the driver's side passenger window. Tara was staring forward, eyes moving left and right, as if trying to comprehend something. Tears were streaming down her face. Karen's hands were in the air.

Brent looked back at Terry and Marta, then back to Eric who fell to his knees weeping. His hands were lifted into the air.

Terry's and Marta's doors quietly opened. They stepped out, not knowing exactly how to respond, until...

All three of them sensed the Holy Spirit's presence. In the humility of the moment, in obedience to the Lord's call, they, too, fell to their knees.

‡‡‡

*But how could You?* Tara couldn't believe the words being spoken to her. *You know too much about me to love me.*

*"My love, I know* everything *about you and still I love you. This is a mystery that you will never fully understand. But know that I cannot lie. My words to you are Yes and Amen.*

*"I made you, Tara. I know the dark places inside where you are afraid to go.*

*"Tara, I love you with an everlasting love. With a love that is greater than you can contain. In Me there is no condemnation. In Me there is forgiveness and hope. In Me there*

*is forgiveness and rest for your troubled soul."*

*Please... Please, don't offer me what I cannot have.*

*"I want you, Tara. May I have you? Will* you *love Me? Will you serve Me? Will you allow My death on a cross long ago be your deliverance?"*

*It's hard, ... God.* She finally admitted it to herself. She allowed herself to fully accept that it was God, Himself, that was making this offer to her.

*Oh, God! Oh, my God! I don't have the words. I can't think of the words. How do I talk with You. I'm not worthy. Oh God, turn away from me. I'm hideous!*

*"Let Me make you beautiful."*

*I'm broken, God.*

*"Let Me make you whole."*

*I'm plagued and filled with impurities, Lord.*

*"Let Me remove your disease."*

*I am so lost, Father.*

*"Let Me show you why I made you."*

Tara was scared. No ... she was terrified. How could anyone survive in such holiness, beside such perfection? How could she be worthy of such offers?

*Jesus ... You* are *Jesus, aren't You?*

*"I Am."*

*Jesus. Forgive me! Forgive me for who I've been to You and to those who recognize You as their God. Please! Oh, I beg You ... PLEASE ... accept me as one of Your own.*

*"It is done."*

Tara looked forward. She blinked her eyes.

The Jeep wasn't moving. Her heart was beating so hard. She reached her hands to her face and felt the tears. She looked down. Her shirt had soaked up dozens of tear drops. She heard a whisper to her right. She turned and looked. Karen was praying; her hands raised.

No, she wasn't praying. She was ... she didn't know the right word. She was ... *adoring* God.

She looked to her left, out the window. Terry, Marta, Eric, and Brent were on their knees adoring God, too.

What had happened? She remembered everything clearly. She remembered every single word.

She grabbed the handle to the door and began to open it. She felt a hand rest upon her right shoulder. Karen's hand. She turned to look at her. She was smiling at her and gave her a slight nod.

Tara pushed open the door. She began to step out and almost

lost her balance. Her legs were weak.

She heard Karen open her door and close it.

Terry, Marta, Eric, and Brent stood up and looked at her.

The tears began to cascade down her face again, as she said...

"He wants me."

## Chapter Thirty Five

### Wednesday, July 1 – 8:00 a.m.

Tara awoke to a new day.

She awoke to a new life! She lay in bed staring at the ceiling. If ever there was proof that she had become a "new creature" as Karen had called her, it was now.

She couldn't remember the last time that she woke up without feeling the dread of going into a new day. Well, dread or the excitement to do something evil. Even then, there was a heaviness; a darkness that followed her out of her bed each morning. *Funny how the darkness isn't as recognizable from the inside. Now that I'm out...*

Tears welled up again. *Goodness! How many boxes of tissues will it be today!*

She was giddy.

She threw the sheet off of her and rolled out of bed. She extended her hands into the air and said, "Good morning, Jesus! I love You!" She said it over and over again. "I love You. I *love* You! I love ... *YOU!*" She laughed and spun around as if suddenly she were a ballerina.

Then she realized... Others might still be sleeping. She cringed.

Last night, after all of the talk of their backpacking adventure and her incredible encounter with none other than *the God of the WHOLE Universe!,* she realized that she didn't have anywhere to go.

Mr. and Mrs. Lawton must have sensed it, because even without asking if she *did* have a place to go home to, Mr. Lawton said, "Tara, it's pretty late. If you're willing, we'd like to invite you to stay the night in Lydia's room."

She had gratefully accepted.

Walking up to the bedroom door she took a robe off of a hook. *I hope Lydia won't be upset that they lent me her PJs and robe.*

She opened the door and quietly stepped into the hallway. The doors to the other two bedrooms were open with no occupants. She walked to the top of the stairs and smelled a combination of coffee and bacon.

"Oh, wow," she whispered.

She used the restroom, brushed her teeth, and grimaced

when she saw her hair. "*There's* something You didn't fix, Lord." She let out a soft giggle as she ran a comb through it. "Well, it's a little better," she sighed.

Walking down the stairs she nearly ran into Brent as he rounded the corner and took a step up.

Startled, they both looked at each other for a moment.

"Sorry," she said.

Brent smiled. "Nothing to be sorry for."

Awkward silence.

"Breakfast is ready," he finally said. "I was just coming up to knock on your door."

"Thank you."

Awkward silence.

"Brent, there are so many things that I need to say..." Her sentence drifted off.

"Okay. But we can talk later." He held up two fingers. "Two things:"

She waited a moment, then took the cue. "And the two things are...?"

"One: I forgive you of everything. And two: I really need to eat bacon, so come on already."

Tara found that particularly funny and erupted into laughter and even snorted; which, then, caused them both to start laughing.

They heard Brent's father say, with a louder-than-needed voice, "Guess he didn't need to knock."

Brent and Tara smiled and headed toward breakfast.

‡‡‡

## Mid-September

The two and a half months that followed were a whirlwind for Tara. On top of the fact that she was still a full-time student, so many things happened that turned her old life upside down.

She started attending church with Marta and the Lawtons. She began to change her wardrobe into something a little more bright. She was reading the Bible that she was given when she made a public confession of her new faith. She and the members of the backpacking group got together again and ceremoniously burned all of her occult materials: books, amulets, tarot cards, horoscope manuals, and many other things. She thought it would excite her to be rid of all of it, but during their burning a strange and uncomfortable physical reaction rose within her. It felt like something inside of her was strenuously objecting. She remembered how nauseated she felt. She covered it up well, though, and made no mention of it to the others.

In addition to all of that ... she prayed.

A lot.

The day after her powerful experience with Jesus, she tried to enter back into the same kind of interaction with Him. And while she could certainly sense His Presence, she couldn't hear His voice the same way she had that previous day. She could feel His love and could sense His encouragement, but couldn't hear His words and it had frustrated her.

Brent later told her that she would probably hear Him as a "still, small voice" from that time forward as she advanced in her walk with Him. He also told her that God had given them His Word—the Bible—to guide them along with a Friend and Counselor called the Holy Spirit, the "third Person of the Trinity."

The Bible had always been the book of her enemy up to that point. She had thought it a book of dos and don'ts; a book full of mythical stories that had no real place in a civilized world. It hadn't dawned on her that many of the writings that she had clung to as a practicing witch were hundreds of years old and full of myth, themselves.

She also had thought the Book would be nearly incomprehensible, with all of the *thees* and *thous* to navigate through. But the translation of the Bible that she received from the church was modern in its text.

She remembered walking out of the "counseling" room and back into the sanctuary of the church along with the other people who had accepted Christ that morning. She walked up to Marta, Terry, Karen, Eric, Brent, and his parents with what she knew was a big silly grin—she couldn't help it!—and showed them her new Bible.

"We're so proud of you!" "Congratulations!" "Welcome to the family!" "We love you!" were accolades that she hadn't expected.

As they had walked out of the church into the parking lot, she turned to Karen and said, "This is a *thick* book!"

Karen had told her that it was actually 66 books, written over more than 1500 years by people, who, for the most part, never knew each other. She said that in spite of the number of people that penned the books and letters, there was not a single contradiction over that span of time; that it was the only book of 'sacred writings' on the planet that had that bragging right.

Karen had then suggested that she not start at the beginning, which seemed a little odd to Tara, but to instead begin reading the New Testament, and to start with the book of John.

That same day, as the whole group enjoyed lunch together at a nearby restaurant, she opened to John and started reading, more out of curiosity than out of intention to actually embed herself within its pages. But the words were like magic to her.

She remembered thinking the word *magic*—or *magick,* in the occult sense—and immediately rebuked herself. Old habits—and old words—were going to be things of which she needed to rid herself.

The words in the ancient text were more like... how had she thought of them? ... more like an infusion of life! The words sounded a little mysterious in the first chapter, which only aroused her curiosity further.

Apparently, as she was reading, food had been placed off the side of her Bible that she hadn't noticed. Brent had nudged her and asked if she was going to eat.

She had said, "I feel like I already am!" She looked at them with eyes of wonder. The group smiled and chuckled. She felt a little embarrassed and said, "I'm sure this is something you're all used to and that it's 'old hat' and all that, but ... wow!"

Eric had responded to her comment. "Never 'old hat'. But when we read it over and over we *do* mostly know what lies ahead. I envy you, Tara. I wish I could go back and experience the Word again as if it were the first time. I remember the affect it had on me, too."

Mrs. Lawton chimed in with, "Tara, Brent's dad and I are still working our way through the Bible for the first time. We're really not too far ahead of you in the knowledge category. That book, for me anyway, has been very challenging. It's like looking into a mirror sometimes and seeing all of the blemishes that need to be gotten rid of." She smiled and absentmindedly raised her right hand to her cheek. "But we serve a good God who takes care of those blemishes in His own time and in His own way. I've read some of the books of the New Testament a couple/few times through, and each time I read, I keep finding things that hadn't struck me the first or second time that I had read them."

The others at the table had nodded in agreement.

Mr. Lawton added, "If you want to read something really interesting, take some time to read the first eleven chapters of the book of Genesis—the first book in the Bible in the Old Testament."

She looked at Karen, who had simply shrugged and smiled, conceding the point.

Mr. Lawton continued. "It will tell you how life started and how everything fell apart. It was important for me to learn that life was meant to be more than it is right now. It'll also tell you where all the different languages and cultures came from. Then you can jump back into the New Testament. Oh! And do you know the account of Noah and the flood? It's in those first eleven chapters, too!"

"Keith, let the girl eat!" Mrs. Lawton declared.

With a light laugh, Tara had then pulled her plate within reach and started forking food into her mouth as she returned to the pages of God's Word. She heard a couple of soft chuckles and she just smiled without looking up. She read, again, John chapter one, concentrating more deeply on the words.

> [1]In the beginning was the Word, and the Word was with God, and the Word was God. [2]He was with God in the beginning.
>
> [3]Through Him all things were made; without Him nothing was made that has been made. [4]In Him was life, and that life was the light of men. [5]The light shines in the darkness, but the darkness has not understood it.
>
> [6]There came a man who was sent from God; his name was John. [7]He came as a witness to testify concerning that light, so that through him all men might believe. [8]He himself was not the light; he came only as a witness to the light. [9]The true light that gives light to every man was coming into the world.
>
> [10]He was in the world, and though the world was made through Him, the world did not recognize Him. [11]He came to that which was His own, but His own did not receive Him. [12]Yet to all who received Him, to those who believed in His name, He gave the right to become children of God— [13]children born not of natural descent, nor of human decision or a husband's will, but born of God.
>
> [14]The Word became flesh and made His dwelling among us. We have seen His glory, the glory of the One and Only, who came from the Father, full of grace and truth.[9]

"Wait!" Tara blurted out, still staring at the words on the page. When she finally looked up she realized she had just rudely

[9] John 1:1-14 – New International Version

interrupted their conversations. She smiled apologetically and said, "Sorry."

"It's okay, Tara," said Brent. "What's up?"

"Okay, it starts off saying that there is this 'Word' and that the 'Word' created everything. Right?"

Several at the table had nodded.

"Then it says after that little number 14, that the 'Word became flesh and dwelt among us.' Is that talking about Jesus?"

"Sure is," said Mr. Lawton.

"Then... wait... *Jesus* is the Creator?"

A couple of chuckles and several yeps and yeses were issued.

"You're telling me, that Jesus, the One that was crucified here on this planet, is the same One who created the entire universe?"

More nods and verbal affirmations.

Terry spoke up then. "And it's not us who's telling you, Tara. It's God's own Word telling you. You don't have to take it from us."

Tara thought for a moment about this new revelation and tears started to well up in her eyes. Softly, she said, "The Creator of the universe..." she swallowed. "The Creator of the universe died for *me?*" It was all she could do to finish the question. Tears fell.

Karen had then put her arm around Tara and the two brought their heads together. "That, my dear friend, is why it's called '*Amazing* Grace.'"

# Chapter Thirty Six

## Tuesday, September 15 – 3:30 p.m.

Marta looked at her watch. Tara's final class of the day should just now be letting out. She was sitting at a table in the Student Union building waiting to have lunch with Tara.

Brent was home sick with a bad cold. *Probably sitting around in those plaid flannel pajama pants and long-sleeve T.* She smiled. *Lord, heal him so he feels better and so we can get together.* She needed to talk with him about a recent conversation that she'd had with Karen.

Karen had told her that even though Tara was now saved, it didn't mean that she wasn't going to have some major challenges soon because of her past occult involvement.

She said, "Tara's enjoying her *honeymoon* with the Lord right now, but as much as she'll want that feeling to remain, I've found that one of two things usually happens with new Christians. One: They begin to get used to the Christian lifestyle, and by seeing what so many other Christians are doing in their walks, she could drift into becoming more of a doer of the Bible than a maintainer of her relationship with Jesus. The second thing is that she could start feeling tugs from the Enemy. The Enemy may have lost her to Christ, but that doesn't mean that the demons won't try to entice her again with things she used to be able to do in her witchcraft past. In fact, there is also a chance that her 'spirit guide'—this Shalinar—is still assigned to her, and may, in fact, still be latched onto her, or even inhabiting her."

"You mean like... You don't mean possessed, do you?"

"No. A true Christian cannot be possessed by a demon, because the Holy Spirit and a demon cannot both occupy the same heart, or core, of a person's being. However, if Tara was anything like me, one of the things that she did to increase her powers over time was to keep inviting the Enemy to enter her. She may have thought she was just calling on her spirit guide, but she was, in reality, giving an open invitation to any spirit that wanted to come in and play."

"So, you're saying that she could still have some of these spirits residing in her somehow?"

"That's right. Understanding that the body is the 'temple of the Holy Spirit' doesn't mean that the Enemy isn't in the courtyard somewhere—which is still part of the temple."

That made sense to Marta. "So, what would need to be done *if* there were still demons in the courtyard?"

"Remember what Jesus did when He went to the temple and found the money changers in there doing corrupt things, causing the worshipers to stumble?"

"He made a whip and drove them out."

"Exactly."

‡‡‡

Tara walked into the food-court area of the student union and saw Marta. *Funny*, she thought, *this scene used to be tainted with hatred as I walked toward Marta and Brent in the past.*

As she drew close, Marta saw her and lit up, waving at her. *God, I love her. Thank You for her friendship.*

"Hi!" said Tara as she sat down.

"Hi! How was Poli Sci?"

"Interesting. I have a pretty liberal professor in that class. I had him for a class my freshman year and I held close to his views on things. I find it amusing, now, how a good dose of truth and reality in my life is causing a shift in my," Tara transitioned into her best male professorial voice, "'political paradigm.'"

Marta laughed. "Something similar happened to my parents when we moved to America. We moved here and saw that real freedom allowed for the voicing of different political views and they shifted from a 'paradigm,'" she said in *her* best professorial voice, "*of having to deal with fear-based militarism* to what in America are called conservative views. They were happy that they were allowed to make as much money as they'd like, spend it how they'd like, and even start a private business without the government breathing down their necks."

"I can only imagine how hard things were in Guatemala." Tara paused, considering whether she should say it or not. *Yep, I have to.* "Especially with all the *gor*-illas."

Marta laughed. "Can you believe that conversation? I about peed my pants when I realized what he thought I was talking about."

Tara laughed, too. Then she suddenly became contemplative. "You know, I hated that I was taking pleasure—from time to time—in the laughter and the camaraderie that all of you were enjoying during that trip."

Marta's smile faded. She leaned forward, folded her hands, and put her elbows on the table, her chin resting atop the back of her hands. "How hard was it, really, to live that double life?"

"Actually, it wasn't. I had such hate for you, Brent, and the others that I didn't consider any true allegiances with any of you. From the moment that I first bumped into the two of you at the student union, I wanted to be trouble for you. The truth is that there are a lot of people that owe me for the stuff I put them through. A lot of them never even knew I was involved in the pain they suffered."

Marta considered her words. "In other words, a double-decker bitch 'n witch."

Tara grimaced. "Yeah. Well said."

Both of them shook their heads and drew in long breaths, letting them out as loud sighs. Looking into each other's eyes, they broke out in laughter.

"Hungry?" Tara inquired.

"Was going to ask you the same thing." Marta looked over at the food court. "The lines aren't too long. Tacos?"

"Actually, I was thinking more along the line of Italian. Serio's? My treat?"

Marta closed her eyes, a soft sound of delight emitted from her throat. She reopened her eyes and said, "You're speaking my language now."

"Isn't your language Spanish?"

"Not today, *il mio amore*."

Tara giggled.

As they were getting up to leave the student union, Marta thought of something. "Can I ask how it is that you're able to afford the life you live? ... and my pasta?"

Tara decided against a full explanation at that moment. "Well, let's just say that the way I got my money is another reason that I had hated God. It's probably a story that you, Karen, and Brent should hear together."

Marta was more curious than ever, now. *It figures that Brent would pick today to be sick.*

‡‡‡

**3:47 p.m.**

"I'm not saying that I felt as if you deceived me. I'm just saying... I thought you would have mentioned it sometime in the past three years that we've known each other." Brent's voice was hoarse from his sore throat and the coughing he'd been doing. He held the phone in his right hand as he reclined in his dad's chair in the family room.

It had been a rough three days being laid up at home. He was going stir crazy, but feeling too weak and lazy to even go sit outside, though temperatures were in the upper 70s. Karen's call was a welcome distraction from the mundane daytime TV shows that he had to choose from.

"In truth, Brent, you are the only one in our close-knit community that I had considered telling. But I felt that if I told you that I would have been deceptive to everyone else."

"I can understand that, I guess. But not one of us was going to judge you because you used to be a witch."

"Okay. Okay. I get that. Embarrassment? The fear of being looked at weird? That I might be shunned... You name it. These things played on my mind. I mean, how many witches do people encounter in real life?"

"In *my* real life? Three! If I can count myself."

Brent could hear Karen stifle a laugh on the other end of the line. "Touché."

"I'm glad you called," Brent said. "I needed someone to talk to."

"About?"

"About? Oh ... no. Not about anything in particular. Just needed the interaction."

"Well, good. I'm glad I could be of service." Karen paused for a moment before continuing. "Brent, I actually called to ask you something. Based on my experience with witchcraft and then becoming a Christian, I was wondering if both of us shared a similar post-salvation experience."

"Talk to me."

"Okay. And this is another reason I don't like to talk about this area of my past. Brent, did you have any struggles or temptations with the occult after you got saved?"

Brent thought for a moment. He'd been pretty much nightmare free since that evening six-and a-half years ago. He couldn't think of any real temptation to do any of the old things he had done. "No, I don't think so. At least none that I'm remembering." He paused. "Why do you ask? Did you?"

He could hear Karen sigh. "I kinda thought you'd say that. As for me ... yeah. I had some terrible struggles."

"Like what?"

"Like waking up in the middle of the night feeling like I'd had a nightmare, but never remembering anything. Times when anger would flare up in such a way that I'd want to strike out at the person who had made me mad. Periodically wishing I could do some of the things I used to do in the craft. A voice inside telling me, 'Go ahead. Just this once. It won't hurt you.'"

Brent couldn't think of a single instance in which he'd struggled like that, except maybe with anger, but not with any sort of real vengeance in mind.

Karen continued. "For the longest time I just thought it had to do with old habits dying hard. You know? But it wasn't leaving me. I mean, a year and a half into my Christian walk and I still felt this overwhelming urge to jump back into the occult. On top of that were the physical things that were happening."

"Physical things? You mean manifestations?"

"Exactly. I didn't know what was going on. Most of the time I was just fine. But when I would get around people who were praying very intensely, some of them engaging in spiritual warfare on another's behalf, I would start feeling sick. Sometimes it would feel like a stabbing pain in my chest or stomach. When I finally couldn't take it anymore, I went to see my pastor. I told him everything that I was struggling with and he said that it sounded like I was being demonically oppressed."

Brent had heard the phrase before, several times, by his own pastor. When he would teach about spiritual warfare and the reality of demons, he'd talk about different types of attacks the Enemy would use in the lives of both believers and unbelievers to keep them bound and ineffective in their Christian walks or to keep the non-believers from being able to hear the Gospel clearly.

"Okay," responded Brent. "I'm following. Your deep practice of witchcraft left some *friends* tagging along with you after you got saved."

"Something like that, yeah. But he told me that with people who have actually called on spirits—demons—to live within them, it's different than what most people who deal with oppressive spirits contend with. He said that because they were actually invited in they had a right to remain in residence, if you get my drift."

"Yes, it's kind of like the Temple illustration that you gave to Marta."

"She told you?"

"Was she not supposed to?"

"Oh, no, it's definitely okay. I just didn't know. Good. I'm glad that you know about that. Did she also tell you that I'm concerned that Tara may have some challenges coming?"

"Yes, she did. And, now that you've told me some of what you've gone through, I'd have to agree. Have you mentioned it to her yet?"

"No, not yet. I need to. But I wanted to talk with you first, to see if you had any similar experiences that might corroborate my belief that she may be in store for a bit of rough road ahead."

"Okay, so tell me... How did your situation get resolved?"

"Brent, it's a story that you probably wouldn't believe. It's hard for me to believe parts of it myself. Suffice it to say that getting rid of my *friends* was no fun."

## Chapter Thirty Seven

**Friday, September 18 – 6:20 p.m.**

Marta and Brent waited for Karen and Tara to arrive. They thought that meeting at the church to talk might be best. It was open and occupied for the first night of play practice so there was no trouble having access. Plus, Pastor Chuck was going to be in the building, too.

Brent had thought it best that Pastor Chuck know what was going on. So, Wednesday morning, before classes, he called the church to speak with him. He asked for counsel on how to best handle the situation.

Should they not say anything to Tara about what may never happen? Would telling her cause her to start second guessing any weird feelings she might have, though none of them were even remotely spiritual in nature? Would giving her heads up be the wise move, just in case demonic symptoms arose?

Pastor Chuck said, “Brent, all of those questions are good ones. However, the one you didn’t ask is probably the most important. What if she starts feeling the draw of the occult again or if she thinks that there is no one that she can talk to that would believe her strange experiences? She might feel like a failure as a Christian. She might be too embarrassed to come to one of you who seemingly have it all together.”

Brent immediately understood.

“Definitely bring her to the church if you can arrange it. You can share with her on your own, but I’ll be there as a backup if you need me.”

“Thank you, Pastor.”

“Brent, one more thing. My son, Pastor Jonathan, he’s dealt with a few cases recently in his own congregation that are very similar to Tara’s. If it comes down to Tara needing to be ministered to in this area, I’m going to ask him to take the lead on it.”

“Okay, Pastor. Thanks again.”

‡‡‡

Tara was grateful that Karen had been up front with her, though she still didn’t know completely what the three of them wanted to talk with her about. Karen would only say that they wanted to discuss some precautions with her as it related to her occult past and they thought that the church would be both a convenient and more appropriate place to get together to talk.

Okay, it was actually weirding her out a little bit.

As Karen turned into the church's parking lot she saw a lot of cars. Surprised by this, she asked, "Why are so many people here?"

"The church is getting ready to start practices for their annual Christmas production."

She looked at Karen. "Like a play?"

"Actually, a full-scale musical."

"No way."

"Yep. Obviously, I've never seen one of their productions, but Brent and Marta say they're pretty impressive."

"Wonderful! I can hardly wait!"

After parking, they walked into the atrium. Sitting at a table near the café were both Brent and Marta.

Tara smiled and waved. Both Brent and Marta lit up. *Shew! Thank God,* Tara thought. *It looks like I'm* not *in trouble.*

After hellos and hugs, Brent suggested that they just stay right there at the table to talk. Everyone was agreeable, though Tara did wish the café was actually open.

Brent asked how everybody was doing. Each shared a little about his and her week, though most of it was already known as a result of being on the same university campus. When the ice was broken, Brent apparently felt compelled to be the one to broach the subject of why they'd all gotten together. Karen interjected that she had mentioned to Tara that it had to do with her prior occult involvement.

"Good," Brent said. "I'm glad this isn't going to come out and hit you from out of nowhere."

"Brent," interrupted Marta, "maybe we ought to pray before we actually start talking."

"You're right. Let's do that."

Brent prayed that God would meet them there, that they would be joined in a spirit of love and caring. He prayed that God would grant them spiritual protection, proper discernment, and that He would give each of them wisdom. He wrapped up the prayer by giving God glory for the work that He had begun, and was continuing to do, in each of their lives.

That's when Tara felt it. An awful twisting in her gut. She grimaced slightly.

Marta noticed. "Tara? Are you okay?"

Tara didn't try to hide it. "I don't know. I'm starting to feel very nervous and nauseated."

Karen took the lead here. "Tara," she began with a look of compassion and a half smile, "That's why you're here." She put a hand on Tara's head and said, "Spirits, be still and be quiet, in Jesus' name."

Tara furrowed her brow in concern. "Okay. The pain and nausea are gone. Are you telling me that they're still in me?"

Karen gave another reassuring smile and said, "That's what we're here to talk about. Was that the first time that you felt what you just did?

"No. It's happened a few times since I came to Christ."

"You okay to go on?"

Tara nodded. She was still feeling nervous, especially now that she knew what the subject matter was going to be.

"Tara?" asked Brent, "How have things been going in your walk with Christ since the day you got saved?"

Tara thought that an odd question, again, considering that all of them saw her on campus almost every day. "Well, things've been great! I love Jesus, and I know that He loves me. I haven't like moved off the narrow path at all. Why?"

"Know this first, Tara. We're all excited for you. We know that your love for Jesus is genuine. There are no accusations here, whatsoever. There is a reason we're asking, and we're going to get to that in a second, but please don't get mad because of the questions. They'll all make sense in a minute."

She looked to both Marta and Karen. Marta's smile spoke of caring. Karen gave her a wink along with her smile, which straightaway made her feel better.

"In truth," Brent continued, "Karen is probably the better person to ask these questions because of her experience. And she's the one who was concerned enough that we get together to talk."

Attention shifted to Karen, who simply nodded and said, "Tara, how have you been sleeping?"

The old, evasive nature in Tara tried to rise up. She initially thought to say that everything was fine. The truth was that every few nights she'd wake up from night sweats. She had initially played them off as the result of bad memories affecting her dreams. But she eventually realized there was something deeper going on.

"I sleep pretty good most nights. Sometimes, though, I wake up in a panic. A few times I woke so suddenly that I didn't know where I was. I couldn't tell you what my dreams were about, just that they had have been bad. Sometimes I have some vague images of things when I first wake up, but like, right now, I can't remember a single one of them."

Karen went to her next question. "How often have you felt sick like you did a few minutes ago?"

"Umm... I don't know. It doesn't happen often. But when it does I get scared." Tara looked at the faces of her friends. "What does it mean? Is there something wrong with me?"

Brent's eyes darted back to Karen as Marta's went down to her own folded hands.

"Nothing that I haven't gone through myself," assured Karen. "It's a common occurrence with those of us who have come out of the occult."

"Brent, too?" wondered Tara.

Brent was both glad and sad that he couldn't relate to what Tara was going through. "My experience was different. I don't know why, but it's like God knew that if He didn't take care of all of my challenges in one extreme act of deliverance, I'd go home feeling like a failure and kill myself. The night that I got saved he completely took away the things that were about to kill me or drive me insane."

"Then why not me, too?"

Tara's question hung in the air for a moment. It was Marta who answered. "I'm the least qualified to talk about any of this. I haven't experienced anything that the three of you are talking about. But I do have experience in relating to people in the areas that God has changed in my life." Marta considered how to proceed. "I was an *extremely* spoiled brat in high school, not to mention materialistic. Being an only child allowed me to guilt my parents into giving me more and more stuff since they didn't give me any brothers and sisters. When I got saved, it was *very* hard to change. I was still an only child and I still wanted what I wanted. But God slowly started to change my heart as I read the Bible and got around other Christians. I started noticing my high school friends with new eyes. The girls that I hung out with were the same spoiled breed, and I started seeing very clearly the whiny, manipulative monster I had been.

"The thing is," Marta continued, "if I hadn't gone through the struggle of change, I wouldn't have been able to help my friend, Lacey, go through it. She came to Christ later the same year I did. Because I could identify with her, I could help her. Everyone else could only watch and pray."

"Yeah," agreed Brent, "that's how I feel now; like an outsider even though I had been involved in the occult, as well. I can't relate like Karen can. She's been through all of this."

Tara understood. Then it hit her. What if Karen wasn't here right now? What if there was no one with whom she could relate at this moment? She looked back at Karen with appreciation in her eyes. "I'm sure glad you're here."

Karen smiled. "Me, too! I love you, chick!"

Tara smiled, too. "Okay, so, if I had to guess, the reason I'm going through this stuff is that the demons that I invited into me didn't leave when I got saved."

"Some of them might have, but the strong man—that's what the Bible calls the ruling demon that controls the rest of them—is still in you. And until you renounce him he has a right to be there. After all, just like I did, you gave an open invitation in order to get more power. Am I right?"

"Oh yeah. Big time." Tara asked the question that she wasn't sure she wanted an answer to. "So, how do I get them out?"

Karen's face became serious. "I'm not going to lie to you, Tara. It's not going to be fun."

Brent interrupted. "You know what? I think that we should have Pastor Chuck answer the rest of this question."

Karen looked at him and nodded. "Definitely."

Brent pushed back from the table and went to find the pastor. A few minutes later he returned with the older man.

Pastor Chuck had a warm smile on his face as he approached the table. It was genuine, Tara could see that clearly.

"Hello, ladies," he said.

The three responded in kind.

"Tara, I'm not going to pretend that I don't know why all of you are here this evening. Brent approached me earlier this week to see if I could help in some way with what you're going through."

Tara was taken aback for a moment. How did they know she was having struggles? Pastor Chuck answered that with his next sentence.

"Brent was working entirely on assumption after a conversation with Karen. We talked and I suggested that you all meet here to talk in case I was needed."

Tara was very aware that all attention was on her. It was making her uncomfortable.

"Brent has already told me that you are having a few challenges, but I want you to know something. This is coming from a man who has years of experience in dealing with spiritual issues. Everything is going to be okay. I can't say that I've had a *lot* of experience with deliverance, but I have had some. And one thing is a foregone conclusion: the demons always lose when the host wants them gone. So, take heart in that."

That last statement gave Tara much-needed encouragement. She took a deep breath, exhaled, and with a look of resoluteness, she asked, "What do I need to do?"

Pastor Chuck smiled. "Very good, Tara." He looked at the chair that Brent had vacated. "May I?"

"It's your chair, Pastor. Literally."

The group chuckled.

"Tara," Pastor Chuck continued, "this is my suggestion on how to make things as easy as possible. Do you know what a fast is?"

"To not eat?"

"That's partially correct. In context, it means to give something up so that you can give the time you'd be using to do that thing to instead focus on God. When Jesus talked about a fast, He wasn't talking about candy or TV—obviously. He was talking about food. He went on a 40-day fast when He was led into the wilderness to be tempted by Satan. Jesus knew that a fast would create discipline and focus and willingness to hold onto the things of God and to fight. A fast can be either a waste of time or it can be used to make yourself stronger as you deny your body what it thinks it needs.

"What I would like for you to do, is consider doing a fast. But first, I want to ask about your availability next week to get together again. All of you."

After a minute of deliberation they all agreed that the following Thursday would work best.

"Thursday it is," agreed the pastor. "Okay, Tara, next Thursday is 'Freedom Day'."

Tara cringed. She felt bile travel up her throat. She swallowed hard to keep it out of her mouth.

Pastor acknowledged her discomfort with a smile that was meant to bring some comfort that he understood. "They've been put on notice and they're not very happy, are they, Tara?"

"Not at all." She attempted a smile.

"Tara, it's a normal part of life that there are consequences that coincide with past actions. You invited them in and they took you up on your offer. Now they want to stay in, and they're going to do all that they can to keep their home."

"I want them out of me."

"Good. That's the first step in getting rid of them. You've got to renounce them." The pastor gave another reassuring smile. "Karen? Marta? Will you lay hands on Tara. We want to quiet these things down for her."

Karen and Marta both got out of their seats to stand behind Tara and lay hands on her shoulders. Brent began to do the same, but the pastor intervened.

"Brent, let the ladies have the only contact."

Brent, slightly embarrassed, stepped back.

"Father, we love You," began Pastor Chuck. "We acknowledge that you are sovereign over all things on Earth and in Heaven. In the name of Your Son, Jesus, we command the spirits residing within Tara to be silenced and to remain still. We take the authority that we've been entrusted with and we bind you spirits with chains that will not let go. We gag your mouths to keep you silent.

"Father, I plead—we plead—the blood of the Lamb to cover Tara. Establish a hedge of protection around her and keep her safe and strong until the day of her freedom next week.

"Thank You, Lord, for the work that You are doing in her life. We are excited about her walk with You and look forward to seeing the things You will accomplish throughout her life. In the name of Jesus we pray. Amen."

The ladies sat back down and Pastor Chuck continued. "Yesterday I spoke with my son, Pastor Jonathan. I told him about you, Tara, and your situation. I hope that was okay."

Tara didn't know what to say, so she just nodded.

"He said that he's available to come into town to minister in this situation. He's had much more experience than I. So has his wife, Jenni. You'll really like her. If it's okay, I'd like to pass on your contact information to the two of them to call you in the next couple of days."

Again, Tara nodded.

"Good. Now, Tara, get into the Word as much as possible. I imagine that you've still got all kinds of classes that you're taking and lots of text books to read, but don't let those things keep you from God's Word. Okay?"

"I won't," Tara said with resolve.

"I know this is scary, Tara. But thousands and thousands of men and women have gone through similar experiences. This isn't something unique. I want you to also be in as much prayer as possible. Stay in an attitude of prayer all day long. Now, the fast that we talked about. I'd like you to fast for at least 24 hours leading into your 'Day of Freedom'. If you think you can manage it, try for 36 or 48 hours. Drink plenty of water, though. When you feel hunger pains, let them remind you of what you're accomplishing. Take that hunger pain and make it a trigger for prayer. Any questions?"

Tara thought for a moment. She had a thousand questions, but they were so jumbled in her mind that she couldn't think to construct a single one, so she just said, "Not that I can think of."

"One last thing, Tara." The graying gentleman smiled broadly. "Get excited. In six days you're going to know what real freedom feels like!"

Tara couldn't help but grin.

# Chapter Thirty Eight

**Thursday, September 24 – 6:21 p.m.**

Tara's salvation and her ensuing struggles led to this night. What would come of it? Brent was feeling edgy; a sort of nervous anticipation of ... of what? He thought back to his own salvation experience. God had delivered him from everything ... *everything* ... in a single night! Was the Lord going to show Himself that big in Tara's life this night?

The ten-minute drive to the church ended with a left turn into a near-empty parking lot. Most of the lights were off in the building except at the main entrance. He saw Marta's and another car already in the parking lot. A car also entered the lot behind him. He couldn't make out the driver's face. Pulling into a parking space the car behind him pulled up beside his. It was George and Cheryl Chamberlin. He knew that Pastor Jonathan and George were close. It shouldn't have surprised Brent that George would have been invited by Pastor Jonathan to help on this night. After all, he'd had his own spiritual problems that were dealt with through deliverance. The drugs and "other" activities in his life had allowed an entrance for his own personal set of demons.

Brent got out of his car and was about to shut his door when George called over to him. "Brent, did you bring a Bible?"

"Yeah, sure did. Guess I need to bring it in?"

"If there is ever a time for a Bible in a church, this is it," George said with a smile.

Brent reached across the driver's seat to grab the Bible sitting on the other side and then closed the door. "Hi, Cheryl. How are you?"

"All prayed up, Brent. How about you?"

"I'm prayed up like a man going to his execution," said Brent with a slight grin. "I've gotta tell you, I'm still a bit nervous."

George angled toward Brent as they approached the entrance to the church and put out his hand. Brent took it and George brought them to a stop. "Brent, this *is* a serious task we're about to engage in, but remember who is in control. Jesus hasn't brought Tara this far to allow the Enemy to get the upper hand now.

"While we've definitely got to be on guard, we've also got to *expect* the victory that is coming tonight in her life. As long as

Tara cooperates she's going to have the experience of her life. She's not going to enjoy the process—neither are we—but I can promise you there will be freedom in the end. Now, we'd better get in there. We've got a very nervous young lady waiting on us."

Brent nodded his head, and with a pat on his shoulder from George, the three of them walked into the battleground.

‡‡‡

**6:23 p.m.**

Brent, George, and Cheryl walked into a room that was normally designated for counseling after altar calls. Brent had seen untold numbers of people enter through this doorway after accepting Christ. Having demons cast out in this room had never entered his imagination.

Standing in the center of the room were Pastor Jonathan, his wife Jenni, Tara, Karen, and Marta. Pastor Jonathan looked up and smiled as the three approached. "Hi, guys… and lady. Looks like everyone's here."

Brent walked up to the small group and took the pastor's extended hand. "Hi, Pastor; Jenni." He let go of the hand and turned to the three girls. "Hi, ladies." Looking into Tara's eyes he said, "How are you doing right now?"

With a squeamish-looking smile she said, "Oh, I just want to run out of here screaming, that's all. Oh … and I want to throw up."

Brent tried to give a light-hearted chuckle at what she had obviously meant as self-deprecating humor.

Marta added, "It's been a difficult day for her. But she's been a trooper. When Karen and I picked her up the only thing she wanted assurance about was that this would be the end of the road for the demons inside her. I told her we were going fight right beside her until every last demon regretted the day it came into her life and was gone. Isn't that right?"

Tara looked into Marta's eyes for the same assurance that she just spoke. Brent could see a twinge of hope mixed with a lot fear. And he didn't blame her one bit.

The three latecomers took off their coats and other belongings and laid them on a couch at one end of the room. Brent set his Bible down and walked back to the group.

Pastor Jonathan took his wife's right hand in his left and said, "Why don't we start things off in prayer. Tara, you're in good hands; I promise you. We're going to give this evening to the Lord, for Him to be in control, for Him to take the lead in all that happens tonight." He extended his hand out to George who took his wife's hand. Marta took Cheryl's, Karen took Marta's and Brent's, and Brent was about to take Tara's when Pastor Jonathan spoke again.

"Brent I'd like for you to change positions with Karen. I'd like Tara to be in the hands of two women during this prayer. No offense, it's just a spiritual precaution."

"Uh... sure," said Brent. Changing places, he took Marta's hand, then Karen's.

Pastor Jonathan then asked George if he would open the evening in prayer.

Brent closed his eyes and heard George's rich baritone voice begin, "Most High and Holy God, we come to You in the matchless name of Jesus, the Christ, our Savior and Redeemer..."

Brent heard what sounded like a wince of pain from Tara. He opened his eyes to see Jenni lean over to her and speak something softly into her ear. Tara's face relaxed and she nodded.

"... This night we come to You expecting Your mercy and power and love to shine through like a blazing beacon, like a lighthouse pushing back the night, producing a great hope of safety in a troubled sea. Holy Spirit, You are Tara's friend. You have taken residence within her because You *want* to be in her. You are *especially* fond of her, and along with her spirit You want to be her body's only other resident. We ask you to prepare the ground upon which we tread tonight, upon which the battle is to be engaged. Jesus, our Mighty Conqueror! Hear us tonight! The battle is Yours! We fight for Your kingdom tonight, for this precious young woman who has accepted Your offer of salvation. Lord Jesus, she has been faithful since that day. She has been fighting these demons the best she knows how. And she is determined that her house, her physical body, Your temple, be rid of them forever."

George paused for what seemed a good sixty seconds. Brent wondered if he meant for people to just start praying as they felt led, but then he spoke again. "Tara, is there something on your heart that you'd like to speak to the Lord right now?"

Brent wanted to open his eyes, to look at Tara. But he didn't want to violate this intimacy should she, too, have looked up at that moment. He heard her begin with a hushed voice. "Uh ... Jesus..." Her voice faltered. "Umm... I love You. I love You. I love *You.*" The first sob broke through. "I ... I'm so scared right now. Please, please, let what these people have been saying be true.

Please, Jesus, rescue me. I need this to work. I so need You to be here for me. Jesus, I know You're real. I've felt You. I've experienced Your grace after all of the ..." She stopped to compose herself. "... oh God ... after all of the horrible things that I've done. Some of them to Your *own people!*" Her voice was getting stronger.

"Father of light, You overcame the darkness in my life. You accepted me in spite of all of it. Tonight, I pledge to You—in the company of my friends—my life. I am Yours. In the name of Jesus Christ of Nazareth, I now renounce every single evil spirit contained in my body, the temple of the ..."

Suddenly Brent heard a thud and a strong vibration in the floor. He and the others looked to where Tara had been standing. She was grabbing her abdomen with her right hand and arm, her other hand was planted on the floor in front of her. Jenni and Marta began to drop to their knees and put their hands on her shoulders. Tara responded by sitting up and getting on her knees. She spoke in a strained whisper, "No ... no ... you're liars! You will *not* win tonight!" She winced again and then looked like she was about to retch.

The rest of the group began to walk toward her and she put up a hand to stop them. "No, I'm okay. It's just my old *'friends'* acting up." Then she looked up to the ceiling and called out, "Jesus, I love *You!* You! I love *YOU!"* She thrust her hands into the air and yelled, "Jesus! I will not allow these ... these *things* to win! Karen told me on the way over here that I need to put fear aside and be willing to let everything be exposed. I need to be willing to let You win this battle for me. I'm Yours, Lord! I'm Yours!" Without warning, Tara lurched forward onto her stomach and began to convulse.

George hit his knees beside her and directed Jenni and Cheryl to help him turn her over onto her back. Tara's back immediately arched, her stomach stretching toward the ceiling. Cheryl brushed the hair away from Tara's sweat-glistened face.

Someone in the room gasped. Exposed by eyelids opened wide in terror were two eyes completely rolled back revealing nothing but white.

Shock and fear permeated Brent's body. His gaze shot upward to Marta, who with her right hand covering her mouth, stifled a scream. Brent was still standing in his original prayer position unsure of what to do. He'd been warned that things like this were likely, but...

"Brent, grab your Bible," said George. "Open it to Psalm 91, verses fourteen through sixteen."

Brent rushed to the couch and grabbed his Bible. He fumbled with the zipper where it had caught the ribbon bookmark. *Great! Come on! There's no time for this!* He finally pulled it past the ribbon and around the cover. Opening the Word he landed in the heart of the Psalms. He quickly found Psalm 91—*Mamaw's Psalm for me!*—and hurried back to the others who were kneeling on the floor. "Got it!"

"Brent, we want to begin speaking life over her. This is a great place to begin. Personalize it for Tara. Change the *hes* and *hims* to *shes* and *Taras*. Understand what I mean?"

Brent looked at the passage and it took hold of what George was saying. "Yes, I understand."

"Okay, start reading it out loud. Be as aggressive with its use as you feel you need to be."

George and Pastor Jonathan laid hands on Tara's head. The ladies laid their hands on her abdomen and began praying. He could hear that Pastor Jonathan was praying in the Spirit as was one of the ladies. Marta was coming to grips with the situation and lent her hand to the mix. Pastor Jonathan took the lead in prayer.

"Father, we first give this situation to You. This is not beyond Your strength and knowledge and wisdom, all of which we call upon now." Then his voice became assertive and powerful. "Foul spirit that is causing Tara to convulse, I *bind* you in the name of Jesus! Release her now!"

Brent saw her body relax for a moment, her back falling flat against the floor. Then with another fit of spasm her stomach arched upward again and a scream escaped her mouth. "AAAHHH!"

"Brent! Don't look, *read!*"

Brent looked at George for a moment then his head cleared. "Uh, yeah. Sorry." He momentarily studied the three Scripture verses and began. "'Because Tara loves Me,' says the Lord, 'I will rescue her; I will protect Tara, for she acknowledges My name. She will call upon Me, and I will answer her; I will be with Tara in trouble, I will deliver her and honor her. With long life will I satisfy her and show her My salvation.'"

In the midst of what was going on, the words of that passage were not lost on Brent. Without being urged to do so, he spoke the Word again with more power, making little changes that he believed would produce an even stronger impact.

"'Because Tara loves Me,' says the Lord Jesus Christ, 'I will rescue her; I, Jesus, will protect Tara, for she acknowledges My name. Tara will call upon Me, and I *will* answer her; I *will* be with Tara in trouble, I *will* deliver her and honor her. With long life I *will* satisfy her and show her the salvation of her God!'"

Again, Brent spoke the words. Again, he changed them slightly, feeling the Holy Spirit fill him and lead him.

"'Because Tara loves the Lord Jesus Christ, she will be rescued! The Savior Jesus Christ will protect Tara, for she acknowledges *His* name. Because she called on *Jesus*, He will answer her! Jesus, the Christ, will be with Tara in this trouble! He *will* deliver her and honor her! Tara's life will be long and Jesus, Himself, will satisfy her and show her His salvation!'"

As Brent continued to read the authoritative Word of God aloud, Pastor Jonathan was taking the authority given to him and wielding it like a finely-honed weapon.

"Spirit, silence! Cease in your activities in Jesus' name!"

Again, Tara's body relaxed. She lay panting on her back, beads of sweat now beginning to run down into her hair.

Pastor Jonathan looked at his wife. "Jen, is the Lord giving you any discernment?"[10]

Jenni was quiet for a moment, praying to hear the Holy Spirit speak a word of knowledge[11] to her. "The strongman[12] isn't witchcraft, or even rebellion. It's rejection." She looked down at Tara who was fully relaxed with her eyes closed.

"Tara? Are you okay?"

She didn't open her eyes, but simply nodded.

"Honey, did you hear what I said about rejection?"

Tara clenched her teeth and nodded again.

"Do you know what might have opened the door to it?"

Tara's response was to stick her tongue out at Jenni. She drew her hand up to stick her thumb in her mouth, but Cheryl gently brought her hand back down to her side.

A male-like laugh belched out of Tara. "Haahaah!"

"Spirit," exclaimed Pastor Jonathan, "I bind you, in the name of Jesus!"

The smile left Tara's face. She opened her eyes and blinked a couple of times. "I'm not liking this," she said softly.

"You're doing great," said the pastor. "Can you answer Jenni's question?"

Tears filled Tara's eyes and she nodded slightly. She

---

[10] Go to Appendix B for biblical information on "discerning of spirits."

[11] Go to Appendix B for an explanation of the scriptural term "Words of Knowledge."

[12] Go to Appendix B for biblical information on the "strongman" and this demon's role in plaguing a person's life.

composed herself before speaking. "My dad..." She stopped.

Marta looked from Tara to Pastor Jonathan. "May I?"

He nodded his consent.

"Tara, you began telling me about your dad. Can you tell me the rest?"

Tara looked at Marta and the tears in her eyes became glassy pools that spilled down both sides of her face. Cheryl grabbed a box of tissues, took one, then wiped away the streams.

"My dad... daddy... left me."

"How old were you?"

"It was just before my thirteenth birthday." She sobbed. "Why did he do it? Why?"

Marta felt the next question was important to ask. "You never spoke with him again?"

Tara's head suddenly craned backward, her back arched again, stomach jutting high in the air. Another hideous laugh. "He is ours!"

Instead of silencing the spirit, the Pastor commanded an answer of it. "I command you, in the name of Jesus, to answer my question truthfully. Who are you speaking of?"

"The witch's father! He's ours," the spirit spat.

Another voice came out of Tara and proclaimed with glee, "I did it! I did it!"

Jenni looked at her husband with mournful eyes and said, "Spirit of suicide."

He nodded.

Brent choked up. "Oh God," he whispered.

The young pastor once again asserted his authority in Christ. "Spirit of rejection. I bind you. I shackle you with strong chains. I command you to be restrained and silent. In Christ's name, I command you. Spirit of death, of suicide, I command you to be silent, in Jesus' name!"

Tara went limp like a rag doll. Again she was panting.

Pastor Jonathan addressed the group. "Okay, we know some of the spirits that we're dealing with. Cheryl, will you grab a pen and paper off of that table over there?" As she got up he continued. "We're going to do our best to determine the hierarchy[13] here. Taking out key characters can cause others to leave without having to be identified. But I want to make sure that any that do reveal themselves specifically are dealt with specifically."

Cheryl was back. "What do you want me to write?"

---

[13] Go to Appendix B for information on demonic hierarchies.

"The strongman is rejection. There's also a spirit of suicide. We know that there is a spirit going by the name Shalinar. She also has at least one spirit of witchcraft. Witchcraft is almost always a follower of a spirit of rebellion, so put that spirit on the list, too."

Turning his attention back to Tara, he asked, "Tara? How are you doing, young lady?"

Tara momentarily pursed her lips then gave a slight nod.

"Okay, I need a little more help. Can you answer another question or two?"

She nodded again.

"Tara, did you have sex as a part of your rituals or to gain more control or more power?"

She delayed in her response, but after a couple of moments she whispered, "Yes."

"Thank you for being honest. It's going to make all of this easier. Don't give in to a temptation to lie. We're all friends here." Pastor Jonathan took that opportunity to look at everyone, making eye contact, to ensure that everyone understood the sensitivity of what was being revealed.

Brent nodded. He noticed others do the same.

Tara cleared her throat and whispered, "Thirsty."

Immediately Karen got up and poured a glass of water from a pitcher that had been brought for this very reason. She returned to Tara and Jenni lifted her head. Tara took the glass in her hand, but it shook too much and water began to slosh out. Karen steadied her hand and helped guide the glass to Tara's lips. She took a couple of swallows. "Thank you."

"John," said Jenni. "I believe there is also a generational curse here."

"Can you be more specific?"

Jenni began to shake her head when Karen spoke up. "I believe the Lord was telling me the same thing. It's like it's..." She shook her head, unable to come up with a concise word. "It's like it's cultural or something."

Pastor Jonathan thought for a moment. "Tara, is there a history of witchcraft in your family?"

"Not that I'm aware of," she responded in a stronger voice.

Karen remembered something; the Triskele tattoo on Tara's right shoulder blade. She looked at the pastor. "Can I ask her a question or two?"

He nodded.

"Tara, your tattoo. It's Celtic, I think. Are you Scottish?"

"Yes. On my mother's side. My dad was part Scot, too."

"How about Stephanie?"

Marta looked up at Brent who just shrugged.

"Yes. In fact, she made a big deal about my heritage when we first met, asking all kinds of questions. At the time it just sounded like she was enjoying that we both had Scottish backgrounds in common." Tara looked up at Karen who was scrunching her brow. "Why? What are you thinking?"

Karen looked back at Pastor Jonathan. "Tara was being groomed as part of a coven. Stephanie was her priestess and mentor. The Celtic tattoo that Tara has is like the one she saw on Stephanie." She proposed an explanation. "A coven of witches with only a certain cultural heritage?"

Pastor Jonathan looked at George who shook his head, not having an answer. "Okay, good. Good discernment, Karen."

He spoke to the group. "It *sounds* like we may be dealing with a form of SRA—satanic ritual abuse. I know Tara wasn't a Satanist, but she was part of a coven that was full of ritualistic, and apparently, sexual practices. Sex is a very effective means for passing spirits from one host to another."

Tara's face showed that she was uncomfortable with what had been revealed about her. Cheryl leaned down and said, "Remember what the Bible says? 'There is now no condemnation for those who are in Christ Jesus.' Sweetheart, don't be embarrassed. Don't give into self-loathing. Not one of us in here hasn't made self-serving, harmful decisions. Okay?"

Tara whispered an "Okay" and gave a slight nod.

Pastor Jonathan went on. "The first thing that we need to deal with is the generational curse. Think of it as a sort of spiritual doorway and container that made it easier for the strongman to enter. We collapse that first, then we deal with the strongman, himself."

Tara began gagging.

Jenni began to turn Tara's head to the right. "George will you help me roll her onto her side, toward Pastor Jonathan?" As they began to move her, Jenni asked, "Cheryl will you grab the towels over there?"

Cheryl moved right away and quickly came back with the towels.

Taking one of them and folding it, Jenni placed it under Tara's head allowing Tara to expel any fluids. Jenni leaned down toward her. "Tara, it's okay. You don't have to fight to keep anything in. We're prepared for this. The less you fight, the sooner you'll be free. Many times a demon will come out through vomiting."

Tara's eyes were closed, but she again nodded.

"Okay, everybody," said the pastor. "Ready to set this princess of God free?"

The seven in attendance around Tara voiced their yeses.

Tara wasn't going to be left out. "Yes. Get'em out."

Pastor Jonathan smiled. "You got it, sister!"

# Chapter Thirty Nine

**Thursday, September 24 – 7:47 p.m.**

The process was labored. The demons were holding on, some of them shouting that they had a right to be there.

Did they? Was there something that hadn't been revealed that gave them something to hold onto?

Pastor Jonathan had halted the attempt to cast the demons out. It was exhausting Tara and they seemed to be getting nowhere. He asked the women to softly sing some hymns over Tara, one of which was "Oh, The Blood of Jesus."

He paced around the room praying for a revelation.

Brent and George were kneeling a little ways off interceding for Tara and the desired end result.

"Father," Pastor Jonathan prayed again, "What are we missing? Please, Lord, help me to hear You. Holy Spirit, help my mind to be quiet enough to hear Your voice." He leaned backward against a bare section of wall. Wrapping his left arm across his chest, he pinched the bridge of his nose with his right hand. *Peace be still*, he thought to himself. *Shh… quiet*.

He was still. He was at peace. His body relaxed. He offered himself to the Holy Spirit as a platform on which to speak. That's when he finally heard Him.

*Pain. Dark and deep. A secret.*

Pastor Jonathan didn't ask for an explanation. Experience had taught him that the Lord always gave what was needed.

He righted himself and whispered to George and Brent, "Guys." He motioned for them to return to Tara. All three of them knelt down again.

Tara's eyes were open and she was showing no ill signs, save for being extremely tired.

"Tara," said Pastor Jonathan in a very caring tone, "tell me about your secret."

Tara looked at him, confused. "What secret?"

"I don't know. The Holy Spirit gave me just a few words. He said, 'Pain. Dark and deep. A secret.' What does that mean to you?"

Tara's eyes began to show signs of panic, darting left and right. Her hands went from her sides and clasped her abdomen. And she screamed!

"NOOOO!!! NOOOO!!!"

The shriek was deafening. Marta and Cheryl covered their ears. Pastor Jonathan was on it. "Hold her. George and Brent on her legs. Marta and Karen take her arms. This is it."

Everyone shifted quickly.

"NOOOO!!! Leave us! Leave us alone!"

"Silence!"

The voice coming out of Tara became very soothing. "We'll take care of her. We promise. We love her."

"I said silence! In the name of Jesus!"

Tara began to thrash. It was all that the Karen and Marta could do to just keep her arms down at her sides. Both George and Brent took to straddling her shins, gripping her knees to hold them down.

Brent exclaimed, "She's so strong!"

"It's not her," said George.

Brent looked at him bewildered, then back down at Tara. His eyes widened.

Pastor Jonathan once again commanded the spirits. "Cease in your maneuvers! In the name of Jesus, release Tara!"

Again Tara's body came to rest like a wet towel. She was panting heavily, hyperventilating.

"Cheryl, give her some water."

Once again Jenni lifted her head and Tara took a long draught of the water. Then another. Cheryl took the glass away when Tara indicated she was done. Tara's stomach tightened and she turned her head toward the third towel that had been laid to the right of her head. She retched and threw up the little bit of content in her stomach.

"Please, make it stop," she groaned.

"We will," Pastor Jonathan assured her. "We will. I need a little more help from you, though. Okay?"

She nodded weakly.

Marta wanted to cry. She hurt so deeply for Tara.

Pastor Jonathan spoke again. "Tara, what was the Holy Spirit revealing to me?"

Her face became a picture of abject misery—absolute sorrow. She tried to draw her hands back up, but Karen and Marta were still holding them down. They looked at the pastor who gave them a permissive nod. When they let go Tara's hands went back to her abdomen again. No one had to ask another question. Her tears and body-wracking sobs told the story.

Her breathing began to stutter. Tiny inhalations, like that of a little girl. She began to weep with such regret that it started to break the hearts of everyone in the room. "My little baby," she said, just above a whisper.

She was now inconsolable. She rolled onto her right side and into a fetal position. She could hardly breathe for the grief that poured from her.

Jenni looked up at her husband, tears trailing down her own face. He gave a small shake of his head, indicating that she should let Tara have the freedom of this moment.

"Oh God. Oohh *God!* ... I killed my baby!" She wailed with such intense grief that the others gave in and began to weep with her.

"Oh God... my little girl..."

‡‡‡

Tara wept for the better part of 20 minutes. No one hindered her. She poured it all out, mourning deeply, with a profound repentance that humbled everyone in the room.

After several minutes of laying on her side, eyes glassy, Tara sat up. She crossed her legs Indian style and positioned her elbows on her knees. She held a wet tissue in her right hand. Her breathing was back to normal. The only discernible after effects were frequent sniffles and a barren stare down at the floor.

Jenni knew it was time to move on. She brushed hair back from Tara's forehead and gave it a kiss. "There's freedom here, Tara. There's compassion with every confession to God. Your baby is in His care." Tara's head went forward some more, chin to chest. "I am not just saying that to try to make you feel better. It's the truth. Know this, too; there is no hate or un-forgiveness in Heaven. Your child will only *ever* love you." She caressed Tara's hair and neck. "Let that settle in your heart. Okay?"

Tara's strawberry-blonde hair wrapped back around to cover her forehead and face as she nodded. She whispered a thank you, then said, "I'm ready."

Brent looked at Tara with eyes of wonder, with such admiration. *She may be the bravest person I've ever known.*

Within a couple of minutes they were in their familiar positions around Tara. She on her back, everyone else strategically placed around her head and limbs.

"You're in the home stretch, Tara," said Pastor Jonathan. "There's nothing left for them to hold on to."

And there wasn't.

Pastor Jonathan decided to cover all of the bases again, just in case. He broke the generational curse over her life, over her lineage. He took authority over the strongman, and commanded him to come out. There was little resistance this time. Tara coughed and gagged and finally, with one large convulsion that arched her back, the spirit of rejection came out with a loud cry.

Suicide was next, followed by demons that represented her years in witchcraft, including rebellion and divination. Unclean spirits were next—spirits of sexual impurity. The demon known as Shalinar resisted one last time, appealing to the friendship he had with Tara before the pastor shut him up and commanded him to leave.

It was difficult to tell the total number of demons that came out of Tara that night. Some of them later estimated between 25 and 30, in all. But regardless of the number, it was finally over.

The end result was nothing less than breathtaking for the few who were blessed to witness it. There were hugs for Tara and amongst one another.

As everyone stood and watched, Tara made her way to the center of the room and knelt. The Presence of the Lord was palpable!

Holiness surrounded Tara—enveloped her. Her hands extended to the heavens as if she might touch the face of God. Radiant love and peace adorned her face, as the last tears of the evening rolled down her cheeks.

It was done.

Her freedom fight was complete.

To Be Continued . . .

*Otherealm: Freedom War*

# Excerpt from Chapter One of

# *Otherealm: Freedom War*

## Chapter One

### 843 A.D. - Pictland (Ancient Pre-Scotland)

### 19 Junius – Approaching Midnight

Drosten ran. He had no choice. What else could he do? He wasn't supposed to see. He wasn't supposed to hear. But he did. All that he could see now were the branches just before they struck his face. All that he could hear was the snapping of twigs and the rustle of underbrush beneath his feet as he ran.

*They are dead! All of them!*

He had to stop and think. He would. But first he had to find a safe place. The river was to the West. If he could make it, he could follow it back North.

His lungs were burning. He had to stop. He had to catch his breath. He ignored the thought.

*I must flee. I have to protect the key.*

Though he tried to press forward, he could no longer take the pain. He'd been running, jumping, climbing at full speed for too long. He slowed and tried to continue by walking, but ultimately he fell to his knees gasping.

He tried to listen. Was he being followed? If his heart would stop hammering in his ears and his lungs would just relax, he would be able to tell.

Drosten, Keeper of the Bridei Key, focused to control his breathing. He stilled his body, closed his eyes, and told his heart and lungs to slow down.

After a few moments he was able to hear clearly again. He concentrated on the woods behind him. He could hear nothing. He concentrated on the high grasses to his left. Nothing.

He lifted his chin and breathed in. A scent. *Water! The river is close!* He got up and began to walk toward the last stand of trees that sheltered the river. Upon breaching the thick woods he released a sigh of relief. He had reached River Tay.

He recognized where he stood. He was at a large bend that jutted eastward before heading back west. He'd been traveling northward the whole time. Good.

Drosten walked to the bank of the Tay and knelt for a drink. The cool water from the highlands relieved his parched throat.

After taking his fill, he stood and surveyed as much of the landscape as he could by the light of the moon. Traveling the river was both wise and difficult. Following the waterways, he would make it from river to loch to river, all the way to Loch Ness.

He was more than a week away from completing the journey before him. But a warrior's allegiance is to his king and his people. And back to his people he would go, because he no longer had a king to serve.

The warrior had no illusions about what had happened. In a matter of just a few minutes the whole world had changed. Drust, king of the Pexa, was dead; betrayed by the Scot, King Cináed mac Ailpin. All seven heirs to the crown were dead, as well. The Scotti may have finally figured out a way to extend their kingdom into the Highlands without another war.

Drosten knew that his king—though barely a year into his reign—was already a beaten man, though the Scot king probably didn't know this. King Drust knew that the only chance that they had to keep their lands was to bargain for peace and to combine their strength with that of the Scotti to defeat the Norse. These raiders from a distant land—these "Vikings"—with their long boats were siphoning away the remaining strength of both kingdoms. When the Scot king sent messengers to Loch Ness to actually propose such an alliance, King Drust breathed a sigh of relief and Drosten had seen hope come back into his eyes.

But now...

The keeper of the key closed his eyes, replaying the events in his mind. He would be required to give detail of what he had seen and why he was the lone survivor of Cináed mac Ailpin's betrayal.

The open grounds of Scone had been selected by both parties as an appropriate site to negotiate a treaty of peace. It had been the heart of the Pexa kingdom several times in their history. It was an ancient place, full of legend; a place that Drosten had always hoped to visit. Now it was a place of agony that he wished he'd never seen.

When the plans had been made to head to Scone, King Drust made it clear that he had no intention of a permanent treaty with the Scot king. He knew that combining the forces of two kingdoms to defeat the Norse would ultimately leave just the one enemy to contend with, and if the treaty between the Pexa and the Scotti held after the war, it would allow for a period of peace, allowing the Pexa armies to heal and grow strong again.

Drust, along with the seven Earls—the remaining heirs to the

Pexa crown— had accepted the invitation to meet with King Cináed mac Ailpin. The royals from both sides of the conflict agreed that they would enter Scone unarmed.

The time that it took to arrange for the seven royal houses to come together for travel and the additional time that it took to actually reach Scone, allowed the Scotti to set a devilish trap.

‡‡‡

**Present Day**

There are certain things a man tries to forget ... things that a man sees only out of the corner of his eye; things that speak to him only in the silence of a darkened room ... things that make him afraid.

He was reminded, again, of an old Scottish prayer that he'd memorized long ago...

From ghoulies and ghosties
And long-leggedy beasties
And things that go bump in the night,
Good Lord, deliver us!

This was more than a bump in the night, and he had hoped he would never deal with *anything* like this again.

## Author Notes on Book Two

In this sequel to *Othrealm: Freedom Fight,* twenty-four years have passed since best friends Brent Lawton, Marta Rosales, and Karen McLaughlin, had their lives rocked and changed through an encounter with Tara Baker, a black witch who was bent on their destruction.

Brent has remained in his hometown of Millsville, Ohio. A police officer now, he raises his family of five within the suburban community that he has been hired to protect.

Not all is well, though. A number of individuals, who have been keeping their fingers on the spiritual pulse of the surrounding area, are now having premonitions.

Something is coming; something evil.

Re-enter Picti High Priests, Brendan Cadeyrn and Stephanie O'Leary. They have finally pieced together the fragments of a culture and religion once so powerful that it had kept the mighty legions of ancient Rome at bay. It is their intention, along with several hundred followers, to reclaim that religion, and along with it, its power. No one will be permitted to stand in opposition to their plan to unleash an evil that has lain dormant for over a thousand years.

Yet a single family *will* stand. They will confront the darkness and put their own lives on the line for the sake of their God, their community, and each other.

With a twist that few will see coming, dive deep into the story of one family's "furious love" for a mortal enemy bent on their destruction.

Can God's love win in the belly of such darkness where its practitioners want nothing to do with Him?

Find out, as you journey again into the *Otherealm* and engage in a war that could one day be your own!

***Freedom War***

**Frank Lattimore** is a graduate of Kent State University, with a B.A. in Political Science. He is an Independent Business Owner, specializing in nutritional supplementation, physical endurance, and skin care. He's active in his "Rockin" church and in his free time enjoys hiking, biking, ziplining, fishing, riding roller coasters, target shooting, and eating crispy BBQ wings.

## Acknowledgments

Thank-yous go out to several people who have been a real blessing in my writing:

**The Three-in-One** - Sometimes I am both humbled and amazed at the capabilities that You have given to me. While I haven't enjoyed all of my experiences in life, I have at least come to value most of them, because You have turned them around for my benefit and the benefit of others. Thank you for the talent that You have given me to write these stories—and the ones to come. I would say that I appreciate You more than You know, but since You know everything...

**Kevin Kaiser** - My first novel rejection came from an all-around good guy. Thank you for pointing me down the right editorial path.

**Allison Chamberlain** – A wonderful gal who contributed a lot of her editing talents in the beginning stages of this book.

**Lori Taggart** – My new friend and final draft editor. Thank you for volunteering your talents to my projects and making them worthy to present to the final decision makers.

**Lindy Stein** – A friend who lent a lot of excitement to my writing. I'd write and you'd respond with excitement.

**Robert Liparulo** – A friend and incredible author. I appreciate the amount of time that I got to spend with you at The Ragged Edge in 2011. Your insights prompted the writing of two novels, rather than a single very long one. Your willingness to provide me with additional wise counsel over the past couple of years has been priceless.

**Tammy Norwood** – My biggest critic and a wonderful friend. You were methodic in the picking apart of my novel. It wasn't easy having my creation poked and prodded, but it was your honesty that caused a more worthwhile end product.

**Mark Russell** – My brother-in-law and all-around great guy. You were also someone willing to give much-needed structural criticism.

**Michele Atwell** – Someone dear to me who emerged from my past. You became my greatest cheerleader.

**The Ragged Blue Monkeys** – Yes, they exist! You are the single-most encouraging group of animals I've ever met. Blue Monkeys in a Brown-Monkey world.

**Ted Dekker** – Someone I've admired from afar for a very long time. Several phone conversations with you inspired a writer. Your Ragged Edge event solidified one.

**Tosca Lee** - Thank you for being someone who is open about who she really is, flawed and perfect at the same time. Those qualities, adjoining your ability to shape words into sentences, and sentences into intricatc prosc, arc hclping me to become a better writer. I appreciate the time I've had in your presence.

**The Reid Art Consortium** - **Angela Reid**, your ability to capture a picture and manipulate its structure provided for some incredible ideas for the cover art. **Hanna Reid**, your ability to be both beautiful and "mean" at the same time created the atmosphere that I wanted convey on my cover. **Megan Reid**, your skills with digital graphics created a finished product of which you should be very proud. Thank you--all three of you--for the time you dedicated. I'm honored to have your contributions!

**Christy Brothers** - A wonderful friend & photographer, who, early on, prompted some needed manuscript adjustments.

# Appendices

## Otherealm – Appendix A

**Footnote 1:**
"Hello, Brent" - Multiple Personality Disorder vs. Demonism

First, let me say that I am not an expert in all things occult, nor do I claim to have a lot of knowledge about inner workings of the human psyche. I do, though, have enough experience in dealing with the "spirit world" to know the difference between mental illness and what I went through as a youth, much like Brent Lawton. I also have experience in dealing with others who have had demonic issues while practicing, and after coming out of, the occult.

A few years ago I wrote an article for an online publication. I called it *The Demonization of America*. Obviously a play on words, but the point I was making was that Americans (Westerners in general) have advanced amazingly far in terms of medicine and technology. We are a "civilized" society that has turned to a more naturalistic observation of life. As a whole, we have naturalized all things that we don't understand, leaving out any possible explanation from the spirit realm. Unfortunately, this is applicable nearly as much to Christians as to our agnostic and atheist friends.

Let me ask you a question. From the time that Jesus walked the earth to today, how many fewer demons and angels are there? The obvious answer is that there are no fewer than were originally created. The Word does say there are some that are bound in the pit awaiting judgment, but understand that that was written in the New Testament of the Bible. And that means that those demons that were *not* bound and continued roaming the earth affecting people's lives at the time of the apostles Paul and John (the Revelator), are still with us today.

Let me ask you another question. Over the past two thousand years, have all of the demons stayed in the area we now call the Holy Land? The answer is no. So where are they? Do they only reside in Third-World countries? Or is it possible that these fallen angels, these harassers of mankind, are global in their reach?

Today, because of how our country has naturalized all things wrong with the human mind/soul/spirit, we've given medical "reasons" for why people act out the way that they do. The Word of God, though, makes it very clear that demons are going to continue hindering people from coming to Christ until the end of the age. If that is so, then demons are all too willing to hide from sight while they cause people to live with many types of afflictions: Multiple Personality Disorder (MPD) a.k.a. Dissociative Identity Disorder (DID), Schizophrenia, Manic Depression, Suicidal Tendencies, Phobias, Panic Attacks, God Complex, etc.

Let me qualify things here a little bit. There *are* mental disorders that are based on completely physical origins. A person can be chemically/clinically depressed. There are stresses that can cause a person's mind to "collapse", and there are some coping mechanisms that can kick in to help an individual separate from traumatic life situations. I personally believe that these are the exceptions, though. And, though I believe that these are exceptions, I am not willing to assign a percentage to how many are spirit-based versus natural/physical-based.

Dr Haraldur Erlendsson—whom I believe to be a naturalist—in his research paper, 'Multiple Personality Disorder - Demons and Angels or Archetypal aspects of the inner self,' comes to this conclusion:

> When alter personalities are asked about whom they believe they are, they say they are: children (86%), helping spirits (84%), demons (29%), another living person (28%), dead relatives (21%) and a person with opposite sex (63%). The two largest case series that have looked into this are by F W Putnam (1986) who described 100 cases and C A Ross (1989) who described 236 cases. Even though the majority of alters claim not to belong to the individual the prevailing opinion is that these are in fact parts of the individual.[14]

When the voices coming out of an individual are calling themselves spirits and demons, the medical establishment puts the patient on medication to control his delusions. Jesus and the apostles cast them out. One is a constantly "managed" disease/disorder, the other is a cure.

Based on my experiences, and those of others that I've had

[14] 'Multiple Personality Disorder - Demons and Angels or Archetypal aspects of the inner self,' Dr. Haraldur Erlendsson ©Haraldur Erlendsson 2003 http://www.rcpsych.ac.uk/pdf/erlendsson_01_jun_03.pdf

the opportunity to speak with who have had similar experiences, I can conclusively state that demons are alive and well in the United States. They are willing to be overlooked as long as they can keep the focus of the "sick" individual off of God. If it's a medical situation that can be managed by a pill, why trust in a God or give credence to a devil?

***To continue reading the novel turn back to page 17.***

**Footnote 2:**
Effective Prayer:

Scripture tells us that we should "pray without ceasing" (1 Thessalonians 5:17), and that "the effective, fervent prayer of a righteous man avails much" (James 5:16). To pray without ceasing really means to maintain an attitude of prayer all day long, not that you've necessarily got to be praying the whole time. But if you've got a relationship with the Lord that is close (not based on doing, but based on intimate love with your Creator), then you are in a position to hear the Lord when He calls you to pray. And when we've got something to pray about, it's not enough to just toss up a prayer for a few seconds and then complain when the answer doesn't come.

*Prayer sometimes means work!* It means *pressing in* to God's Presence. Coming "*boldly*" before Him and remaining there in the throne room until He moves on our behalves or on the behalf of the individual that we are praying for. The parables of the Unjust Judge (Luke 18:1-8) and the Friend at Night (Luke 11:5-8) show that it is persistence that pays off.

***To continue reading the novel turn back to page 19.***

## Otherealm – Appendix B

**Footnote 3:**
Tara's items for ritual spellcasting:

A **grimoire** (pronounced /ɡrɪmˈwɑr/) is a textbook of magic. Such books typically include instructions on how to create magical objects like talismans and amulets, how to perform magical spells, charms and divination and also how to summon or invoke supernatural entities such as angels, spirits, and demons. (From Wikipedia)

An **amulet**, similar to a **talisman** is any object intended to bring good luck or protection to its owner. (From Wikipedia)

A **pentagram** (sometimes known as a **pentalpha** or **pentangle**) is the shape of a five-pointed star drawn with five straight strokes. The word *pentagram* comes from the Greek word *pentagrammon*, a noun form of *pentagrammos*, a word meaning roughly "five-lined" or "five lines".

Pentagrams were used symbolically in ancient Greece and Babylonia, and are used today as a symbol of faith by many Wiccans, akin to the use of the cross by Christians and the Star of David by Jews. The pentagram has magical associations, and many people who practice Neopagan faiths wear jewelry incorporating the symbol.

Satanists use a pentagram with two points up, often inscribed in a double circle, with the head of a goat inside the pentagram. This is referred to as the **Sigil of Baphomet**. They use it as a connection with Tartaros, which literally translates from Greek as a "Pit" or "Void" in Christian terminology (the word is used as such in the Bible, referring to the place where the fallen angels are fettered). The Hebrew letters ל ן י ח ך form the name Leviathan as in Tara's pentagram (right). (From Wikipedia)

A **casting cloth** or altar cloth is used in ceremonies to aid in the conjuring and casting of spells. Typically the instruments of the witch's spellcasting rest on or around it. Tara's casting cloth contains the pentagram above.

***To continue reading the novel turn back to page 89.***

**Footnote 4:**

Pastor Jonathan's sermon on "The Ten Virgins & The Wedding Feast of the Lamb":

"This is a subject that cannot be empirically defined. The matter is, in many ways, subjective, but only from the standpoint of mankind. God knows exactly what He's going to do. And when the Rapture takes place most of us will slap ourselves on the forehead with an 'Ohhhh ... *that's* what the Bible meant!'" He then mimicked a slap to his own forehead.

The congregation chuckled again now that the mood had been lightened a bit.

"I wanted to make the point that you cannot make yourselves good enough for Heaven. But—and this is a massive 'but'—you *do* need to make yourselves right for the Wedding and Wedding Feast of the Lamb. Jesus has bought your ticket into Heaven by what He did on the cross, but as we're about to find out, the Rapture and the Wedding Feast are up to the Christian.

"As Christians we can live our lives one of two ways: 1) as believers outside of intimacy with Jesus Christ. 2) as believers *in* Christ with a relationship *based* on intimacy. There is a whole lot of difference between the two. I believe that in either situation you will make it to Heaven, but I also believe, based on the parable of the ten virgins that we're about to look at, that the ones who don't have a genuine relationship with Jesus—who are not living expectant lives and being a light in the darkness—may be left behind when the Rapture takes place.

"Usually it makes sense to share a parable first, then to exegete for the meaning. But I find that sometimes a little shock value pulls us into the parables a little better."

Pastor Jonathan began to flip through his Bible. "Okay, everyone take a deep breath and let it out. *Relax,* people! You look all uptight!" Laughs and a lot of deep sighs could be heard throughout the sanctuary.

"Okay, those with Bibles, turn with me to the gospel of Matthew, chapter 25, and follow as I read. These words are straight from the mouth of the Savior:

'Then the kingdom of heaven shall be likened to ten virgins

who took their lamps and went out to meet the bridegroom. Now five of them were wise, and five were foolish. Those who were foolish took their lamps and took no oil with them, but the wise took oil in their vessels with their lamps. But while the bridegroom was delayed, they all slumbered and slept. And at midnight a cry was heard: Behold, the bridegroom is coming; go out to meet him!' Then all those virgins arose and trimmed their lamps. And the foolish said to the wise, 'Give us some of your oil, for our lamps are going out.' But the wise answered, saying, 'No, lest there should not be enough for us and you; but go rather to those who sell, and buy for yourselves.' And while they went to buy, the bridegroom came, And those who were ready went in with him to the wedding; and the door was shut. Afterward the other virgins came also, saying, 'Lord, Lord, open to us!' But he answered and said, 'Assuredly, I say to you, I do not know you.' Watch therefore, for you know neither the day nor the hour in which the Son of Man is coming.'

Moving away from the lectern, Pastor Jonathan began to preach in earnest. "Notice that all ten are virgins, and all ten are waiting for the return of the Bridegroom, whom we know to be Jesus. So, we can gather that all ten are believers. We also see that all ten fell asleep due to the delay of the Lord's return for them. The only difference between the five wise and five foolish virgins is preparation for the delay.

"Maybe all of them were tired from service to the Lord, making preparations for the feast and the wedding. Maybe they all deserved to have a good rest while waiting for the Bridegroom." He began to walk back and forth along the edge of the platform as he continued to speak. "So, all ten virgins fell asleep, but the foolish virgins fell asleep with a different mindset than the wise. My guess is that they grew tired of the start again / stop again of waiting for the Bridegroom to fulfill His promise to come for them. Imagine them thinking, "Yeah, yeah, we've heard it many times before, but He's never shown. What makes you think this time is any different?'

"The wise virgins, on the other hand may have responded with, 'He *is* coming back. It doesn't matter how many times we're disappointed with further delays, we're going to be ready.'

"Let me ask you, family, are you getting distracted to the point where the Wedding Feast and Heaven are not prevalent on your mind? Are you putting things before God on your priority lists? Paul instructed us to keep our minds 'on heavenly things.' Are you doing that?"

Pastor Jonathan paused for a moment before continuing.

"What is the price for allowing yourselves to be distracted by all of the sparkly things that the world has to offer? Do you understand that 'the earth is the Lord's and everything in it'? That means that for those of us who go to Heaven, we're not going to be losing anything, because Jesus is going to restore this earth to its pre-Fall condition. We'll get all the sparkly things, and then some. But the priority now, here on this fallen planet, is people. It is people and *your* relationships with Christ. It is having a heart for the lost and eyes fixed on Jesus.

"The benefits are unfathomable when you're heart and mind are fixed on Jesus and on the lost that need Him. You store up wealth in Heaven by focusing on what Jesus focuses on; and that *what* is really *who*. Two people are losing out when you're distracted by the world's priorities: the person going to hell and the person you stare at in the mirror.

"'Where your treasure is, there your heart is also,' said Jesus. Make your treasure people *and* your relationship with Christ. The result for those who do not do this is going to be emotional devastation.

"As we've read—and I'm going to put this all in the future tense now—the foolish virgins will come pounding on the door of the Wedding Feast of the Lamb after having finally gotten themselves right. But, after the Rapture takes place it will be too late to call for entry. You will be stuck here with all of the rest of the lost to endure the tribulation period that is described in both the Old and New Testaments.

"What percentage of the total virgins did the five foolish make up?"

Several voices perked up with shouts of "Half!" and "Fifty percent!"

"Fifty percent," said the pastor. "Those of you who said half were pretty close."

Laughter and ribbing dominated the moment.

"Listen, folks, I'm not trying to scare you into right relationship with Christ, and I'm not saying that you can't enjoy life and have fun. After all, Christ came to 'give us life, and life abundantly.' So, go to an amusement park, go to a shooting range, go to sporting events. Take some time to relax. Enjoy the freedoms and the joy of the Lord. What I *am* trying to do is coax you to reevaluate your priorities in this life. If this message scares you into that frame of mind, so be it. But know that I'm not a preacher of fear. I'm a preacher of hope! And the hope of which I speak comes from intimacy with Jesus Christ, the Father, and the Holy Spirit; each one of them the same God, each one of them an individual person. Get to know all three intimately.

"Okay, now, here's the tricky part to the parable of the ten virgins: I'm going to try taking a stab at this, but let me first reiterate two things: First is my belief—my guess—that all ten virgins represent born-again Christians. My second guess is that those with the wrong mindsets toward the delay of the Bridegroom aren't going to be taken into the Wedding Feast of the Lamb—the greatest celebration that will have ever taken place, up to that point.

Pastor Jonathan raised his left hand to his mouth as if to contemplate his next words, then dropped his hand to his side. "Okay. Now, the tricky part: Notice what is *not* in this parable, but is in other parables; a phrase that says something to the effect of, 'Now depart from Me cursed ones into everlasting fire where there will be weeping and gnashing of teeth.' My assumption is that the five foolish virgins did not—will not—lose out on Heaven, but they are not going to be recognized by the Bridegroom as having a right to the celebration; hence the phrase in verse twelve 'I do not know you,' which could be translated as 'I don't recognize you,' or 'I don't recognize you're right to be here.'"

Pastor Jonathan walked down from the platform to the main floor. He walked a few steps up into the aisle on which Brent and Marta sat and continued. "Listen, folks, after hearing what I've shared so far, your guess is as good as mine. On the one hand, Scripture makes it very clear that the Enemy cannot snatch you out of the hands of God. You *are* secure in your salvation. But there is nothing in Scripture that indicates, at least to me, that every single one of us who is born again will be caught up to meet the Lord. So, for those who are indifferent about the Rapture, those who want to go do something else because He's delayed too long, it's time for a checkup from the neck up.

"I think that to have a celebration feast means to have something to celebrate. The celebration is as much about you 'enduring to the end' of the Lord's delay as it is about the consummation of your relationship with Christ. So here's what I'm going to leave you with: Get your walk right. What in your life is so doggone important that it's worth sacrificing the Wedding Feast of the Lamb for it?

"You may ask, 'Pastor Jonathan, what if Christ doesn't come back until after I die, and I wasted all this time focusing on the Rapture and on Heaven?' And if you do ask me that, I may very well pop you on the forehead."

A hearty laugh erupted from the congregation.

"You can never waste time keeping your mind on heavenly things. You will never be anything but blessed because of it. You can hardly go wrong while looking to the source of your hope and strength. Amen?"

"Amen," came the response of the crowd.

"Now, please understand, I'm not talking about you going out and getting all legalistic and becoming so works based that you're no good to anyone. I'm talking about all of you pressing into a deeper relationship with the King of all kings, the Lord of all lords, the Creator of all that exists. This Man, Jesus, who is also Yahweh-God, loves you with a passion. Love Him back. Talk with Him. Discuss your day with Him. Share your joys and your sorrows with Him. In other words, make Jesus your Best Friend and your First Love. Get *intimate* with Him. You will not regret it here, and you certainly won't regret it when you've been accepted into the wedding feast."

***To continue reading the novel turn back to page 143.***

**Footnote 5:**

The authority of the name of Jesus Christ:

Acts 4:12 says, "Salvation is found in no one else, for there is no other name under heaven given to mankind by which we must be saved." That is the greatest explanation of the power of His name. The reason that no other name can save is that the name of Jesus represents one of the co-equal persons of the Trinity. According to the book of John, chapter one, Jesus, "The Word," is the Creator of all things, including all of the angels. This includes Lucifer before he was cast out of heaven with one third of the angels that followed him into rebellion. As the Creator of all things, Jesus' authority reigns supreme. All powers will one day bow to His name, but until that day, all demons are still subject to the authority of Christ's spoken name. One thing to make clear is that Christ's authority is His own. He allows us to use it as representatives of His kingdom. Wielding that authority is something that is your right as a child of God. However, we are warned about picking fights with demonic powers with an example: Jude 1:9 says, "But even the archangel Michael, when he was disputing with the devil about the body of Moses, did not himself dare to condemn him for slander but said, 'The Lord rebuke you!'"

If the Archangel of the Lord will not pick a fight, don't think yourself wise to do it yourself. Respect the use of the name of the Lord. Use your authority to rebuke the Enemy wisely. Spiritual Warfare is certainly not a game.

That said, the authority of the name of Jesus can not only be used to mute, rebuke, and cast out demons (and people), but also for physical healing. Search the Scriptures and find out how the apostles used the authority given to them in, and with, the name of Jesus!

***To continue reading the novel turn back to page 160.***

**Footnote 6:**

A brief history of the Picti people:

Information on the Picts, the "barbarians" who so often ravaged the Britons from the north, is somewhat scarce. The only text left to us by the Picts is their king-list, which gives the names and the lengths of the reigns of 60 or more Pictish kings. The list ends with Causantin mac Cinaeda, who died in 876. Thereafter, this record of the Picts was no longer used. The only other written source from around the Arthurian era is Adomnan's Life of Columba. Archaeological evidence for their lifestyles is also scarce.

The domain of the Picts was what we consider today to be Scotland. The terms "Picts" and "Pictland" were used in speaking of the inhabitants and the area up until 900, when the country began to be called "Alba."

The Picts had a warrior society, "and warlords needed strongholds. When Columba visited the Pictish king, Bridei, son of Maelchon, in 565, he went to one of the royal fortresses; it was 'near the river Ness' and the most widely accepted identification is Castle Urguhart on Loch Ness... where the medieval castle overlies earlier occupation..." (Nicoll 23) Several Pictish forts have been excavated, revealing that the warlords lived in style, wearing great silver chains and beautiful jewelry. A Pict's life was not altogether different than that of his southern Celtic neighbors; they all spoke a very similar language, as the Pictish language is convincingly argued to have been P-Celtic or Brittonic.

Some archaeological information comes from uncovered Pictish hoards (prior to safe-deposit boxes and banks, a method used to protect valuables was to bury them; inevitably, some remained unclaimed). Brooches and dress-pins have survived from these hoards. The absence of grave-goods, indicating that the Picts did not think much of the practice of burying valuables with the dead, "presumably has implications for their pagan concept of death" (Nicoll 25).

Small painted stones used as charms, distinctively Pictish, have also been found.

For an exhaustive bibliography and a small over-view of the Picts, as well as a continuation of the information on this page, check out A Pictish Panorama: The Story of the Picts and a Pictish Bibliography, edited by Eric H. Nicoll, printed by Pinkfoot Press in 1995.

Taken directly from: http://www.eons.com/groups/topic/1111219-Picts?page=1

***To continue reading the novel turn back to page 163.***

**Footnote 7:**

The "still small voice":

It would be wonderful, albeit terrifying, if we could hear the very voice of God with our own ears. Though God certainly reserves the right to speak with an individual in that manner, He has made it clear that we would have the counsel (what Brent is encountering at this moment), companionship, and friendship of the One that Jesus called the "Comforter" or "Advocate" (John 16:7). Also, Jesus said, "But when the Father sends the Advocate as my representative—that is, the Holy Spirit—he will teach you everything and will remind you of everything I have told you" (John 14:26).

The Holy Spirit, living within us, may prompt you to do something; He may put a check in your spirit so as to prevent you from doing something, but He may also, when you are quiet in your spirit—while enjoying or pressing into His presence—whisper something to you. In that moment, you recognize the words, but you know that you didn't hear them audibly; you just *know* that the Lord has spoken to you (1 Kings 1:11-13). That is the "still small voice" of God. I find it interesting that God, Himself, tells us to "be *still*, and know that I am God" (Psalm 46:10).

It is my personal opinion that the Lord speaks to us often through His still small voice, but we are so caught up in distractions that we often don't hear what He has to say.

But if you put aside distractions in order to hear, or call on Him to speak and actually listen, you may just find that the voice of the Holy Spirit will calm your fears or give you strength or even move you to do a good work.

If you are willing to spend enough time with God—in relationship, not in "doing" or "not doing"—you can become sensitive to His voice. You will also be at an advantage in your walk with Christ.

When dealing with situations that require that you "test the spirits to know whether they are from God" (1 John 4:1) you must first know the voice of your Shepherd. If you recognize *His* voice, you'll know when the Enemy is trying to trap you.

***To continue reading the novel turn back to page 174.***

**Footnote 8:**
Praying in the Spirit

This is an arena of prayer that is greatly misunderstood by many in the Body of Christ. It has been mocked by opponents and sometimes misused by those who believe in this gift from the Holy Spirit. Let's first make some things clear: First, the New Testament church made evident and purposeful use of this gift as documented in Scripture. Second, Scripture does not say that these gifts have ended. On the contrary, Paul makes it clear that "until the perfect comes" the gifts of the Spirit will persist.[15] We do not live in the perfect time, yet. And my guess is that we won't until, at the very least, the Millennial Reign of Christ. That said, there is Scriptural basis for all of the Gifts of the Holy Spirit. Third, if the gifts that are received, such as the gift of praying in the Spirit, come as a direct result of asking the Holy Spirit to give them, then how can anyone dispute that they are gifts from God? As Jesus said, "What father among you, if his son asks for a fish, will instead of a fish give him a serpent; or if he asks for an egg, will give him a scorpion?" [16] You can trust the Father, through the Holy Spirit, to only give what is a benefit to you. Fourth, and finally, praying in the Spirit is very similar to, but *not* the same as, speaking in tongues.

The gift of praying in the Spirit is talked about by Apostle Paul. He mentions the ability in no less than three of his letters, to the believers in Rome, the churches at Corinth, and the churches in Ephesus. Obviously he wanted this gift to be utilized widely and often. "In the same way, the Spirit helps us in our

---

[15] 1 Corinthians 13:8-10
[16] Luke 11:11-12

weakness. We do not know what we ought to pray for, but the Spirit himself intercedes for us with groans that words cannot express." "For if I pray in tongues [or a tongue], my spirit prays but my mind is unfruitful. What am I to do? I will pray with my spirit, but I will pray with my mind also; I will sing praise with my spirit, but I will sing with my mind also." "And pray in the Spirit on all occasions with all kinds of prayers and requests. With this in mind, be alert and always keep on praying for all the saints." [17]

Does Paul make this sound optional? Why would Paul speak this as a necessary component to the believers if God was going to just strip it away sometime after the believers of the First-Century church died off? The answer is that God didn't remove the gift. Rather we moved away from the gift with corruption in the church that lasted for generations, disallowing Christians to even know what was said in the Scriptures. [18]

Paul wasn't the only one of the church fathers to teach it. Jude also made it clear that this was an important practice when he said, "But you, dear friends, build yourselves up in your most holy faith and pray in the Holy Spirit."

For those who think that praying in the Holy Spirit is in your modern-day English, re-read what Paul said to the Corinthians. He said that "if I pray in tongues, I don't understand what I'm praying." That means that he wasn't praying in any earthly language that he understood. And it would be impossible for him to pray in a human language that he had never learned. So, what the answer to that? Pray in the spirit (without human understanding) and pray with my mind (with human understanding). The same goes with praising God in song! How about that?!

This gift has to be asked for from the Holy Spirit. Some teach that it only comes from the laying on of hands, but I won't limit God in this respect. Ask for the gift, and if you attend (or find) a church in which this gift is practiced, ask the believers there to pray for you to receive, first, the *baptism* in the Holy Spirit, which is step one to receiving the gift of praying in tongues.

Practical Usage:

If you feel a burden from the Holy Spirit to begin praying, or maybe you just have a situation weighing on you but are unsure about how to pray, just launch into your gift of praying in the Spirit (praying in tongues). Keep praying until the burden

---

[17] Romans 8:26; 1 Corinthians 14:14-15; Ephesians 6:18

[18] Jude 20-21

subsides and you feel at peace. Sometimes you'll know in your mind what to pray, so pray in English (or your native language). Don't think that only one or the other type of prayer is best. Use all the tools that the Lord gives you.

***To continue reading the novel turn back to page 204.***

**Footnote 10:**
Discerning of spirits:

The Apostle Timothy speaks to a need for Christians to be alert to false doctrines: "Now the Spirit expressly says that in latter times some will depart from the faith, giving heed to deceiving spirits and doctrines of demons ... For the time will come when men will not put up with sound doctrine. Instead, to suite their own desires, they will gather around them a great number of teachers to say what their itching ears want to hear. They will turn their ears away from the truth and turn aside to myths."[19] We live in the times of which Timothy prophesied. Because of that God has given us another gift that comes from the Holy Spirit called discerning of spirits. This very specific gift is not given to everyone in the body of Christ. Each believer is given his and her ministry gifts as the Lord sees fit.[20] Let me qualify the previous two sentences by saying that while the "gift" is not given to everyone, the ability to discern whether something that is being done is good or evil must first start with studying and getting to know thoroughly the Word of God. This is essential to *anyone's* growth as a Christian.

The actual gift of discerning of spirits gives the individual the ability to know, without seeing, whether another individual is being influenced by either the Holy Spirit (because the Holy Spirit would obviously recognize Himself and His own works) or by a demonic spirit. This gift is valuable in that it can allow a person to sense that something is wrong even when nothing has happened in the physical world to make it evident.

***To continue reading the novel turn back to page 260.***

**Footnote 11:**
Words of knowledge:

---

[19] 2 Timothy 4:1, 3-4
[20] 1 Corinthians 12:10

Here we have yet another gift from God the Holy Spirit. This is a gift or a happenstance that can occur out of the blue. Suddenly you have insight into another human being or a situation. But with knowledge comes responsibility. God may speak into your spirit that a certain individual is going through a certain circumstance. Don't think that God gave you that tidbit of knowledge so that you can sit on it. God is not a gossip! If He speaks a word of knowledge to you, pray about what you've learned. Ask the Lord if He wants you to approach the individual that He spoke about. Maybe He wants that person to know that He cares, and speaking to that person about something you should have no knowledge about may be the key that opens the door. It may be that a person is going through a difficult time and has no way of knowing if he'll make it through. God may want you to just let that person know that God sent you to speak comfort to him; that he's not forgotten.

The point is that God can use this gift however He wishes, but you've got to be willing to ask for, and operate in, this gift.

***To continue reading the novel turn back to page 260.***

**Footnote 12:**

The strongman:

Here is the being that causes the possessed or oppressed to be unable to rid himself of the demons. Jesus spoke about this spirit and is recorded in three of the four Gospels: Matthew, Mark, and Luke.

Jesus had just cast out a demonic spirit that was causing a man to be unable to speak. Jesus cast out the spirit and then was quickly accused by the religious leaders of the day of being in league with the devil in order to have such power over demons. Jesus made it clear that the only way that the house (the inside of a man) could be cleared out of demonic influence is to first get rid of the strongman (who could also be the lone demon causing the problem). This demon sets up shop and "protects" his host from any other intruders, except those allowed in by the host and the strongman. Jesus went on to say, "But when one stronger than he attacks him [the strongman] and overcomes him, he [Jesus or the one using the authority of Jesus] takes away the armor that he [the strongman] trusted and divides the spoils.[21]

Once the strongman is eliminated, the remaining "spoils"

[21] Matthew 12:22-29; Mark 3:21-27; Luke 11:14-26

can be divided. To me this means that the other demons within the host can be cast out after the armor/strength of the strongman is eliminated. That person can now have the peace that he or she has been seeking. But there is a warning that Jesus gave. He said that if the house is left unoccupied after the strongman is cast out, that demon will come back to check on his old "home." Understand that demons are under strict command by other demons of higher rank. Losing a host to the Enemy [Jesus Christ] is not tolerated. The strongman *will* come back to see if that individual made a decision to accept Christ or not. If the Holy Spirit now dwells within the individual, the strongman cannot re-enter. However, if the strongman comes back and sees that the individual did not invite Jesus to reside where the strongman once did, that demon will re-enter and will set up shop again, and will invite even stronger beings than himself to reside within the host, as well. This creates an ever worse situation that before the strongman was originally cast out.

When doing deliverance, the team must first be assured of the individual's desire for Christ prior to the act of deliverance. Otherwise it is actually more compassionate to leave the person in his current state. It's best to lead the individual to salvation first, then do deliverance, but in some cases in which the demons within the individual hold great sway, at least get some sort of acknowledgment from the host that he (or she) *wants* to have Christ. Otherwise the entire event could be, at best, pointless; at worst, far more dangerous.

***To continue reading the novel turn back to page 260.***

**Footnote 13:**
Demonic hierarchies:

There is much speculation on the exact structure of the demonic hierarchy. Some scholars believe that it is the same structure that the angels hold to, except that the demons are evil. However, there is also the belief that the demonic structure of command is much more complex; after all, it is a kingdom of beings that cannot be trusted. Many demons have been put into such positions of unimportance that they are called "imps"; demons that hold little influence over other demons outside of their own rank.

The Bible does speak to command levels of demonic forces, though. Paul deals with this in his letter to the churches at Ephesus. He writes, "For our wrestling is not against flesh and blood, but against the principalities, against the powers, against the world-rulers of this darkness, against the spiritual hosts of wickedness in the heavenly places."[22]

During my research into how best to describe this hierarchy, I found a website that got into a lot of terrific detail about demonic rankings. The owner of the site dutifully sought out the meanings of certain words in the Greek and Hebrew to make sure that proper defining of roles was included. I've put the link to that site below. Understand that all websites are subject to the owner's removal at any time.[23]

It is believed that "Principalities" hold the second-highest ranking within the demonic kingdom, second only to Satan, himself. Below Principalities are "Powers and World Rulers of Darkness." I believe that these Powers include "Powers of the Air."

Paul goes onto mention "Spiritual Wickedness in Heavenly Places." It's possible that this is not so much a classification of class, but rather the whole of the demonic realm, including the weakest of impish demons.

Satan is portrayed as a god (a false one), a prince, and a king in Scripture. But there is One who is greater, who, in fact created all of the angelic realm in which Satan and his minions exist. It is He, Jesus, who is the True God, the Prince of all princes, the King of all kings, and the Lord of all lords. He reigns as the Second Person of the Godhead, who is supreme commander of all that exists.

**To continue reading the novel turn back to page 261.**

[22] Ephesians 6:12
[23] Battle in Christ dot com

3152060R00162

Made in the USA
San Bernardino, CA
10 July 2013